THE GHOSTS OF

CUMBO FLATS

A NOVEL

MACE THORNTON

Personal Chapters
PUBLISHING

The Ghosts of Gumbo Flats © 2025 by Mace Thornton

Cover Design by Marco Primo

PUBLISHING

Wakarusa, Kansas
www.personalchapterspublishing.com

Printed in the U.S.A.

Paperback ISBN: 979-8-9927670-1-8
Ebook ISBN: 979-8-9927670-2-5
Hardback ISBN: 979-8-9927670-3-2

Library of Congress Control Number: 2025918791

DEDICATION:

For my loving and patient wife, Denise Brazier Thornton. You are my blessing and inspiration every day. Thanks for believing and always persevering. And to all my family and friends, who empower me with courage that is deeper than Doniphan County topsoil and as formidable as the wide Missouri itself.

CONTENTS

CHAPTER 1

October 1865

UNHEALED SCARS

MOSES WATSON STARED AT HIS UPTURNED HANDS, scarred and calloused, clenching and unclenching in slow repetition like a well-worn prayer, too sacred to forsake, but too familiar to deliver its original grace. The scars marked his place within life's design, etched into his flesh by men who mistook chains for order, silence for obedience.

Was this the handiwork of the Great Unmoved Mover, the eternal one who shaped life from dust, only to cast it into endless struggle, fated to crumble back into dust once more?

Moses shook his head, sweat dripping, as he wrestled with the question.

Why shape existence as a battlefield, body and soul at odds, both bracing beneath the world's relentless weight? And why? Why would the Creator grant one man the power to shackle another, flesh binding flesh, as if sanctioned by divinity?

"Lord?" His voice broke the hush. "What kind of holy justice lets the strong crush the weak and puts chains on people too heavy for their bodies and hearts to carry?"

Moses lifted his gaze to the darkening sky. "Did You see, Lord? Were You watching?"

No answer came, but in the stillness, a storm rose in Moses, not from heaven, but from his own will.

Moses stretched his legs and rocked forward in his porch chair, the cane rocker cracking like brittle bones. Questions nibbled at him like a smoldering ditch fire.

Slavery had twisted a divine gift into blind, bloated power. Freedom's arc was broken, leaving Moses not just a victim, but a witness watching free will, sacred and rare, turned into a mocking curse. It lingered in bloodlines, in names, in the quiet between breaths.

These truths bore into his mind, but Moses refused to let them define him. Even here, in the freedom of his Kansas homestead, his hands were living reminders that slavery haunted his every fiber.

Freedom was a field yet to be cleared, untilled land, a seed yet to be sown. The abolished institution remained a matter of flesh, blood and family. The time for reflection was over and Moses was done with silence.

Now was his time to act.

Moses was shaped by the land from which he sprang, sturdy and enduring, yet vulnerable to forces beyond his reach. His broad shoulders rippled, but they also bore the aches of relentless toil. The gray creeping from his temples was the only hint of age. A dimple creasing his left cheek softened his rugged face, a hint of the gentle spirit within.

Moses was known as much for his unyielding work ethic as for the gentle care he showed to every living thing under his hand. From the horses that pulled his wagon to the livestock he raised, each creature garnered his respect. In every task, Moses revealed a reverence for life that echoed his deep ties to the land.

To those who knew him, Moses was a steadfast friend and farmer. His loyalty extended to the land itself and the resources it shared. Stewardship was his second skin. There was a quiet dignity in his work, a pride in his labor that no challenge from man or nature could diminish.

Moses looked down at his hands, broad as woven baskets for gathering crops. His scars, peculiar in their pattern, crisscrossed from the meat of his thumb to the base of his fingers, resembling tangled reeds left behind after the rush of a flood. Though they stood witness to his suffering, Moses no longer felt them. His nerves, damaged beyond repair, had not healed with the skin. The physical pain was gone, but the visible reminders lingered.

Six months had passed since two monumental events swept across the land. On April 9th, 1865, Robert E. Lee surrendered to Ulysses S. Grant at Appomattox, marking the end of major Civil War battles. Yet, days later, the victors' joys were shattered when Confederate sympathizer John Wilkes Booth fired a pistol into the back of President Lincoln's head.

Moses recalled Senator Charles Sumner's words shortly after Lincoln's death on April 15th: "Mourn not the dead, but rejoice in his life and example. Rejoice that through him Emancipation was proclaimed."

Seated in the cane rocker, Moses rested his hands on his knees. "Rejoice? How can we rejoice when they killed the man who gave us freedom? I'll celebrate when my family can walk in peace, no longer looking back in fear, waiting for the shackles to return."

Moses knew Lincoln's murder bore a dark warning. Freedom's birth would be met with blood and betrayal. The road ahead would be long, shadowed by those still clinging to the Southern cause, their hearts set on turning liberty back into bondage.

For months, echoes of gunfire and resistance reverberated through a nation that was still very much divided. Civility was delicate and fragile. Confederate forces continued to trickle in their surrenders, but the hate and bitterness of war hung like a fog. Some rebel soldiers refused to lay down their arms. Others schemed in the shadows, unwilling to accept defeat. The North remained cautious, unsure when or if the bloodshed would truly cease. President Andrew Johnson did not proclaim the war's end, leaving a lingering sense of ambiguity that stretched across the nation like a musty quilt, frayed at the edges.

For Moses, that uncertainty was like a festering wound. More than six years had passed since he and his son, Gabe, had left Gumbo Flats and a plantation there called Riverview Grove. Freedom papers in hand, it still felt like an escape. Though he and Gabe had been freedmen farmers for more than half a decade, true freedom remained as elusive as a shadow at high noon.

Gumbo Flats was a wide bottomland nestled between the bluffs and banks of the Missouri River west of St. Louis. Moses was born on the plantation and had labored in its sticky gumbo soil for more than 50 years. Even after gaining his freedom, no amount of liberty could wipe away the nights of pain or the memories of endless days under the baking sun, back bent, dropping seeds, cutting weeds and harvesting the plantation's crops.

The recollections flooded his mind, the pungent smell of fish rising from the riverbank, blending with the thick, humid breath of the midday heat. The memory of a cracking whip splitting the air still made his shoulders tighten. Moses stood in Kansas, but Missouri mud still squished between his toes. Part of his spirit remained bound to that cursed plantation. From that plantation, every member of his family except Gabe had been ripped away and sold downriver by Old Man Manchester like merchandise, their names reduced to scratches on an inventory ledger.

Sitting on the front stoop of the Kansas house he and Gabe had built to stake their claim on freedom, Moses felt the ache of absence. His wife, Sally, and sons, Michael and Samuel. Where were they now?

Moses' urge to go back to Gumbo Flats, where his life and the story of his family all began, consumed him. Could his family be found? He did not know. But his soul would not rest until he tried.

He spoke into the empty air, his voice low. "I will undo what has been done."

After feeding the cattle, Gabe knelt beside his father on the porch.

"Talking to yourself again, Papa? That ain't gonna change things."

Gabe ignored what had become his father's incessant habit of rubbing his palms together. Gabe had his own scars, both physical and emotional. He moved to the front step and stretched his legs. Gabe had returned from the Civil War Battle of Leavenworth a hero. He'd fought for the Union as a Jayhawker and almost died. Now, both men, alive and strong, lived in an uncertain and divided world. Freedom had not yet settled into the cracks of the nation's soul.

"I'm going back," Moses said. "Back to Gumbo Flats. But not you, Gabe. You've fought your war, spilled enough blood to damp the soil. You stay here. Tend the farm, build the future. I'll walk this road alone."

In the momentary silence, Moses scanned the horizon, his gaze searching.

"My soul's tethered to that place, to that damned, sticky gumbo soil. But the barest of all truths is I will never be free if I leave behind those I love, as if they never were. I've carried their absence too long. I won't let them stay buried in the past, forgotten like they were shadows in time."

Gabe rose and leaned on the porch rail, shaking his head.

"Papa, going back there? That's foolish. You've built somethin' here. We both have. We have found what the runaway slaves before us called their Maroon, their places of freedom and safety. This is what they dreamed of—land of our own, freedom carved from soil and sweat, far from whip and chain. They made Maroon communities, hidden and defiant. We did the same, only out in the open. This life wasn't handed to us. We fought for it. And now you want to walk back into Gumbo Flats? That's like stepping into the jaws of a wolf in pursuit of your ghosts."

"Ghosts? No, son. They're flesh and blood, same as you. I know they're out there, somewhere. You'd have me sit here and let the world forget them, let time bury them like they never lived? No, Gabe. A man don't turn his back on his own. If I don't go looking, who will?"

"I'm not sayin' they ain't real, Papa. But you go back there alone and you might not come back. The war might be over in the headlines, but it's less than half a year. People ain't done fightin'. You've said it yourself. Ain't no place for us now, not with the slavers carryin' grudges. The Union Army might be occupying the land, but those wounded bastards still have all the secret power."

"What do you mean, secret power?

"What I'm saying is, Yankee reconstruction holds no loyalty. The masters are lickin' their wounds. Schemin'. The talk in our very town of Lowland is that throughout the Deep South, those bastards are formin' clandestine clubs. Union Army or not, they rule the South. Their grudges grind on."

Moses' hands balled into fists. "You think I care about their wounds, their grudges? I carried their chains, Gabe! I wake up every morning thinkin' about our family, knowing they're alive, wonderin' if they have yet tasted freedom. You're my beloved son, and I am thankful you're by my side, but don't tell me what or who I should leave behind."

Gabe ran a hand through his hair, exhaling sharply. He looked away, jaw tight, the tension between him and his father thicker than a slab of pork belly.

"You're right, I don't know what it's like for you. I miss them too. But I fought my own damn war, Papa, and I almost didn't come back. Plus, I killed Old Man Manchester before we left Gumbo Flats. If people put two and two together, they might hold you to reckon for the rash actions I took."

Gabe's words stirred memories that Moses had tried to bury as deep as the Missouri River had buried Old Man Manchester.

It had been a sweltering day of field work when Gabe's anger boiled over against Manchester. His fury erupted as he raised a shovel and brought it down, splitting Manchester's skull. That action sent the man crashing to the ground, never again to rise.

Moses remembered the sickening thud, the way Gabe's breath had come in ragged gasps, the disbelief in his mind as he stared at Manchester's lifeless body sprawled across the gumbo dirt. Gabe's hands trembled but there had been no remorse in his eyes, only a cold rage.

They had worked quickly, silently, loading Manchester's body onto a cart. Together, they wheeled him to the river's edge, the dark water lapping at the shore like an indifferent witness. Moses had helped because there was no other choice. He never supported Gabe's rash decision. As they rolled the body into the river, it disappeared into the murky depth. A weight had settled over Moses that still remained.

Moses knew he was forever bound to that secret, and secrets always had a way of floating to the surface. He could neither forget nor forgive his son, or himself.

Moses' thoughts lingered on that dark day by the river, but Gabe's voice pulled him back with a bitter edge.

"Old Man Manchester had it comin', you know that. That snake would've sold every last one of us to fill his pockets." Gabe spat the words, as if they could erase what he'd done. For a moment, the same fire from that fateful day flickered in his eyes. It was the same blaze Moses had seen the day the shovel came down. "But I ain't proud of it, and I'm not lookin' to lose anyone else because of some foolish cause. You think I want to forfeit you to the folly of some rebel's errand?"

Gabe stepped closer. "I understand, Papa, I do, but you're not thinkin' straight." He shook his head in a mix of frustration and fear. "This fight, it ain't worth the cost, and you know it."

Moses' face flushed with anger, his pulse quickening, but before he could reply, Gabe stepped even closer, a last attempt to bridge the divide.

"Look, I ain't sayin' don't go. And forgive me, Papa, but just don't go alone like a fool. Talk to our neighbor, Perry. He's a solid thinker and he's traveled down harsh roads. Just talk to him. See what he thinks. If anybody can help you make it, it's him. Hell, he's practically kin at this point, the white uncle I never had, and he ain't gonna let you walk into a swamp of trouble blind and alone."

Moses grumbled, pacing the length of the porch. His thoughts a storm, swirling in uncertainty, driven by the bitter taste of freed slaves caught in the traps of Confederate sympathizers. Going back to Missouri, and possibly beyond, meant walking into the belly of a beast that wasn't ready to die. Gabe's words echoed in his mind. Perry Adams, their neighbor and friend, was a white man who had carved out his farm in nearby Jawbone Holler. Perry had made his own harrowing journey to Kansas from his native Indiana, and he would know the risks of the road, the terrain, and maybe, just maybe, he could be the ally Moses needed for the journey.

"You think Perry understands my pull to go back there? To erase a wrong?" Moses finally asked.

"I know Perry lost his mama, so he knows that pain, but he's never walked in your shoes," Gabe crossed his arms as he returned to the porch rail. "Perry's a good man. He put his life on the line for our cause, beside me with the Jayhawkers at the Battle of Leavenworth. He's got a level head, and he knows those backwoods, just like you. Two such minds might better your chances. You goin' back is your call, but you don't gotta go it alone. Ain't no shame in havin' a friend like Perry watchin' your back."

Moses paused, staring out at his cattle as they grazed the close-by meadow. There was no denying that this farm had given both he and Gabe new life and purpose. It had provided them their Maroon, but not the finality of peace. Moses rubbed his palms together again. He gave Gabe a reluctant nod.

"I'll talk to Perry. But Gabe, you struck out at Old Man Manchester as payback. If I didn't try, your action would be for naught. Just like you felt that day, I ain't lettin' go of this. I can't."

"I don't expect you to. Just don't let it be the death of you. Go talk to Perry."

Moses pulled the worn leather saddle tight around his horse. The air was thick with the musty scent of decaying hardwood leaves in autumn.

Moses hoisted himself into the saddle, his horse shifting beneath him. He gave a gentle nudge with his heels, and together they set off for Jawbone Holler.

The route wound through hills that rolled like the folds of an old blanket, rising and falling, draped in golden grasses and clusters of half-barren oaks. The autumn air carried the scent of fallen leaves, and the sky stretched wide and open, a perfect blue dome punctuated by the occasional drifting cloud. As Moses rode, his eyes scanned familiar surroundings. This was the place that hosted his first steps as a free man, the same hills and hollers that had offered him and Gabe sanctuary before, and now after the war.

The earth here felt solid, steady, and yet his heart was pulled in another direction. For now, his focus was Perry Adams, a friend who might offer counsel, maybe even help, to traverse a path toward the reclamation of stolen years.

Moses crossed a small stream, its waters trickling over smooth stones, the soft burble mingling with the sound of birds flitting between the branches of maple trees. The woods around him were alive with the hum of life. Rabbits darted through the underbrush. Squirrels leapt branch to branch, their bushy tails flashing in the dappled sunlight. A red-tailed hawk circled above, its sharp eyes scanning the ground for movement. There was energy in the wilderness, a pulse that ran through it like blood through a man's veins.

It reminded Moses of why he was on this journey. Nature never forgot. Every creature in these woods knew its place, its purpose. Even the stream, winding through the hills, only strayed from its course at its most abundant. It made him think again of Sally, Michael and Samuel. Somewhere, they were out there, like buried roots ready to be unearthed, waiting to be remembered. Moses wasn't going back just for answers. He was going back to reclaim what had been taken from him.

As he rounded a bend in the road, the hills opened up to a small meadow, golden with late-season wild sunflowers swaying in the breeze. In the distance, a family of foxes, two adults and three kits, skittered through the grass, their fiery coats bright against the muted earth. Moses stopped for a moment. The scene kindled memories of a family, united, whole, and five-members complete. He squinted his eyes in marvel of their movements, swift, purposeful, protective. The mother nosed her kits forward, ushering them toward a patch of shade under an old persimmon tree, the father standing watch at a distance.

The scene stirred a fierce, primal resolve. Like those foxes, Moses had a duty to his own, a pull stronger than fear or pain. The mother fox didn't abandon her young to the wilds, didn't leave them to fend for themselves. She kept them close, safe. Moses had been forced to leave his own behind, but he couldn't rest until he knew their fate, until he had done everything in his power to find them.

The foxes disappeared into the brush as Moses urged his horse forward, the steady rhythm of the ride matching the growing determination in his chest. He crossed another ridge, the land dipping into the valley known as Jawbone Holler where Perry's farm sat nestled between two river bluffs. The Adams place wasn't much different from his own, with rail-fenced meadows, neat crop fields, a simple but sturdy home.

Moses' mind was clear. The wilderness around him had spoken. Just as the foxes protected their own, so too must he. Whatever awaited him in Gumbo Flats, he couldn't forego the search. The land had taught him that much. Nothing forgotten stays buried forever.

With a deep breath, he pressed toward the Adams farm, where a longer journey might begin.

CHAPTER 2

October 1865

FERTILE GROUNDS

THE GRASSY ROAD TO PERRY ADAMS' FARM was one Moses and Perry had traveled together many times as neighbors, friends and brothers in struggle. Each journey strengthened their bond, forged by hardship and hope that came with farming's relentless demands.

The cold bit into Moses' fingertips as he rode, but Perry's humble homestead, sturdy barn, and dormant cornfields always reassured him. Here, hope grew alongside the crops. Though the months after the war had changed much, one consistent truth was that Perry's hands, like Moses', still knew the honesty of laboring in the soil.

Archibald, Perry's old, floppy-eared hound, was the first to notice Moses' arrival. He let out a deep familiar bark that rang through the still air. "Uh Roo Roo Roo!"

Moses chuckled and slid off his mount. He leaned down, scratching the dog's ears.

"Archibald, you old hound. Still barkin' at friends, I see."

A team of Belgian draft horses crested the hill pulling a wagon stacked high with corn. Perry Adams guided the horses, Beulah and Barney, his hands firm on the reins. Perry sat tall and lean, a man at ease with the land. The wagon rattled toward the farmstead, the wheels kicking up dust as it rolled along the dirt path.

Perry's service in the Union's Jayhawkers unit and his years of farm work in Jawbone Holler had carved him into a masterwork of sinew and resilience. Still too young to have lines in his face, his eyes gleamed. Moses knew his friend was sharper now, more seasoned than when they first met. Perry was a man marked by the past but leaning hard into the future. A wide-brimmed straw hat rested atop his head and a red bandana was tied around his neck.

Perry smiled and raised a hand in greeting. Beulah and Barney stopped and Perry climbed down from the wagon, dusting his hands off on his trousers.

"Moses, this is a surprise."

"My soul led me here. I came to seek your counsel."

Perry wiped his forehead with the red bandana, his face flushed with the effort of the day's labor. He looked over at his overflowing wagon, his smile widening.

"Every day is a blessing my friend and the Lord has blessed this land. It's still early, but this looks to be the best harvest I've had in years. I'll be corn-rich till next summer."

Moses cast an approving glance at the wagon. The golden ears of corn were stacked high, each ear with full rows of kernels from end to end.

"You've always had a way with the soil, Perry. Few can draw this bounty from the good earth like you."

Perry chuckled, shaking his head as he brushed dust from his pants.

"Nothing teaches success like a good old-fashioned ass-kickin'. Nature's handed me plenty. I also want to let you in on another little secret. It ain't just the corn that's been productive around here."

"What's that mean? Your old mare Beulah expecting another colt?"

"Bigger than that. Millie's expecting. And you'd sure enough be in all kinds of trouble if Millie heard you comparing her to a mare. Our best guess is that right around mid-March we'll be welcoming a little one."

Moses broke into a broad smile. His laugh shaking loose the tension he had felt during his short ride northward.

"Well now, that's news worth celebrating! You and Millie are blessed. A child to carry your name forward, and a spring birth too. Your family will be abloom like the land where it's planted."

Perry nodded, impending fatherhood already resting on his shoulders and visible in the bright blue of his eyes. "It's a new season for us, Moses. This land has given me much, but a child, well, that's different. Deeper. Godsent."

Moses grew quiet. He looked out toward the distant hills that met the sky in a jagged line. "You're a lucky man, Perry. You'll find out. There's much to be said for having family at your side. My life wouldn't be the same without Gabe."

"I feel the same, Moses. Gabe's like a kid brother to me. He proved that kinship when we fought side-by-side. But now, the two of you have also built something solid and lasting out here. And Gabe continues to grow into a fine man, just like his father."

"Gabe's settled in well enough here, I suppose. He's taken to the farm life. I can't deny he's a diligent worker. But there are still moments when sparks of stubbornness arise. He gets it straight from me. It's in his blood. But he's also fiercely loyal, just like his mother. That's the balance. He may be headstrong, but he's as steady as they come. Sometimes, he pushes boundaries, but he's still finding his way. I can't always rein him in, and I'm not sure I want to. A man's got to learn from blunders."

Perry leaned against a nearby fence post. "Life's lessons come hard and fast out here, Moses. They don't much care if you're ready. This land doesn't coddle. It teaches with both the hand of man and God. But more often than not, it's the quiet moments that teach you the most. Out here, a man learns to bend or break, to work with the seasons or fight against 'em. And when the lesson comes from above, well, you've got no choice but to yield. It's just the way of things. No matter how strong you think you are, the land and the Lord have a way of humbling."

A shadow crossed Moses' face at that moment. "I am humbled, indeed. You know my boys, my wife, Sally, they were taken from me before the war. I miss them, Perry. Gabe thinks it's foolish to hope I can find them now, and maybe he's right. But I need your wisdom. If there's any chance of saving them, or saving myself, I need to know the way forward. I reckon I don't know if they're alive or dead. And there are some days I don't care if either is my own fate."

Perry looked at his friend, seeing the pain etched into Moses' face. He had heard the story but knew the wound would only heal with resolution.

Moses continued, his eyes distant. "Now that the war's over, I've been thinkin' it's time I try to find them. The world may be free, but my heart ain't, not without knowing for sure."

Autumn whispered around the farm. The dry rustle of fallen leaves and the distant clucking of chickens filled a lull in the conversation before Moses spoke.

"It's been a good six months since Appomattox. But a man like me, a freed slave with a mind of my own, I ain't sure if now's the time for me to go looking for them. But I know I won't be able to rest until I've tried."

Perry didn't answer right away. He leaned against the wagon. Freedmen like Moses still walked a perilous road. Perry understood the pull. From his experience in leaving Indiana, he knew family wasn't forgotten, and the burden of not knowing was heavy.

"Moses, hostile guns are still at the ready across the South, and they've already killed President Lincoln. Folks are angry, and they're clingin' to the old ways. But I know this. You've got a right to search. Blood ties can't be cut by time or distance. If you feel this is what you must do, there should be no hesitation. But we have to acknowledge the danger. Caution must be our guide."

Moses expected as much. Perry's words brought him some comfort. He trusted Perry's judgment, and his friend's support meant the world. He ignored the fact that Perry had used the word "we."

"I know it won't be easy," Moses said. "I've no illusions. But I've been through worse. Hell, we both have."

Perry tilted his head, his eyes narrowing as he considered the situation. "If you're set on goin' back, Moses, we can't go unprepared. We'll need a plan. Have you thought about where we'll start?"

There was that word again. "We." Moses selectively ignored it. He rubbed his chin, the rough texture of his beard familiar beneath his fingers.

"Gumbo Flats. That's where I'll start. It's where I was born. It's the place that stole my family. It's where the trail starts and goes cold all at once."

"Gumbo Flats makes sense. But there needs to be more than a place for us to start. We need people we can trust, folks who can help along the way. People in the South, both black and white, are feeling their way around in a new world that hasn't yet been formed."

"I've been thinking about that too. I don't want to bring Gabe into this. He's fought his war. This is mine."

Perry straightened up, a glint of resolve hardening in his eyes. "And that, my friend, is why I keep using the word 'we.' I'm goin' with you."

Moses blinked, taken aback. "Perry, no. Millie's expecting. You've got a child comin'. This is my road."

"Millie and I have been talkin' about this for months, ever since our wedding day when we saw Sally's name on the poster at the church about misplaced and lost families."

"I put her name on that list."

"Since reading it, we knew sure as sunrise this day would come. Millie and I are in union. I've traveled some of those roads already, and I know how to handle myself if things turn ugly."

Moses opened his mouth to protest, but Perry raised a hand.

"You listen now. I know the kind of men we might run into. I've got a good eye and a steady hand. If trouble finds us, it will tuck tail and run. We haven't sweated for years on these river bluffs just to piss it away tilting at windmills. You need me."

Perry's eyes carried a stubborn resolve. Moses wanted to argue, but deep down he knew Perry wouldn't be swayed. He sighed, the fight leaving him as he shook his head.

"You're a stubborn man, Perry Adams," Moses muttered.

Perry grinned. "That I am."

Moses couldn't help but smile in return. "Honest. I'll need all the help I can get. But I still worry about Millie."

"Ahh, Millie's tougher than you give her credit for. She's got the heart of a hawk, always observing, sensing things unseen. She knows what we're about to face."

Perry continued. "Before we head out, there's something, or rather someone, we need to consider. I think there's another fella who might want to join us on this journey. You met him at our wedding, though you wouldn't have thought of him as a man who ever wanted to travel South again. Pete Fontaine, the bartender over in Roubideaux."

Moses blinked, his mind racing back to Perry's wedding. Pete had been the man with the waxed handlebar mustache and a chest as thick as a rain barrel. That day, Pete had been quick with a laugh, and eyes as sharp as his tongue.

"Pete Fontaine? Oh yes, I remember him well. We struck up a friendship. He brought out that bottle of rot-gut rum to the wedding. Said it was the reason you drew a liking to Millie in the first place."

"Yep. That's Pete. But there's more to Pete than meets the eye. He may pour drinks over at his tavern in Roubidoux now, but he's no stranger to the land we're heading toward. He's a son of the South. Grew up in Arkansas, working fields like both of us. His father was a sharecropper, but Pete wanted more. He left, looking for something better, but his southern roots still run deep."

Moses' interest piqued. He'd sensed something more to Pete during the brief moments they'd exchanged words and handshakes at the wedding, but he hadn't thought much beyond that. Now Perry was speaking of Pete like he was a man who could tip the scales on their dangerous journey.

"He knows the South, then," Moses said slowly. "Knows the people, the land?"

"Knows them inside and out. He understands how they live, how to work around the twisted roots that tangle so deeply in that part of the country. And more importantly, he knows how to get himself out of tight spots. He's a damn fine shot with a rifle, and he's got the kind of instincts you can't learn from books or tavern talk. Pete's lived through struggles, but he also had the wisdom to walk toward a brighter horizon, just like us."

A spark of excitement thumped in Moses' chest. Pete wouldn't be just another gun. He would be a compass crafted on a southern work bench. Having Pete along would give them a speaking map of the terrain ahead, one with a southern accent.

"Sounds like the kind of man we need on a trip like this. But you're holding something back. What's his stake in all this? Favors don't come free, and he barely knows me."

"Well, Pete and I had some long conversations when we first met. He was raised in a place where division was passed down like an inheritance. When I first met Pete, I wasn't sure where he stood on a lot of things. He played devil's advocate, made me spill my guts on the war and on slavery. But it didn't take long to see where he stood. He understood the wrongs that needed to be righted. And that is what stands before us now. He knows more about you than you realize."

Moses listened, nodding as Perry continued.

"And there's more to him. He can be trusted. You remember Marcus Mixon, don't you?"

Moses' eyes flashed with recognition. Marcus Mixon, the owner of the trading post in Roubideaux, had risked his life to help Moses and Gabe get across the Missouri River to Kansas Territory all those years ago. He'd been one of the hosts for the Underground Railroad, a man who had moved countless souls toward freedom under the cloak of secrecy. And though Moses and Gabe held freedom papers in hand, such a passage remained critical to their ultimate freedom.

"Marcus got us to the river and after that he didn't walk away. He staked us with tools, seed, and hope. What we built here started with his kindness, his belief that men like us deserved more than just survival.

I've repaid him for his generosity, but I still owe him everything."

"Well, Pete's one of the few people who knew Marcus's secret. He kept that knowledge close, never letting it slip, not even when the war was tearing this country apart. He understood the importance of what Marcus was doing and protected it, even when he had no direct stake in it himself. That's the kind of loyalty you can trust. The kind of man we need at our flank."

"He kept Marcus's secret? That says a lot. When I met Pete at your wedding I could tell there was something about him. He had that spirit in his eyes, like he'd seen things most men don't speak of, but never let that stand in the way of doing what's right."

"And it's why I'd trust Pete with my life. He may not have walked exactly the same roads as either you or me, but he's fought his own battles. Made his own escape. I know he'll be an asset. I don't think it will take much convincing."

Moses couldn't help the smile that spread across his face. The idea of Pete joining their dangerous, uncertain mission filled him with renewed hope.

"Pete's seen his share of darkness, but he's not the kind to run from it," Perry said. "He faces it head-on, like a man should. For a long time, he stood on the thin line between right and wrong, but then he chose his side."

"So," Moses said, "when do we leave?"

"Soon, my friend. Soon. I just need to finish this harvest, make a few plans for Millie's care and the tending of this farm and then we'll be ready. But until then, I need you to prepare yourself. You're about to face your past head-on, and it won't be easy. But know this: the day of redemption is close. I believe that with every fiber of my being."

Moses looked out across the fields. His heart was heavy, but it was also lightened by hope, a hope that had felt so distant for so many years.

"Together," Moses said softly, more to himself than to Perry.

"Together," Perry echoed, as steady as the land beneath them.

CHAPTER 3

October 1865

ECHOES IN THE HOLLER

MOSES SHOOK PERRY'S HAND, their eyes meeting in a wordless pact forged by shared burdens. Perry cleared his throat, breaking the silence. He watched as Moses turned to check the saddle straps on his horse.

"Before you ride out, I've been thinking, do you reckon Gabe might look after Butter while we're gone? That old cow's taken a liking to him, and he's got a knack for keeping her calm."

"Butter, huh? I think you're more worried about her than yourself."

"Well, her and Millie. I think Millie will have plenty of friends to help, but Butter, she's kind of on her own. But Gabe's got a way with animals."

"Don't worry. Gabe's got a soft spot for that cow."

Perry nodded, reassured, but Moses wasn't done. "But what about your horses? You'll probably be riding old Appy, your saddle horse, but what about your draft Belgians? Are you leaving them behind?"

"No, I've been thinkin' it over. With the distance we've got to cover, and the supplies we'll need, it's better to be safe. We should ask Marcus if he can help us wrangle a Conestoga wagon. Beulah and Barney can pull it. They're strong and steady, and with a wagon, we can carry enough provisions without needing to stop too often. Plus, we can use it as shelter if need be."

"You're right. I never considered that. The only time I traveled overland, Gabe and I moved light, but there's no need to do that now."

"And I don't plan on coming back empty-handed. We'll need somewhere for Sally and your boys to ride on the way back."

Moses nodded. The real possibility of bringing Sally, Mike and Sam back was beginning to sink in. "You're right. We'll need room for them if…no, when…we find them. So, you takin' Appy too?"

"You're damned right I am. The value of a good, well-broken, fast horse cannot be overestimated. Never know when we might need to move swiftly."

Perry's eyes caught the doubt that crossed Moses' face. "We will find them, Moses. I can feel it. That's why we need to be prepared. Appy will follow behind the wagon, tethered and ready if we need to make a quick move, but Beulah and Barney'll keep us steady through the tough terrain."

"No ground will be too rough for those two."

"We're going to do this right. Lessen our risk. We'll have good horses, a strong wagon, and the determination to see it through. Gabe will take care of things here—Butter, the farm. And Millie's got friends in town. Everything will be in good hands."

Moses' face hardened with resolve. "Then there's no turning back."

They stood in silence for a moment longer. Their mission would take them straight into the heart of a large mine with unstable timbers in search of three tiny flakes of gold.

Perry broke the silence. "I'll head over to Marcus's place as soon as my last ear of corn hits the bangboard of the wagon. I'll ask him to find us a proper Conestoga wagon and supplies. He'll understand. He knows the stakes. And while I'm there, I will have my discussion with Pete about why we need him."

"As soon as you get back to these hills, you stop by my farm and let me know how it went."

"I know it'll test your fabric, but give me at least two, maybe three weeks. Need to finish harvest, and I want to make sure Millie is on board."

"You got it."

Moses mounted his horse. He cast one final look at Perry, gave a quick wave and nudged his horse forward down the return trail.

Perry watched as Moses' silhouette dissolved into the fading daylight. The stillness of the evening wrapped around him, but his mind was far from quiet. As the cool air settled in, Perry turned and led Beulah and Barney toward the barn. There was still work to be done before he could call it an evening. The day's last wagonload of corn needed storing. His hands worked automatically, shoveling the golden ears into the crib, but his mind was elsewhere.

With the last scoop, he patted down the mound of corn, making sure it was secure before leading Beulah and Barney into the barn. The two horses nickered, knowing the day was done. Perry scooped generous portions of shelled corn for them and for Butter. The animals were Perry's family, of sorts, and, still thinking of Moses, a rush of guilt tugged at his heart for leaving his four-legged friends behind for the night.

He patted each of his horses, the feel of their strong muscles beneath his hands. "Won't be long now," he whispered, more to himself than the horses.

With a deep breath, Perry walked toward the farmhouse, beckoned by the warm lantern light spilling through the windows. Millie waited inside, and there were still a few maters to talk over. But tonight, he would hold her close, savoring the moments of peace before the storm that awaited.

The sound of his boots on the wooden porch echoed as Perry opened the door, stepping into the warmth of the home he planned to soon leave behind.

The familiar scent of ham hocks and navy beans hit his nose as he opened the door. Millie stood over the wood-burning stove, stirring the beans with a wooden ladle. Her face, flushed from the heat of the fire, glowed in the dim light. Perry smiled as he stepped inside.

"You're radiant," he said.

Millie turned, a playful blush rising in her cheeks. "If I'm glowing, it's because of my passion for you, Perry Adams."

Perry's face reddened slightly, a rare moment of shyness overtaking him. "I'm hoping what I'm about to tell you won't dim those embers."

Millie's eyes sparkled with curiosity as she set the ladle down and turned to face him eye-to-eye. "Go on then, what is it?"

Perry took a deep breath. "Moses and I, we've got a plan. A mission, really. He's been carryin' the weight of losing his wife, Sally, and their boys for too long. We're goin' South to find them, to bring them back if we can."

Millie's face grew serious, her hand resting on her belly, where their child grew. "Perry, I know we've been talking about this since our wedding day, but that's no small task. The timing could be better, but there is no question that you need to be by Moses' side."

"I do," Perry said, nodding. "But Moses and I can't do this alone. We need someone else. Someone who knows the land and its people. Someone to ride shotgun and watch our backs. I'm thinking about asking Pete. He grew up in Arkansas. His father was a sharecropper. Pete knows the South like the back of his hand. He left that life behind, but he hasn't forgotten anything and he's wise in the ways of defusing situations. And if push comes to shove, he also knows how to handle himself in a fight."

At the mention of Pete, a warm expression spread across Millie's face. Pete had been like an older brother to her, ever since she first set foot in Roubideaux, before moving to Kansas.

"God forbid your trip from including any form of violence, but you're right about good old 'Awesome Possum' Pete. When I was on my own, Pete and Lucy made sure I was safe. They offered me a job playing piano at The Outpost. Even gave me that little room upstairs. If not for that, I never would have met the strikingly handsome hermit I ended up marrying. Pete will stand by Moses and you without question, just like he's always stood by me."

Perry reached out and squeezed Millie's hand. "I hoped you'd see it this way. This journey is about building something better for all of us."

Millie considered this for a moment. "It's a long journey, Perry. How long do you think it'll take?"

"I expect it'll be a matter of a few months, but no longer. Harvest is nearly done, and it's the fallow time of year on the farm. All we'll need is someone to look after Butter. Moses thinks Gabe can manage that while we're away."

Millie's eyes flickered with one final thought of concern. "What if it takes longer than just a few months? Our baby's due in mid-March, Perry."

"I'll be back by then, Millie. I promise you. In addition to our young one, I have corn fields to prepare in March."

Millie gave a small, uncertain nod. "And if something goes wrong?"

"I know. If danger's the biggest concern, my mind's already made up. We're going, Millie. I'll make sure you're looked after while I'm away. We can rent a place in Lowland, closer to town and the church, or..."

He hesitated as Millie again stirred the pot of beans, the ladle scraping its bottom in a slow, methodical rhythm. "Or what?" she asked.

"Or, maybe you could spend the time over in Roubideaux, maybe stay in your old room above Pete and Lucy's place at The Outpost. You and Lucy are like sisters, and with Pete away, I bet she could use help running the place. I know you are with child, but I am guessing you could play piano like you used to, maybe help out just a little in the kitchen on weekends. It'd be like old times."

Millie's face lit up at the mention of Lucy, her eyes sparkling with the thought. "Lucy would love that. And I could help her. Maybe even play their fancy new piano."

Perry smiled as the excitement returned to her eyes. "It's not a bad setup, is it? You'd be close to friends, to the church where you taught, and you wouldn't be alone."

"It could work. But make sure this doesn't take longer than it needs to. You come back to me before this baby arrives."

Perry reached out, pulling her into his arms. "I swear it, Millie. I'll be back in time for the birth. Moses and I will find Sally and his boys, and we'll bring them home. It won't be easy, but I've got a good feeling in my gut."

They stood hugging for a moment. Then, with a deep breath, Perry pulled out a chair for Millie. He walked over to the stove and brought back the pot of beans and the cornbread, setting them down with care. Perry sat across the table from Millie and tore off a piece of cornbread, slathered on some butter, and ladled some beans into his bowl. As he sopped up the rich broth from the beans, his eyes locked on Millie.

"You know. I love you more than anything in this world. More than heaven itself."

Millie smiled, warmth settling over her like a quilt. Before she could respond, a piece of warm, buttered cornbread slipped from Perry's fingers, falling to the floor with a soft thud. Archibald, never one to miss an opportunity, lunged for it, devouring the bread in a single gulp.

Perry chuckled, shaking his head. "Guess Archy loves cornbread as much as I love you, more than heaven itself."

Millie laughed, the sound filling the small kitchen with a sense of calm, despite the storm brewing on the horizon. The journey ahead would be long, and it would test them in ways they couldn't yet foresee, but for now, they had each other and that was enough.

"You mentioned Gabe taking care of Butter, but what about your horses and old Archy here?"

Perry reached down and scratched Archibald behind the ears, his hand moving in a slow, thoughtful rhythm. "I've been thinkin'. We'll be taking a wagon with supplies, so Beulah and Barney are going for sure. And I've also been thinkin' that Archy would be a suitable road companion."

"Archy? You sure about that? You think he might slow you down?"

"Well, he can just ride in the wagon."

"What if something happens to him? He's your hunting companion but after our child is born, I think he might be even more important."

"I know. He's more than just company. You know how good he is at tracking, finding trails that no human could spot. If we need to track someone or something out there in the wild, he'd be invaluable. His sense of danger's better than ours. He could save our skins. If things go sideways. If we run into trouble, Archibald might just be what gets us out. He's got the instincts of a survivor."

As the words left his mouth, a shadow seemed to pass over the room. Millie bit her lip, turning back to the stove. "Well enough, Mister Adams, I guess you have a deal."

Perry gave Archibald a final pat on the head. "Uh Roo Roo Roo." The hound barked and looked up at him, as if already understanding a journey was looming and his place would be by Perry's side.

CHAPTER 4

Late October 1865

A CHANGE IN THE AIR

TWO WEEKS HAD PASSED since Perry had started the fall corn harvest of 1865. Now, with winter whispering on the edges of the wind, his hands bore the rough signs of the season's labor. Each night, the ache in his bones settled deeper, but there was a quiet satisfaction in the rhythm of his days, a sense that despite everything looming on the horizon, the land still yielded its gifts, stubborn but abundant.

As Beulah and Barney plodded along before him with wagon in tow, he reached for another ear, the metal shucking hook on his hand shining in the sun. With a quick stroke, he cut through the husk, peeling it back to reveal the ear of corn beneath. The snap of the husk was sharp and clean. The ear flew from his hand, like a quail flushed from cover, arcing through the air before landing with a soft thud atop the wagon's heaping pile.

Again, he repeated the motion. Hook, snap, toss. The rhythm was meditative, ingrained so deeply it left little room for thought. And yet, his mind wandered. The familiar quiet of the field, usually a comfort during a long day's work, stirred his unease. Tomorrow, he'd take Millie to Roubideaux. Plans would be discussed, strategies that reached far beyond the fences of his farm.

Another ear of corn snapped free, its journey ending in the wagon with the others, but Perry's thoughts were miles away. Moses' mission tugged at him, a shadow at the threshold of his mind. And Millie, he'd promised her they'd set things right, or at least set them in motion. He didn't yet know if all would come together.

Reaching the final cornstalk on the last row, Perry snapped the last ear free with a crisp, satisfying crack. He paused for a moment and tossed the ear into the wagon with a thud that echoed louder than the rest. The field, once alive with green and gold, now lay stripped and barren. Wiping sweat from his brow, he climbed into the wagon. With a soft click of his tongue, Perry urged the horses forward, the rustling of the harness marking the quiet end of another season's toil.

Reaching the corn crib with the season's last load, Perry leaned into the wood as if to prop up both himself and the structure. The crib groaned under its golden cargo, ears of corn stacked high, spilling over the top like a harvest too proud to be contained. Perry's breath rose in the crisp autumn air. The mist dissolved before him, much like the fleeting satisfaction of a task well done because there was a much larger undertaking ahead.

Perry's eyes again traced the overflowing bounty, each ear another small reward for his long hours under the sun. But where pride should have settled in his chest, a flicker of anxiety lingered. The crib was full, and with each passing year, his yield had expanded. He would have to add storage for the added bounty to come with the next year's harvest. The thought nibbled at him like a mouse at a grain sack, small but persistent.

He muttered under his breath, barely louder than the rustle of barren cornstalks in the distance.

"More than I bargained for," the words falling flat as he looked out to his field, the stalks swaying in the breeze like tan waves against a rocky cliff of yellow and orange trees. The conquered stalks stood brittle and tired. Perry could not admire the scene. Not yet.

He stretched his fingers, trying to ease the stiffness. The harvest was done, but there was always more work. The wheel never stopped turning. Farming allowed no time for stillness, no time to marvel at the bounty, only the next season, the next task, the next burden. And now, more than ever, his mind was pulled elsewhere.

Perry leaned more heavily against the corn crib. A grit of dirt clung to his skin, his hands raw and weathered. They looked like they belonged to an older man, someone who'd raised more crops and worked more years.

Perry put his horses into their stalls, grabbed his shovel and began to scoop the season's last load of corn into the crib. The soft, steady rhythm of each shovel-load echoed the closing of one chapter and the unsettling start of another.

After the last shovel was heaved, Perry dusted off his hands.

Millie, in her fourth month of pregnancy, appeared in the barnyard, her small frame dwarfed by the buildings around her. She walked toward Perry with purpose.

"You could've stopped by the house and told me you were finishing up," she said, with playful disappointment. "I might be carrying our child, but I'm no porcelain doll. I'd still rather wield a shovel by your side than sit indoors fussing over packing for tomorrow's trip. There's a certain poetry in unloading the last wagonful of the year, Perry, and now I've missed out on all that ceremonial spirit."

"My deepest apologies for robbing you of that joy, my lady. But I did think you might be finding some joy in preparing for tomorrow's excursion."

Millie stopped a few feet from Perry, wrapping her arms around herself against the cool evening. Perry bent to the ground to pick up an errant ear of corn that failed to reach the crib's interior. He handed it to Millie.

"Here you go, my love. The last ear of the harvest. Give it a toss to its proper home, and you can claim authorship to the happy ending for this year's harvest."

Millie smiled as she grabbed the corn, reared back and flung it through the corn crib's open door.

"Makes me feel much better, kind sir."

"How's it going with the preparation for tomorrow's trip?"

"Almost done, but I'm a little worried. What if Pete and Lucy don't agree with the plan? This is asking a lot, and things are changing so fast. We might be putting them in danger too."

Perry walked over to her and placed a comforting hand on her shoulder.

"Pete's always stood by us, and he will know what's at stake. Lucy too. They'll understand why we have to do this."

Millie sighed, gazing toward the distant horizon.

"I know, I know they will. But I keep thinking about what it'll be like being away from you while you're gone, especially now, with the baby coming. I've always been strong, but this time I feel so anxious."

Millie pressed a hand to her stomach, her voice trembling.

"It's different now. I support what you and Moses need to do, but I'm scared, Perry. Scared of what could happen to you and scared of being here alone."

Perry pulled her close, resting his chin on her head. "Millie, I know this path ahead is full of dark clouds and angry floods. But there are some storms from which you don't run. You stand in them, ride it out because on the other side, there's a calm. I wouldn't step into this if I didn't believe what's waiting for us is worth the rain."

She nodded against his chest but didn't say anything for a moment. Finally, she whispered, "I just don't want to lose you. Not now. Not when our family is just beginning."

"This journey is about bringing peace to what's been torn apart. We need that peace in our holler and beyond. Once we help Moses find that rest, we all might have a future burdened and blessed by farming."

Millie pulled back, still smiling as she looked deep into Perry's eyes.

"I know. And I'll be strong while you're gone, but it doesn't stop me from worrying. About you, about the baby, about Archy. About everything."

"Millie, worrying isn't a very Christian thing. We don't carry these burdens alone. We are walking this road with help from above. It's only human to be worried, but we've got to have faith that we'll all be guided through this."

"Just promise me one thing, Perry."

"Anything."

"Promise me that when things get hard out there, you'll think of us. Of me and our soon-to-arrive baby. And that you'll come back no matter what."

"Indeed, I will," Perry replied, his mind racing ahead. "I've been thinking tomorrow would be a good time for us to make a quick run over to Roubideaux to talk with Pete and Lucy. You up for the trip?"

"I'm ready for anything. Just don't go thinking I'll let you face trouble without me. I may be pregnant, Perry, but I'm still an Adams."

As dawn broke the next morning, Perry harnessed Beulah and Barney to the wagon and he and Millie set off toward Roubideaux. Strapped to Perry's leg for security was his Colt revolver, while his Burnside carbine rifle was tucked under the wagon seat. The road was firm beneath them, its path smooth from many journeys past. The trip was quiet, a kind of uneasy stillness. As they rode, the conversation between them was light, but Perry could tell Millie's thoughts were elsewhere.

After a few miles, dark clouds began to roll in behind them. The wind picked up, bringing a chill that cut through their coats. Perry glanced up at the sky. "Looks like a storm's coming," he muttered.

As the wind howled around them, a dark figure rode toward them. Perry squinted, slowing his horses as the rider came into view. The man's face was hidden beneath a black, wide-brimmed hat, shadowing his features. But as the rider drew closer, the distinguished posture and fine coat gave him away. Perry's eyes widened.

"Judge Merriweather?" he called out.

The rider tipped his hat back revealing the weathered but sharp face of Judge Virgil Merriweather, the mayor and elder statesman of Lowland, Kansas.

"Good morning, Perry, and a blessed morning to you too, Mrs. Adams. This is a pleasant surprise."

Perry extended his hand. "Good to see you, Judge. What brings you to this path this early morn?"

Judge Merriweather reached out and shook Perry's hand, his eyes sparkling.

"Got wind of some news about our recovering nation, and I wanted to measure the tone across the river. Spent the night there, but now heading home. Are you heading Missouri way yourselves?"

"We are," Perry nodded, then hesitated. "You mentioned hearing some news about the state of things, about the nation recovering. What exactly have you heard, Judge? I'd like to know what we're up against, especially with all the unrest stirring. Seems like folks around here are on edge."

Judge Merriweather, ever the eloquent speaker, straightened in his saddle and began with a measured tone.

"Ah, Perry, we all know we are living in a moment of transition, one where the tides of change pull at our reconstituted nation. Word travels with swiftness across the winds. The Union Army, which has stood as both a shield and a symbol of hope for our like-minded southern cousins, is retracting its presence. Reconstruction—our great national endeavor to mend what was torn asunder—is beginning to falter. And, as with any fragile endeavor, cracks are showing where we most need stability."

"What do you mean by 'falter'?"

The judge leaned forward. "The Union presence has been the binding force, ensuring the rights of the newly freed are upheld, matters like freedom and citizenship."

Judge Merriweather drew a deep breath, his voice as somber as a preacher at a deathbed.

"The heart of our recovering nation is much like a field after the harvest, capable yet spent for the season. The Union, while steadfast in its intentions, is facing the inevitable weight of weariness. The soldiers who have safeguarded this fragile peace are eager to return to their homes, to reclaim their lives from the long shadow of war. And therein lies the danger."

The judge paused to catch his breath. "With fewer guardians to enforce the laws of this new order, we may find ourselves standing in a perilous void. Where justice is not rooted, there are those who will seek to plant the seeds of discord. The old guard, those clinging to the remnants of a fractured past, will snag opportunity in the absence of authority. And, my dear friends, when such forces move unchallenged, unrest is not just a possibility. It is a certainty."

The judge's eyes narrowed. "This is the moment when vigilance is not just a virtue, but a necessity. For a nation unguarded in its rebirth is ripe for those who would return it to its former chains."

A tightness tickled Perry's throat. "So, you're saying trouble's brewing?"

Judge Merriweather's eyes darkened as he nodded. "Trouble, my dear friends, is quiet and insidious. We must all tread with care, for not all those you meet on this road share our commitment to what is just and righteous."

Judge Merriweather paused, letting his words settle before his expression softened.

"But let us not lose heart, Perry. For every shadow cast, there has to be a light that breaks through. The seeds of justice have been planted deep, and though the winds of resistance may blow they are but a light breeze. Those seeds will take root. We stand at the edge of a new dawn, where freedom can flourish, if we, together, tend to it with courage and resolve."

"Well, you know, Judge, I am a farmer, quite good at things like tilling soil and nurturing seeds."

At that moment, the skies above opened up, releasing a sudden and chilling downpour. The rain, cold and relentless, pelted the earth as if to underscore the challenges still ahead. Perry and Millie pulled their collars tighter, while the judge simply adjusted his hat, smiling through the torrent.

"Ah," Merriweather said with a touch of wry humor, glancing upward. "It seems the elements wish to remind us that even in the face of hope, we must weather our trials."

The judge doffed his hat and continued, giving a small nod to Perry and Millie.

"Before I forget, Perry," he added, almost offhandedly, "how are things with Moses and Gabe? I received a curious telegram yesterday from a St. Louis attorney, a person unknown to me, asking if either of them were residents of this county. Strange, wouldn't you say?"

"Who sent it? What did it say, exactly?"

Merriweather paused, a shadow passing over his face. "That's all I can share for now, I'm afraid. Confidential legal matters. But it gave me pause." He shifted in his saddle, the warmth in his smile fading.

Perry frowned with unease. "Does it sound like good news or bad?" he pressed, trying to catch any hint in the judge's expression.

Merriweather remained stoic, the rain beading on his weathered face. He held Perry's gaze for a moment, unblinking, his lips twitching as he considered the question.

"I couldn't say," Merriweather replied, his tone flat and unreadable. "Matters like these have a way of unfolding in their own time."

Perry's frustration flared, but he bit it back. "But, surely…"

The judge cut him off. "Perry, some things must remain behind closed doors, but a matter from the past has resurfaced." His eyes held an unreadable flicker. Good or bad, he masked it behind his usual calm. "We'll speak again when the time is right."

With that, Merriweather tipped his hat once more.

"Well, my friends," he said, pulling the brim of his hat tighter against the rain, "I shall leave you to your journey. May it be a safe one, despite the storm clouds, both in the sky and, perhaps, on the road ahead."

"As for me, I must return to Lowland before my absence becomes more conspicuous than the weather. My wife, bless her heart, has planned quite the feast for today's noontime meal—duck and rabbit from my last venture into the thickets. If I don't make it back in time, I'll never hear the end of it. Farewell and may Providence guide you both."

With a warm smile, Judge Merriweather turned his horse toward the road. With a gentle nudge, his horse trotted off into the rain-soaked distance. The good judge slowly vanished into the gray mist, leaving Perry with more questions than answers.

CHAPTER 5

Late October 1865

RECKONING AT THE RIVER'S EDGE

THE DOWNPOUR SUBSIDED as Perry and Millie approached the ferry dock on the Kansas side of the Missouri River. The river was a roiling expanse of muddy water, swollen from heavier rains upstream that had turned its gentle currents into a swirling maze of floating logs. Perry coaxed the horses aboard the riverside ferry as it creaked and groaned. The ferryman steered it against the current, logs bouncing off its bow. Perry stood in the wagon to gain a better view, his hand resting on Millie's back, steadying her as they crossed. The water boiled in eddies and ripples, its surface a turbulent reflection of the situation they soon might encounter.

The wind whipped at their cloaks, carrying with it the cold bite left by the quickly departed storm. The dark clouds gave way. Millie appeared calm, her eyes steady as she gazed across the water.

"Feels like the river knows what we're up to," she said, pulling her cloak tighter around her shoulders. The wind whipped at the loose strands of her long black hair, sending them dancing around her face.

Perry glanced at her, and nodded, his eyes fixed on the far riverbank of Roubideaux. He drew out his brass spyglass that had once belonged to his great, great grandfather, a shipmate aboard Blackbeard's infamous pirate ship that terrorized coastal Carolina.

"Maybe the river does know. Nature often has a way of sensing things before we do."

"I can't shake the feeling that this is just the beginning. Everything feels like it's teetering, about to be swept away by a sneaky storm. But I have no doubt, we are doing the right thing, Perry. I know it."

Perry's hand tightened on her back.

"We've weathered storms, Millie. We'll weather this one too."

Millie looked at him with a fierceness that startled him for a moment.

"We've faced plenty. And we've never run, except for maybe when I ran away from my exploration of the religious life in the convent. But this time, it's more about the people we're pulling into this, the people we care about. Pete and Lucy have their own worries, their own lives. And here we are, asking them to risk everything for Moses."

"All we can do is appeal to them about what is right. We can make a difference, and that's the kind of world I want for our child, one where people don't turn their backs on each other."

Millie didn't react at first. Her gaze fixed on the approaching far bank, lips parted like she'd left certainty across the water. The ferry jolted against the dock on the Missouri side of the river, wood groaning, ropes thudding. She clutched her satchel tight.

The ferryman threw out the ropes, securing the vessel to the worn wooden pilings, and shouted a word of caution. "Mind yer wagon folks. The planks 're slicker than a weasel in a butter churn."

Perry tossed the ferryman a coin for fare, snapped the reins, and the horses moved forward onto a muddy path before hitting the plank streets of Roubideaux. The wind rattled the chain-suspended wooden signs from the front of businesses lining the street. A scent of smoke and damp earth flooded their nostrils. The town was hunching its shoulders, and the streets were quiet, except for the occasional gust of wind that sent the few remaining autumn leaves skittering across the ground like startled birds.

They took the straightest route to Pete and Lucy's Outpost Tavern, where it most definitely would not be quiet. It was late Saturday morning and everyone in town knew the breakfast fare at The Outpost could not be missed.

Horses and carriages crowded the street as they approached the establishment. After lifting Millie from the wagon, Perry held her hand as they approached. With each step they edged closer to Pete and Lucy's, their thoughts were warmed by the promise of coffee and hot food, a much-needed break from the tension of the ferry ride. The sound of laughter poured out the swinging door, which Pete had not yet replaced for the winter season.

As Perry swung open the door, the tavern was humming with life. Locals filled the tables, chatting over the clinking of plates and forks, and the rich aroma of frying bacon wove through the scent of fresh bread. Pete and Lucy were in full stride serving their typical Saturday breakfast and brunch to the fine townsfolk of Roubideaux.

Bar owner Pete Fontaine spotted them first, his eyes narrowing as he took in Perry and Millie standing at the entrance to his bar. Pete's voice boomed across the room, "Well, awesome possum, look who's come blowin' in with the wind. It's been months. Perry, Millie, what a surprise this is."

Pete leaned against the scuffed oak bar with his usual commanding presence. He wore a rugged but jovial look that let patrons know he'd seen more bar brawls than he'd care to admit. His thick, barrel-like chest was clad in a faded flannel shirt with rolled-up sleeves, revealing his signature ace of spades tattoo—the death card, an unspoken warning that, if necessary, he could do more than just serve drinks. His waxed handlebar mustache flared out like a small pair of wings that matched his bushy mutton-chop sideburns. Pete was in his late 30s, his jet-black hair thinning slightly. His formidable build hadn't softened much, save for the belly that hinted at his habit of sampling the bar's finest brews.

Pete grew up the son of a poor sharecropper near Jonesboro, Arkansas. He was all too familiar with hard labor, but he spoke of his past with pride rather than bitterness. He'd inherited a slow, deliberate Southern drawl that he wielded to full effect, calmly spoken but unmistakably firm, the kind of voice that could quiet a room if things got rowdy. Pete held onto his southern roots without much nostalgia. Though he respected where he'd come from, he had little patience for the darker legacies of the past.

"Great to see you, my friends. I thought you'd be hunkered down on the farm this autumnal season."

"Just wrapped up harvest, so we thought it might afford us time for a quick trip away from the holler," Perry grinned, exchanging a nod with Pete.

"Well, I just happen to have two final chairs left, the fancy table with the candles in the corner. I'd be honored for you to join us. And, Perry, you might be interested in knowin' we've improved on your slipshod recipe of biscuits and gravy. It's been selling out every Saturday. And, we've added flapjacks."

"I can't say whether I am honored or insulted by your upgrades to my recipe, Pete. Guess I might have to try it, but only if it comes with one of those delectable mixes of beer and tomato juice—a 'mater beer as I recall."

"I would expect to serve you no less, Perry. It's my greatest contribution to frontier society, at least thus far."

As Perry and Millie took their seats at the fancy table, Lucy bounded around the corner in her trademark apron and a warm smile breaking across her face. Pete called her his blond-haired spitfire. A constant spirit of intensity poured from her presence. Just over five feet tall, she was the room's true commander. Lucy's calm, unwavering gaze could still a crowd as surely as any shout from Pete. Her ash-blonde hair, swept into a loose braid, framed a fine-boned face with striking pale green eyes that missed nothing. Moving through the tavern with practiced grace, she managed lively patrons and clinking glasses as if it were second nature.

Her only flaw was a strong aversion to smoked salmon. Her dislike stemmed from a fateful day at Marcus' trading post, years earlier. Lucy had trekked there eagerly, craving the smoky delicacy, only to find the shelf bare, a casualty of Marcus' famously lax inventory management. Frustrated and salmon-less, she'd spun on her heel and blamed Pete, who was the unfortunate young man stocking the shelves. Pete met her ire with an easy grin that melted her annoyance at him, but from that day, she forever swore off smoked salmon as a symbol of her spunky defiance.

Just like that day, Lucy's voice was sandpaper scratchy, but it carried a confident firmness. Lucy's loyalty to Millie ran deep, her warmth matched by her resilience. She commanded a rare strength of spirit that held the tavern together as surely as Pete's physical presence. She was the heart of the place. Pete was the muscle.

"Good to see you two," she said, setting steaming mugs of coffee in front of them. "How long's it been? Four, maybe five months? Sure hope you're hungry. We've been bakin' since dawn."

"Lucy, do I smell your cinnamon rolls?," Millie asked. "I swear, I have dreamt of them since Perry told me we were going to make a visit."

"So, yes. That will be one steamy cinnamon roll for the lady. Anything else?"

"They're as big as a plate. I don't think I would have room for much more."

"And how about you, Mr. Adams?"

"Well, Pete tells me you have tried to perfect what I already considered immaculate recipes for biscuits and gravy, so I reckon I had better find out."

Lucy's eyes sparkled with a mix of mischief and pride as she wiped her hands on her apron. "Coming right up, you sweet talker. But don't go thinking a little flattery's gonna earn you a second helping," she teased. "Though if Pete's been runnin' his mouth about my improved recipe, you'd better brace yourself, Mr. Adams. I've added a little extra kick, so you remember whose recipes are truly flawless."

She winked, already heading back to the kitchen with a light laugh. "Hope you've got a hearty appetite, Perry—this isn't for the faint of heart!"

"Hey, Lucy," Millie interrupted. "Can you come back for a second? Perry and I would like to spend some time with you and Pete after the breakfast rush has died down. You know, sit and chat about some things."

Lucy paused, her smile playful yet touched with warmth as she looked at Millie. "Well, now, you two planning to steal me away from my own kitchen? I must be in for some special news or at least some worthy gossip." She gave Millie a gentle pat on the shoulder, glancing between her and Perry.

"Tell you what," Lucy continued, nodding back toward the stove, "I'll whip up the best breakfast this side of the state, then we'll sit down together. Just the four of us. You know I don't get out of my kitchen often enough. Let me finish fattenin' up this crowd first, and then I'm all yours. Plus, I have some news to share with you as well. Just don't plan on wearin' me out with too many stories, or I might put you to work! Be right back."

She bounced into the kitchen and then, just minutes later, Lucy carried out two plates and placed them in front of her honored guests.

Millie's plate was dominated by a cinnamon roll. It was a golden-brown swirl that spilled over the edges. Its surface glistened with melted butter that soaked into the soft dough. The roll's spirals, packed tight with dark cinnamon sugar, unraveled under the warmth, revealing gooey pockets of sweetness. A generous drizzle of creamy icing pooled in the crevices, mingling with the butter in a decadent dance. The outer edges had a slight crispness, but the center remained soft and pillowy, promising each bite to be melt-in-your-mouth perfection. The aroma of cinnamon, butter, and sugar filled the air, drawing Millie's eyes to the indulgent masterpiece before her.

Perry's plate was also a sight to behold. Two biscuits sat at the center, each one split open and smothered in thick, spicy pork sausage gravy. The biscuits, fluffy and buttery, soaked up the rich gravy, which was flecked with bits of sausage, hints of cracked pepper and other red spicy bits. It was a creamy, velvety sauce with a strong hint of heat, far more flavorful than the bland chipped-beef variety that bore Perry's trademark. The spicy kick of the sausage melded into the smoothness, offering a perfect balance of warmth and richness in every bite. The plate was a heap of hearty, indulgent satisfaction.

"I could have had Pete bring this out to you, but I wanted to soak in the honor myself," Lucy said.

"Oh, Lucy, you have outdone yourself. I can't wait to dig in," Millie said.

"I must also endorse that assessment," Perry said. "I see you have changed the recipe by dumping the chipped beef for pork sausage. Wish I would have thought of that."

"All in a day's work," Lucy said. "Now let me fetch that 'mater beer for Perry."

She returned with a thick glass mug filled with a rustic concoction of beer and tomato juice, Pete's signature mix. The amber liquid frothed to the brim of the mug with a light fizz that leapt at the surface. The drink had a deep, earthy hue somewhere between amber and rust. Perry's mouth watered at its sight.

"Now, I'll leave you two at it," Lucy said. "Once the rush grinds to a halt, I'll bring Pete over so we can get caught up."

"No rush, Lucy," Millie said. "I think it's going to take us a while."

As the number of guests began to dwindle, Lucy came by to cart off the plates.

Perry's plate was clean, not a speck remaining. Try as she might, Millie could finish only about half of her cinnamon roll.

"Millie, I'm proud you were able to finish what you did," Lucy said. "And, Perry, you left only a ghost on your plate. So, what's your verdict?"

"Well, Lucy," he began, drawing out his words as she glanced over her shoulder. "Just another affirmation that every day is a blessing. I gotta hand it to you. This was downright perfection."

Lucy smirked as she stopped her work and faced him fully. "Oh, really now?" she teased, crossing her arms. "Is that what I'm hearin'? Go on, Perry, don't stop now."

Perry chuckled and gestured to his plate. "I've spent years tryin' to get this right. I always used chipped beef 'cause I thought it had that old-world charm. But this," he pointed to the plate, "this spicy pork sausage was the stroke of genius I never thought of. You didn't just improve my recipe, Lucy. You perfected it."

Lucy's eyes lit up as she clapped her hands together, laughing triumphantly.

Perry raised his hands in mock surrender, grinning. "OK, I admit it. You've got me. I'll never be tempted to make chipped-beef gravy again." He leaned forward with a mischievous glint in his eye. "Of course, if you really wanted to take it to the next level, maybe start a culinary trend, you might consider an option for smoked salmon."

Lucy's smile faded the instant Perry mentioned smoked salmon, and she turned around, hands on her hips, eyes narrowing in a way that made it clear he'd just crossed a line. "Smoked salmon! Of all the things you could suggest, smoked salmon? You know I've hated the stuff since that day I met Pete at Marcus' store. It was the only thing I had on my shopping list that day—and don't you dare forget, there wasn't a scrap of that so-called 'delicacy' in the entire frontier region back then! Marcus and Pete, his flunky, failed me that day. It was more than I could handle. Might as well have been askin' for unicorn steaks!"

Lucy glared at Perry, her arms crossing as she leaned forward. "I've put up with a lot, Perry Adams, but you reminding me about smoked salmon? That's where I draw the line."

Perry, barely containing a laugh, again raised his hands in the air. "Very well, I take it back. No smoked salmon."

Lucy shook her head, muttering, "You're a rascal, Perry, a proper, no-good rascal. If I never hear those two words again, it'll be too soon." She shot a smile and with a victorious crow, she spun back toward the kitchen. "Told you, Perry. Stick with me and you'll never go hungry, or wrong! Just don't push your luck with that smoked salmon nonsense!"

CHAPTER 6

Early November 1865

BONDS OF TRUST

THE CROWD AT The Outpost TAVERN began to thin. The lively chatter and clinking of dishes faded, leaving behind a quieter, more intimate atmosphere. Lucy, wiping her hands on her apron, caught Perry's eye and nodded, signaling it was time. She beckoned to Pete from across the room. Pete, still leaning against the bar, gave her a nod, then grabbed two nearby chairs.

The chairs scraped in protest as Pete dragged them across the rough hardwood floor. He positioned the chairs beside Perry and Millie's table before retrieving mugs and a fresh pot of coffee.

"Hope you don't mind the racket," Pete said with a chuckle, motioning for Lucy to choose her seat first. He stretched his broad frame, resting an arm across the back of Lucy's chair as she joined him. "Since it's been a few months, I figured we'd better get comfy for this little interaction."

"Good move, Pete, because we have considerable news to share," Perry said. He and Millie exchanged glances, both beaming about the unshared news that was too good to hold back.

Pete grinned. "Spit it out already. You two have that look. What's goin' on?"

Millie's eyes sparkled as she reached for Perry's hand. "Well, since you asked, come spring there's going to be an extra seat at our table. We're expecting a little Adams."

For a split second, Pete and Lucy were speechless, then their reactions exploded in pure joy. Lucy clapped her hands, her face lighting up as she leapt from her chair.

"Millie! Perry!" She reached over and squeezed Millie's hands, her eyes shimmering with happy tears.

Pete let out a booming laugh, his hand slapping down on the table. "Well, I'll be damned! A little Adams, huh? That's the most awesome of all possums."

Millie laughed, squeezing Lucy's hand back. "We're thrilled, too. Nervous, but excited."

"That's the best news I've heard all year. Almost!" Lucy said.

"Almost?" Millie asked, almost offended.

A glint of mischief returned to Lucy's eyes as she glanced at Pete. "Well, we've got our own news to share."

Pete chuckled, shaking his head as he looked at Perry and Millie. "Guess the good news doesn't stop with you two. Doc Anderson gave us some news of our own."

Lucy's smile deepened. "After all these years of trying and hoping, Doc Anderson tells us that we're expecting too. We've finally planted the seed."

For a moment, it was as if time froze at the table. Millie's jaw dropped, and Perry's eyes widened with surprise. Then, almost in unison, the joy erupted again. Millie sprang from her chair to embrace Lucy, laughing and crying at the same time. "Lucy, that's incredible! I can't believe it. You and Pete! We'll both have little ones running around soon! When are you due?"

"Doc Anderson says probably mid-March. I'm just now beginning to feel the difference."

Perry, grinning from ear to ear, reached over to shake Pete's hand. "Looks like we're both in for some sleepless nights, old friend. I couldn't be happier for you two. We're in this together, huh?"

Pete's eyes gleamed with pride and emotion. "We might not be as young as you and Millie, but I reckon we've got a few tricks left in us," he said with a wink. "Doc Anderson says it might be tough, but we're ready for it. We've been ready."

The table buzzed as joy wrapped the friends in warmth. The tavern shrunk around them, four friends, soon to be parents, anticipating the most important chapter of their lives.

After the initial excitement simmered down, the conversation shifted to a quieter, more reflective tone. Perry leaned back in his chair, his hand still resting on Millie's. "You know, it's funny how life works. We spend so much time chasing after things—money, success for our businesses, even a little bit of happiness now and then. But when it comes down to it, none of that matters."

Pete nodded. "Ain't no riches in this world worth what we got sittin' right here."

"When the world feels too heavy, friends make all the struggle worth it," Lucy said.

Millie nodded. "It's about knowing that when the tough times come, and they always will, we've got each other. That's the real treasure."

The four friends sat in silence. The fireplace crackled nearby, the sound a gentle reminder of the warmth and comfort they found in each other's company. The future, uncertain and full of challenges, was more approachable knowing they would experience it together.

"To family," Pete said, raising his coffee mug in a toast.

"To family," the others echoed, clinking their mugs in a moment both simple and profound.

As the warmth of their shared joy settled, Perry's expression shifted, the joy fading from his eyes. He leaned forward, his hand resting on the table as he cleared his throat. The sudden seriousness in his demeanor caught Pete's and Lucy's attention. Millie, sensing the change, placed a hand on Perry's arm, her face now solemn as well.

"You know," Perry began, "the theme of family is the real reason Millie and I came to see you both."

Pete's eyes narrowed as if trying to read the fine print of Perry's thought. "What do you mean?"

Perry paused, glancing at Millie before continuing. "It's about Moses. You both met him and his son Gabe at our wedding. By all accounts you really hit it off. You know how much he's been through, what he's sacrificed." Perry drew in a long breath. "Moses has made a decision; one that neither he nor we can take lightly. He's going on a mission to rescue his family, back to the plantation over by St. Louis to gather any clues and then head into the deeper South to find them, all of them."

Lucy's hand flew to her mouth, her eyes wide with shock. "His family?" she whispered, her voice trembling. "I didn't even know he had family other than Gabe."

"Oh yes," Millie jumped in. "Has a wife and two other boys. They were shipped off to Memphis and sold before the war. But Moses, he has always carried the promise in his soul that after the war, he would go find them and bring them back to his new home. That time has come."

Pete's face grew hard, his jaw tightened. "I reckon Moses has been carrying that burden a long time. Quiet about it, though. I doubt he wanted to tell me about it to cast clouds over your weddin' day."

Perry nodded. "He doesn't talk about it much, except with me. I don't think he wanted to put any of us in harm's way with just holding that knowledge. Moses has always been one to bear the weight alone. But now he has a chance. He knows in his heart that his wife, Sally, and sons, Michael and Samuel, are alive. He means to extricate them from the dangers they still might face. He's not sure where exactly, but he's determined to find them."

The room fell into a heavy silence, the crackling fire the only sound as Perry's words sank in. Pete leaned back, his eyes dark with contemplation. "That sounds like searching for a needle in a haystack. And he thinks he can do this alone?" he asked, though the question sounded more like a statement.

"That's what he wants," Perry said. "But you know as well as I do that he can't. It's too dangerous, especially for a spirited freedman like himself. There are too many unknowns out there, especially with the way things are now. He needs help, and that's why we came to you."

Millie's voice cut in. "Moses has always put others first. He's always been there for us. Now it's our turn to be there for him. This mission, this rescue, it's about doing what's right, no matter the cost."

Perry leaned back, letting the moment of silence hang in the air, his expression serious once more. He glanced at Millie, her eyes filled with a quiet but steady resolve, before turning back to Pete and Lucy.

"We've made a decision. Millie and I talked it over, and I'm going with Moses on this mission. He's going to need someone to watch his back, especially out in territory that might still be hostile. With everything Moses has been through, he shouldn't be doing this alone."

Pete thought for a second before jumping in. "I figured you'd want to help him. But you're talkin' about a whole different kind of risk now, Perry. You sure this is the right action for you and Millie?"

"It's the only action. Millie and I both agree. It's just the right thing to do. But we can't do this without some extra help."

He paused, awaiting Pete's reaction. "I've been thinkin' about this for a while now. Your knowledge of the South could be crucial, Pete. You know the land, the people, how to travel through places where tensions are still high. You've dealt with the rough edges of this country. We could really use you on this."

Lucy's eyes widened, her gaze flicking over to Pete. "You want Pete to come with you?"

Pete sat back in his chair, rubbing his chin. "Perry, that's askin' a lot. You know I'm not one to shy away from a challenge, but this is different. Just like what we're facing with our wives pregnant and all. This would be like untangling a knot in a spool of twine in the dim light of a flickering candle."

"I know it's a big request, Pete. But you've got the experience we need. If we're going to succeed here, we need someone who knows the land, someone who can read a situation when things get tense. And that's you."

Pete looked over at Lucy, his expression conflicted. She gave him a small nod, her face tense with worry. "Pete, you always stand by what's right when trouble breaks out here at the tavern. You have a good scale of truth and fairness, even in a split second. I think standing by our friends on this comes down heavy on the side of right," she said, disregarding the other factors she and her husband were facing.

Pete leaned back in his chair, the initial thought of the proposition pressing on his mind. He looked at Lucy before his eyes shifted to Millie, who sat with her fingers interlaced. "But what about you two ladies? Both of you are expectin' come March. How would we keep y'all safe if we're out there on this mission? What about your health?"

Lucy glanced at Millie, the unspoken worry clear in her eyes. Millie smiled, her calm demeanor meant to reassure.

Perry was quick to jump in, sensing the rising concern. "We've thought about that, Pete. We expect to have this entire journey done and dusted well before your little one, or ours, arrives. We won't be out there long, just long enough to search for and hopefully to bring Moses' family back. We may come back empty-handed. If we don't find them, at least Moses will know he's done everything in his power to make that happen. I do have an idea or two that might make it work for all of us."

Pete leaned forward. "Go on. But understand that you're not just asking for my time or help. You're dragging Lucy, me and even our unborn child into it, so you better have more than an idea or two. You better have a damn good plan."

The room hushed around them. Pete's gaze locked on Perry, having seen the consequences of risks taken lightly. "I need to know you've thought this through. My biggest concern is leaving our wives alone."

"How about Millie moving in with Lucy, just for the time we're gone," Perry suggested. "They could look after each other. Millie could help out around The Outpost, maybe even play the piano again for your patrons like in the old days. It'd give both of them some company and support while we're on the road."

Lucy's eyes lit up at the thought, her face breaking into a wide smile. "Millie, playin' the piano again? Oh, I can already hear it. It'd bring such life to this place, just like old times." Her mind raced with happy possibilities. "You and I could make it work, Millie. I'd love the company."

Pete shot Lucy a frown after her premature exuberance.

Lucy's smile held firm, though her eyes sharpened as they locked on Pete. "If Pete goes with you, then you'd better watch his back. I'm not scared. I just know what danger looks like, and I don't take it lightly. He comes back, or you don't come back at all. Understood?"

Millie leaned in, her grip on Lucy's hand steady, resolute. "I've thought the same about Perry. But fear doesn't run this show. We do. This mission matters, and I believe in them. Pete and Perry know what they're walking into, and they'll make it back. We don't wait in fear— we stand ready."

Lucy gave a sharp nod, blinking away the sting in her eyes before dabbing them with her apron. She drew a deep breath, her jaw set firm. "You're damn right, Millie. It's hard, but that doesn't mean we flinch. I trust Pete with my life, and if this is the path we must walk, then I'll march it. No second-guessing."

Lucy's eyes shifted to Pete who was secretly yearning for the possible adventure despite his outward facade of concern.

"Pete, you should know by now I don't take guff from fools. The tavern will be fine, and Millie and I will be fine too. I love you dearly, but I think I can live without your chivalry for a couple of months, as long as you promise to come back safe. I'll take care of things here while you're gone, and Millie and I will keep each other company."

"You're a strong woman, Lucy, my love. As for the trip, don't worry about me. I'm tougher than saddle leather, and if I come upon a sword imprisoned in stone, I'll pull that bastard out quicker than Arthur. Among me, Perry, and Moses, we'll handle whatever's out there, and your knight shall return."

Perry grinned. "That's exactly the plan, Sir Pete. You've got the knowledge and the instincts that we'll need. I wouldn't have asked anyone else. Your skill, your experience, it'll make all the difference.

The risks are there, but we can manage them. And the reward at the end will make it all worth it."

Lucy smiled with pride in her eyes as she looked at Pete, and then at Perry. "If you do this, you both better swear a sacred oath that you will be careful."

"We will," Perry said, before Pete could reply. "You have my word."

"We'd be goin' in smart and comin' out safe, or we wouldn't go at all," Pete replied.

Pete leaned back, his eyes locking with Perry's, and for a moment, the two men shared a look of understanding. "You got it," Pete said. "I'm in. Let's bring Moses' family home."

Perry thrust his fist into the air and quickly returned his thoughts to practical matters regarding the trip.

"Pete, you know the route as well as I do. What's your time estimation for how long the travel part of our mission will take? We head over to Saint Louie and down to Memphis. Only the Good Lord knows how long our actual search might take."

Pete rubbed his wrinkled forehead, his gaze drifting to a dark corner of the room as he mapped out the journey in his mind. "Well, Perry, reckonin' the mileage and the stops we'll need to make along the way, I'd say the travel part from here to St. Louis is probably going to be two, maybe two and a half weeks. It's pretty rough. But once we hit St. Louis, we can shoot south to Memphis using the Memphis and Hernando Plank Road. That's probably a very dependable two weeks, as long as we don't meet any setbacks."

"That's kind of what I was thinking too. If we throw in some time to resupply and rest the horses for a couple days near Gumbo Flats, I'm thinking for travel time alone from here to Memphis is just a little over a month. Then figure another month to get back here and another month, maybe two, for our search. By that point, we should know if Moses' family can be traced and found. That gives us about four months. Regardless of our success, I figure we're back here by late February at the latest, and I can get my fields plowed and crops planted by the end of April."

"And we'll both be home by the time we become papas in mid-March," Pete said.

"No doubt about it," Perry said smiling, looking at Millie.

Pete glanced toward Millie and Lucy. "No offense to you two ladies, and I don't doubt either of your capabilities, but while we're gone, I would like to make sure there's an extra measure of security around this place. The Outpost gets lively on the best of days, and if folks catch wind that I'm out of town for a spell, well, I reckon we'll need someone to help keep the peace. A little local muscle. Someone trustworthy."

Lucy shot Pete a curious look. "Nobody can cover for you, Pete, but do you have someone in mind?"

Pete nodded. "Yeah. I know just the person. Lucy, you know Hank Crowder. Comes in here occasionally for a quick glass of beer and conversation."

"Oh yes, I know Hank. He'd be perfect."

Pete looked to Perry. "He's been doing custodial work over at the mission school for a couple years now. He's trustworthy and knows how to handle himself. Plus, he's well-mannered with all the Sisters who teach over there."

"I know Hank too," Millie added. "He's a solid and upright man. Never met a problem without a solution. Plus, he's a large imposing gentleman."

"He grew up tough a little east of here in Hamilton, used to wrangle cattle, and spent some time as a deputy in a small town out that way before he came here," Pete added.

"Sounds like a good choice," Perry replied.

"I've seen him break up a few disputes before they got out of hand without ever raising his voice," Pete said. "He's good with people, firm but fair. More importantly, he's got the build to make sure no one thinks twice about actin' up in the tavern."

Lucy nodded, a thoughtful look crossing her face. "The last thing we want is trouble brewin' here while you two are off on your southern crusade."

Pete chuckled. "I'll talk to Hank Monday morning."

"Well, sounds like you've thought it through," Perry said, smiling. "It's good to know the tranquility of this place will be in capable hands. And Lord knows, if anyone gets past Hank, they'd still have Lucy to deal with."

Lucy, still looking thoughtful, let out a long breath and smiled. "Pete, if you trust Hank, then I trust him. But if there's any doubt, any hesitation, at the first hint of trouble, I'll send him packin'."

Pete laughed. "Don't worry, Lucy. Hank can handle himself. He'll keep the security detail of The Outpost runnin' smooth as silk while we're gone, under your watchful eye of course."

The plan was set, and a sense of ease washed over the group. While Pete and Perry prepared for their mission with Moses, they knew The Outpost Tavern, and the two women they cared most about, both expecting children in March, would be doubly safe with Hank behind the bar.

CHAPTER 7

Early November 1865

BARGAINS AND BARTER

"WELL, PETE, WE'VE GOT the will and a broad plan for our mission, but now we need the means," Perry said. "The way I see it, we're going to need a solid, covered wagon stocked to the brim with supplies for the trip."

Pete nodded, taking a sip from his coffee. "Not to mention a few extra things along the way. I've been thinkin' about some new armaments—maybe a couple of shotguns. Might need 'em to hunt along the road, and, well, you never know what we might run into out there."

Perry chuckled. "Shotguns, a wagon and supplies. That sounds like a job for our old friend Marcus."

"Ah, Marcus. That slippery old dog. Dealing with him is like trying to wrestle a greased hog." He leaned forward, tapping the table with his finger. "We'll need to go see him together. You know how he is, trying to squeeze a bargain out of him solo is like walkin' into a swamp blindfolded."

Perry laughed heartily, nodding. "Yeah, dealing with Marcus is about as dangerous as this rescue mission. It's more than one man should handle alone for sure."

Their laughter rang out through the tavern, and on cue, Millie and Lucy, who had been lost in their own conversation, glanced over. Millie grinned, her eyes twinkling. "You boys seem to think everything's a grand adventure, even when it's just getting supplies."

Lucy snickered, nudging Millie. "Oh, let them have their fun. Besides, it's good practice. I hope that Marcus turns out to be the toughest challenge they face on this trip."

Pete waved a hand in mock defeat. "You're not wrong about that, Lucy. Marcus can make you feel like you've just paid double for half the goods."

Millie leaned toward Lucy. "And while they're off wheeling and dealing, we'll be making our own plans. Think of it, Lucy, time for just us. I can't wait to play that song, Shenandoah, like the old days. Your patrons loved that one."

Lucy's eyes lit up, her face bright with excitement. "Oh, I'd love that. You'll help keep me sane while Pete's off playing hero. Having you here with me is the best possible remedy."

Plotting their time together, the women giggled like schoolgirls while Perry and Pete stood up from the table.

Perry grabbed his hat and slapped it against his thigh. "Pete, no time like the present. Let's go see how much trouble we can get into with Marcus."

As the wind whipped through the dusty streets, Perry and Pete approached Marcus Mixon's Trading Post. The weathered wooden sign swayed in the cool breeze, creaking above the door. Inside, the shop was cluttered but organized, with barrels of grain, stacks of leather, and rows of goods from floor to ceiling. Marcus stood behind the counter wiping his hands on a worn apron, his shrewd eyes gleaming as the two men entered.

Marcus, the wily proprietor of frontier goods, was a squat, balding man whose sharp eyes missed nothing. His sleeves were always rolled up, held in place by arm garters like a blackjack dealer preparing to shuffle from the bottom of the deck. His smirk suggested he was always a step ahead in any deal. He moved with the confidence of someone who had seen it all on the frontier and could out-negotiate just about anyone, his stout frame built to weather both harsh elements and harder bargains.

Marcus had a knack for turning even the simplest conversation into a performance, talking about the weather, local gossip, or whatever trivial matter crossed his mind. It was all part of his strategy. The more insignificant he could make things seem, the more people would let their guard down, which was exactly when Marcus would strike, securing the upper hand in negotiations. He could haggle over a crate of oats or a rifle with the same casual ease, all while his calculating mind ticked away under the surface.

"Well, well," Marcus drawled, crossing his arms over his chest, "what brings you two gents here this early? Must be somethin' big if Perry and Pete both arrive in my humble shop together. You two looking for a fight or a bargain?"

"Neither one of us have ever seen a bargain walk out of your fine establishment, with maybe the lone exception of the John Deere plow I managed to steal from you at a cut-rate price a couple years back," Perry replied. "But we are not here for a fight, at least not beyond a little good-natured haggling. We have a mission before us, Marcus, and very clearly, we need your help, if such an act of charity is possible."

"Look no further, gents. I am your friendly purveyor of both assistance and goods." Dollar signs began to dance in Marcus's eyes.

Pete leaned against the counter. "There's a reason we need your help, Marcus," he said. "The mission before us is goin' to take us into my old territory. We're headin' south."

"It's a short-term trek, but not for just a change of scenery," Perry added.

Marcus glanced back over his shoulder, curiosity flickering in his eyes. "Only fools would wander that direction for the mere change of venue. Neither of you are fools. I figure you have somethin' brewing.

What's the story?"

Perry approached the counter, tipping his hat as he stepped forward. "You know our friend Moses. Well, he needs help from Pete, me and even you, Marcus. You've helped him before and it's time to step up again. Pete and I are joining Moses on a mission to find his family and bring them back. Turns out they were transported and sold down south. Memphis, specifically."

Marcus straightened, his usual playful smirk fading. "Memphis?" he repeated, his voice tinged with surprise. "Now that's a trip, and maybe a bit dangerous too. You might find some sympathetic scallywags along the way, but for every one of them, there are probably two or three of the opposite persuasion."

"Scallywags? Sounds like a pirate word to me, Marcus. Has it taken a new meaning?" Pete asked.

Marcus leaned in, pulling up his sleeves. "It has, at least that's what my trading partners tell me. A 'scallywag' is what folks down South have been callin' white Southerners who've sided with the Union, or at least with the new laws comin' from Washington since the war ended. See, now that the Confederacy's gone under, there's a whole lotta change comin' down on the South—new laws, new ways of doin' things, and the government's lookin' to rebuild.

"The scallywags are standin' with the Republicans who're runnin' things up North, tryin' to help freedmen get rights and such," Marcus continued. "The old Southern loyalists, though, they see 'em as traitors, sayin' they're turnin' against their own kind just to get ahead under the new order."

Marcus chuckled, though it was humor tinged with bitterness. "Some of these fellas really do believe in buildin' a better South, one without slavery and all that. Others are just lookin' for a way to make money or get a piece of power under the Union. I'm not one to judge any pragmatic businessman trying to make a buck, but 'scallywags' ain't meant as a compliment."

"Well, I'm quite pragmatic myself," Perry said. "We would accept support from anyone willing to offer, including you, Marcus."

"Right now, all we know is that Moses feels as much hellbent as he is heaven-sent to bring his family home," Pete chimed in. "We figure it will be about a three-and-a-half-month commitment, maybe a little less. What we know for sure is that we can't let Moses wander into the South alone. You yourself should understand since you've been by his side ever since before he and Gabe crossed the river to the real freedom offered in Kansas. We've got the workings of a solid plan, but we need the right supplies to make it happen."

Marcus stood silent for a moment. "That's a hell of a thing," he finally muttered. "Moses is a good man. You boys make sure you're ready for what's ahead."

Pete nodded. "That's why we're here. With your help, we'll be ready."

"We're going to need a lot of supplies, and a sturdy means to haul them," Perry said. "I'm thinking a Conestoga wagon with strong wooden roof hoops and a heavy canvas cover, the kind treated with oil to repel the elements."

Marcus smirked as his ruthless side began to take hold. "A covered Conestoga, huh? Those don't come cheap, my friend. And stocked, you say? I think I might have what you need."

Pete cut in, "We're also gonna need a couple of shotguns, Marcus. Some firepower for huntin' and, just in case things get rough out there. We've already got rifles and pistols, but shotguns would also come in real handy."

"I've got a wagon that'll suit your needs on my back lot down by the stable. As for the shotguns, I've got a few choices in the back. But like I said, this probably won't be cheap."

Perry nodded, but his eyes stayed sharp. "We're not asking for a handout, Marcus, but I know you have a strong streak of humanity running through your cold bones. Pete and I have always been good customers, and we know you will cut a fair deal considering the situation."

"Business is business, fellas. At the very least, I know you're good for it. A Conestoga wagon with a good roof, at least a month's supply of goods and a couple of shotguns? That's a tall order. I can't just hand it over without a little somethin' in return."

Perry glanced at Pete, then leaned closer, dropping his voice just a notch. "How about this? You give us a good deal on the wagon and supplies, minimize your profit margin, and when we return, we'll owe you a favor. You know we don't make promises lightly."

Marcus tilted his head, a glint of interest flashing in his eyes. "A favor, huh? Now you're speakin' my language."

Pete stepped forward, resting his hands on the counter. "You know we don't back out of our word, Marcus. We'll make sure it's worth your while. But you've got to give us something fair in return, or this deal and our rescue mission goes nowhere."

Marcus studied them both for a long moment, then let out a long breath, the smirk returning. "Fine. I'll give you the Conestoga at a price that won't send you home broke. And the shotguns and supplies? I'll throw 'em in for what I paid for 'em, plus a small stocking fee, of course."

He held out his hand. "Make sure you give me a little humanitarian credit when you tell Moses. And, boys, don't forget that favor. I'll be callin' on you for it."

Perry smiled, shaking Marcus's hand firmly. "Deal. We're going to be leaving in a week, so that should give you plenty of time."

"Hell, I could get you on the road today. Don't let anyone ever tell you that Marcus Mixon doesn't deliver the goods in St. Joseph."

"Just what in the hell does that mean, Marcus?" Perry asked.

"You mean to tell me that Pete didn't clue you in on the latest maneuverings of our local lawmakers?"

"I know nothing of this. Is Roubideaux no longer Roubideaux?"

"Yup," Pete replied. "It's St. Joseph now. The town fathers changed the name about six months ago. Surprised you didn't see the new sign as you were coming into town."

"It was pretty windy this morning so maybe the sign had blown sideways in the breeze. I've heard of towns changing their names before. Hell, my hometown changed its name from Salt Spring to French Lick, Indiana, after I left town. Fellas, I was quite the hellion in my youth, breaking hearts, going on drunken benders, damaging property that belonged to others, all sorts of mischief. I even stole from my own father, though full restitution has since been made. I suspect part of their motivation for renaming my hometown was so I might not ever find it again."

"A hellion? Surely not our mild-mannered country gentleman friend, Perry Adams," Marcus laughed.

"Oh, yeh. I will not go into all the sordid and sundry details, because that person is no longer me. But that's one of the reasons I ended up here. I didn't feel like I had much of a choice. It was either head west to the land of opportunity or be tarred and feathered and rode out of town on a rail. Though I'm not much good at it, I think it's always best to leave on your own terms. That way you can look back and thumb your nose at those who shunned you."

"And then you came here as a wild-eyed Hoosier abolitionist to steal some government land in Kansas Territory and farm as a squatter. It's all consistent with your pattern of vagrant behavior," Pete laughed.

"I guess you could describe it that way. However, as you gents know, I am much reformed. Now, let's get back to the name of this unpresuming little burg. Why change the name?"

"When it first started, they decided to name the settlement after its founder, one Joseph Robidoux, an old fur trapper and trader," Pete said. "Hell, it wasn't much of an honor for old Joe because the guy who made the signs and maps spelled it wrong. So, a few months back, our town leaders decided that might be part of a perceived image problem, plus it was too hard to say and even harder to spell."

Marcus chimed in, "It's not that Ol' Joe was a problem himself. He was the first owner of the Trading Post. Hell, I learned a lot of the retail trade under his wing."

"I find it humorous you call your profession a trade," Perry smirked. "It requires the charm of a preacher, the cunning of a poker player, and the flexible ethics of a raccoon rummaging through a trash dump at midnight. Did Ol' Joe really teach you all your haggling skills?"

"He most certainly did. Taught me all the ropes."

"So, if he was such an honorable fella, why didn't they just correct the spelling instead of changing the name? What exactly was the problem?"

"Not a problem. A solution. They still wanted to honor Ol' Joe by keeping his name. On top of that, as you know, St. Joseph was the earthly father of Jesus. He was the embodiment of protection, humility, and steadfast loyalty—qualities our officials thought might go a long way after the mixed messages our village put forth during the Civil War. They want our town to represent a place where families seek shelter and build a future, much as Joseph provided for Mary and Jesus in uncertain times."

"It's all kinda ironic if you ask me," Pete said. "Funny thing is, this town ain't seen much protection, not from the likes of war or hard times. Even our old mayor up until just five years ago, Meriwether Jeff Thompson, the 'Swamp Fox of the Confederacy', he sure didn't protect this place from gettin' tangled up in the war."

"The Swamp Fox himself," Perry said.

"Born in Harpers Ferry, but he made his name here," Marcus said. "On the surface, he was a good fella. He didn't have much at first, but he worked his way up. Ran the gas works, a couple railroads, even sent off the first Pony Express rider. But when the war came, he turned all that fire into fightin' for the Confederacy. He led his men through the marshes down south, outfoxing the Union at every turn."

"He may have lost in the end, but he didn't give up. Neither will we," Pete said.

Perry was quiet for a moment, absorbing the story. "Seems like this town, regardless of name, has had its share of people willing to fight for what they believe in, though maybe not always on the right side.

That stands in pretty sharp contrast to the role you played, Marcus, in the Underground Railroad. I guess I understand why the town's image might need a little remodel."

Perry leaned back and crossed his arms, looking toward Marcus.

"You've got a week, oh fine purveyor of the best goods St. Joseph has to offer. Here I thought you were just a regular tradesman, but now I see you might be our first scallywag collaborator."

Marcus chuckled, shaking his head. "I reckon that's about right. A scallywag and proud of it." He shot Perry a sly look. "I'm on the right side of history with this crew."

CHAPTER 8

Early to Mid-November

LOOSE ENDS

THE RIDE BACK TO JAWBONE HOLLER was comparatively quiet after Perry and Millie brewed their big plans with Pete and Lucy. The sky above was a soft shade of purple twilight. Perry and Millie sat side by side. Everything they'd set into motion swirled in their minds in contrast to the stillness of the river bluffs.

As their small farmhouse came into view, nestled among the rolling fields they'd worked so hard to tend, Perry let out a long breath. "Things are falling into place. One step at a time."

Millie nodded, leaning her head against his shoulder. "I believe they are. But there's always the unexpected."

Perry grunted in agreement, his mind already turning to the next step. "I'll go see Moses and Gabe first thing tomorrow. I think they might like a Sunday visitor. I might even stay for dinner, if invited and if you don't mind. We've got to get every last detail in order before we head out."

Millie smiled, lifting her head from his shoulder and giving him a soft nudge. "Of course I don't mind, Perry. I think you having dinner with the Watsons is a grand idea. It might put them more at ease, especially with everything they've got on their minds. Plus, you're going to need time to relay all the details. I know Moses will have questions."

"You're right. I'll stay, give them the space to ask anything they want. And there's that troubling message from Judge Merriweather. I better make sure Moses secures as much information as possible before we take off. No sense heading out on this mission with mysteries and loose ends hanging over our heads."

"If there's anything more to that message, it could change things. The last thing you all need is a surprise creeping up behind you while you're trying to mount a rescue."

Perry sighed, running a hand through his hair. "It's strange, though. That message from an unknown St. Louis attorney, it's just too vague. I don't like it. Could be legal trouble, or something bigger. Either way, Moses has to face it before we go."

Millie wrapped her arms around Perry's waist, leaning into him. "You'll figure it out, Perry. But just be careful. With all the pieces moving, things could turn faster than we expect."

He kissed the top of her head. "I will. Don't worry. I'll get everything sorted, and we'll keep this mission as clean as we can."

They stood in silence for a moment, and then Perry pulled away.

"I need to put the wagon and horses in the barn. Might give Beulah and Barney each some extra grain tonight. They're gonna need to gather their strength over the next week. I might even give Archibald some extra scraps."

"While you're doing that, I'll go in and throw together some suppertime magic."

An hour later, Perry stepped back into the farmhouse after tending the horses. The savory aroma of the evening meal greeted him, tickling his nose with comfort. He hadn't expected Millie to make anything elaborate, especially in short order after the long day they'd both had.

Millie stood by the stove, stirring a pot of rich, meaty stew. Lanterns lit the room. The soft light reflected off Millie's piano in the next room. It was the piano she had played in secret at The Outpost Tavern while serving at the Mission School as teacher, a taboo to which nobody had called attention. Millie called the room her parlor, but it wasn't much more than a hastily added side-room Perry had built onto the home before their marriage.

Back in the kitchen, a loaf of fresh cornbread was cooling on the table, its golden crust cracked just enough to show the soft interior. A small crock of butter sat nearby, alongside a bowl of roasted root vegetables—carrots, turnips, and potatoes—all tossed with herbs and glistening from the oven's heat. She turned, smiling at Perry as he wiped his hands and took a seat.

"I didn't expect you to whip up a feast," Perry said, as he looked at the spread. "But I can't say I'm complaining."

Millie laughed, wiping her hands on her apron before sitting across from him. "It's nothing fancy, just a quick meal that's hearty enough to keep you going before you head out in the morning."

Perry reached for the cornbread, breaking off a chunk and slathering it with butter. He took a bite, savoring its warmth and richness.

"Quick or not, it's good enough to make a man count his blessings. I'm a lucky man. But to top it off, perhaps you can play a few tunes on your piano later."

Millie smiled as she ladled the stew into bowls, the steam rising and filling the air. "It's just a simple beef stew, some root vegetables we had stored, and the cornbread baked while the stew cooked. My piano playing, however, will always be the dessert."

Perry dipped his cornbread into the stew, taking another bite. "A meal like this doesn't need dessert, Millie. But I'll take it. Your playing, like your cooking, is a masterpiece."

As they ate, the warmth of the food and the fire in the hearth created a sense of peace. Above the fireplace, the jawbone of Perry's late mule, Luke, anchored the scene. Amidst the looming uncertainty, the relic of Old Lukey brought calmness to the house. After a few moments of silence, Millie spoke again.

"I'm looking forward to staying with Lucy. I hope you trust that."

Perry looked up from his bowl. "Yeah? You seem pretty excited about it."

Millie nodded. "We don't get to spend much time together like we used to, and I think we both need it, especially with everything coming up. It's going to be exhilarating and comforting at the same time, sharing the experience of being pregnant together. I wouldn't dare tell Lucy this, but it reminds me of the biblical story of Mary and her cousin Elizabeth. Mary was young and Elizabeth was much, much older. Through heaven-sent miracle, they were pregnant at the same time. I'm not sure Lucy would appreciate my musing about her age in such a manner because she's not elderly like Elizabeth was, but it's still a blessing that we get to go through this side by side."

Perry slurped the last of the stew from his bowl and smiled. "I think you two will be good for each other. Lucy's tough, but maybe motherhood will soften her up just a little."

Millie's eyes blinked as she reached across the table, resting her hand on Perry's arm. "And I'll be a lot less worried about you, knowing Pete will be with you."

Perry's thoughts turned to his impending visit with Moses and Gabe. He stood, gathering the dishes from the table. Millie rose to help him, but he waved her off.

"I'll take care of this. You've done more than enough."

Millie smiled, leaning against the supper table. "No complaints from me. It's been a long day. The first of many. But I still owe you at least one song."

Perry chuckled, shaking his head as he worked the pump handle at the sink and rinsed the dishes.

Millie approached and sat down at the worn, upright piano, its keys yellowed with age but still resonant and tuned. She began to play the most popular saloon song of the day, a haunting ballad called "Beautiful Dreamer" by composer Stephen Foster. The gentle melody captured the melancholy created by the assassination of President Lincoln. Like the song's lyrics, many people wanted to escape into a world of dreams and peace.

Millie's fingers danced across the keys. Each delicate note floated through the air like a feather. Her playing was flawless. Each stanza built on the song's bittersweet mood, the song evoked dreams of distant loved ones and the hope of better days. Millie thought it appropriate given Moses' current situation.

Perry stopped pumping water and listened, drawn in by the melody. As Millie played, her expression calm and focused, her grace reflected as though she were playing in the world's finest opera hall. But it was still a modest farmhouse, one filled with the simple joys of their shared life. It was their sanctuary—a place where, no matter what happened beyond its walls, they could always find their way back to each other.

The next morning, as the first light of dawn stretched across the horizon, Perry saddled up his horse, Appy. The chestnut gelding pawed at the ground, eager to get moving, and Perry patted the horse's neck with a soft chuckle. "Let's go, boy."

The world was quieter, as if gathering its breath for the cold months to come. The bare trees stood like sentinels, their branches clawing at the pale blue sky. A squirrel scurried into a hollow tree, and in the distance, a deer moved through the underbrush, foraging for whatever remained before the deep freeze set in.

As Perry rode through the countryside, he marveled at the beauty of the fall morning. The countryside, though bare and preparing for the long sleep of winter, held a peacefulness that settled his spirit. The natural world was quieting, animals retreating into their burrows, preparing for survival, just as he was preparing for the journey ahead.

Perry's thoughts returned to the visit that lay in front of him. He would soon be sitting down with Moses and Gabe, delivering news that wasn't comforting. The cryptic message from Judge Merriweather, sent by an attorney in St. Louis, weighed on his mind. As peaceful as the scene was, the uncertainty of what that telegram might mean loomed over Perry like a storm cloud waiting to burst.

He clicked his tongue, urging Appy forward as the trail curved through the hills and hollers. Moses had enough on his plate and Perry wasn't eager to add to his burdens. But whatever this message from St. Louis was, it needed to be addressed.

As they crossed a shallow stream, Perry filled his lungs with the cool air of resolve. "One thing at a time," he muttered to himself. "We'll figure this out."

Ahead, the familiar outline of Moses' homestead came into view, smoke rising from the chimney, and a separate one from his smokehouse. Both plumes of smoke curled into the orange morning sky. Perry slowed Appy as they neared the house, already bracing himself for the difficult conversation to come.

Stepping down from the saddle, he tied Appy to the porch rail and gave the horse a reassuring pat. "Rest up, boy," he whispered. "We'll be headin' back soon enough."

With a final glance upward, Perry strode toward the house. As peaceful as the morning had been, he steeled himself for the conversation. Moses was out front after finishing his morning chores. He leaned against the rough-hewn wood of his porch. Gabe stood nearby, sharpening a knife with deliberate strokes focused only on that task. Moses glanced up and smiled.

"Good morning to you, Perry. I can't wait to hear the news of your visit to Roubideaux."

"I have a lot to cover, Moses. But for starters, the city fathers changed the name of the town. It's now St. Joseph. They wanted to shed the image of the town being less than hospitable, given Missouri's pro-slavery past and the fact the town produced a few heroes for the Confederacy."

"I see. What was the tone there? Has it shifted with the change in name?"

"All seemed peaceable enough. But there are whispers of continued resistance in locales further south."

"I bet there are," Gabe chimed in. "I pray you gentlemen keep that thought at the forefront of your minds at all times."

"Oh, we will, Gabe," Perry replied. "I will face the terrain with the same intensity you and I mustered during our joint action with the Jayhawkers during the Battle of Leavenworth."

"Well, Perry, as you might recall, I earned a medal during that skirmish, but I also got a hole shot in my leg, and our good friend Constable Dan was sent to the great beyond."

"I'll never forget. But listen, Gabe, you've gotta have some faith in the mission. Negative thinkin' has a way of spoilin' life's good things."

Gabe huffed and then smiled. "You're right, Perry. Faith will help carry you and Papa through this mission. And maybe this time, it won't just be about survivin'. Maybe this time, you'll come back with more than you left with, my mama and brothers. That will change everything in life for the better."

The depth of Gabe's words surprised Perry. "That's the spirit, Gabe. You've got a way of putting things that makes a man think."

Gabe shrugged, the hint of a smile returning. "I've seen enough darkness to know that light's always just around the corner. It's there, even when you can't see it. We just have to keep goin' until we find it."

Moses jumped in. "Okay, Perry, details. I need details. I need to hear about our plan."

"Pete's in," Perry said, cutting straight to the point. "We've got Marcus on board too. He's setting us up with a wagon and all the supplies we'll need. We figure we are looking at three or four months. It's all comin' together. While Gabe looks after Butter and keeps an occasional eye on my farm, Millie is going to stay with Pete's wife, Lucy. And get this, Lucy is pregnant too."

Moses breathed out slowly. "Good. That's a relief. I'm happier than a hog in shit to hear this. So, when we leavin'?"

"We can leave in a week, if that works for you, but first, there's another little matter I need you to handle."

"Sure, Perry, what is it?"

"This is the troubling part. During our trip over to St. Joseph, we ran into Judge Merriweather on the trail, and he relayed a puzzling message related to you."

Gabe's hand paused mid-stroke on the knife before he resumed sharpening, though the rhythm had slowed.

"What did the judge want?" Moses asked with a flicker of unease in his eyes.

Perry shrugged, leaning forward. "Not much. Just mentioned he got a telegram from an attorney fella from St. Louis. Some legal matter. He said it involved you, Moses."

The porch fell into an uneasy silence. Perry noticed the way Gabe stiffened, his jaw tightening. Moses, to his credit, kept his expression neutral, but his hands clenched just a bit tighter around the porch railing he gripped.

"A legal matter, huh?" Moses said, his voice measured. "Did the judge say what it was about?"

Perry shook his head. "He was cryptic. He said the telegram wasn't clear. I suggest that before we leave, you should stop down in Lowland and talk to him. He wouldn't share any details with me, but since it sounds like it involves you, I think you're entitled to know the full scuttlebutt. Could be nothing, but I'd feel better if you got ahead of it. Just to be safe."

Moses and Gabe exchanged a glance, their silence sharp enough to cut, a message Perry couldn't decode. Gabe's face hardened, the humor gone from his usual smirk, while his eyes widened just enough to signal alarm. Perry felt the weight in the air shift. Neither father nor son spoke, leaving Perry to wonder what they weren't saying and why.

Perry leaned back. "Anything I should know about?"

Moses forced a smile, shaking his head. "No, nothin' to worry about. Just sounds like more legal dust-ups, probably related to the freedom papers we were given before we moved out here. The man who issued those papers is an attorney named John Manchester and he lives in

St. Louis. He's the son of the man who shipped my family off for sale before my very eyes. In spite of his father's cruel streak, John's just the opposite. We grew up together like brothers of different colors."

Perry wasn't convinced, but he let it slide. "If you can, just get your matters in order with Judge Merriweather. This trip might take longer than we plan, and I don't want anything hanging over your head while we're gone. And Lord knows, we don't need any distractions."

Moses nodded. "I'll make sure everything's set."

Perry turned to Gabe, offering a nod of appreciation. "And, thanks for your help, Gabe. With Millie moving in with Lucy, I need someone reliable to keep an eye on Jawbone Holler. You've always been good with the land."

Gabe gave a brief nod, his hands never stopping their work on the blade. "It's no trouble."

Satisfied, Perry rose to his feet, dusting off his pants. "We'll head out soon. Just be ready."

"Since you're here, why not stay for a spot of dinner?" Moses asked. "Gabe and I butchered a fine market hog yesterday. I fired up the smoke house before sunrise and I have two full racks of ribs that are far more than we can eat. Won't you stay, Perry?"

"I could smell that smoky pork goodness from a mile away, Moses. I never thought you'd ask. I'd be honored to break bread with you gentlemen."

The three friends feasted and talked more about shared memories, as well as the possible future.

"Hate to eat and run like this, fellas," Perry said, his shirt buttons almost popping from the meal, "but I have plenty to prepare back in Jawbone Holler before the trip."

As he left, Perry paused at the edge of the porch, turning back toward Moses. "Don't ignore what the judge said. Better to meet trouble head-on than wait till it's breathing down your neck."

Moses smiled, though it didn't quite reach his eyes. He opened and closed his hands to feel the hollow sensation of his scarred palms.

"You're right. I'll handle it."

As Perry began his trek back to Jawbone Holler, a thought tugged at the back of his mind. It was the near-panicked look he saw in Moses' eyes, the tension in Gabe's posture. It didn't sit right with him. But Moses was a private man, and Perry respected that. For now, he'd focus on the mission ahead and hope that whatever was lurking beneath the surface wouldn't come back to haunt them.

As Perry rode away in the distance, back on the porch, Moses turned to Gabe.

"What do you think the judge knows?"

CHAPTER 9

Mid November

OF BLOOD AND BOND

THE QUIET TENSION ON THE WATSON'S FRONT PORCH was thick between father and son. The silence pressed down like wet canvas on a storm-beaten tent. Gabe returned to his chore of knife sharpening. He paused mid-motion, the sharpening stone still in his hand as he laid the knife down on the table. He cast a sideways glance at Moses.

"If that telegram's about Old Man Manchester," he said, "things could get ugly real fast."

Moses stood. The mention of Manchester's name was a punch in the gut. It was a mix of anger and rage, about his family and how Manchester had physically violated Sally on many occasions. He turned to Gabe, meeting his son's gaze with the hollow stare of a man who'd faced too many shadows of grief.

"Don't worry about Manchester. That asshole deserved his fate. Whatever this is with the judge, I'll handle it. Right now, our priority is getting our family home. I seriously doubt it has anything to do with our freedom papers from John-Man. Though I trust Perry like a brother, there's no need to pull him into any of this."

Gabe exhaled, his shoulders sagging and ribs tightening as he chewed over his father's words.

"Well, what if…" Gabe paused, casting a glance at the distant hills. "What if the old man's body washed ashore before the river rats could do their work? They'll know it was a blow to the head. A hit like that doesn't just happen naturally, and everyone knows we were the last folk to see him alive."

Moses paused. "Do they? I'm not so sure. We were careful. Careful enough, I'd say. And most wouldn't think twice about what might happen to a boozing man like Manchester out there in the wild riverlands."

"Maybe. But Papa, if they do suspect something, it's on me. It's my fault. I shouldn't have acted on impulse, shouldn't have…" He broke off, his eyes narrowing with regret.

Moses stepped forward, placing a heavy hand on Gabe's shoulder, steadying him with a father's quiet strength. "Son, there are days I'm glad you did it, but upset that I didn't do it myself. Listen to me. Whatever is known, we'll face it. You didn't do anything but what you had to do. I didn't agree with it at the time, but the old bastard deserved it. And think about it this way. If it's the ghost of Old Man Manchester wanting revenge, I'm not sure we would be atop his list. As for the telegram…" he hesitated, glancing toward the table where the knife lay like an uninvited guest. "Until I see Judge Merriweather, we won't know for certain what the attorney's after."

"But this attorney. You think it could be from John-Man himself?

"I don't know, but somebody is sure as hell looking for us with intention. But it still hasn't changed my mission. And if the news in the telegram runs that dream off the rails, then I'll face the consequences alone."

"I can't let you do that. This was all my doin'." Gabe's knuckles popped as his hand tightened on the table's edge. His gaze flicked back to the hills, then to the dark line of the treetops where dusk was beginning to settle in. "Papa, we're in this together. If vengeance is coming, let it come for both of us."

"I know you mean well, son. But it's one thing to want to stand with me, and it's another to face what may be coming. I know the wake we left on the river that day, and I'd rather not have you feel its ripples. You're a young man with much to live for. I am merely the embers of a fire to watch over as it turns to ash."

Gabe blinked hard as his father's words sank like stones tossed into a pond. But he didn't waver. "I'm the one who started the fire."

"You didn't, son. I admit you carry the fight of ten men. But what I need you to do is focus on what matters now. It's not the battles we've fought in the past. It's the family we're trying to bring home."

The silence settled between them again, but this time it wasn't heavy; it was laced with a shared understanding, each man standing firm, knowing the other would be there when the time came. The knife lay still on the table, the fading light catching its edge as if sealing a pact.

Moses broke the silence. "Son, just remember, we need to be wise. We've come too far to let dark memories swallow what future we still have. One step at a time."

"The first step, Papa, is to find out who the telegram is from."

"I'll find out tomorrow when I meet with Judge Merriweather. You keep an eye on things around here. If I don't like what I hear, I'll cancel the entire rescue mission."

"Just don't keep me in the dark. As soon as you find out, you get back here. I don't want to sit here wonderin'."

Moses nodded. "You're right. When I know, you'll know. But until then, don't let this weigh on you more than it has to. Focus on the future, not the past. The real battle is the one ahead."

Gabe gave a stiff nod, as Moses returned his gaze to the fading light over the fields. Despite his words, he couldn't shake the feeling that the past had come knocking, and this time, it might not leave without a reckoning.

Moses rose before dawn and tied his sidearm to his right leg. He saddled his horse. Gabe was already up, watching from the porch with a mixture of worry and determination. No words needed, they exchanged a nod. Gabe knew better than to offer again to join his father. This was a matter Moses wanted to face solo.

As Moses rode down the long, winding path that led from his farm to the main dirt road, he couldn't shake the uncertainty. The seven miles into town felt longer than it ever had before. He replayed Perry's words in his mind about the telegram from an attorney in St. Louis and the mysterious tone of the message. If it had been urgent enough to contact Judge Merriweather, then it had to be more than idle inquiry. Yet why now, after so many years of he and Gabe keeping to themselves, trying to live quiet lives?

The road to town was mostly empty, except for the distant drumming of a woodpecker and the soft rustle of a rabbit darting through the roadside underbrush.

Moses hit the patch of flatland at the foot of the river bluffs that fell into the outskirts of Lowland. An autumn mist obscured his view for much of the trip, but it began to lift as the town came into view. Small, familiar wood-frame houses and larger brick buildings greeted him in the stillness. The general store, the blacksmith's shop, the telegraph station, all tucked around a square that was intentionally left vacant.

While the young town had already been designated county seat, Judge Virgil Merriweather and other local officials wanted to wait until they could afford to build a stately courthouse worthy of that designation. For the time-being, a nondescript, two-story brick building nestled among the businesses along Main Street claimed the honor. Judge Merriweather's office included a large window that looked out over the street from the second floor.

Moses rode his horse up the gravel street and wrapped the leather reins around a hitching post in front of the building. He pulled open the large oak doors and was greeted by a prim young woman at the front desk. She jerked her head up in a startled motion, like she had never seen a man of African descent.

Moses strode assertively toward the grand oak staircase. The young woman, a look of worry etched on her face, rose from her chair.

"What brings you here today, sir?" she asked, her arms crossed and her gaze sharp. "And what, sir, might be your given name?"

"Moses Watson. I'm here to consult with the judge," Moses replied, his face unreadable. He waited for her reaction.

"Do you have an appointment, Mr. Moses?" she pressed.

Moses frowned before forcing a faint smile. "It's Mr. Watson, and I didn't realize an appointment was needed, considering I served the good judge as a peacekeeper at the town hall events not too long ago."

Her eyes softened as she stood and moved toward the stairs. "I'm sorry, Mr. Moses. I didn't know. I was just a little girl back then."

"No need for apologies. It seems like a lifetime ago."

The young woman glanced at the gun strapped to Moses' leg. "I'm sorry, but if you want to see Judge Merriweather, you're going to have to check your gun at the desk. Judge Merriweather doesn't have much affection for firearms since that rebel insurgent tried to shoot him during a town hall meeting a couple years back."

"I remember. The slug hit the Bible he was waving around. Sent holy confetti all over the stage. Likely saved his life. I not only saw it, but I was the one who wrestled the assailant to the ground."

"Oh, well then, I'm certain the judge will welcome your visit. He's in his office, savoring his morning coffee."

Moses removed his holster and handed it to the young lady. She glanced toward the stairway and gestured with a quick nod.

Moses nodded with a polite smile. "Thank you kindly."

Moses climbed the staircase, each step sounding like a measured heartbeat in the stillness. Whatever the news carried by the mystery telegram, Moses wanted to hear it straightaway from Judge Merriweather.

At the top of the staircase, Moses paused, taking in the hallway that stretched out before him. Shadows played across the walls, where paintings from what looked like a foreign location presided over the hallway. Ornate wallpaper, dark and elegant, lined the walls, interrupted by brass sconces casting a warm, flickering glow. The interior of this temporary courthouse lived up to the name, unlike its plain street-front facade. The hallway had an air of quiet authority, as if it bore a solemn secret.

He reached the judge's outer office and paused, letting his gaze sweep across the empty room. Rows of dark leather-bound ledgers lined the shelves, their spines faded, holding years of knowledge and authority. A heavy oak desk sat unoccupied, its surface pristine and orderly, a few papers stacked in one corner, a quill resting beside an inkpot, as if waiting for the next signature to seal another fate.

The faint aroma of coffee mingled with the earthy scent of leather and the subtle woody smell of polished furniture, hinting at a building still carrying a touch of newness.

Moses took a moment to collect himself, his hand resting on the desk, his scarred fingers tracing the smooth grain of the polished oak. Here, he was just one more folder of legal paperwork, yet his purpose felt urgent, more than a mere visitor's stature. Moses looked to the inner door that led to the judge's chambers, the silence amplifying the pulse of anticipation.

Steeling himself, Moses knocked once, a firm but respectful rap on the door, then waited. He took a breath, squaring his shoulders, his hand steady on the brass door handle. He straightened his coat with a practiced motion, smoothing out any wrinkles.

The room fell back into stillness, his heartbeat the only sound. After a moment, he heard a deep voice from within call out. "Come in."

With a final glance, Moses opened the door and stepped into the judge's chamber, prepared for whatever details might be ahead. His eyes adjusted to the morning sunshine flooding through the big glass window. He scanned the office knowing the conversation ahead could shape much more than just the morning.

The distinguished judge sat behind his desk, coffee cup in hand, eyes lifting to meet Moses' with a mixture of curiosity and recognition. The judge stood, looking almost shocked, his spectacles perched low on his nose as he took in the sight of Moses standing in his doorway.

"Moses," the judge said. "I wasn't expectin' to see you today."

Moses stepped inside, removing his hat as he met the judge's curious gaze. "Morning, Judge. Sorry about not making an appointment, but Perry made it seem like this matter couldn't wait. He said there was a telegram from St. Louis with my name on it."

Judge Merriweather shut the door behind them, nodding as he took a seat at his cluttered desk. "Well, it's true there's a telegram, and it's not every day I receive one inquiring about a Freedman in my county. You're right to be concerned, though I have to admit, the message itself is, well, less than clear."

Moses' jaw tightened. He took a seat across from the judge, his gaze steady. "Who's it from?"

The judge exhaled, pushing his spectacles higher on his nose as he shuffled through a stack of papers on his desk. He produced the thin slip of paper and handed it across to Moses.

"It's from an attorney in St. Louis. A man by the name of John Manchester."

CHAPTER 10

Mid November

A TELEGRAM'S OMEN

MOSES' STOMACH DROPPED as he reached out and took the telegram from Judge Merriweather's spindly fingers.

Sure enough, it was from St. Louis Attorney John Manchester, the man Moses had grown up with on the plantation in Gumbo Flats. John-Man was the son of the slave master who was secretly struck down by Moses' own son in a fit of rage. John-Man was the same man who had extended Freedom Papers to both him and Gabe. Why was he looking for Moses? Had the river currents divulged the secret killing? John Manchester's name stirred within Moses mixed emotions of friendship and possible foreboding. Moses sat down and kept his face impassively frozen as he slowly read the telegram aloud:

"REQUESTED WHEREABOUTS OF FREEDMAN MOSES WATSON STOP NOT A MATTER OF FELONY OR MISDEMEANOR STOP BUT A MATTER OF MYSTERY STOP SHOULD THIS MAN LIVE IN YOUR COUNTY, PLEASE RESPOND ONCE YOU HAVE BEEN ABLE TO CONTACT HIM REGARDING MY REQUEST FOR INFORMATION STOP KINDLY J. MANCHESTER ESQ. 111 LUCAS PL ST. LOUIS MO STOP"

Moses read it again, letting the words sink in. There was no accusation in the telegram, no direct threat, only a vague request, unsettling because of what it didn't say. Moses glanced up at the judge and handed him back the paper.

"So, he's askin' about me. But he doesn't say why."

Judge Merriweather sighed, nodding. "That's the part that doesn't sit right with me either, Moses. He goes out of his way to say it's not about any criminal charges, but that doesn't mean it's good news. When an attorney from St. Louis goes out of his way to find a man, there's a reason behind it. I'd be lying if I said I wasn't concerned."

Moses sat back, his gaze drifting to the window, then to the street below. "John Manchester," he muttered, almost to himself. "Haven't heard that name in years. We grew up together, almost like brothers. He called me 'Watty,' and I called him 'John-Man.' His papa was the man who owned me. He was an evil man. Sold my Sally and two sons and I couldn't do a thing about it. Got drunk one day and wandered a little too close to the river."

The judge's expression was both curious and cautious. "You know him, then?"

Moses nodded. "I did, once. He's, well, let's just say he's someone I used to know, back when life was a little different. Haven't heard from him since he gave me and Gabe our Freedom Papers. We left all that behind. But even then I thought his papa's disappearance might somehow cast a shadow over Gabe and me. I pray this is not the case."

Judge Merriweather leaned forward, his gaze piercing. "Then I reckon this is more personal. But he says up front this is not related to any crime. But if it's just a friendly inquiry, there wouldn't be a need for all this mystery. You have any idea what he might be after?"

Moses shook his head, though his mind was already turning over the possibilities. "No way of knowin' for sure, Judge. But whatever it is, it's probably tied up in some legalities about my freedom that I'd rather keep in the past."

The judge paused, his gaze never leaving Moses. "I don't mean to pry, Moses, but if this man says you're not in any kind of trouble, would there be any reason for him to conceal his true motive for wanting to find you?"

Moses shook his head firmly. "No trouble that's followin' me, Judge. Least, not as far as I know."

The judge sat back, folding his hands. "Well, you let me know if there's anything I can do."

"Well, if I can beg your assistance, Judge. I think I would like to draft a response you can send back. Remember the matter I just told you about my missing family? I'm fixin' to go back to Gumbo Flats and start a search for them."

"Is that wise, Moses?"

"I know, Judge. I'm taking every precaution. Perry's going with me, and we're taking Pete the bartender from over in St. Joseph. He's from the South and knows his way around the terrain and the people."

"I have to admit, I've had a pint or two at Pete's establishment. He is a fine and honorable man."

Judge Merriweather reached out and put his hand on Moses' shoulder. "With unwavering resolve, you will be treading into shadows where peril lies, guided not by ignorance of the risks. You know the dangers, but true valor is born out of embracing it for a purpose greater than your own. You, Moses, have ample purpose for this venture."

"That's why I'd like to reply to John-Man's telegram. Let him know I'll meet him at the old plantation site in Gumbo Flats. That's where the trail has to start and maybe he knows something that can help. Maybe that's why he's looking for me."

"Maybe, Moses, but keep in mind that in a world painted with shadows, the man who clings solely to brightness sees hope but is sometimes blind to truth. Only when you face possible darkness with clear eyes can you find the light that truly endures. Let's draft that reply."

The two men sat at a common desk and began making strokes with quill dipped into ink well. After completing the message, the two men strode next door to the telegraph station and handed the slip of paper to the telegrapher.

"TO J. MANCHESTER ESQ. 111 LUCAS PL ST. LOUIS

MO STOP PLEASE BE INFORMED THAT MOSES WATSON
DOES RESIDE WITHIN MY JURISDICTION STOP HE
HAS BEEN MADE AWARE OF YOUR TELEGRAM STOP
HE INTENDS TO JOURNEY TO GUMBO FLATS WITH
EXPECTED ARRIVAL IN ABOUT 25 DAYS, GIVE OR TAKE
STOP HE WILL TRY TO HELP ADDRESS YOUR MYSTERY
STOP KIND REGARDS JUDGE VIRGIL MERRIWEATHER
LOWLAND KS STOP"

After the agent click-clacked the message across the wire terminal, the two men departed, stopping in front of the courthouse door.

Moses paused, turning to the judge. "Thank you, Judge. For everything. I couldn't do this without your help."

"Moses, there's no need for thanks. Sometimes, a man must walk paths others wouldn't dare, not for glory but for a deeper purpose."

He rested a hand on Moses' shoulder. "Remember, in this venture, stay vigilant. There are those who see your journey as a step into darkness, but you and I both know it's a step toward a shining light."

Moses returned the judge's steady gaze, absorbing his words. "I understand, Judge. I'll keep my eyes open. We all will, Perry, Pete and me."

"Good. Then Godspeed, Moses. And remember, sometimes we're called to find light not just for ourselves but for others, even if it means wading through the shadows. Stay safe."

Moses nodded, tipping his hat. "I will, Judge. And I'll be back to see you soon enough."

The judge watched him go, his expression a mixture of hope and concern as Moses strode off, the veil of mystery somewhat lifted, purpose driving his each and every step.

Moses rode back to his farm under a flickering afternoon sky, the sun playing hide-and-seek behind restless clouds. The farm sprawled in uneasy silence, broken only by the sharp crack of splitting wood. In the yard, Gabe swung the axe with a fury that left sweat slicking his brow, each blow a little too wild, a little too desperate.

Moses slid from his saddle, his boots hitting the dusty ground with a thud. Gabe didn't hesitate. The axe thudded into the ground, forgotten, and he sprinted toward Moses, raw panic flashing his eyes.

"What did the judge say?"

Moses sighed, running a hand through his hair. "Just as we suspected, the telegram was from John."

"Was it about the old man?"

"All the telegram asked was if I lived within the judge's general jurisdiction. Didn't give any details, other than it mentioned a mystery, but sounds like there's somethin' he's uncovered that involves me."

"A mystery? How can that be a good thing?"

"Hold on, son. It went on. It said it was not about a matter of felony or misdemeanor. So, at least on the surface, it is not addressing any kind of crime. That would include murder."

"Don't remind me by using that word, Papa. It will haunt me the rest of my life."

"Sorry, Gabe. Just wanted to share the full effect of the message. That's all. I'm thinking it might be in John's character to share information he's come across about the whereabouts of our family."

"But you can't know that. Just make sure you aren't being overly optimistic. Even though he says it doesn't have anything to do with a crime, that could be a ruse. You and I know what happened in that place. What I did in that place."

"I know Gabe. I think it's time we both forgive ourselves for what happened that day. I am certain in my heart this is not related to the old man. Plus, remember, John is the man who gave us our freedom."

"So, now what?"

"Well, the judge and I wrote out a reply telegram and sent it to John. I wanted to let him know I would meet him at the old plantation site in about 20 or so days, and if possible, I would help him with whatever mystery is haunting him. It might be about his old man's death, but it might be a clue about our family. Either way, I'm meetin' him in Gumbo Flats to get to the bottom of it."

Gabe's hands trembled as he picked up the axe again. "If it's about his father, about what I did, you have to tell him it was all my doing. At least I am here, not at his doorstep."

Moses stepped forward, his eyes filled with fierce love. "I'll say it again. You've got your whole life ahead of you. I've lived mine."

Gabe shook his head, his voice rising in protest. "No, Papa, you don't need to…"

"Enough," Moses said. "You don't have a choice in this, son. I made up my mind the moment we dumped that man's body in the river. If there's a price to pay, I'll pay it. I won't let you throw your life away."

Gabe closed his fists, his jaw tight with frustration, but he knew better than to argue. His father's word was final.

Moses placed a hand on Gabe's shoulder. "We'll get through this so don't worry. I don't think John would misrepresent his intent to me. We've known each other too long. Let's continue to focus on the rescue. And if John Manchester's got answers, good or bad, I'll face him."

The next morning, Moses rode to Jawbone Holler to share the news of the telegram with Perry. Moses found Perry loading a wagon of ear corn near the storage crib. Between scoops, Perry looked up, his eyes widening with relief.

"Well, you're still walkin' tall, Moses, so I take it you're not in any kind of trouble."

"Not in the way you're thinkin'. Turns out, the telegram was from my old friend, John, and it isn't about any kind of negative matter, far as we can tell. No mention of Freedom Papers or anything like that. Just said there was a little mystery he's trying to clear up." Moses leaned against the wagon. "The judge and I sent word back, told him I'd meet him in Gumbo Flats in about twenty-five days."

Perry let out a slow relieved breath. "Good to hear. Still, I can't shake the feeling that 'mystery' means trouble. You're sure John's not hidin' anything?"

"Unlike the old man, I have never known John to have secrets. He's no liar. His actions have proved that. He gave us our freedom, Perry. I believe him, and I think he might have a clue or two for us."

Perry nodded, tapping his fingers on the wagon. "So, Gumbo Flats it is. You think he has some information about your kin?"

"Maybe. There's only one way to find out."

"No matter what it is, I'll be right there with you," Perry nodded with determination and glanced around the farm. "I'll need about four days to get things squared away here. Millie's belongings need packing up, and the house will need some winterproofing if we're gone as long as I expect. Normally, I'd be out plowing the fields this time of year, gettin' the soil ready for spring. But I decided it's best to let the land rest a bit this season. I'll just double up in the spring."

"Smart thinkin'. And we'll have a lot to haul back if things go well."

"Right. Next stop, St. Joseph. Gather our wagon and supplies from Marcus, drop off Millie, pick up Pete and we'll be on our way. You can't pack for every storm, but we're as ready as a squirrel's pantry in December. Meet you back here in four days, bright and early. We're ready to roll, come what may."

CHAPTER 11

Late November

ST. JOSEPH'S PROMISE

JAWBONE HOLLER LAY QUIET in the early dawn, like an old sheepskin map waiting to be unfolded, its dormant fields stretching out under a sky tinged with the golden promise of new trails. The Adams house stood like a stoic guard over the packed wagon. The last whisper of smoke rose from the home's chimney, lingering as though hesitant to leave. The house was hunkering down for hibernation, before the arrival of a new family member the next year. It never again would be the same quiet abode.

In the nearby fields, the stripped corn plants, brittle and bare, whispered in the wind as if they were bidding farewell for the season. Each corner of the farm held its breath, as if it, too, understood this was no ordinary morning for its caretaker but a first step into the unknown.

Perry's footsteps fell heavy as he moved around the wagon, securing the last of Millie's belongings.

The early light cast long shadows across the lane leading to the main trail that looked more like the spine of a wild beast, deformed and stretching beyond sight. A lone crow cawed from the fence post a sharp, haunting note that echoed, "It's time."

Perry tightened the wagon straps, each pull sealing memories of the farm, as Moses approached down the spiny trail. Archibald greeted him, "Uh Roo Roo Roo."

Perry adjusted the harness around his horses, Beulah and Barney, as

Moses arrived and dismounted his horse.

"Mornin', Perry. Gabe'll be by for Butter later today. I think she'll settle in right nicely over at our place. Gabe will do his best to keep her fat and happy."

"Yup, all we need to do now is focus on the road ahead."

Millie emerged from the house, a lace bonnet shading her eyes as she walked toward the wagon, her gaze lingering on the home she was leaving. Perry extended a gentle hand, guiding her up to the wagon seat. She settled in, glancing at the men with a soft smile.

"I trust you gentlemen are ready."

Perry squeezed her hand. "Ready and raring to go, Millie."

Moses tipped his hat to Millie. "Miss Millie, you're like the steady flame of a lantern on a cold night. No matter how rough the road or dark the path, you bring light and calm that keeps us steady. Maybe we should take you along for the longer trip?"

Millie laughed. "That's not exactly a trip I'm up for at the moment, Moses. I'll be quite content to make it to St. Joseph."

After tying Appy to the rear of the wagon and boosting Archibald into an open spot in the wagon's bed, Perry took his seat and flicked the reins. The wagon wheels rumbled, carrying them down the road toward St. Joseph and the first minor leg of the long journey ahead.

The trip to the frontier river town was brisk, the wagon rattling over rough roads under a slate-gray sky. Conversation was light, each mile pulling them, all of them, closer to their daunting missions ahead. For Millie, it was childbirth. For Moses and Perry, it was a quite different objective. Yet, there was a growing energy, a shared determination. By the time they reached St. Joseph, the town was alive with noise, crowded with folks huddled together in the warmth of Pete and Lucy's Outpost Tavern.

As Moses, Perry, and Millie stepped through the door, laughter from the crowd mingled with the smell of pipe smoke, stale beer and aged whiskey. The roar quieted as Moses stepped forward. A tense hush fell over the room. The crowd's eyes were cold, some glances toward Moses were downright hostile. Pete, tall and broad at the bar, noticed the sudden shift of tone across the tavern. Without pause, he turned, raising his glass and booming over the crowd.

"Now, listen up! This man here, Moses Watson, is as good as family to me. Anyone got a problem with that, they can walk their asses right out that door, and don't bother comin' back!"

A few disgruntled murmurs rose up, and two men got up and shuffled toward the exit, muttering under their breaths. Pete gave them a curt nod as they left.

"Good riddance, you sonsabitches."

Once the room settled, Pete grinned and walked over to embrace Moses. "Glad to have you here, brother. Ain't nobody gonna give you trouble now."

Pete put his hand on Perry's shoulder, a broad smile breaking across his face. "With all of us together, we're like roots digging deep, holding strong no matter what tries to shake us loose."

Lucy poured drinks for everyone, including two glasses of fizzy sarsaparilla for herself and Millie.

A wide grin shot across Pete's face, and a spirit of fire jumped from his eyes. He hoisted his mug of beer.

> *"Here's to friends, to dirt and grit,*
> *To takin' ours, not givin' a shit.*
> *On the road, as scoundrels pass,*
> *If trouble shows, we'll whup its ass!"*

A clinking of glasses rippled across the tavern. The patrons knew of the mission and those about to undertake it, bound not by luck but by conviction deep in their bones.

Pete threw back his drink with a laugh, and the group erupted in cheers, each person strengthened by the fierce resolve of the toast. It was the kind of spirit that could carry the rescue party all the way to Gumbo Flats and back.

"There's someone here I want y'all to meet," Pete said. "Hank, come over here."

A mountain of a man arose from a table near the end of the bar. It was Hank Crowder, a broad-shouldered and thick-limbed man, with hands that looked like they could snap a board in half without a second thought. His face was framed by a wild, dark beard streaked with a hint of silver, giving him a rugged, almost grizzly-bear-like appearance.

Yet there was a gentleness to him, a calm, thoughtful way he moved, as though every action was considered. Hank's eyes, a deep, steady brown, held a warmth that put folks at ease, revealing the peaceful spirit beneath the rugged exterior. But those who knew him understood that beneath that calm lay a fire. Hank was slow to anger, but once riled, he was a force you didn't want to cross. A perfect candidate for keeping The Outpost peaceful in Pete's absence.

Pete grinned. "Folks, meet Hank. He'll be the one makin' sure no one gets too rowdy while I'm gone. Best man for the job, if you ask me. The very def'nition of 'Awesome Possum.'"

Hank nodded. A broad smile broke across his face as he recognized Millie. "Howdy, Miss Millie. Been a while."

Millie nodded back with a smile.

"Pete, I appreciate the trust," Hank said, "because scrubbing youngster puke off the floor at the mission school's been testin' my patience. Some days, I'd rather take a man's fist to the face. I can duck that, you know? But when it's a mess on the floor, there ain't no dodging it."

Everyone chuckled, and Perry gave him an approving nod. "Sounds like you've got the kind of grit we're gonna need here. Thanks for stepping up, Hank."

Hank shrugged. "Happy to do it. Least here, if someone over-imbibes and tosses their supper, I can kick 'em right out. At the school,

I just got handed a mop."

Pete laughed, raising his glass again. "To Hank. May his days here be puke-free and his nights free of fists!"

A voice rang out from the far end of the bar, smooth as honey but sharp enough to slice bread. It was Jeptha Nichols, nursing a sarsaparilla with a sly grin. Once known as the town drunk, Jeptha had a peculiar gift, or so he believed when intoxicated, that he could turn himself into a genie to charm free drinks from customers, always in exchange for a fabled wish.

"Hey, Perry, Millie, Moses. Great to see you. If Pete and Lucy haven't told you by now, I'm a changed man. Gave up the devil alcohol and even got a fulltime job now, working for Marcus at the Trading Post. However, if you want to slide me a sarsaparilla, I'll still grant you a wish."

The room chuckled, knowing Jeptha's "wishes" came with a twist more often than not. But in those earlier days, that didn't keep people from buying him rot-gut drinks—half out of superstition, half for the stories he spun.

Perry almost ran to the end of the bar and greeted Jep with a bear hug.

"Welcome back to the world, Jep," he said. "You look healthier than I have ever seen you. I know it takes a while for the fog to lift, but damn, I am proud of you. And, unlike during our previous meetings, you even know me by name this time."

"Why, hell yes, Perry. I always did, but I didn't want you to feel too special back then. Even an old drunk like me knew who Perry Adams was," Jeptha replied with a wink. "Back then, I figured it kept you on your toes if I pretended not to know ya."

"Here's to knowin' each other clear as day now, Jep, without any fog hanging' between us."

Jep raised his sarsaparilla in a mock toast. "And here's to that. But remember, my friends," he said, his voice lowering to a conspiratorial tone, "if you find yourselves in need of somethin' that regular folks can't manage, Old Jeptha's still got a little genie magic left for those bold enough to ask. All for the mere cost of a sarsaparilla."

Hank chimed in, catching Jep's playful spirit. "Just as long as that wish don't turn on us like a snake in the grass, Jep."

Jep laughed, tapping the side of his nose. "Oh, I only grant the wishes worth the risk."

They all raised their glasses, and Hank joined them with a wide grin, enjoying the promise of a cleaner, quieter kind of trouble.

"I'd love to stay here and socialize all day, but we have some business to conduct," Perry said. "Pete, we need to take a quick ride to your house so we can unload Millie's things. Don't worry, we didn't bring back your old piano."

"I trust it will be safe back in Jawbone Holler."

"It will be. Gabe's going to check on things every day or two to make sure. But, Pete, that old piano, it still sounds as sweet."

"I'm sure the bulk of that credit must go to the player."

Millie smiled, as much about the compliment as having a safe place to stay with Lucy.

"Fella's you better not break anything or there will be hell to pay," Lucy piped in.

"Don't worry, my love," Pete said. "We'll treat each item with the same care I take when washing our beer mugs."

"That's the scary part, Pete. On more than one occasion, I've heard your precious glassware tinkle into pieces as it hit the floor."

After unloading Millie's belongings, Perry, Pete and Moses took the straightest route possible toward Marcus Mixon's Trading Post, expecting the merchant to fulfill his promise to provide the goods for their mission.

As the wagon rolled into a spot outside the store, the three men barely had time to dismount before Marcus bounded out waving his hat with enthusiasm.

"There they are!" he called, his voice booming. "You fellas are gonna be mighty proud of me today. That Conestoga wagon is greased up and the canvas cover's freshly oiled. All she's missin' is a team of horses to get her goin'!"

Marcus grinned and continued. "Every supply you're gonna need is loaded up. Since Old Jep's conquered sobriety, he's turned out to be a hard-workin' son of a gun, let me tell ya."

"We're thankful for your diligence, Marcus," Perry said with a smile. "I trust you've drawn up an itemized receipt. Not that we don't trust you, but we know business is business. Each of us decided to chip in to make sure you're fairly paid."

"You fellas are just like the three musketeers, aren't you? All for one and one for all!"

The three men burst into laughter, and Pete shot a whimsical glance toward Marcus.

"I still can't figure why they called them musketeers since they mostly played with swords. I damn sure don't know anything about wieldin' a sword, but we won't be totin' muskets either. Thanks to you we'll have better arms."

Perry shook his head in agreement. "You can still call us musketeers if you like, Marcus, but I prefer to think of us as three avenging angels. I hope others see us as three simple vagabonds. It's good to be underestimated."

Pete rubbed his chin. "Let's just hope we don't end up like the Three Little Pigs. As I recall, there was some serious trouble with a big bad wolf."

Marcus roared with laughter, slapping his knee. "Well, if you're the pigs, this wagon's the sturdy brick house to keep you safe! I made sure of that. Solid as a rock."

Perry's smile softened. "Jokes aside, fellas, we are pilgrims, and this wagon is our Mayflower. This Conestoga and everything in it could be the difference between success and failure out there. If it falters, we're in trouble."

Marcus nodded. "I hear you, Perry. I've gone over every inch of this wagon myself. Tucked a few spare parts in the back too. She's got fresh timber reinforcements, thick iron wheels, and secured rations. She'll get you there and back. We triple-checked everything, every last sack of flour and drop of lamp oil. You've got the best we've got."

"We'll look after it, and after each other," Moses said. "Feels like there's a good startin' spirit here already. You and Jep have set us up right, Marcus."

Pete clapped his hands, grinning. "Well then, let's get that team of horses and hit the trail! Adventure's callin', and the Three Musketeers are ready to answer."

"Let's get a good night's rest and leave at dawn," Perry said. "The road's going to make us weary enough before all is said and done." He gave Marcus a firm nod, a gleam of satisfaction in his eyes.

"Marcus, we'll make sure this Conestoga sees its way there and back, with all of us safe, and, God willing, Moses' kinfolk in tow. I hope you'll keep my buckboard wagon safe here in the meantime. We switch Beulah and Barney over to the new rig, and we'll be on our way."

Moses slapped Marcus on the back, and Pete gave a playful salute. They stood for a moment, an oath hanging among them, each man understanding that they were, indeed, all for one and one for all.

With Beulah and Barney pulling the fully stocked wagon, a quick stop was made at The Outpost to collect Lucy and Millie before the night's destination, the Fontaine home. Archibald and all the horses bedded down for the night in Pete's adjacent barn, as the friends retreated for one last night of rest and comfort inside the house, which Pete called "Lucy's Palace."

CHAPTER 12

Late November, 1865

PARTING AND PROMISE

JUST AS LUCY'S PALACE offered a warm embrace the night before, it also granted a last hug on departure morning. Lucy stood by the wood stove. She grabbed the handle of a new-fangled percolator coffee pot and lifted it from the stovetop. While her arm moved with a calm, fluid motion, her shoulders were tight with tension she tried hard to conceal.

The soft clatter of ceramic mugs echoed across the kitchen and adjacent parlor as she poured steaming coffee from the pot. A cloud of aroma curled upward, filling the space with its familiar, satisfying scent, a stark contrast to the uncertainty that loomed ahead for the gathered friends.

"Drink up, gentlemen. It'll be a long while before you savor coffee like this again."

Pete accepted the mug and cradled it, savoring the warmth before taking a cautious sip. "Best coffee I've ever had, Lucy. Reckon I'll be thinkin' about it every cold night out there along the trail."

Lucy frowned, and she placed her free hand on her hip. "That's not all you'd better be thinkin' about, Pete Fontaine. There's a baby growin' in me, and we had better be guiding your every action and idle thought. Before taking any step toward danger, you'd better remember the responsibilities you're going to have under this roof. You go rescue Moses' family, but don't you dare do anything that will cause me to raise this child alone."

Pete stepped closer, setting the mug aside to take her hands. "Darlin', I'll remember you and the baby every step of the way. You're my anchor, Lucy. You keep me steady, and I swear I'll come back to you both."

In the corner, Perry tugged on his boots, the motion deliberate, almost stalling. Millie stood by the window, her hands fiddling with the ribbon tied at her waist. She stared out at the frost-covered yard, her stoic mask slipping as Perry crossed the room and took her by the hand.

"Millie, I know this is hard. It's hard for me too. But I need you to trust me."

Her fingers tightened around his. Millie's eyes met Perry's in a momentary flicker, and for an instant, her emotions took over. "Don't take any chances, Perry. Let time be your ally, not your enemy. We'll manage here, but you keep yourself safe."

"I promise," Perry said. He reached up with his calloused hand and brushed a tear from Millie's cheek. "I'll be thinkin' about you every step of the way. You're my north star. I'll follow you home with more eagerness than a pirate's homecoming."

Millie hesitated, then reached into the pocket of her apron. She pulled out her rosary, its beads worn smooth from years of prayer. She pressed it into Perry's hands, her voice trembling but resolute. "Keep this in your heart pocket, every minute of every day of the journey. You know how strong my faith is, but my rosary has been through miracles that outnumber even my prayers."

Millie's eyes glistened as she squeezed Perry's hands around the beads.

"It's not just a constant reminder of faith. It'll be a shield, an embrace in the chaos, and a prayer for you to find your way back."

Perry swallowed hard. "I'll guard it like it's your heart, Millie."

Lucy watched the exchange and with trembling hands removed a small golden locket from around her neck. She opened it, revealing a small fragment of a dried rose petal from her wedding day. She stepped forward and placed it in Pete's hand. "Take this, Pete. I'm not sure it carries the same holy blessings, but it's been through all the struggles we've overcome together. It'll damn sure rekindle the strength you've always carried and remind you of the love that took us down the road together."

Pete stared at the open locket and the fragile rose petal. His throat tightened. "I'll keep it close," he said, slipping the locket into his shirt pocket. "Not just as a reminder, Lucy, but as a piece of you I'll carry with me. No matter how far I go, no matter what I face, this comes back to you because I will. Awesome possum forever."

Moses looked at Lucy from across the parlor. "You can count on that, Miss Lucy, as sure as the sun rises in the East and sets God's truth upon the West." Moses held his coffee mug close, the warmth seeping into his scarred hands as he looked at the two women. His eyes welled up as he continued to watch the quiet exchanges.

A clock on the parlor wall chimed six. The men bundled up. One-by-one they walked out the door as the women followed them to the porch. The morning air was sharp and cold. The men saddled their horses, hitched Beulah and Barney to the wagon and tied Appy's halter with a lead rope to the end of the wagon.

The horses flicked their tails in anticipation, sensing the mission ahead. Archibald barked and jumped into the back of the wagon.

Pete tipped his hat. He and Perry gave their wives final hugs before returning to their respective rides. Lucy and Millie clung to each other as the men mounted their horses and Perry climbed into the wagon seat. Archibald jumped through the wagon and joined him. Perry snapped the reins and the horses began to move. The wagon crawled forward. The women remained, hugging on the porch. The men glanced back one last time before the road curved, and the house disappeared from view.

The road lay open before them, long and uncertain. The warmth of their farewells clung like a woolen coat as they began the first leg of their journey toward Gumbo Flats.

The first day's journey through the Missouri River bluffs was unforgiving. Limestone jutted from the earth like jagged teeth, and tangled roots clawed at the wagon wheels. The horses strained against their harnesses as the men pressed forward, each mile a test of endurance.

As the next days passed, the river bluffs rose and fell on either side. Unpredictable gusts of wind swept among the bluffs, whistling through the vacant trees and biting at their faces. On the fourth day, the path grew steeper, winding through the bluffs. Loose limestone rocks tumbled down the slope with each turn of the wheels. The men kept their eyes fixed ahead. Moses and Pete gripped their horses to steady themselves as Perry negotiated the wagon over the rough trail with the skill of a seasoned muleskinner.

On the sixth day, the land opened to rolling prairies. The Conestoga moved more easily, its creaks quieter. A faint sense of relief washed over the men as they found their rhythm on the open grassland, the first trials of the journey behind them.

For the next several days, the trail stretched thin, desolate and cold. They came upon a band of weary travelers huddled together as the three friends approached a grove of barren trees. The travelers' clothes, little more than rags hanging from their gaunt frames, told a story of hardship that needed no words.

Children clung to their mothers, silent and sullen, their small faces streaked with dirt and a hollowness that spoke of empty bellies and restless nights. The men shuffled along, each step an effort, clutching the last symbols of their lives before ruin—a rusty rifle, a threadbare sack half-full of meager provisions, a worn Bible held between trembling hands.

Perry pulled the wagon to a halt. The three friends dismounted, each moved by the sight of the trail's broken souls. There was no need for discussion. An understanding passed between them as Moses went straight to the wagon's supplies. He reached in, pulling out a package of salted pork and a sack of dried beans, and handed them to Pete.

Pete approached a frail woman who stepped forward hesitantly, clutching a small bundle in her arms. Her hands trembled as Pete held out the provisions. "Take this," he said, pressing the food into her hands. "It'll give you strength for the road ahead."

She looked down at the offering as though it were a miracle, her eyes filling with tears that cut through the dirt on her cheeks. Her voice quivered, barely above a whisper.

"Bless you, sir. We lost everything down south. Our land, our homes, all burned to the ground. Blankets and sticks is all we got, and whatever else we can carry. We're just tryin' to find somewhere to build somethin' again. Maybe to find a little shelter from the cruelties of life. Somewhere we won't be run off."

Pete stepped closer with a sincere warmth in his eyes. "Ma'am, I never faced the ruin of war, but I've been where you are now. Nothing but the clothes on my back. There's always hope for a fresh start. If you keep traveling due west, the City of Kansas ain't far from here. It's a place full of new chances, or so I hear. Railroads need buildin', fields need tendin'. Work that'll put honest pay in the hands of your menfolk and food in the bellies of your young'uns."

An older man in the group, tall but bent with exhaustion, looked up, his eyes hollow and hopeless. "Reckon it can't be worse than where we come from. Nothin' grows right down there no more. Fields dried up. Towns turned to dust and ashes." He shook his head, the memories etched deep in the lines of his face. "Ain't nothin' left to go back to."

Another woman, clutching a thin bundle—a few worn clothes and a faded photograph—looked up, her face drawn and haunted. She held her child's hand as though afraid his life would slip away. "Everywhere we go, folks tell us to keep on movin'. Sayin' they can't spare even a crumb. It's like we're ghosts. Somethin' folks'd rather just forget."

Perry moved closer. "The City of Kansas is different. It's a fair place. My wife's from there. Folks with grit like you will find a way." He glanced at the child's threadbare blanket. "You're not ghosts. You're survivors."

She looked into his eyes, her lips trembling into the faintest hint of a smile. "God willing, we'll make it."

One of the children, a girl with wide, solemn eyes clutched a shredded blanket. She looked up at Perry, her voice barely audible. "Mister, you think they'll let us stay in this City of Kansas?"

Perry knelt to her level, smiling with a warmth that softened the worry in her gaze. "I don't just think, sweetheart, I know they will. Good folks like you and your mama are gonna find a place there. The City of Kansas is made for folks who've fought hard and want somethin' better. You remember that."

The little girl nodded, a flicker of hope igniting behind her eyes. The group stood in a moment of quiet understanding, hearts lightened by shared strength. The family, their arms a bit fuller and their steps a touch lighter, continued on the trail.

As they climbed back onto their horses and aboard the wagon, Perry looked at Pete and Moses. "We can give 'em what we have to spare, but it ain't near enough to mend what they've lost."

"Ain't about mendin' the past," Moses said. "It's about pointin' them toward somethin' ahead. We all need somethin' to keep walkin' toward."

Pete settled into his saddle, gazing down the road. "The city may be a short trek away for them, but it'll give them a fresh start. Sometimes a road with hope at the end is all folks need."

The three men exchanged a quiet look as the wagon rolled onward, the weary family fading behind them on the trail, each step now carrying a glimmer of possibility in the desolate prairie dawn.

The early road had been a long stretch, fighting through rough land littered with logs and boulders before hitting the prairieland. In the stillness of the trail, Moses broke the silence.

"This is the kind of trip that makes a man question his soul. It's almost like our shadows are just waiting to see if we'll break before each sunset."

Perry gazed toward the grassland stretching to the horizon. "I thought I'd seen hard times before this. Turns out, that was just a little rehearsal for whatever God or the Devil's put ahead of us now."

Pete leaned forward in his saddle and let out a heavy sigh. "The question's not if it's hard. Hell, it's been hard since day one. The question is if we're made to see it through."

Moses nodded. "Gumption's a fine word when you're standin' at the start, full of fire and ideas. But it don't mean much unless you've still got it when all that's left is ashes."

Perry raised his hand to feel the rosary in his heart pocket. His thumb traced the smooth surface of a bead. "Day after day, I keep thinking: What if we're foolin' ourselves? What if the finish line isn't as clear as we had planned?"

Pete met Perry's eyes. "And what if it is, Perry? What if it's just over that next ridge, waiting for the last man stubborn enough to keep going?"

Moses nodded. "Ain't nothin' worth having that comes easy, fellas. Maybe the road's just testing if we're still as committed now as when we started. My life is on the line, but I am sorry to have asked you to make that same bet."

Pete looked at them both, his jaw set. "We didn't get this far by giving in. If the road's testing us, then let's prove it wrong. Day one, I was ready. Today, I still am. What about you?"

Moses grinned. "I've got no other plan. As long as my horse keeps moving forward, so will my resolve."

Perry pocketed the rosary. "To hell with any doubts we've had to this point. We'll see this through, even if it takes every last ounce of grit we've got."

The men fell into silence again, the challenges of the road ahead undeniable but so was their determination.

Along the prairie trail they met other weary travelers with eyes darkened by hardship, searching for a mere scrap of redemption. Most were broken souls, looking anywhere but forward, and the three men offered what kindness they could—a word of encouragement, a small provision. Beyond these encounters, the journey was quiet, almost monotonous.

Still days away from their first destination of Gumbo Flats, the prairie path entered dense woods pressing in on both sides. Moses scanned the edge of the forest, his senses pricked by an unnatural stillness. A rustling sound broke through the air, followed by the unmistakable shuffle of horse hooves through undergrowth. Archibald, let out a low, warning bark that turned into a menacing growl. Perry's hand went to his rifle, his grip firm as he glanced at the trees.

A sharp, angry yell cut through the woods. Six riders appeared, their faded Confederate uniforms as tattered as their stares were hard. The leader, a wiry man with a jagged scar, spat as his gravelly voice cut through the silence.

"You're on Confederate land," he snarled. "And it'll cost you if you hope to pass."

Pete held his gaze and stared at the man with intensity. "Ain't no such thing as Confederate land no more. We're just passin' through, same as anyone else on this trail."

The leader sneered, kicking his horse forward a step as he sized them up. "Passin' through don't matter to me. It's our land to protect, and if you're on it, you pay a toll or you turn back."

Pete, sensing the danger in the man's stance, worked to keep his expression calm. He offered a smooth, easy smile, his Southern drawl rolling out like warm molasses. "Now, hold on there, friend. Ain't no need for this to get ugly. Hard times have hammered us all. Just tryin' to help these folks get to Saint Louie to find a bit of peace with their families. That's somethin' I think a decent man like yourself can understand, isn't it?"

The leader's eyes narrowed, suspicious but curious. "Where you from? You don't sound much like a damned Yankee."

Pete held his gaze, nodding with pride. "Arkansas. Fought with the Fightin' Fifth Arkansas here in the western theatre myself, but same as a lot of good men, I was forced to serve the side I inherited."

Moses and Perry looked at each other, amazed by Pete's performance.

"Seen more than my share of trouble," Pete continued. "I figure we all got more in common than we don't. We're just tryin' to move forward, same as you."

For a moment, the leader's expression softened with a hint of understanding. Around him, the other men shifted in their saddles, some nodding as war memories pulled at their hardened faces.

The leader's grip on his rifle loosened. "Arkansas, huh? Most of us are from Tennessee. Moving north with one eye on opportunity and another on vengeance. Just not sure yet where we're putting down roots."

The stranger paused, looking Pete up and down, then jerked his chin. "Today's your lucky day. Go on through. But don't expect no more charity on this road. And if I were you, I'd be careful where you set your foot next."

With a final, hard look, he turned his horse, and the others followed, disappearing back into the trees as quietly as they'd come. The tension left as quickly as the vanishing horses. Each man let out a slow breath as silence settled back in.

Perry shot Pete an appreciative glance. "That was a hell of a close one," he muttered. "And you, my friend, are quite the thespian. This road's sure got a broken edge of despair and meanness that none of us had expected."

"It's a different kind of wilderness out here now," Pete said. "Folks aren't just fightin' for land. They're fightin' for what little's left of themselves." He paused, looking down the trail. "We'll keep our heads low and our words soft. But if that don't work, next time we'll have to…" He let the words hang in the air, grim and unspoken.

Moses looked at Pete. "That silver tongue of yours saved us a world of trouble today. I don't think they even noticed me. Best we stay ready for the worst, 'cause the peace out here feels as threadbare as that little traveler's blanket."

With a final look back toward the trees, each of the friends carried a new weight of caution, knowing the journey would demand more grit and resolve than they had expected.

"I figure we have several more days to go," Moses said, setting his eyes toward a spot on the horizon leading to Gumbo Flats.

The prairie stretched out before them, its vast emptiness both daunting and oddly comforting. The air was cooler now, carrying the scent of winter. The men spoke little, each lost in their thoughts, but there was an unspoken determination that drove them forward.

As the miles rolled by, the memory of their farewells lingered. Perry occasionally reached into his heart pocket, feeling the rosary Millie had given him, its presence a constant reminder of home, of the people waiting for them, and of the promises they had made. Pete occasionally touched the locket tucked inside his coat, a small comfort against the uncertainty of the road.

They were three days from Gumbo Flats when the weather began to change. Clouds gathered on the horizon, heavy and gray, and the wind picked up, whipping through the open fields. The horses snorted nervously, their steps quickening as though they sensed the coming storm.

Moses rode ahead to scout the path, his silhouette dark against the ominous sky. When he returned, his expression was grim. "Storm's coming fast," he said. "We need to find shelter."

The men pressed on, their eyes scanning the horizon for any sign of cover. As the first drops of rain began to fall, they spotted an old barn in the distance, its roof sagging but intact. They hurried toward it, the wagon wheels churning through the mud as the rain turned into a thunderous downpour.

Inside the barn, the men worked quickly to unhitch the horses and secure the wagon. They lit a small lantern, its light flickering against the weathered wooden walls.

Pete leaned against a beam, wiping rain from his face. "Well, we've had better nights, but at least we're dry."

Perry nodded and Moses sat near the lantern, his hands resting on his knees as the storm raged outside.

"This trip's testing all of us, but our first stop is close," Moses said. "It's closer than the bark on a walnut tree."

CHAPTER 13

Early December

GHOSTS OF THE ROAD

DANVILLE, MISSOURI WAS DEAD AHEAD. As the rescue party and their Conestoga rattled toward the town, a sense of unease settled over the three friends. The town crouched under the gray afternoon sky, its buildings weathered and worn from more than just years of hard sun and rain. The air was thick and smoky, burdened by a history of violence that seeped from the wood and brick of every storefront.

Pete took in the town with a hardened gaze, the hair on the back of his neck standing at attention. "I'll tell ya, gentlemen, if ever a place was cursed this'd be it, all because of Bloody Bill Anderson. Back at The Outpost, I'd hear whispers about what he did here and across the region, not that long ago. Folks'd huddle together, voices low as if just sayin' his name could summon evil. But there was always one guy in the crowd who idolized him for refusin' to let go of the fight."

"I've read the stories," Perry said, leaning back in his saddle. "From here to all that shit back in Lawrence. He was an unholy terror, but still today some folks see his actions like some twisted kind of gospel. How he'd ride through a hail of bullets without so much as a scratch. For me, the worst part is he grew up in Kansas."

"He might have grown up in Kansas, but he sure as hell wasn't a free-stater," Pete said. "He was out for revenge from the day his daddy got shot down by a judge in a dispute over stolen horses."

Moses scanned Main Street and the cold hard stares from the board sidewalks. One man glared from a store window, another whispered to his friend, pointing toward the three strangers.

"No man can dodge death forever," he said.

"He did long enough to bring that fate to others," Pete said. "He tracked down the judge, shot him twice. Not just him, though. Dragged a sixteen-year-old boy into it too. Left 'em both bleeding in a cellar and tossed barrels in on top like they were burying their own sins. Not far from here, he lined up Union soldiers, fresh recruits, unarmed. Gunned 'em down like buffalo exhausted after a stampede. One by one. About two dozen. Pulled the trigger himself."

"That's no soldier's act. That's the work of a monster," Moses said.

"But, like you said, Moses, nobody can dodge death forever," Pete said. "Union Army had enough of his shit. Tracked him down and put a bullet right behind his ear, but that was after he charged at them full speed. Happened October of last year, up near Albany."

"And now, rebel sympathizers see him as a martyr. That's the only curse he left behind," Perry said.

Perry's words faltered as a sudden, violent uproar shattered the quiet. Across the street, three men had trapped a lone Black man against the splintered façade of a weather-beaten building. Before anyone could react, a noose was flung over the freedman's neck, tightening like a serpent. Taunts erupted from the attackers, each venomous syllable piercing the silence. The freedman stood defiant, trembling yet unbroken.

The leader, a grizzled brute, jabbed a finger sharply into the man's chest and knocked him to his knees. "Think you got rights here? This is Danville, boy. You ain't welcome."

Moses' voice was dark and strained. "We can't just watch this, Pete. You've got the voice. Use it before he swings from that rope."

Pete nodded, dismounting and approaching, boots scraping gravel like steel on flint. "Mornin', gentlemen," he drawled. "Seems you've mistaken cruelty for justice."

The grizzled man sneered. "Butt out mister. Just who the hell are you givin' orders? Another damn Yankee apologist, or maybe a scallywag."

Pete's gaze hardened, his hand resting on his holster. "I'm just a man who's done watchin' good folks bleed for hate. War's over, friend. Let that rope go, or I make sure you swing from it."

A younger attacker lunged at Pete, knife blade flashing. Pete drew his gun in defense. A single shot echoed, sharp and decisive. The attacker collapsed in a heap of hate, lifeless eyes wide in surprise.

After the gunshot's echo, silence, raw and heavy, gripped the street. The remaining men backed away, rage turning to fear. Pete holstered his gun, his voice cutting the tension, "Anyone else feel like challenging my Southern heritage?"

They scattered like rats in a flood, muttering curses under their breaths. Pete knelt beside the freedman, gently removing the rope. "You're safe now," he whispered.

The freedman gasped, eyes flooded with gratitude. "Thank you, sir. Not many white folks would step into that hellfire."

Pete nodded solemnly. "Peace ain't easy, but it's ground worth dying on. Do me a favor. Get on your horse, gallop out of here and don't look back."

Moses stepped forward. "You saved us all from a hornet's nest, Pete."

Pete rose from his knees, his voice dropping to a whisper. "I don't take a shinin' to killin', even when in self-defense. And now they'll gather up his body, call him a martyr, and light their torches with his memory. We need to mount up and make that wagon roll as fast as possible. Those men'll return with twice the hate and double the guns. We cracked their pride, and they'll be hungry for blood."

"Agreed. We need to travel fast and silent," Perry said. "By nightfall, this place might be burning with hatred, and we need to be far beyond the fire's glow. Let's get the hell out of here and keep going into the approaching dark of night."

They rode hard, the horses sensing the urgency in every taut rein and sharp command. Danville faded into the dark horizon, but its threat clung to their backs like smoke. Even miles out, the men stole wary glances over their shoulders, scanning the shadows for pursuers. When the moon rose high and the road grew cold, they slipped two rolling hills off the beaten path, seeking shelter beneath a stand of twisted oaks.

They were a good, hard two days' ride from Gumbo Flats, and despite the dangers lurking in every shadowed town and stretch of trail, they would not be deterred.

That night, the early December moon felt uneasy. It was bright enough to cast nighttime shadows and illuminate the frosted roadside grass with a ghostly sheen.

"That moon looks closer than it ought to, like Old Man Winter's cold hands pulled it down just to keep us company," Perry said. "But that glow feels more like a warning than a lullaby."

Moses and Pete set up lanterns close to camp but shielded by the wagon. Their minds remained darkened by the memory of the Danville incident earlier that day. It might have been the grit of the town's dust still stuck in throats. Pete broke the silence.

"Reckon we made the right call leaving before it got dark. That moon makes it damn hard to hide from anyone."

Perry shook his head. "Yeh, and that one fella, the young one, was just itchin' to pick a fight with anyone. No sympathy extended, but he picked the wrong man for his petty quarrel."

Pete sat by the crackling fire, his eyes distant. "A man ought to stand for somethin' bigger than his own conceit. Pride and hate—that ain't a cause worth dying for. I didn't want to take his life, but he gave me no choice."

Moses stirred the fire. "Maybe so, Pete. But from where I stood, you didn't take his life. You spared another's. That young fool aimed to murder, and today he paid the price a killer earns."

A rustling stirred from the shadows just off the trail, a reminder of the lurking danger. Perry grabbed his rifle, his eyes scanning the trees. "This whole trail's haunted by ghosts. Some actions, thought just, stick with you, no matter how far you ride to leave 'em behind.

An owl's hoot shot through the night air.

Perry perked up. Archibald heard it too and he let out a whine.

"Shit, never like to hear the sound of night birds. I heard a whippoorwill's call the night after my good friend, Constable Dan, was killed by a rebel's bullet at Leavenworth. That song just cut right through the air, sharp and cold. That bird knew somethin' was gone from this world, like it was mourning him. Ever since, whenever I hear the call of a bird under a bright moon, I can't help but feel a chill. Reminds me how close death always is, even on a night so calm."

The owl's hoot echoed again, trailing off into night sky. Perry exhaled, shifting his grip on the rifle. "Some folks laugh at omens, but I don't. The world's got a way of whispering warnings if a man knows how to listen."

Archibald let out a low whine, ears twitching.

Pete cleared his throat and chuckled. "Perry, you're startin' to sound like a witch doctor, conjuring up stories just to spook the rest of us. And clearly, your superstitions are rubbin' off on your dog. Maybe it's the long road gnawin' at your nerves."

"I ain't making this up, Pete. Folks claim the night birds, owl or whippoorwill, can sense a person's soul slipping away, maybe even trying to capture it as its own before it leaves the body. Some believe their song's a death omen."

Pete shot Perry a playful grin. "Might be best turning in for the night, before you start seeing shadows dancin' and spirits lingerin' in the trees."

Perry gave Pete a sideways glance, half a smirk breaking through. "Laugh all you want, Pete. Just don't come running to me when that owl starts screechin' over your tent tonight."

"Wouldn't think about doing such a thing, Perry. I think that bird's just hungry for scraps, not spirits. Let's douse those lanterns and settle in."

The campfire's glow pushed back the December chill. The troubled trail behind them felt miles away.

Pete broke the silence. "Adams, listenin' to you talk earlier like some old mystic, you were startin' to sound like a curse yourself. You had my nerves all twisted up."

Moses laughed at the bickering.

Perry gave Pete a side glance. "I like to think about it not as a curse, but rather as a man with his eyes wide open, seeing the world without blinders. Apologies, Pete, but the warmth of this fire's chased those shadows clean outta my mind at least for tonight, but my eyes will hold forth the watch."

Pete shook his head, laughing. "Maybe we don't gotta dig so deep. Even with your eyes open, we need to get some sleep before dawn. We've got miles to ride. And even tomorrow, we need to watch our backs."

The three men settled back into silence, each staring into the flames as though hoping they'd burn away the bitter memories lingering from the day.

By noon of the second day after the ordeal in Danville, the dense trees thinned, giving way to rolling hills and a widening sky—signs of the river drawing near. The wagon moved more easily over the smoother ground, and the road ahead stretched like a ribbon of quiet promise.

"Gentlemen, if memory serves, Gumbo Flats should be just over the next couple ridges," Moses said. "I don't know what we'll find there, but there's a ferry up ahead at Boone's Crossing."

Pete gave a quiet nod. "They say there's good folks out this way, tryin' to start fresh. I'd like to think that's true. It's just hard to tell sometimes."

Perry smirked. "Woah, there, partner. Who's soundin' like a pessimist now?"

Moses shook his head. "Regardless of what we find, no man's gonna tell us where we can or can't go. We've come too far to turn back."

The men pressed on, the stress of the past two days settling behind them like dust in the wind. Somewhere beyond the final ridge and the ferry crossing, there was food, maybe shelter, and perhaps a chance to lay aside something heavier than just their saddlebags.

Whatever waited at Gumbo Flats, they'd be ready.

CHAPTER 14

Mid December

RESPITE FROM THE ROAD

"HERE WE ARE, FELLAS. Gabe and I rode out through this same break, when we left this place behind," Moses said, rising in his stirrups as he passed through a gap in the hedgerow ahead of Pete and the Conestoga. "This is Gumbo Flats, the place where my dreams and nightmares shake hands."

Perry pulled the wagon up beside Moses sensing his friend's thickness of memory. "Question is, which one's got the firmer grip on you, partner. Funny thing about a place like this is that if you step through once, it's an escape. Step back through again, and it's a reckoning. This was your way out, Moses. It was the gate you slipped through to freedom. And now? Now it's callin' you back. Measuring you up, asking what kind of man dares to cross it again."

Pete jumped in. "I'd say a sure-as-shit honorable man. But, either way, you just crossed that gap in the hedgerow for an entirely different reason."

The sky was cloudy and desolate, echoing the moment's somber mood. At the edge of the plantation's first field, they climbed down in silence. The land around them was raw, a bare expanse in the dead of winter that held for Moses memories of backbreaking labor and bitter endurance. Perry drew out his brass spyglass to get a better view.

Moses dismounted his horse and walked three paces forward into the dried remnants of last season's corn crop. He crouched down and reached into the dirt, running a handful of the gritty, sand-riddled soil between his fingers. The coarse granules fell through his hand, and he remembered every ache, every blister that resulted from his struggle to scrape the ground clean of river sand.

"The flood came," Moses said, speaking from another time. "River overflowed and dumped sand all over this field. Covered up the gumbo topsoil, buried everything we'd planted. Washed away the plantation house too. Old Man Manchester didn't see a disaster, only a chance to get more work out of us. Gabe and I spent weeks out here with shovels scrapin' that sand off foot by foot, loading it into a wagon and carting it off, sunup to sundown. Had to have it ready for spring plantin'. It didn't matter how our hands looked by the end, raw and bleedin' from the grit. To Manchester, we were lower than mules pullin' a plow."

Moses paused. "Only problem was he never got a chance to see that spring plantin'. The old man got drunk one afternoon and wandered too close to the river. Nobody saw him again."

He looked at his friends, his eyes concealing his real memory.

Perry shook his head in disgust. "That man sounds like he didn't possess a shred of decency. Expectin' men to work the land like that. Why not just mix the sand in with the topsoil during the next plowing pass?"

"The sand was way too deep in places. And, well, in places where there was only gumbo soil, it just doesn't scour too well, not even off the face of one of those fancy John Deere plows like you have. Mixin' in that sand might have loosened it up a bit, but the old man was beyond logic."

Moses rubbed his scarred hands, feeling the roughness of those old wounds.

Perry climbed down from the wagon and walked forward, scanning the field. He bent down, inspecting the crop stubble left atop the soil. "This biggest plot looks like it was all corn. Corn grows well in soil like this. But from the looks of it, this land's been worked hard, stripped bare."

His eyes narrowed on two scrappy patches hugging the main field. He walked toward them. The stalks there, brittle and bleached, hugged the earth tighter than the larger cornfield. He crouched, fingers brushing the crisp remains. He cracked open a couple of small pods left among the stubble, small oval beans spilled into the palm of his hand. "Soybeans," he said. "Didn't think I'd ever see a whole field of 'em. Moses, come here, you gotta see this."

Moses walked toward the smaller field, as Perry waved him on.

"Back at the Battle of Leavenworth, the Army cooks roasted and ground these things up and made 'em drinkable. Called it conflict coffee. Kept the shakes off, helped us Jayhawkers feel almost human again."

"Soybeans? Aren't they startin' to grow a few test plots around our area?"

Perry nodded. He picked up seven more pods and cracked them open before standing. He held the handful of beans out to Moses. "Yeh. Just look at these little buggers. They're good for the soil and keeping it fertile. All the journals say it's the next big crop. Whoever's farmin' this place now is settin' the pace. Tryin' their hand at somethin' new. Anythin' that might turn a profit without suckin' the land dry."

Moses let out a low, bitter laugh, shaking his head. "Old man Manchester never introduced ideas. He stuck with the old ways and leached as much as possible out of the land's abundance, never puttin' anything back."

"The current owner must have an eye for innovation, at the very least."

"Yeh, it's gotta be John. This farm was his escape from the hubbub of his St. Louis law office."

Perry held his bean-filled hand closer to Moses, then glanced back at the vast stretch of the exhausted cornfield. "That land over there, it's got ghosts, that's for sure. Old man Manchester might be gone, but it feels like he's still got his claws in that soil, like his spirit's still drainin' it. But you and Gabe, and every man who worked it, you left pieces of yourselves here. You are the true ghosts of Gumbo Flats."

Moses looked out over the desolate cornfield, his face a mix of anger and sorrow. He reached into his pocket and pulled out a small leather bag. "Perry, would you drop those soybean seeds into this bag. Think I'll lace 'em up tight and keep 'em as a good luck charm for the rest of the trip."

Perry cupped his hand and rolled the soybeans into the bag like little marbles. "You got it, my friend." He reached into his pocket and drew out Millie's rosary. "With a little luck added to the Lord's grace, we'll press on."

"This land knows me better than I know myself. I spent so many years in these fields, pushin' myself to exhaustion. Every ache in my bones and every scar on my hands sprouts from this dirt. But now, I'm taking a little piece of what came from this land with me."

Listening from a distance, Pete kicked at the dry stalks as he ambled over. "Funny, ain't it? Like spittin' 'backy juice in the ghost's eye. Taking a handful of beans to bust the curse off this damn place."

Moses nodded, as he cinched the bag tight. His shoulders straightened as he looked out over Gumbo Flats with a new resolve. "I like the idea of lettin' this dirt know we came here on our terms, not to relive the past, but to claim somethin' better. I'm gonna tuck this little bag of beans into my saddle bag. They're goin' home with me."

Perry looked toward the wagon. "We're about to finish the first long leg of this journey. I say we make our way over to the old homesite and stay a couple days. We find John and you can visit. See what he wants to know. See if he has any clues to share. We can restock the wagon in Gumbo Flats and rejuvenate the horses. Just remember, Moses, you came back here to see it for what it is. It's just a place. Not the prison you knew before."

Moses inhaled deeply, the cold air bracing. "That chapter is sure as hell closed."

With a final look, the men returned to their respective rides. Moses tucked the lucky bag of beans into his saddle pouch. As they climbed aboard, Perry cast one last glance back at the barren fields. They began their ride across the flat field toward the far river bluffs to the south.

"If nobody objects, let's set up camp near the site of the old plantation house," Moses said. "As much as I detest the recollections, that place still holds a lot of good memories for me too."

The wagon wheels groaned through the rutted field, hooves stirring up the moldy scent of decaying crops. Moses gripped the reins of his horse tighter as they neared a small rise, his knuckles pale against the worn leather. The spot ahead pulled like a whisper from under the skin. He didn't speak, just stared. Over the rise a clearing appeared. Expecting to see an old foundation and emptiness, wide, raw and quiet, the little hill gave way to an entirely different sight.

Moses pulled back the reins and his horse stopped dead in its tracks.

Where the old house should have been, a structure he remembered as a flooded-out skeleton, crumbling and bare, stood a grand Victorian home, its steep gables and ornate trimmings catching the late afternoon light. Built atop a raised mound of soil, it commanded the eye, towering over the surrounding fields. Bold columns primed in pale hues with dark, freshly painted trim supported a wide porch wrapping the home's front.

A sturdy carriage house stood on the site that Moses remembered as the location of the slave quarters, the only home he had known at the plantation.

"Must be six, maybe seven bedrooms in that house," Perry murmured, taking in the sprawling home atop the tall, mounded yard.

Moses stared, unsettled. "This was nothing but ruins when I left. Not a single board of that old house remained. Only the rock foundation. So why here? Why build atop bones?"

Pete squinted at the house, then turned to Moses. "Maybe the past doesn't matter to whoever owns it now. Or maybe it does. From the looks of that elevation it's built on, whoever built this home must know the perils of living alongside a river. A man with coin looks at land like this and sees what he wants it to be, not what it was."

The men dismounted and Pete walked up the porch stairs and knocked on the door. He waited a moment, then called down the steep lawn. "Nobody's home. I don't know if John or somebody else lives here, but there's a brass plaque on the door that reads 'The Manchesters.'"

"As in plural? Maybe John has a family now," Moses said.

The three men set up a small camp at the bottom of the Victorian home's sloped yard.

The men moved quietly after an exhausting day on the trail. Pete and Perry led the horses to a small patch of grass near the grove, removing the tack and feeding them from their dwindling stores of grain. Moses gathered nearby boulders and made a fire ring and Archibald claimed a spot near it. The dog gnawed on a strip of salted meat Moses tossed him as he walked toward the grove to retrieve firewood.

Moses glanced back at the empty fields that stretched out toward the river. It was quiet here. Too quiet, almost as if the land itself was holding its breath. He returned to camp, his arms filled with dry wood. He handed it to Pete, who set to work building the fire.

Pete struck a match, the small flame catching on the kindling, and soon a warm glow crackled in the darkening air, its light casting shadows that flickered across their faces. They settled down around the fire with Archibald as the chill of the December evening settled in.

"Feels good to rest our bones for a minute," Perry said, stretching his legs. "We've come a long way. But I also know our journey's just begun."

Moses nodded, his gaze fixed on the flames. "Ain't that the truth. We've got a roof of stars and a fire to warm us, but in order to move on with open eyes I need to find out the roots of that telegram inquiry John sent to Judge Merriweather."

Pete took a long breath, stirring a pot of beans over the fire. "We know John Manchester was just like kin to you, Moses."

"Can't wait to see him. John's as close as a brother. I'd trust him with my life, and I reckon I have more than once. We grew up side by side. His momma taught me letters and scripture same as him—defied every rule her world laid down. The old man didn't like it much, but she stood taller than any man I knew."

Moses continued. "Whatever John's got to say, it's bound to be worth hearin'. He's holdin' the keys to somethin' we need to understand. And if there's even the slightest hint about my family and where they ended up, or a road back to them, it's worth every step it took to get here."

"We're here for all of that, Moses," Perry said. "But it sounds pretty clear that John also has some kind of mystery he wants to clear up."

"Whatever it is, gentlemen, good or bad, just know my gratitude for getting' me this far."

The fire crackled and popped as Pete ladled beans into tin bowls, passing them around. "Here," he said with a grin, handing Perry his plate. "A warm meal on a cold night. That might be the best we get if John's got more on his mind than just a reunion."

They ate in comfortable silence, each man contemplating what lay ahead. The road had brought them here, to a place heavy with history and secrets, and they hoped that tomorrow they might finally find some kind of resolution.

After a while, Pete broke the quiet. "I'll tell ya, boys, there's somethin' about this place that feels like it's watchin' us. That plantation ground, it's got stories buried in it, even if the house is gone. Makes you wonder if John's got answers to questions we don't even know to ask yet."

"I hope we'll know tomorrow, but tonight we rest. We need to renew our strength," Perry said.

After setting up their tents and securing their horses, the men settled in as the fire crackled. Above their tents, the stars shone cold and distant. The smell of Gumbo Flats loomed like a shadow in the night, a place of hidden secrets and distant memories. As they drifted into a watchful calm, each man felt the anticipation and gravity of what lay ahead, ready to face whatever John Manchester might reveal.

Perry stirred, blinking groggily as the first light of dawn crept into his tent. He felt a cold, wet nudge against his cheek. He opened his eyes wide to find Archibald's eager face inches from his own, the hound's nose pressed against his skin, sniffing intently.

"What the..." Perry murmured, rubbing his hand over his face. "Can't let a man have five more minutes, can ya?" Archibald let out a low, contented whine, his tail thumping against the side of the tent.

Perry chuckled, scratching behind Archy's ears. "You're the only one who'll wake me up this early and not catch an earful," he muttered, sitting up and stretching. "You hungry, boy? You thinkin' it's time we rustle up some grub?"

Archibald let out a short, eager bark, "Uh Roo Roo Roo."

Perry pushed Archibald aside and rolled out of the tent, shaking the chill of sleep from his bones. He gave the hound a gentle pat. "Let's get some food in your belly, old fella. You know, Archy, with any luck, today's the day we get some real answers."

The hound tilted his head as if listening, his intelligent eyes fixed on Perry. "Archy, you've got more sense in that furry head of yours than most of the folks I've met."

He glanced over at the tents of his sleeping friends and then back to Archy. "C'mon, let's see what we can rustle up for breakfast before the others catch wind of us."

With Archy trotting beside him, Perry started the campfire, his mind already turning toward what the day might bring. They'd need mindful strength for the questions that might lay ahead. He moved around the campsite, gathering supplies. He reached into the wagon for a bag of flour, a slab of pork belly and coffee.

As Perry made breakfast, Archibald sat nearby, soaking in the scene with hungry interest.

Satisfied, Perry glanced at Archy, whose nose twitched at the smells. "Time to wake up the others. Breakfast is served."

"Uh Roo Roo Roo."

Pete and Moses were jolted awake by Archibald's sharp bark, his tail wagging as he darted between their tents, eager to start the day.

Moses rolled out quickly, stretching his arms wide to take in the cool morning air. He knelt down to give Archy a good scratch behind the ears.

"Mornin', Archy! Guess you're better than a morning rooster," he said, chuckling as Archy let out a happy whine.

Pete, however, emerged from his tent with a groggy scowl, rubbing the sleep from his eyes. He shot Archy a look that was both affectionate and annoyed. "Mornin', Archy," he muttered. "Next time, how 'bout givin' a man a little more peace before the sun's barely up?"

The smell of breakfast drifted, and Pete sniffed the air. His gaze shifted to Perry, who stood by the fire, a smile spreading across his face as he stirred a skillet of gravy.

Pete crossed his arms, feigning skepticism. "Last time you cooked, I was chewin' on lumps of flour for days, and I damn near cracked a tooth."

"Oh, ye of little faith," Perry teased, handing Pete a tin plate stacked with biscuits smothered in gravy. "Go on, give it a try."

Moses had already settled onto a nearby log with his plate, chewing contentedly. He glanced up, grinning with his mouth half-full. "I don't know what you're grumblin' about, Pete. Perry's outdone himself. Best thing I've tasted since we left St. Joseph."

"If Moses hasn't keeled over yet, I guess it's safe enough." Pete eyed the plate, poking at the biscuit with his fork. He took a tentative bite. The gravy and biscuit melted in his mouth.

Perry ladled up a small bowl for Archy.

"I'll be damned. It ain't Lucy's, but it will damn sure do." Pete said, unable to hide his surprise. "I hate to say it, but your culinary skills have improved immensely."

Perry gave Pete a playful shove. "Now that's about the closest thing to a compliment I've ever heard come outta your mouth. Must be a good sign for the day. And just look at Archy. He likes it even more than you do."

Moses set his empty plate aside, his eyes bright with anticipation.

"Fellas, enough eatin'," he said, slapping his hands together. "Let's get this camp cleaned up a bit. I'm hoping we meet up with John today. Then we find out what he's got to say."

Pete chuckled, handing Archy the last bite of his biscuit. "You're eager enough for all three of us, Moses. Let's hope your buddy John's ready to deliver."

The three friends shared a look of determination, fueled by the meal and the promise of answers yet to come. They set to work organizing the camp, ready to face whatever the day, and John Manchester, had in store.

CHAPTER 15

Mid December

HEARTS ON THE HOMEFRONT

BACK IN ST. JOSEPH, the early Saturday morning sun filtered through the lace curtains in Lucy's cozy kitchen. The light cast a glow over the table where she and Millie sat, hands embracing steaming mugs of coffee. Each woman's eyes carried a ponderous gaze. It was not a secret they were missing their husbands.

Millie placed her cup on the table with bold resolve. "Lucy, you know as well as I do—our men can handle whatever trouble they might have found."

Lucy stared hard out the frosty window. "They're out there chasing justice, not just survival. While every mile between Pete and me burns like fire, I won't let fear steal my strength." She tightened her grip on the mug. "I think we're steadier than they would ever imagine."

Millie reached across the table, her voice steady, firm. "I feel that ache too, every morning, but I won't let it break me. Those three— Perry, Pete, and Moses—there's not a stronger trio. And they'll find their way home. One way or another, they will."

Lucy nodded, fighting back emotion. "Sometimes, I think they might come walkin' up to the house, but I realize that's months away."

Millie grabbed Lucy's hand. "It's going to take time. But until then, we'll hold down the fort."

Lucy let out a small, quiet laugh. "You're right. We've got a job of our own, don't we? The Outpost, the community, growing our babies, taking care of each other." She gave Millie a warm smile. "And I'm grateful to have you here. I may spout off a lot of bluster, but I don't think I could face this alone."

Millie chuckled, taking a sip of her coffee. "Well, thank the Lord we don't have to. Between you and Hank at The Outpost, and Jeptha with his steady wisdom, I reckon we're as secure as the Pony Express station during its heyday."

They sat together, watching the dawn break like a challenge they were ready to meet. The strength between them wasn't loud, but it was unshakable, rooted in grit, shared purpose, and a fierce refusal to let fear or uncertainty write their story.

Outside, an approaching rumble reached Lucy's front porch. The sound grew louder, accompanied by the rhythmic sound of horse hooves. Lucy raced to the door. Doc Anderson's worn, horse-drawn buggy came to a stop in front of the Fontaine home.

The doctor sat straight-backed in the driver's seat, bundled against the chill in a brown coat that had seen as many years as he had, more patches than original fabric. His face was weathered, tanned and wrinkled from decades of wind and sun, his silver beard cropped neatly. Hands as calloused as a farmer's gripped the reins, steady as the hands of a clock, and his piercing gaze took in the scene, as it always did, with an attentive calm.

Lucy opened the front door, and she and Millie watched from the porch.

As Doc Anderson climbed down from the buggy, he tipped his hat with a smile. "Good morning, ladies. I know it's Saturday morning, but it's time for your six-month checkup. Growing babies don't pay any mind to days of the week, so I make my rounds as needed, rain or shine, regardless of hour."

Millie and Lucy met him at the door, their smiles hiding quiet worries they both held. Doc Anderson had been delivering babies, curing illnesses, and patching up farm injuries and war wounds in the community for decades, and his presence at the Fontaine home was as familiar as family.

Doc nodded toward the sitting room. "Shall we start?" he asked, glancing from Millie to Lucy. "No need to waste this fine morning with me jawing at the doorstoop."

Inside the cozy home, Doc Anderson settled onto a short stool, his presence filling the space with a sense of calm that had guided countless families through uncertain times. He patted Millie's hand and gave her a smile, his eyes wrinkled by both experience and wisdom.

"Let's see how you're doing, Millie," he said, settling her back on the sofa as he took her hand in his. His fingers found her pulse, counting to himself as he nodded in concentration. He checked her color and the brightness in her eyes. He moved his hand to her abdomen, pressing with the light but sure touch of a man who'd delivered countless babies.

After a moment, Doc Anderson gave an approving nod, leaning back with a grin that sparkled beneath his beard.

"You have a powerful pulse. I'm guessing that baby's growing steady. It appears you've been eating right, caring for yourself. Baby seems to be growing as expected at this stage."

Millie rested her hand protectively over her midsection. "I'm glad it's all goin' as it should. Feels like I've been carryin' the weight of two for weeks now."

Doc Anderson chuckled. "That's what I like to hear. You keep doin' what you're doin', Millie. This little one's got strength in 'em, and so do you." With a final, approving glance, he patted her hand. "You're right on schedule."

He turned to Lucy, his face tinged with seriousness since she was experiencing her first pregnancy at an older age. The look made Lucy's pulse quicken.

Lucy settled herself, glancing nervously at Millie before leaning back. Doc Anderson moved forward, placing his hand on her wrist to check her pulse. His expression shifted, his fingers lingering a bit longer than usual. He saw the slight pallor and the tension in her eyes. His experienced gaze noticed every small detail. He pressed his hand over her abdomen, his touch gentle.

"Miss Lucy, have you been eating right?" He sat, his face thoughtful as his fingers stroked his beard in contemplation, searching for appropriate words.

Lucy's smile faded, her gaze locked on him. "Doc? Somethin' wrong?"

Doc Anderson sighed, setting his weathered hands on his knees. "Lucy," he began, his voice gentle but firm, "The degree of fullness I would expect at this early stage isn't quite right. Not ideal. I'm not sayin' there's anything wrong just yet, but we need to stay vigilant. Your body's gonna need every bit of strength it can muster for that baby to grow healthy."

Lucy's face fell. Her voice trembled with worry. "Are you sayin' my baby's in trouble, Doc?"

Doc shook his head, his tone steady as he met her gaze. "No, Lucy. Not yet. But we want to make sure it stays that way. You've got some catching up to do, so here's what I want: keep your meals hearty. I know it's difficult with the menfolk away, and I know your schedule is demanding, but try to rest as much as you can. Eat lots of butter, milk, eggs—anything rich and filling. And stay clear of stressing yourself."

Lucy nodded, her face pale, though she forced a small smile. "Easier said than done, Doc, but I'll do whatever it takes. I want this baby to be healthy."

Millie reached over, her voice resolute as she placed a hand on Lucy's arm. "Starting today, I'll be keepin' a closer eye on you. You'll be eatin' what I eat, and then some."

Doc Anderson smiled. "That's the attitude. Between the two of you, these babies have more strength around 'em than half the town. And don't let anxiety weigh you down, Lucy. Keep your mind as steady as your meals. You and your baby will both be better off for it."

He rose, giving Lucy's shoulder a reassuring pat. "I'll be back in a couple weeks to check in on you. And if you feel poorly, you send for me straight away. You understand?"

Lucy stood and hugged him, her eyes bright with gratitude even as concern lingered. "Thank you, Doc."

Doc Anderson returned her hug, his voice gruff but kind. "No need for thanks, Lucy. Just doin' my job. We'll make sure you and that little one get on the right track." He tipped his hat to both women and smiled as he turned to head back to his creaking buggy outside. The sound of the wheels faded as it rumbled down the street.

Millie looked at Lucy and took her hand. "Doc gave us our orders, and I'll be right here to make sure they're followed to the letter. We'll strengthen you up and that baby too. We'll find power in each other during the weeks ahead. Rest and faith will bring us through the challenge."

Lucy looked at her friend, feeling a flicker of hope amid her worries. "With you here, Millie, I know I can manage. But I think rest might have to wait until tomorrow. It's Saturday morning, and The Outpost calls. My focus'll be on fryin' bacon and scramblin' eggs."

The jingling sound of an approaching carriage drew their attention. It was Hank Crowder, their morning ride. Hank labored his mountainous body up the stairs and knocked. Lucy skipped to the door, bracing herself for the day.

"Mornin', ladies! Your carriage awaits. Ready for a big morning at The Outpost?" Hank's voice boomed with cheerful enthusiasm.

Millie gave Lucy a smile. "Let's get to it, then. That breakfast crowd isn't gonna feed itself. We can rest tomorrow."

They climbed into the covered carriage, settling onto the worn wooden bench as Hank gave a mighty snap of the reins. The vessel lurched forward, bumping over the gravel street.

Hank glanced back through the lowered cloth curtain, noticing a pensive look in Lucy's eyes.

"Now, don't tell me you're thinkin' about Saturday's rowdy crowd already!" he teased, a grin spreading across his bearded face. "You two make that place hum like a beehive."

Lucy managed a small smile. She didn't want her worries to dampen the mood, with Millie and Hank doing their best to cheer her up. "You're right, Hank. I guess I was lost in thought."

"We'll make it through the busy morning, Lucy. We always do," Millie said.

Familiar scenes rolled by. Modest homes stretched in every direction, smoke rising from their chimneys. As they neared The Outpost, Lucy's shoulders relaxed. No matter her worries, the tavern had become her lifeline with Pete away. It was a place that brought people together, a place where she could lose herself in the simple routine of cooking and serving, of sharing laughter and stories with familiar faces.

Before long, the familiar clapboard building came into view. Hank brought the carriage to a stop.

"Here we are, ladies," Hank said, tipping his hat. "Go show that crowd what you're made of."

Lucy and Millie exchanged a final determined glance.

Minutes later, a crowd began to gather on the board sidewalk outside. It was clear the fine citizens of St. Joseph were eager for the tavern's famous Saturday morning breakfast. The Outpost's wooden sign swung in the morning breeze as the scent of hearty cooking began to drift outside through cracks in the window frames. Mingling and chatter grew by the minute.

Inside, Lucy and Millie jumped into action, moving around the kitchen as they prepared The Outpost's signature breakfast fare. Thick slices of cured ham sizzled in the pan, corn grits bubbled on the stove, buttery biscuits baked to a perfect golden brown, and eggs fried fresh with a satisfying sizzle.

Lucy was inclined to go above and beyond with each order. If a patron ordered two eggs and ham, it came with three eggs and two pieces of ham. If a simple order for scrambled eggs and bacon hit the kitchen, it was returned with double eggs, bacon…and ham. Ham was always on the plate. It had become a tradition, but Lucy always put her customers on notice that it should not be expected. She never knew when the ham supply might dry up unexpectedly.

Millie stirred a pan of grits with focused care as they thickened over the heat, glancing over her shoulder. "Lucy, you mind passin' that butter? We're gonna need it."

Lucy, rolling out biscuits at the counter, handed over the butter. "Here you go," she said, glancing out the window at the crowd gathering outside. She couldn't help but smile a little, despite the long day ahead. "Guess they know where to satisfy their hunger."

Hank moved around the dining room with his usual booming presence before grabbing the handle and swinging the front door open for business. He greeted each customer with a hearty laugh as he guided them to their tables. Hank tossed out friendly jabs with the regulars, his deep laugh ringing through the room. Catching Lucy's eye, he winked, grinning. "See? The whole town can't get enough of you two. But knowing your conditions, say the word and I'll jump in. While I know I'm here to crack heads if necessary, I've cracked an egg or two in my day."

Lucy laughed, shrugging off a bit of the tension. "You already do half the work out here, Hank. But we'll keep that in mind."

"All I do is keep the peace, Miss Lucy!" Hank joked, his eyes twinkling. "Y'all are the real reason folks line up."

As the morning rush filled The Outpost, Jeptha Nichols strolled in. He approached the bar. "Hank, please pour me a sarsaparilla, kind sir," he said.

As he sipped the beverage, his usual mischievous grin softened as Lucy slipped out of the kitchen to take a quick breather. Noticing the weary look in her eyes, Jep ambled over and took a seat across from her.

"Now, Miss Lucy," Jeptha said, "I've seen many a worry cross a person's face, but none quite like what you've got today. Care to share with an old fool like me?"

Lucy sighed, looking down at her hands. "Doc Anderson says I'm not gaining size like I should be at this point. Says it could be a sign of trouble for the baby."

Jeptha nodded, his face shifting from curiosity to concern. "I'm not a lady, but I'm guessing there ain't nothin' easy 'bout carryin' a child. But you've got courage in spades. I've seen it with my own eyes. And don't forget, you've got Millie and this whole town behind ya, too."

Lucy looked at him, the worry in her eyes replaced by gratitude. "Thank you, Jep. I'll remember that."

With a gentle smile, Jeptha raised his mug of sarsaparilla in a small toast to Lucy. "To you and that little one, may you find strength and God's peace in every step."

"Was that a genie wish?" Lucy asked.

"Nah, just a prayerful thought from a friend."

The crowd noise settled into a steady hum, laughter and conversation filling The Outpost along with the clatter of plates. Lucy and Millie moved through the room, lifted by the fellowship around them, a reminder that they were part of something bigger.

As they caught a moment at the counter, Millie nudged Lucy. "We've got this, you and me. And when the boys get back, they'll see how resilient we've been."

"They better. Sometimes, I think life's like this old Outpost—built sturdy, wearin' a little weather, but holdin' folks in a big hug. You can't always patch up the cracks, but you can fill them with laughter and warmth enough to keep the roof from fallin' in."

CHAPTER 16

Mid December

BURIED TRUTHS

A FINELY APPOINTED CARRIAGE, blacker than night, rolled up to John Manchester's sprawling Gumbo Flats estate. The polished wood gleamed in the late morning sunlight.

The carriage came to a stop at the home's front porch, the spirited laughter of children pouring down the hill toward the morning campers. A carriage man hopped from his seat and swung open the door. The dapper John Manchester jumped out first, followed by a woman dressed in a long winter coat. John wrangled a small boy and his younger sister from the carriage. They twisted and squirmed as he lowered them to the ground. The children ran wild with shouts of joy like a couple of young puppies as they bounded up the porch stairs.

After a long, grueling week of mind-taxing legal maneuvers in his St. Louis law office, John looked forward to a weekend, perhaps longer, of reprieve in the comfort of his country home. He deserved it.

Looking down onto the campsite, John's eyes narrowed with curiosity, then his face softened into amusement. Near the bottom of the gentle slope, three figures squatted at the edge of his lawn. Even after more than six years, he immediately recognized Moses. The other two were strangers. John let out a quiet chuckle, tipping his hat in their direction as the carriage pulled away.

John climbed up the stairs and assisted his wife and children to the porch. He approached the thick oak front door, grasped the knob, inserted a long skeleton key and twisted. He swung the door open and motioned his family to enter.

"Lizzy, go on inside, dear. I'll be right in to start a fire. We left St. Louis before dawn and I'm sure you and the young'uns need to warm up. Get some rest. I have a few gentlemen to meet and some business matters to attend to."

Lizzy approached the door and kissed John on the cheek. Even from a distance, the visitors saw that John had married well. Lizzy was a beautiful woman. Her countenance radiated the elegance and poise of a city woman accustomed to refinement. She stepped toward the door, her silhouette wrapped in a luxurious velvet cloak of deep burgundy, its edges trimmed in soft fur that framed her body in warmth and grace.

With a gentle smile, John reached out his index finger and gave playful taps to the noses to his children.

"Now settle down and obey your mother. I've got quite a bit of business to handle. I'll be inside as soon as I can."

John crossed the lawn with an easy gait and a smile. Moses stood, brushing dust from his trousers, and stepped forward. His hand went out as John drew near, their eyes meeting before Moses's grin spread wide.

"Well, now, look at this sight, and right on time as promised!" John said, laughing as he grabbed Moses' hand. "Didn't expect to find you camped out on my lawn though, Watty."

"This place, though it's changed, is still like home to me, John-Man. It warms my soul to see you doing well and with family in tow," Moses replied, a spark of joy bounding off the lone dimple on his left cheek. "With the old house gone, I didn't expect you would be so easy to find, my friend. All I did was follow the field. Looks like you're doing well on all fronts. I think you've made quite a name for yourself over in Saint Louie."

John shook his head, a sparkle in his eye. "A bit of legal wrangling here and there. You know how it is. But tell me, Watty, how was your travel?"

"A couple of inconsequential dust ups, but we made it in one piece. That's the important part."

"How's my buddy, Gabe?"

"You'd be proud, John. He came back from the war a hero. He's settled in nicely at our farm in Kansas. Works harder than me most days. John, I'd like you to meet my friends, Perry Adams and Pete Fontaine."

"Sooo, you brought associates?"

"I did. As you can imagine, a trek to these parts as a solitary African man would not have been wise."

"Wise is what you are, Watty. Always have been."

Pete and Perry stepped forward. Pete tipped his hat with a wry grin and shook John's outstretched hand. "Been a long journey. Great to meet you, Mr. Manchester. Moses has told us a lot about your kindness and generosity."

"Call me John. Mr. Manchester was my father, though I still am unsure if he deserved that level of respect."

Perry then reached out his hand to John. "From the telegram you sent to Judge Merriweather, is sounded like you have some private matters you need to discuss with Moses. We won't pry or contribute unless invited."

"Consider yourselves honored guests here in Gumbo Flats. I no longer call this place a plantation. Only a farm. I'm glad you're here as witnesses, gentlemen. That flood buried a lot of secrets here and we're going to try to uncover them."

"We figured both you and Moses might have some information for each other that made all these miles from St. Joseph worthwhile," Perry said.

"Yes. Something quite interesting that came to the surface not long ago and Moses holds the key to the mystery," John said, his smile fading into a blank gaze.

Moses' knees buckled, picturing Old Man Manchester's body rising from the muddy river. The air evacuated his lungs, and his spirit shook as though trying to flee. Moses knew through John's choice of words that this secret mystery might hold dire implications. If so, the next words from John's mouth could start a grave consequence. He braced himself.

"I have plenty of information to share, but I need to tie up some loose ends first," John's tone was ominous. "I reckon it's time I told you why I've been lookin' for Moses."

Moses refilled his lungs with two deep breaths. "Well, go on, John. We're here for a reason. It's time for whatever atonement might come," he said.

"Let's settle in. This is a long story." John motioned for them to follow him up the slope. They climbed to a shaded area under a sprawling oak. The four men sat on two benches under its boughs. John continued, "There's something I found recently, gentlemen. Rather, something that was discovered, like a ghost from the past hidden away for years. It could be of major consequence."

"What is it John-Man? Just say it," Moses said, bracing himself for the worst scenario.

John glanced at Moses and began.

"Before the construction of my home, the crew preparing this elevated site first had to do major excavation of the old plantation house. Inside the old foundation, as they were digging through the silt and debris left by the flood, their shovels hit a hard spot. They used their fingers to scratch and claw the dirt around that area and uncovered a small, sealed chest. About a square foot in size but hefty in weight."

Pete and Perry exchanged glances, curiosity piqued. "A sealed chest, huh? Did they open it?"

"What was inside?" Pete asked.

"They did not open it because there was a small brass plaque on the lid that read, 'To be opened only by John in the presence of Moses.' I knew right away it was a decree from my father. Rightly or wrongly, in my professional practice I always treat such directives, whether formalized or not, as a matter of intended contract. That's particularly true if the originator is deceased."

The crushing burden of mystery lifted from Moses. It had been as weighty as Atlas' eternal punishment of holding aloft the heavens for opposing Zeus. Moses' feet shuffled as though he was prepared to soar, untethered from the earth.

Moses spoke with shrouded jubilation. "John-Man, surely your papa left you a will spelling out his final wishes. Did that document not mention this mystery box?"

"He did leave a will, but it said nothing about the box. Lex non scripta."

"Hold on, John," Perry said. "Who the hell is this Lex fella, and how did he get into the script?"

"Ah, Perry, that's just fancy lawyer talk. Means total silence. The box wasn't mentioned."

"That indeed is a mystery," Perry said, he and Pete focused on Moses.

"I have the box stored away in the carriage house, tucked under a canvas tarp. It's biding its time, holding a fate either radiant or ruinous. I say Moses and I open it together, like my father intended. You two gentlemen can be our official witnesses."

Moses stared at the carriage house, knowing the ghost of Old Man Manchester could tell no tales about his own demise, but perhaps this mystery chest might hold a clue.

"Sounds like a plan," Perry said, looking at Pete. "Pete and I, we'd consider it an honor to bear witness for you in this box-breaking proceeding."

"The chest has endured the ravages of flood and the degradation of burial, leaving only God to know the contents or the state of that content that lies within," John said. "It appears sturdy. By my observation, its construction is of thick iron sealed by an overlapping leather gasket. It's heavy, much heavier than such a chest should weigh alone. It was destined to remain intact to reveal its contents at the proper time. Gentlemen, that time is now."

John removed a pair of jeweled cufflinks and rolled up the sleeves of his fine linen shirt. "Allow me to retrieve the mystery box and bring it into the light, making our actions transparent and beyond impeachment."

John walked away, each man following his steps as he disappeared into the carriage house. Even before seeing the chest, their thoughts swirled around what secrets it might hold. Anticipation hung thick in the air, as if the very earth itself held its breath contemplating the arrival of the chest that had been buried beneath its mud of time and Old Man Manchester's decree.

Pete leaned over to Perry. "I can't decide if we're about to crack open a treasure or a heap of trouble. This box sounds heavy, both in weight and consequence."

Perry nodded, his gaze fixed on the carriage house. "Either way, it's a piece of the past comin' back to life, and there's no stopping that once it's set in motion."

Moments later, John reappeared, the mystery box clutched in his arms, its dark iron casing dulled by years. While sturdy, flecks of dirt clung to its corners where the leather gasket protruded. A small brass lock secured the lid.

Under one arm, John carried a small sledgehammer and under the other a black pry bar. He dropped the box with a thud on a sturdy picnic table under the old oak. John brushed the dirt off his hands and glanced at his witnesses. John's face was calm, but an unmistakable spark shot from his eyes, a tension that portrayed both excitement and a measure of unease. He drew a coal chisel from his pocket and placed a steadying hand on the box.

"This is it, gentlemen. This box, hidden for who knows how long, is ready to divulge its quarry," John pointed to the plaque on the lid. "It's time to discover just what my father meant by this message chiseled in brass."

John looked at Moses. "Ready, Watty?"

Moses drew a breath from his marrow. He stepped forward until he stood shoulder-to-shoulder with John. "Yes, sir. Whatever's in there, I'm guessin' it's part of my story here, and maybe my life yet to come."

John picked up the hammer and chisel and offered them to Moses with a faint smile. "I think it fitting that you take the first whack at that lock. What lies within is likely as much yours as it is mine. Whale away!"

Moses set the chisel's edge against the lock's shackle and drew back the hammer, its heft familiar in his grip. He swung with measured care and struck the lock. The metal-to-metal crack echoed sharp in the still air. The chisel jolted back, barely scratching the shackle."Give it another whack," Pete said.

Moses again positioned the chisel. He placed the hammer at his waist and delivered a full-clock swing. The hammer's head struck the chisel with a clang. Sparks flew. The chisel's edge cut through the brass lock like a knife through butter. Dust and grit shook free from the box's leather-sealed edges, but the lid itself held fast.

Moses passed the hammer to John. "It's time for me to pass the honor to you, John-Man."

John rerolled his sleeves, smiled and wedged the pry bar into the lid's seam, between iron and leather. He brought back the hammer and slammed it into the trailing edge of the bar. The lid bounced.

Pete and Perry stood nearby, their gazes fixed on the lid, hardly daring to blink. The moment of truth was at hand.

John again gripped the pry bar. With gritted teeth and a bead of sweat forming at his temple, he jabbed the bar into the leather seal. He pulled the bar down with biting leverage. The seal broke and the lid flew up.

A rush of stale air escaped in a blast of sandy dust before the lid fell shut. John glanced at each of the men, then leaned forward, gripping the edge of the box. He dug his fingers under lid and lifted. All four men gathered around. Rays of the late morning sun echoed off the box's contents and a glow bounced off each of their faces. They stood in awe, their eyes widening in unison.

CHAPTER 17

Mid December

GILDED MYSTERY

ATOP THE BOX, A DEEP LAYER of gold coins glistened. John's mouth dropped. He glanced at Moses who staggered back at the sight. John hesitated for five seconds before plunging his right hand into the gilded hoard.

"Bloody hounds of hellfire! These are $20 Double Eagles. There must be at least several hundred."

Perry and Pete stepped closer as John ran his fingers through the pile. It took up about a full third of the box's interior. John brushed the coins to the left side. Under it rested a trove of perfectly preserved but yellowing documents. Legal documents.

Pete broke the silence, a piercing whistle escaping his lips.

"Damn. There's not a lick of logical sense in any of this. A store of gold coins left by a man y'all thought to be flat ass broke after the flood." John dragged his hand down his jaw, eyes fixed ahead, unblinking. "All these years, my father always said this place was barely afloat. After the flood, he swore up and down everything had been lost, every dollar sunk or washed away. Yet here it is. Squirreled away. Untouched. The box had to be put in place before the flood occurred. That's the only explanation, but he still knew it was there all along."

Perry shook his head, crossing his arms. "It wasn't just a little stash for the down times, John. This is a fortune. It's enough to rebuild a whole new plantation."

Moses' eyes narrowed as he took in the cache of gold, his voice edged with a doubt that turned into anger.

"He let us believe the plantation was done for, but he socked away this fortune all along. He never needed to sell a single member of my family. Not one of them."

John nodded, his face hardening. "Greed must have been in his veins deeper than I ever realized." He hesitated, looking at Moses with a question in his eyes, "There has to be more to this. He didn't just hide this gold. He left instructions that it could be opened only by you and me, together.

Moses' jaw tightened. "It's a box of lies. All the pain I've been through. The separation. The loss. For what? So he could hoard this fortune and make me witness its unearthing?"

John squinted, wrestling with memories of his father. "He was ruthless, no question about it. He always harbored some twisted plan. He wouldn't have gone through all this trouble, left the clues and instructions, if it were about money alone. He was deliberate to the point of obsession. Perhaps he had some change of heart. Then again, if that were true, he wouldn't have sold Moses' family. Before you return home, I need to decipher this mystery, but I will do so with great haste."

Perry nodded, his gaze fixed on the box. "Those documents beneath might give you some answers. It's strange that he hid all of this and left you both tied to it. There must be something else he wanted you to know."

"It's as if my father wanted us to dig up his sins, like a final slap across the face. But why? What was he hoping to prove? Or maybe he wanted to punish us with this perplexing plunder in his wake."

Unanswered questions deepened the mystery. Each man stared at the open chest as if it held not just gold, but the twisted judgement of a man long gone.

John scooped out the coins and placed them in a canvas bag.

"Must be about 25 pounds of gold here. And these documents, I can't believe they're all still intact. I bet they've been in that box a good

15 or 20 years, not to mention them withstanding the flood from seven years ago."

John's eyes flickered with a sense of duty, a determination now burning behind the initial shock. "I'll be burning the lanterns all night to uncover the truth."

He pulled out the first few documents for closer examination, his fingers tracing over the spidery handwriting.

"People often leave secrets in their choice of words, and I've made a career out of interpreting the meaning of obscure documents. If there's an answer here, I'll find it."

Moses stared at the chest as if trying to peer through the years-old mysteries lying within. "I've been waitin' to learn what happened to my family. I'll wait a little longer if it means those documents might get us anywhere closer to the truth." John gave a slight nod, his face growing more upbeat.

"Actually, there is something," John chose his words with care. "That telegram I sent to Judge Merriweather looking for you. You might say it carried double intent, but I wanted to settle the mystery of the sealed chest first."

Moses exchanged glances with Pete and Perry, and his eyes grew wider.

"John. I haven't been completely open with you either. Perry, Pete and I didn't come here just to turn around and go home. Even before Judge Merriweather told me about your telegram, we had already made plans to travel to Memphis to search for my kin. We were going to stop here all along to look you up, but when the judge got your telegram, it all kinda fell into place."

"I think I might be able to help. This is where our grand stories converge, Watty. Now that we've opened that chest, my other damn sure intent is to fortify you with the knowledge of a few other things I've uncovered."

Astonishment bounced off Moses' dimpled cheek as he looked at John.

"My father never left me a shred of meaningful information in his will, but during a recent search of estate records at the courthouse, I found a whole file full of clues. Documents. Bills of sale tied to your family. They were in St. Louis records, overlooked by everyone but still as real as the day the ink dried. Those documents, they include names of purchasers, dates and destinations. That should be more than enough to guide you on an informed path."

Moses' eyes widened, the substance of John's words sinking in. His face shifted, cautious hope returning. His voice caught as he spoke. "John, that's the real treasure. You have no idea what this might mean. For years, I walked in darkness, thinking there was no hope of findin' them. No trace."

"You're going to have much more than a trace. I've even drawn up a map. I really didn't think you would come all this way just to turn around and go home."

"We'll bird-dog that trail as far as it runs."

John looked at the three weary men.

"You gentlemen have a long road still ahead of you. You're gonna need a night to rest up and restock. I'll work all night to dig through those papers from the chest. I'll have that answer by morning light, at which time I will wrap everything, including the map, in a pretty little bow."

John continued. "I'd like to offer you the comfort of my home for the night. You need to refresh. The house is warm and homey and I'm sure the food will be better than what you consumed along the trail."

The three men looked at each other and chuckled, but a degree of hesitancy washed over Moses.

"There's plenty of room, more than enough bedrooms, and a fireplace that'll chase the chill from your bones better than any campfire." John said, gesturing toward the house.

"John, that map you've drawn is more than enough. But I'll wait one more night so you can get the answers you need from the documents in the chest. I didn't come here lookin' for comfort. I came for answers, and that map is all I need."

Perry, attuned to the peril of spurning a man's offer of hospitality, jumped into the conversation.

"We're right here with you, Moses. No offense, but we've spent enough nights on the trail and there are more ahead. One night in a fine house would be a godsend. I think it would be right suitable for us to take John up on his offer."

After Perry spoke, Moses hesitated again, casting a wary glance toward the stately home. Moses shifted his feet, looking away as if to gather his thoughts.

"John, all I ever knew of this place was the cramped quarters of the slave cabins. A fine house like yours..." He trailed off, searching for words. "I wouldn't even know how to act inside those walls."

John's face tightened, and he placed a firm but gentle hand on Moses' shoulder. "Moses, if that's the way of it, then you've earned more comfort than any room in that house offers. I think you might even enjoy soaking in a warm bath to soothe your bones. You're rightly entitled. I want you to stay inside as my guest, and that's not a request."

John gave Moses a pointed look, but one punctuated by the hint of a smile. "You, Perry, and Pete. All of you."

Pete met Perry's gaze. Perry gave a slow, deliberate nod, his lips pressing together in approval. Without a word, they both turned to Moses.

Seeing their quiet encouragement, Moses relented, nodding in hesitant appreciation.

John's smile widened as he continued. "There's space in the carriage house for the animals. Full access to grain and fodder, safe from the elements. They'll be able to rest up, get their strength back for what's still to come. After we're all settled in, I'll dig into these documents."

John again placed his hand on the stack with reverence, as though each page carried both treasure and burden. "These papers will have my full attention."

"Holy damnation! What a day!" Pete exclaimed.

CHAPTER 18

Mid December

HEARTH AND HOME

AFTER FEEDING ARCHIBALD and tending to the horses in the pre-dawn hours, Pete, Perry, and Moses gathered in the parlor, hands stuffed in their pockets and arms crossed, their gazes drifting toward the front door and their path beyond it. In his office, John rubbed sleep from his eyes as he stacked the mystery documents. Each page had revealed to him in the quiet of night a faint whisper of the past.

Moses scanned the parlor, his eyes lingering on the cheerful trimmings of the approaching Christmas season. Evergreen garlands hung above the doorways, dotted with bright red berries. A small, festive Christmas tree sat in the room's corner, adorned with handmade wooden ornaments and tied ribbons. The faint aroma of a cedar tree cut from the pasture filled the room.

A woven basket beneath the tree held small gifts wrapped in paper and tied with string, waiting to be opened in little more than a week. The sight warmed Moses, but it also stirred an ache, reminding him of the meek slave-quarters holidays he'd once shared with his own sons.

Moses walked toward the door of John's office. "John-Man, you know we're grateful for your overnight work, but the fellas and me, forgive us, but we're getting' antsy. We're hankerin' to hit the trail. They left families behind, and I still need to find mine. We're itchin' to get back on the road toward Memphis."

John looked up from the stack of papers, his eyes bloodshot, but gleaming.

"I know, Watty. And I've got news. Real news. I've cracked it. The chest, the mystery, it's all here. I know you'll want to be on the road by first light, but I'd be honored if you and your two companions joined me for breakfast first. I will tell you all about what I found."

"That's great news John, and I think I can accept that breakfast invite on their behalf."

John lifted the stack, the pages trembling slightly in his grip. "These papers, journals and letters, every thought my father had before hiding that chest. Every reason he never said out loud."

"I'm all ears, John. I can't wait to hear what his motivation might have been."

"And don't forget about this more important information," John said pointing to the corner of his desk. "These are the documents that really matter, bills of sale, names and locations of the buyers. These are the papers that provided information for the map I drew up. It's all here, and now that information is sorted nice and neat."

Perry tapped his foot in a restless rhythm outside John's office. "John, you don't know how happy I am to hear that. I was afraid we might start pacing holes in your floor."

In the kitchen, John's elegant wife, Lizzy, grabbed a coffee pot as it finished percolating atop the wood stove. She pulled out four delicate china cups and saucers from the cupboard and filled each one to the brim.

"Let's take our leave to the dining room, gentlemen," John said, clasping the two stacks of documents in each hand.

After Pete, Perry and Moses were seated, Lizzy sat each cup of coffee atop a matching saucer in front of John and the houseguests.

Lizzy smiled as she placed the last cup in front of Moses. "I thought a warm cup would be fitting," she said. "I don't know how you gentlemen do it. I'm completely spent after the little ride out here from St. Louis. I do hope deep in my soul you will find your Sally, Moses. And you two," she said, looking at Pete and Perry, "your wives have to be saints."

"Right you are ma'am," Pete said. "Saints Lucy and Millie."

"God be with them," Lizzy said. "Now, I will leave you gentlemen to your business. John, the floor is yours. The children and I will be in the parlor if you need us."

"Thank you, my dear," John said. He cast a glance at Perry and Pete before his eyes settled on Moses. While his eyes glistened, his face was solemn, aware of the importance of what he was about to share. Perry and Pete sat back, witnesses, feeling the tension in the room.

"Moses," John began, "I want to get straight to the heart of this matter, the reason you came all this way. The documents I retrieved from the St. Louis courthouse, the ones tied to your family's sale, are all here."

He stuffed that stack into a brown leather portfolio.

"I've compiled everything I could find, organized with points of sale, buyers, and locations. I've detailed each of them as much as possible, right down to directions from Memphis."

Moses' gaze remained fixed on the portfolio in John's hands, a glimmer of hope in his eyes as he took in John's words.

John continued, "It's all here, Watty. Every step of the trail. Here's what might be the best news you've heard in a long time: there are only two locations listed in this paperwork. Just two. One buyer, a man named Silas Henson, a farmer near Germantown, purchased Sally and Michael together. And another buyer, Jeremiah Collins, a cotton planter in Mississippi, bought Samuel."

John paused. "With these two locations, all within a day or two ride from Memphis, it means your search won't be as scattered as we feared. You can focus on Germantown first, then south to Mississippi. You've got a clear path."

Perry let out a breath, his face reflecting Moses' relief. "That's a blessing, Moses. We've got a real shot at findin' them in short order."

John nodded. "Call it a stroke of luck, or providence. Either way, it's enough to give you a fightin' chance." He handed the portfolio to Moses, whose hands shook with a rush of adrenaline. Moses swallowed hard. He gripped the portfolio like a lifeline, his fingers tracing the leather.

"John, you didn't just give me names, you gave me a map. I've spent my life chasin' whispers and dead ends. But this gives me a way forward. A real place to start."

John cocked his head. "That's only the first part, Watty. Now, as for the documents inside the chest..." He took another deep breath, preparing to reveal additional information.

"My father, the cruel-hearted man that he was, wrote a will, a last testament of sorts. What he left out was any mention of our mystery chest. The documents inside covered that. There, within those directives, he named not just me, but also you, Moses, as recipients. Guilt riddled his soul, about how he treated you and Sally."

Moses looked up in astonishment as John continued. "He admired you, Moses. He just didn't have the spine to say it. He credited you with the plantation's success, but he couldn't free you. Not during the time of slavery. Unfortunately, not when it would've mattered most."

John glanced away, his jaw tightening.

"The document, though, it came later. After you and Miss Sally jumped the broom, after he started calling you a 'breeding pair.' His words, not mine. Crude, cruel. But that's when he sealed the chest. It was a brief, strange window in his life. Quiet. Regretful. Reticent."

John looked directly as Moses.

"He wrote down the rest, too. The ugly part. I won't drag us both through it, but we know what happened. After my mother died, he became fixated on Sally. Obsession, not affection. He took liberties."

Moses shivered. The past lingering like smoke.

"My father knew that Sally could never be his. An old white slaveholding widower and a young slave girl would never be accepted. So, he pushed you to find a mate, knowing it'd be her. Knowing you'd treat her right. Two-thirds of the chest's gold, he meant it for you. So you could protect her. Call it twisted. Call it guilt. But maybe, just maybe, call it a blessing disguised as penance."

John continued, "Of course, you and I both know the ugly, monstrous part that came after his change. That part was not found anywhere in the papers. The chest had been sealed many years prior. Everyone around him, you included, saw his demise. Unlike most, you felt the consequences upon your skin. Doctors called it an irreversible case of senile dementia. I would never have thought of him as a pleasant man in any way, but as his affliction progressed, it ate into his brain and changed him into the hostile, violent man he became at the end."

Pete and Perry listened in silence, spellbound by John's stylish summation, as if he were presenting evidence to a jury in a murder case.

"Once that dementia set it, in his case fueled to some degree by his hard-drinking ways, there was no turning back on his hellbent path to frustration, anger and hate. He wanted to fight everyone like he was some kind of noble crusader. For those of you he controlled, it was even worse. He thought he was some kind of vengeful god. He saw what you and Sally had together. He could never accept it in his state of mind."

John drew a deep breath. "You and I both know how it ended. I like to think that him drowning in the river was likely a work from the hand of the angel of mercy leading him unseen up to the river's edge."

Moses sat motionless, harboring the secret that Gabe had been the true angel of mercy that fateful day.

John continued. "That's all I discovered Moses. So, bottom line is that a full two-thirds of that gold is yours. The face value alone comes to about $5,300. He left the other third to me, but I don't need it or want it. To me, it's blood money. I have this farm and that's enough. For me to accept it would suggest I carry the same level of addiction to wealth that drove him into the ground."

He looked directly into Moses' eyes. "I want you to have it all. The grand total's about $8,000. You can use at least part of it to finance your rescue mission from this point forward. Use it to find and care for Sally and your boys." Moses was speechless. Never in his life had he even considered such riches.

"I don't know what to say, John-Man. I know all that you say is true, but it's a bitter reality. You are a kind and generous man, and I shall be indebted to you for the rest of my days."

"You will not. Any debt that might have ever existed, you paid long, long ago."

"How can I manage this situation, John? I can't carry this amount of gold on the road. There are only three of us and who knows the kind of men who lurk ahead on the trail."

"I have a suggestion, Watty. You may not have heard about it, but the Union Government earlier this year set up what they call the Freedman's Savings and Trust Company. This isn't just any bank. It was created to help folks like you who'd just gained freedom. The idea was to give freed slaves and Black veterans a place to save and manage their money as they found their footing. Congress set it up, and President Lincoln, rest his soul, backed it personally."

John paused and drew a sip of his coffee between thoughts. "You can imagine how many folks stepped into freedom with nothing—no land, no money, and no support to speak of. The Freedman's Bank is meant to be that support, to give freed men and women a chance, to start saving and planning for their futures. It's one small step toward independence. A way to help people survive in this new world with the pay they are now able to earn with their own hands and hard work."

Perry interjected. "Hell, I still keep my treasure at home under a floorboard. I don't trust banks. Leastwise, not yet."

John looked at Perry and Pete and then his gaze stayed on Moses. "With Watty's permission, I would suggest you gentlemen take a sufficient amount of the money with you so you won't face any unnecessary hardships along the rescue trail. Watty, again, with your permission, I will deposit the rest on your behalf at the Freedman's Bank in St. Louis. Upon your arrival back in Kansas, we can make a transfer."

John leaned in, sensing Moses' puzzlement. "They can send money from place to place without you having to carry it physically. Secure from the highwayman and other assorted low-life types. Let's say a man in St. Louis wants to get money to someone in the City of Kansas. The money itself isn't exactly sent down there, like you'd think of sending a letter."

"Then how does it work?"

"The banks use the telegraph. They'll send coded instructions over the wire. These messages tell an allied bank to release a specific amount of money to the recipient. The cash stays put, and they deduct the amount indicated in the telegram. All that travels is the instruction itself, and the banks settle things between themselves afterward."

Pete and Perry stood in confused silence. Neither had heard of this telegram banking option. "Interesting," Pete said. "I bet I could use that when I order stuff for the tavern. Of course, I only do that for stuff that Marcus doesn't stock. Gotta keep the old buzzard fed."

John continued. "After the correspondent bank on your end receives the message, all you have to do is walk in, give your name, prove your identity and pick up your money."

Moses whistled. "That's pretty impressive, John. After the message is sent, all that's needed from me is say-so?"

"Gentlemen," Perry said after finishing the last sip of his coffee, "thanks to John's generosity, hospitality and keen legal mind, I think we have all we need, John. Moses, Pete and I are greatly respectful of your relationship, but we best be hitting the trail."

CHAPTER 19

Mid December

A CITY OF PROMISE

PERRY, PETE, AND MOSES moved with purpose as a morning mist hung over Gumbo Flats. The three men had the answers they had come for. The mystery of the telegram was answered. A chest of treasure was unsealed. They had a portfolio full of details and a mission map. It was time to continue their trek.

As John looked on from the edge of his lawn, Perry hitched up the horses to the Conestoga, patting both Beulah and Barney on the neck with a reassuring hand. The leather reins squeaked as he tightened them, and the horses stamped their hooves with renewed energy. The men were refreshed and informed but still faced several unknowns.

Pete saddled his horse nearby, pulling the straps tight, his usual humor softened by the finality of departure. Moses stood beside his own horse, lost in thought as he stroked the animal's neck. The land still burdened him with memories, but now hope had joined the team. He was stepping out from behind Old Man Manchester's shadow.

Moses gave John a nod of gratitude, extending a hand. "I would have been wandering in circles if it weren't for your help. Thank you for openin' your home and for all you've shared."

"It's your road now, Watty. Go find them. After you do, take them home and grow that farm. But you'll always have a place to bring them back to, if you ever need one."

Before Perry could climb to the driver's seat of the wagon, John spoke again.

"Perry, if you could spare a private moment, I'd like to give you some specific guidance for the road between Saint Louie and Memphis."

"Sure thing, John," he turned to Pete and Moses. "Fellas, hold tight. As the navigator for this trip, duty calls."

John led Perry a few paces away from the others, his voice dropped as he gestured toward the south. "I want to give you a heads-up about the Memphis route. Along most of the route, you will want to take the Memphis and Hernando Plank Road as I drew it on the map I gave Moses. You familiar with that road?"

Perry nodded.

"Heard of it, but I haven't traveled it myself. I understand it's an old stagecoach route? But I have to say, if it's a plank road, it should be smooth sailing compared to what we've already traversed."

John folded his arms, glancing back to make sure Moses and Pete were out of earshot. "Well, yes and no. The road is smoothed with wooden planks to keep it passable when the ground turns to mud, which is more often than not. The route drew heavy movement during the war. Troops, supplies, and every kind of traveler you can imagine passed through. Thing is, that road's got more wear and tear than most. You might still run into abandoned debris, traps laid down that folks never cleared."

"Abandoned traps? What're we talking here?"

John sighed, leaning in. "Military traps, craters, broken plank stretches and hidden pits. Let's say some folks still make a business out of raiding travelers caught unaware. While things are calmer now, I don't trust that whole stretch. You need to keep your eyes peeled."

Perry's face tightened with understanding. "So, this isn't just about directions. We'll need to stay sharp, like we're crossing enemy lines."

"Precisely. Stay vigilant. Take no chances."

Perry extended his hand, a higher level of respect shining in his eyes. "Much obliged. You can count on us to watch out for each other."

"I've a final point to share too. A confidential matter. Can I ask for your discretion?"

"Yes. You have it. What's troubling you?"

"There's another matter I did not have the heart to divulge to Moses, but I wanted to get your opinion on it since you are so close to both Moses and Gabe."

John glanced over his shoulder at Moses then leaned in closer to Perry. "Those papers from the chest, they drew a strange narrative. One document read, 'I hereby bequeath a full two-thirds share of this gold to my most loyal slave, Moses Watson, the custodial caretaker of the one called Gabe Watson, a bastard son.'"

Perry frowned. "Your father actually wrote it like that?"

John nodded. "I found it puzzling. My summation is he believed Gabe to be his own son, born from his blood. I have no way of confirming it, but I wanted your opinion. Everyone knows he knew Sally in that sense."

Perry scratched his chin. "It's true, Gabe's lighter-skinned than Moses, but so is Sally, as Moses described her to me. Doesn't tell us much either way. But, that dimple on Moses' left cheek? Gabe's got one in the exact spot, same size. That, to me, says plenty about Gabe's true lineage. Credit to your father for thinking of Moses, but between you and me, I think he was madder than a mule in a pepper patch."

John nodded. "No offense taken. Let's keep this between us. Moses has enough on his plate without adding my father's eccentricities. The old man was crazy in his later years, and who knows when his wits first started to slip the reins. For my own sanity, I'm chalking it up to that."

"Understood. Mum's the word. You have my promise."

"I know." John gripped Perry's hand and handed him the folded map. "Take this map. If Moses asks the tenor of our talk, tell him it was about the road ahead. Not the whole truth, but it's not a lie, either. We lawyers know how to walk that line."

Perry grinned, giving John a firm handshake. "Reckon you do. Thanks for the heads-up. Now it's time for us to hit the trail."

John raised his voice so all could hear. "Safe travels. As I said, keep your eyes sharp all along that plank road to Memphis."

Perry turned and strode back to the wagon still pondering the suspicion John shared about Gabe's parentage.

Moses had a steady grip on the reins of his horse as he tucked a small leather bag of coins from the chest into his saddlebag, next to his smaller bag of soybean seeds. The coins would make the road ahead smoother, even if they faced a broken plank here and there.

The three men began to snake their way up the river bluffs as the morning mist began to lift, parting like the veil of the past as they left Gumbo Flats behind.

Their mission remained the same: to prove Moses' kin weren't ghosts. With every clue in hand, the summoning was set to begin.

The trio hit the main road to St. Louis on the higher ground above the river bottomlands. The road was rough, lined with skeletal trees stripped bare by the season. The air held a crispness, almost cleansing after the drama of the past few days.

Perry rustled the reins, guiding the wagon along the winding path toward St. Louis, while Pete and Moses rode alongside. After five hours, they began to encounter shanty homes on the outskirts of St. Louis. A sense of hope sparkled within each of them, optimism that they were on the verge of making real progress after their brief respite.

Pete glanced at Moses, a grin breaking across his face. "I reckon St. Louis makes a man feel like he's on the boundary of somethin' big. It's a city where folks start somethin' or start over. They build themselves up. I think it's an encouragin' sign."

Moses looked ahead. His mind wandered down the path. "A fresh start. I've been searchin' for that all my life, Pete. I found that in Kansas, but here I am, searching again."

Cresting a hill, they caught their first glimpse of St. Louis, sprawling and busy even in winter's grip. From atop the hill, the Mississippi River snaked along the city's edge. It shined like a ribbon of steel, abuzz with flatboats and paddle steamers carrying goods and passengers from all parts of the nation.

Unlike the wild, untamed Missouri, with its swift currents and muddy waters, the Mississippi flowed with a lazy, calm majesty. The Mississippi was a river of purpose and strength. It teemed with commerce and stories, from places far beyond St. Louis.

Christmas spirit was in the air and the city was alive with movement. As the men drew closer, the sights and sounds of the city intensified. Merchants lined the streets, their wagons overflowing with barrels and crates. Children darted among the crowd, laughter mixing with the calls of hawkers selling their wares. The Union force was alive and well in St. Louis. Blue-uniformed soldiers lingered by the docks, casting watchful eyes over the rushing scene.

Pete pointed to the riverfront, where a grand paddle steamer was moored, its brass trim shining. "There she is, boys, the Belle of Missouri," he said. She's somethin' to see, ain't she? Makes the old boat I worked on dealing blackjack look like a leaky washtub."

Perry nodded, as a plume of steam billowed skyward. "I'll be damned. Imagine floating on that beauty all the way to Memphis. Feels like the river could carry you clean off the edge of the world."

Moses took in the flurry, the clang of iron and call of river hands. "St. Louis feels like a gateway to bigger things."

Perry patted his coat pocket. "Then it's good we've got directions. John handed me the map. Stick with me, gents. We may not ride the river's currents, but this chart won't lead us astray."

As they walked along the crowded streets, they passed a row of modest but well-kept houses. In one yard, a young Black family worked together, raking the last remnant of fallen leaves into neat piles. Bundled against the cold, a child laughed as she tossed a handful into the air, the golden flakes swirling before settling again. The father shared a prideful glance with his wife.

Moses slowed his steps. The rhythm of the family's work, the warmth in their faces, the way they moved with unspoken unity, stirred his emotions. A life ahead could be built, not with grand gestures, but with small, steady moments. It was possible.

Perry leaned toward his friend. "That will be you one day soon. A family around to care for. A home you have built they can call their own. But with a couple new farmhands, I doubt you'll be content with rakin' leaves. Don't let go of hope, not for a second."

"I won't. That's the kind of future I want."

They approached a stable to temporarily board their horses, then made their way to the lively Market Street to restock the wagon. The air was thick with the scent of roasted chestnuts and fresh bread, vendors shouting out their holiday goods to the crowd of passersby.

Pete elbowed Moses, nodding toward a modest shop with a hand-painted sign that read, "Missouri & Pacific Telegraph Office." The shop was crowded with customers and onlookers eager to send season's greetings to far-off friends and relatives.

"Now there's a sight. Word travels fast in this city. I bet if we sent a wire, by sunset folks would know our names and about our little trip, from New Orleans to New York."

"Well, maybe not quite that, but it's good to know the world's a little closer here. Ain't it somethin', how connections can bridge miles?"

They continued down the street. Perry caught sight of a preacher standing on the street corner, his voice carrying over the din. The man's words were strong and resolute, promising a future of peace and prosperity for all willing to pray and work. Perry turned to his companions.

"Hear that? Even the preachers in St. Louis talk about new beginnings," he said. "Ain't nothin' better than my farm in Jawbone

Holler, but I'll admit, this place has its own kind of pull."

Moses looked around, the hum of life and hope all around him. For the first time in years, he pictured a future he could shape with his own hands. He glanced at his friends, the bond they shared strengthening in the presence of this grand city.

"Then let's make the most of it," he said. "This city's given us a glimmer of shining hope, and I don't plan to waste it. Let's load up the wagon with the best things Saint Louis has to offer and hit that plank road to Memphis."

CHAPTER 20

Late December

A SOLITARY CHRISTMAS

A WEEK BEFORE CHRISTMAS, as snowflakes drifted down on a hushed afternoon, a familiar figure ambled up the path to the Fontaine home dragging a tall scrub cedar tree. Millie and Lucy exchanged glances at the commotion. They rushed to the front door.

"Jeptha Nichols, what on earth are you doin' with that tree?" Millie exclaimed.

Jeptha, bundled in a threadbare coat, tipped an imaginary hat to them, his eyes twinkling.

"Ladies, allow me to present to you a fine, festive cedar, courtesy of Mr. Marcus Mixon," he announced, giving the tree a playful shake so snow dusted off its branches. "It's a gift delivered by your friendly Outpost genie, here to grant you Christmas tidings!"

Lucy laughed, her cheeks flushed with delight as she shuffled aside to make room for Jep and the tree. "Jep, you never fail to surprise us. How did our friend Marcus come by this tree?"

"Oh, he saw it growin' on the edge of town, all lonesome-like," Jep said with a wink, dragging the cedar over to a corner by the hearth. "He asked me to dispatch it with a mighty sharp axe. We talked about it and figured we'd give it a new home, someplace where it might spread a little joy. Who better to give it to than you two ladies?"

Millie clapped her hands, excitedly. "Jep, you're an angel sent by the good Lord himself. We were just saying we wished we had a tree to make things more festive.

Jep set the tree upright and nailed it to a wooden stand. Dusting off his hands, he gave the tree a final inspection. "Well, a genie's job is never done," he said, feigning a grand bow. "Now, you'll need somethin' to decorate it with. Got any ribbons or such around here?"

Lucy and Millie shared a glance, then hurried to gather buttons, bits of ribbon and strips of fabric. Together, the three of them decorated the tree, Jep chattering away with tales from The Outpost, where he claimed he'd granted a dozen more wishes this holiday season in exchange for pints of sarsaparilla.

They tied a final bow on the cedar. Jep stepped back, nodding in satisfaction. "Look at that! If that don't invite some Christmas spirit, I don't know what will."

Millie, overcome with gratitude, gave Jep a quick hug. "Thank you, Jep, and please express our gratitude to Marcus."

Jep's expression softened, his usual jovial demeanor fading. "Ladies, a lot of folks have come through The Outpost, and I've seen power in all shapes and sizes. But you two, waitin' here, keepin' the home fires burnin', I reckon that takes a different kind of strength."

"We take it one day at a time, Jep," Lucy said.

Jep nodded with understanding. "Remember now, every wish you make, a genie's out there listenin'," he said with a wink. "And until those men come home, you got friends like me here to remind you you're not alone."

The three of them shared a moment, their laughter and gratitude filling the small room as they admired the cedar tree standing proudly by the hearth, a little symbol of inspiration to carry them through the season.

Jep took his leave, tipping his imaginary hat with one last flourish. Lucy and Millie exchanged a look, their spirits lifted.

The simple tree, decorated with scraps and bits, glowed in the soft light from the fire, reminding them of the power offered by friendship and small gestures, even in the hardest times. The warmth left by Jep's kindness filled the room, carrying them forward with a spark for what lay ahead.

A week later, Christmas morning landed on the doorstep of the Fontaine home in St. Joseph with a thud muffled by a blanket of snow. Though a Saturday morning, The Outpost Tavern was closed for the day. The townsfolk would have to fix Christmas breakfast for themselves, and Millie and Lucy reveled in the holiday respite.

The soft chime of bells from the nearby church floated on the cold morning breeze, and Lucy glanced at the clock, its hands inching close to 8 a.m. She sighed, settling beside Millie on the parlor sofa.

Lucy's face brightened as she set a warm mug of cider in Millie's hands. Yet beneath their warm smiles anxiety stretched further than the miles separating them from their husbands.

"Do you suppose they've made it to St. Louis by now?" Lucy asked, her eyes drifting to the frost-laden window. "It's a considerable distance from here, and with the snow, travel can't have been easy."

"Absent any trouble along the trail, I would guess they hit St. Louis about a week ago and are plodding toward Memphis. They would be south of us, so I doubt they are facing the same snowfall the Lord has brought to our doorstep. I tell myself maybe they're sittin' by a fire somewhere, thinkin' of us."

"Sometimes, I feel this tiny weight, like a promise taking root inside me. It's strange, this knowledge that a little life is growing within. Yet, with Pete so far, it feels like I'm carryin' this little person all by myself."

Millie's hand reached over to cover Lucy's, her eyes warm and compassionate. "You aren't alone, Lucy. We're carryin' them together, you and me. And I reckon in some ways, our menfolk are carryin' us, too, wherever they are. I can almost sense Perry's arms around me, holdin' me close though he's miles away. This is our Christmas, Lucy.

Maybe it's not the one we'd hoped for, but it's ours to make beautiful."

Lucy rummaged through a bag, drawing out a carefully wrapped bundle, handing it to Millie with a smile. "I stitched this up for you. Well, for your little one, actually."

Millie's hands trembled as she unwrapped the bundle, revealing a tiny pair of knit booties, edged with delicate stitching. She traced her fingers over intricate patterns stitched by her friend.

"Lucy, it's beautiful. Boy or girl, they're simply perfect. I don't know how to thank you. I've got nothin' like this to give you back, but I swear to you I'll be right here with you, every step of the way."

Lucy wrapped her arm around Millie's shoulder. "That's all I need. Just knowing I'm not by myself."

As the candles flickered and the day wore on, they told stories of past Christmases, of families and laughter, of the years when life had been simpler. They laughed, sharing memories from childhood, moments that shaped them, flashes reminding them of why they waited, of the resilience it took to hold fast.

The evening settled around them, peaceful and serene, the snow blanketing the town in thick silence. Millie looked out the window. "I think when our little ones hear of this day, they'll know their mothers were strong. That we waited, not just for their fathers, but for the world they'd one day inherit. It's a world we're buildin' with our hearts this very day."

The room grew quiet as they shared a moment that transcended words. They didn't know when their husbands would return or what the months ahead would bring. They found strength in the promise of a brighter Christmas, and in the still, certain knowledge that love and friendship would carry them forward.

On Christmas morning Gabe woke to the creak of the rafters as the cold wind brushed against the walls of the Watson home. Frost on the windowpane glittered like white lace. Gabe watched his breath rise in the dim light. He reached over, wrapped himself in a worn wool blanket, and made his way to the hearth.

Gabe lifted a bundle of kindling into the grate and blew into it to coax the embers from the previous night's fire back to life. Soon, the small flames danced, warming the room and casting a glow over the simple furnishings.

He straightened, staring into the fire. The heat thawed his fingers but not the restlessness in his chest. Since his father left, a stillness had crept into the house, as well as his spirit. The silence was ominous, like the first shovelful of dirt thrown over a grave, and it ate at him. This solitary life, it wasn't natural. He'd grown up surrounded by his father's steady presence, by the rhythms of shared work and conversation, by voices filling the empty spaces.

Gabe's eyes remained fixed on the flames, his thoughts churning as he rubbed his hands, not from the cold but from the ache of isolation. Emptiness swirled around him, each quiet corner of the house echoing his own doubts. The calm was unnatural, an uneasy reminder despite all his strength and resolve, and he wasn't sure it was enough to hold everything together.

"I should be used to this by now, shouldn't I?" he whispered to himself. "I've fought battles alone. Lived through storms. But this silence, it's different. What if that pull takes me down?"

He shook his head, frowning. "You're thinkin' like a child now, Gabe. Papa's done all he can to teach me strength. He's not lost, not like he was back then. He knows the risks, and he can handle them. But can I handle this?"

The question hovered. In this new silence, he saw visions of choices yet to be made, of a future he wasn't sure he could shape alone.

"Am I supposed to carry on without him? Keep things steady here while he faces whatever waits for him out there? I've come to depend on him. The shared promise binds us. It always has, good times and bad."

Gab had no way of knowing what lay ahead for Moses at the end of this journey. Whether his father would come back changed in some way, or whether he would come back at all.

With a sigh, Gabe pulled on his boots, grabbed his coat, and went outside to tend to the animals. The morning light was magnified by the snow. The chickens clucked in their sheltered hutches. The cows stirred, plumes of steam rising from their breaths as he filled their troughs. Even among the animals, loneliness blanketed Gabe. As he went about the chores, he caught himself again talking aloud.

"I wonder what Papa's found down there in Gumbo Flats. Has he run into trouble?" He shook his head. "Well, I reckon if anyone could handle himself in that pit of misery, it'd be him."

The thought should've comforted him, but it didn't. His mind felt untethered, as if he were drifting, waiting for news that could change everything. The questions nagged him, and the quiet didn't help. Gabe longed for some sort of connection, a reminder that he wasn't alone in the world.

He finished his chores and leaned against the fence, letting his thoughts wander. "Maybe today's not the day to be by myself," he murmured. Then, with a sudden determination, he made up his mind. It was Christmas, and though he rarely set foot in a church, an African church sat a mere mile outside of Lowland. He'd heard its congregation was capable of sending their voices soaring straight to heaven.

Inside, he threw on his cleanest shirt, then saddled up his horse. The journey was tranquil, the snow-packed ground muffling the sounds around him. The closer he drew to the church, the more alive he felt, like his soul was lifting.

The whitewashed church came into view, a modest wooden structure with a weathered cross hanging above the door. From a distance, he heard the murmur of voices, the sound warming him from within. He dismounted, brushing snow off his coat, walked up the steps and pushed open the door.

At the entrance stood the pastor, a tall, dignified man with a warmth in his gaze that put Gabe at ease. The pastor extended a hand.

"Welcome, son. I'm Reverend Ezekiel Hayes. Come on in, we've got plenty of room for all God's children here."

Gabe shook the pastor's hand. The strength of the pastor's grip extended an unexpected jolt of comfort. "Thank you, Reverend. I don't usually come around these parts, but today, well, I was drawn here."

The pastor nodded. "Christmas season has a way of calling folks to gather for rejoicing, especially those in need of a little company." He gestured toward the rows of wooden pews, filled with families in their Sunday best, dark faces, but bright and hopeful despite the cold. A dozen people in all. "Find yourself a seat, son, and let the Good Word settle over you."

Gabe nodded, slipping into a pew near the back. The room was alive with greetings, children whispering to each other, the rustle of hymnals being opened. The shared warmth of a congregation, bound by race but not necessarily by blood, offered a sense of belonging. The most common characteristic in their faces was spirit.

The service began with a hymn, the voices rising in unison, filling the small church with a sound that wrapped Gabe like a blanket. Each note, each voice, added to the fire inside him, stirring embers he hadn't felt in a long time. He closed his eyes, letting the music wash over him, feeling his spirit lift in a way it hadn't since his father left.

When the hymn ended, Gabe kept his head bowed, loneliness settling back over him. Barely above a whisper, he offered a solitary prayer. "Lord, if you hear me, I could use some company. Someone to fill this space, even for a brief while."

He paused, his arm resting over his chest to staunch an ache. "If it's in your plan, let my papa be safe, and let me find a way through this on my own if I have to."

The Reverend's voice rang out, steady and sure, breaking through the quiet reflections of the worshipers. Gabe opened his eyes. His cheeks flushed with warmth. He had been lost in thought during much of the sermon, praying to God as though the Reverend's words were his own inner voice. Embarrassed, he hoped no one had observed his extended period of distraction.

"Brothers and sisters, as we celebrate the birth of Christ, let us remember that every dawn brings a new day. The light that broke over Bethlehem so long ago still shines for us. It tells us that no matter how dark the night, how heavy the burden, God's love will guide us. His grace will sustain us."

The pastor leapt forward, his eyes sweeping the small church. "As free people, we are the keepers of this flame. Freedom is not just the breaking of chains but the opening of doors, to faith, to unity, to a brighter future. Yet, we must walk through those doors together. Trials will come, yes, and tribulations may bend us, but they cannot break us if we stand firm in our faith. Prayer is the lantern we hold high to light our path, and unity is the hand we extend to one another when the way grows steep."

The Reverend lifted his hands toward the heavens. "This Christmas, hold fast to the hope that lives in your hearts. Let it be a flame that cannot be extinguished. For every hardship a stronger blessing. For every shadow a brighter light. Walk forward in the knowledge that we are never alone. God is with us, in our joys and in our struggles, and through Him, we are bound to one another. Today is a day of rejoicing, but it is also a day of renewal. It's a day to step toward what lies ahead, with courage, faith, and love."

The congregation stood to sing a final hymn, Gabe's eyes scanned the room, landing on a young woman sitting near the front. Her delicate profile, framed by soft curls and a bonnet adorned with a simple ribbon, struck him with quiet force. She wore serenity like a crown, her hands folded in her lap, her lips moving softly to the hymn. Gabe's breath got tangled with his heart. It had been a long time since he had noticed someone in that way.

She sensed his gaze and looked up, catching his eye with a shy smile that made Gabe's heart skip.

When the service ended, Gabe lingered near the door, his heart racing as the young woman gathered her things. Mustering his courage, he stepped forward and tipped his hat.

"Good morning, ma'am," he said. "I don't reckon we've met. I'm not much of a church-goin' man but today was a wonderful day to make an exception. Most often I commune with the Lord in the peace of nature."

She turned to him, her dark eyes meeting his with a gentle curiosity. "Good morning, sir. What made today different?" she asked.

"Well, that's a fair question. I could say Christmas, but the truth is for some reason I felt a pull. The name's Gabe Watson."

"I'm Naomi. Naomi James. My family and I usually worship at home, but we thought it'd be good to visit the church for Christmas. It feels more connected."

"It does. Sometimes you don't realize how much you've been missin' that connection until you find yourself in the middle of it."

They stood for a moment, the warm hum of the departing churchgoers around them. "Well, Mr. Watson," Naomi said, "I'm glad you came today. It's nice to see a new face."

Gabe smiled, a warmth spreading through him that was different from the fire back home. "And I'm glad to have met you, Miss James. Maybe I'll see you here again sometime."

"Maybe you will," she said with a gentle laugh, her cheeks dimpling as she turned to leave.

As she walked away, the emptiness in Gabe softened, giving way to a cautious but welcome hope. For the first time in ages, loneliness did not dominate his thoughts. For today, that was enough.

CHAPTER 21

Late December

HOLIDAY HUNKER-DOWN

SOUTH OF ST. LOUIS, a sagging stretch of The Memphis and Hernando Plank Road groaned under the heavy wagon wheels as Perry, Pete, and Moses made their way through a frigid and snowy Christmas day. The falling flakes grew heavier, swirling in erratic patterns as a biting wind whipped through the trees.

The men pressed forward as morning passed to afternoon. Clouds of steam from the horses' snorting nostrils rose fast in the cold air. Archibald trotted alongside, his usually wagging tail tucked low, bracing against the chill.

The men were wrapped tightly in their coats, their heads bowed against the icy gusts. Perry drove the wagon as Pete and Moses followed to the rear. Conversation had dwindled to grunts and murmurs, each man lost in his own thoughts as they fought the elements. The wagon groaned ominously, the planks of the road slippery beneath its iron-bound wheels.

"Old Man Winter's tryin' to freeze us out," Pete muttered to Moses, his voice muffled by a bandana.

Moses nodded grimly, clutching his bridle with gloved hands. "This ain't the worst of it, but it's bad enough. We'll need shelter by nightfall. Why don't you ride up and express those sentiments to Perry."

Pete brought his horse up to a trot, and rode up alongside Perry, his breath visible in the frigid air. Perry looked over from the wagon seat as the vessel topped a hill.

Pete pulled the bandana down from his face and raised his voice so it could be heard above the creaking wagon and the howling wind. "Moses reckons we oughta find shelter. It will be dark soon and I gotta agree with him. We keep goin' much longer, we'll be icicles by morning, plus it's Christmas."

Perry squinted against the wind, his gloved hands tightening on the reins. "Shelter isn't exactly growing on trees out here. You see anything that might keep us from freezing to death?"

Pete scanned the horizon and shook his head. "Nothin' yet, but it's gotta be better to stop and make camp than keep pushin' till the horses drop. We ain't got the sky on our side tonight."

Perry nodded. He pulled out his brass spyglass, but the lens could not cut through the freezing fog. "I'll keep an eye out for anything, a barn, an abandoned cabin, maybe a thicket sufficient to break the wind. Go back and tell Moses we'll stop as soon as we can. Till then, we keep moving. The worst thing we can do is sit still."

"I'll tell him. Make sure this wagon don't give out first. It sounds like it's startin' to preach its own squeaky funeral."

Perry fixed his ears on the groaning wheels and his eyes on the shifting planks beneath them. "Well, if it is, we'd best hope it's a long-winded homily. I'm not ready to carry this load the rest of the way."

Pete reined his horse back to the rear as the day turned to twilight and the plank road became hard to see under the accumulating snowfall.

Perry snapped the reins to urge Beulah and Barney onward. The crack of leather was met with a sharper, booming snap, like thunder after a tree split by summer lightning. Behind the wagon, Moses and Pete flinched, mistaking it for a gunshot.

Suddenly, a burst of snow shot up from beneath the wagon as the road gave way. A three-inch plank had shattered, launching splinters and jagged shards into the air. One chunk shot within inches of Pete's head. The wagon jolted violently, its back right wheel taking the full brunt of the collapse.

Perry brought the wagon to a stop and walked back to check on his friends.

"You gentlemen okay back here?"

"We're fine, but that was a close one," Pete said. "A piece of that plank came sailing past my noggin faster than a swoopin' night hawk."

"I wonder if that was one of the traps John warned me about," Perry said. "If so, it sure picked a helluva time to spring."

Moses glanced back at the wagon, his eyes catching a slight tilt.

"Perry, you might want to take a gander at the right rear. Shelter ain't the only thing we'll be needin' before we go on. Looks like somethin's fixin' to give."

Perry knelt in the snow to examine the wheel. There was noticeable play in the right wheel. An axel linchpin had loosened. He slammed the heel of his hand into the wheel to knock in back into place.

"Damn. Looks like you're correct. That loose plank damaged the right side. If we don't stop soon, we're gonna be walkin' to Memphis. It's a good thing I tethered Appy to the left side, otherwise, we'd have a bigger problem, like a dead horse, on our hands."

"Nothing against Appy, my friend, but if he had been on the right, that projectile might not have come as close to me as it did," Pete said. "Better a dead horse, than a dead Pete."

Perry scanned the horizon's darkness, his heart sinking as trees were weighed down by snow to impede the view. "Keep your eyes peeled, gentlemen, as will I. We're gonna need a Christmas miracle tonight. What I did to the wheel is just a temporary fix."

As if receiving a divine cue, Moses raised his arm, pointing through the flurry to the faintest light glimmering in the distance. "There," he said. "Between those trees, a house or at least a barn."

Cresting the next hill, the men squinted through the snow, their spirits lifting as they caught clear sight of a modest farmhouse and its sturdy barn. Smoke rose from the chimney, a warm invitation against the snowy backdrop. They could see the barn's double door ajar as they approached, offering a hint of hay piles inside.

"Awesome possum," Pete said, breaking into a grin. "It's like it was sent from heaven. Let's hope whoever's in that house is in a holiday mood."

As they pulled up to the house, Pete dismounted, pulling his coat tighter as he trudged through the snow. He climbed the porch and knocked on the weathered door, the sound echoing through the snowy night.

After a moment, the door creaked open, revealing a wiry man with grizzled hair and sharp eyes that took in every detail at once. His face was lined with years of hard living, and his patched coat hung loosely on his thin frame.

"Merry Christmas, sir," Pete said, tipping his hat. "We're travelers lookin' for shelter. A place to bed down for the night. Your barn would suit us fine. Got a wagon, some animals, and not much else but cold bones."

The man leaned against the doorframe, squinting at Pete. "Depends. Is your lot Union, or former Confederate?" he asked, his tone sharp.

Pete held his ground. "We're from the border states. Always been loyal to the Union, if it matters now that the war's over."

The man's face softened into a sly grin. "Well, that's somethin'. Some of my neighbors call me a scallywag for not bowin' to the Confederacy. Proud of it, too. Never had much use for their highfalutin talk about states' rights, not when it only meant keepin' colored folks in chains."

Pete nodded. "Glad to hear it. Now about that barn. We'd be mighty obliged."

The man rubbed his chin, his eyes flashing with mischief. "Well sir, everything these days comes with a price. Two dollars a night for each of you, and I'll throw in the animals. Fair price, seein' as how it's Christmas."

"Two dollars a night? At that rate, I reckon we oughta be stayin' in the finest hotel in Memphis, with room service, roses and a brass band to boot."

"You want shelter, you pay the fee."

Pete reached for his pocket, but the man's gaze shifted past him to Moses, standing near the wagon. The man's expression darkened.

"It'll be an extra dollar on top for the colored fella," he said coldly. "Only fair to the host, considerin' the trouble it might bring. Folks 'round here already suspect my allegiance. Plus, I got standards to uphold."

Pete forced himself to stay calm. He handed over seven dollars without a word, the tension thick in the air. The man pocketed the money and stepped aside.

"Barn's yours for the night. Keep it tidy, and don't go spookin' my goats."

Pete scoffed and gave the man a tight smile. He tipped his hat just enough to keep his tone from spilling into defensive venom and turned to walk back to the barn, muttering, "Well, ain't that the spirit of Christmas generosity. Chargin' us a showboat rate for river raft accommodations. Spoutin' off about enlightened ways and then tackin' on a penalty for a man's skin color."

"What's that, Pete?" Moses asked. "Some kind of problem? That man got a concern about my race? Even me just bein' in his barn?"

"All's I'll say is that if old Charlie Dickens were still cranking out novellas about Christmas, that fella right there would utter the biggest humbug of all. At least we have that Scrooge's barn for the night."

Pete looked over his shoulder. "Come on, gents. We've got ourselves the bottom floor suite, complete with hay mattresses and all the barn cats we can chase. It's a downright holiday miracle."

The men rode to the barn and lit lanterns before they unhitched and unsaddled their horses and led them inside.

Moses reached into his saddle pouch, fingers brushing the small leather bag of Gumbo Flats soybeans. He gave the bag a gentle squeeze. Still there. Just a handful of seeds, but somehow, they felt heavier than gold. He wasn't sure why. He just knew they mattered, at least to him.

The warmth of the hay barn was a welcome relief, even with a herd of goats fenced into a pen toward the rear.

Moses lifted his lantern and slipped its handle over an iron hook nailed to a wooden post. The flame wavered, then steadied, spilling a warm, amber pool across the worn boards and dust-flecked air. Shadows danced against the post. A sharp musk of animals tangled with the dry, musty sweetness of old hay, thick enough to taste.

"I'm going to go out and take a closer look at that wagon wheel before I turn in," Perry said. "I'm hoping we might find some spare parts Marcus packed in the toolbox. We'll fix it come morning."

Perry snagged one of the lanterns and stepped outside, its light bobbing as he made his way to the wagon. He crouched low, fingers tracing the rear wheel before giving it a firm tug. A sharp rattle answered. He exhaled through his nose, stood, and headed back toward the barn with an answer that was less than perfect.

"Gentlemen, we got lucky, but it's just as I suspected. Looks like the plank that flew up from the roadbed jarred the wheel hub loose. She's a bit wobbly but should be fixable by light of day. Good old Marcus packed a few spare lynchpins in the back of the wagon, so all we'll need to do is hammer in a new one and it should tighten things right up."

"At least we're out of the snow for the night," Moses said.

The men worked to move hay to create space for their horses and make sleeping room for themselves. The barn door opened with a groan. A woman stepped inside carrying a steaming pot of coffee and three mismatched cups. She was sturdy yet graceful, her dark hair streaked with gray and neatly pulled into a bun. Her face was kind, though lined with years of worry.

"Evenin', gentlemen," she said, setting the pot and cups on a nearby crate. "Thought you might like somethin' warm to drink. Coffee's fresh, and there's plenty of it."

Pete straightened, tipping his hat. "Much obliged, ma'am. That's mighty kind of you."

She waved off his thanks and poured the coffee. "Don't mind my husband. He's a hard man, but he's got a good heart underneath all that bluster. Just don't tell him I said that," she added with a wry smile.

Moses accepted a cup and out of habit gave an indirect nod of thanks. "Much obliged, ma'am. Means a lot on a night like this."

She glanced at Moses, her eyes softening. "Name's Cora. My husband can be set in his ways, but I don't hold with his nonsense about an extra fee. You're just as welcome here as any man."

Moses smiled faintly, her words easing some of the tension in his chest. "Thank you, Miss Cora. Pete never told me he paid an added fee because of the color of my skin, but I appreciate your kind words."

Pete, not admitting the unintended transgression, stared at the ground and sipped his cup of coffee in silence.

Cora stayed for a while, chatting with the men about the weather, the road, and the hardships of farm life. Her laughter filled the barn, a bright contrast to the storm outside.

"Y'all take care of yourselves. The world's a hard place, but a little kindness can go a long way. Don't let the cold get to your hearts. That road to Memphis is narrow in places and so are the minds of some of the folks you might meet along the way."

After bedding down the animals, the men settled into the hay, the barn's warmth and Cora's coffee easing the chill from their bones.

Archibald nosed around in the hay, his sniffing punctuated by soft snorts of curiosity. Suddenly, with a sharp hiss and a blur of motion, a black barn cat exploded from the shadows like a bolt of lightning. Startled, Archy sprang to life, barking with wild zeal. "Uhh Roo Roo Roo!" His houndish bark echoed through the barn as he bounded after the streak of fur, hay flying behind him.

The cat, sleek and practiced, sank its claws into a nearby barn pillar and climbed to the safety of the loft above. Perched just out of reach, the cat stared down with disdain, its tail darting in triumph.

Archy stopped at the base of the wooden pillar, his nose pointed skyward as he let out a few indignant huffs. He pawed at the post in one last show of determination before letting out a resigned grunt. With a dramatic shake of his floppy ears, he trotted back to his pile of hay beside Perry, his nose twitching in doggish indignation.

Perry reached down to pat the dog's head. "Well, Archy, that cat's got you figured out. Reckon you'll dream about this one tonight."

Pete laughed from across the barn. "If that bark wasn't enough to wake the whole countryside, nothin' will. Guess he's got his Christmas excitement in for the night."

Archy flopped onto his side, letting out a heavy sigh that made the men laugh harder. The dog, though defeated, was unbothered as he nestled into his spot, the warm hay and his companions lulling him into contentment.

Perry leaned back against a haystack, his hands behind his head. "This has been a strange Christmas."

Pete nodded. "I wonder what Millie and Lucy are doin' tonight. Probably sittin' by a fire, talkin' about us, worryin' like they always do."

Moses stared into the lantern. "Christmas was about the only day we didn't worry back in Gumbo Flats. We'd even get an extra helping of soup. We always sang holiday hymns until the wee hours of the morning because the soup warmed our voices."

Outside, the snow fell steadily, wrapping the world in a deeper blanket of white. It was a night of contrasts—cold and warmth, distance and connection, hardship and hope.

Perry dimmed the lantern, and Pete began to hum the melody of Silent Night. Perry and Moses joined in, and the song carried softly through the barn, blending with the wind outside. It was a small act of defiance against the cold night. The world eased into tranquility as man and animal alike drifted gently into slumber.

Moses was the first to drift off as his eyelids grew heavy, the warmth of the barn lulling him to sleep. Then, in a heartbeat, his mind was somewhere else entirely.

He stood on a rise above the wide Mississippi River, stretching before him like a great, unyielding wall. The sky above boiled in furious shades of crimson and black, as if the heavens themselves warred over his fate. Behind him, his family huddled together. Sally was dressed in a gown of rags. Michael and Samuel stood bravely at her side, casting fearful glances over their shoulders.

Beyond them, the earth trembled beneath the hooves of a hundred angry horsemen, their torches licking at the wind, their cries carrying a terrible chorus of vengeance. The family was trapped.

Moses turned to the river, his breath rising in ragged clouds. There was no escape. His right hand clutched a shepherd's staff, long and curled. The staff pulsed in his hand with an energy not of this world. He had not chosen it, but it had chosen him.

A voice, deep and infinite, thundered from the heavens, "Strike the earth, Moses, for I am with you."

Terror twisted his gut, but he had no choice. Raising the staff high above his head, he brought it down with all the force his soul could summon. The ground quaked. The air hummed. A deafening silence swallowed the world.

Before him, the Mighty Mississippi split in two, its mighty waters drawn back like curtains revealing a path of dry land stretching to the opposite bank. Great walls of water towered on either side, shimmering like liquid glass.

His family gasped, but he did not wait. "Go!" he commanded, leading them forward. Their footsteps pounded against the earth as they fled into the miraculous corridor.

Behind them, the horsemen surged forward, their steeds wild-eyed with fury, fire shooting from their nostrils. They would not be deterred. The men saddled on the horses shouted ahead for the Watson family to surrender their exodus to freedom, before being drowned out by a howling wind.

The wind, stern and dreadful, whispered a warning into the Watson family's ears. "Look not behind thee, my children, lest ye be swallowed whole. For in thy wavering glance, judgment shall claim its toll."

Moses reached the opposite riverbank, but his family trailed his advance by twenty yards. He spun to see Samuel glance back over his shoulder at the advancing horsemen, anticipating their impending verdict of doom. Moses' chest heaved in a drumbeat of desperation, as the voice returned. "It is finished. The test is lost."

The river roared. The waters collapsed. A monstrous wave surged over the riders, as well as Sally, Michael and Samuel, consuming each soul in a crashing fury. Their screams of futility drowned in the flood.

Moses stood alone on the bank of freedom, water crashing around him. The staff in his hand turned to dust. The sky above him cleared, and the world fell to an eerie, endless silence.

Moses dropped to his knees, his voice a raw whisper. "No. No, Lord, no." He screamed aloud as he felt a warm wetness on his face. He gasped awake, his body drenched in sweat, his breath ragged. The dimmed lantern flickered enough light that Moses saw Archy standing over him, tongue out and lapping at his cheek with earnest concern.

Moses jerked upright, a choked cry escaping his lips.

Perry and Pete shot up from their makeshift beds of hay, hands instinctively reaching for their guns. "Moses!" Pete rasped. "What the hell was that? You good?"

Moses panted, his mind clawing back to reality. His fingers reached out as if searching for the staff, for the river, for his family that had been swallowed by the waters. There was only the barn, the scent of hay, the quiet murmurs of resting horses and Archy.

Moses buried his face in trembling hands, shoulders shaking as he whispered hoarsely, "It was a terrifying nightmare, like livin' through hell itself."

Pete exhaled sharply, running a hand through his hair. "You sounded like you seen the Devil himself."

Moses swallowed hard. "Maybe I did. He was on horseback." His voice was hoarse, the vision still flattening his words.

Perry rubbed his jaw, studying Moses. "Must've been a bad one, huh?"

"I dreamt I was him—Moses from the Bible, the one I'm named after. Except I wasn't leadin' Israelites and splittin' the sea. I was guidin' my family though a similar split of the Mississippi River. But the river rose up like a wall and swallowed 'em whole, every last one, along with the horsemen chasin' us straight from hell." His voice broke on the last word.

A heavy silence settled among the barn's interior.

Rekindling the lantern, Pete scratched his chin. "That's the trouble with dreams. They ain't real. But this?" He gestured around the barn, the soft rise and fall of their horses' breathing, the comfort of their companionship. "This is real. And we're here, watchin' your back, day and night."

Perry reached out and placed a reassuring hand on Moses' shoulder. "There's not a vengeful horseman around that's going to take you or your family. Not while we're here."

Moses exhaled, grounding himself in their words and presence.

Archy wagged his tail and let out a soft, contented huff, as if satisfied that his charge was safe once more. Moses reached down and scratched the dog's head. "Guess you were tryin' to wake me up before I drowned." Archy licked his hand in reply. "If I'm ever in real, trouble, Archy, I hope you're there to pull me out."

Moses, his heart still rattling in his chest, let out a weary chuckle, steadied by the presence of his friends.

"Well," Pete muttered, settling back into the hay, "if you have any more biblical nightmares, try to keep 'em quiet, huh?"

Perry smirked, lying back down. "Yeah, least till morning. We need our rest for whatever's ahead. Plus, that snow's really piling up outside."

Moses nodded, his breath finally steady. While memories of the nightmare lingered, they no longer crushed him. He glanced up at the barn's rafters. It was just a dream, but even then, the vengeful waves of the Mississippi River still raged and crashed in the corners of his mind.

CHAPTER 22

Late December

GOOD TIDINGS TO ALL

THE MUFFLED SOUND of an approaching horse through the snow stirred Pete from his interrupted sleep. He nudged Perry, who rubbed his eyes and sat up.

"What's going on? Moses have another nightmare? What's that sound?" Perry quickly stood and squinted through a crack in the barn wall.

Outside, a figure on horseback approached, their silhouette blurred by the dark. The rider dismounted and knocked on the door.

Perry opened the door cautiously, revealing a young woman wrapped in a heavy cloak. Her cheeks were flushed from the cold, and her eyes shone with a mix of urgency and relief. She pulled back her hood, unveiling light auburn hair tied into a loose braid.

"Sorry to trouble you, this day after Christmas," she said, her breath fogging in the air. "I'm Virginia, Virginia Carter. I live down this lane a bit. My father's ill, still recovering from the war, and we're snowed in. I'm not asking the cranky old man in this house, but I saw your wagon and I thought you might be willin'. I could sure use a few extra hands."

Perry glanced back at Pete and Moses, who were already on their feet. "What kind of help, Miss Carter?"

"The barn doors are blocked by a four-foot drift, and my animals need tending. The snow's blocking my entry."

Pete exchanged a look with Moses, then let out a low whistle. "A snow pile that big is gonna be a job and a half."

Virginia nodded, her voice laced with determination. "My father's not well enough to lend a hand, and I can't manage it all myself. I hate to impose, but if you could spare a few minutes."

Moses stepped forward. "We'll help. Lead the way, Miss Carter."

Virginia's eyes flickered to Moses, her hesitation brief before a grateful smile warmed her face. "Thank you, sir."

Perry grabbed a pair of shovels from the barn's corner, handing one to Moses. "Looks like we've got some work ahead of us. Let's saddle up. We'll follow you, Miss Carter."

As they began the short ride to the farmhouse, Perry pondered the meaning of this morning-after-Christmas encounter. Strangers, bound only by the simple truth of shared humanity, stepping forward in kindness. It was a reminder that small gestures could chip away at the coldest hardships and make the world a little warmer.

When they reached the barn, Perry let out a low sigh. The drift was taller than he'd expected, its hardened surface crusted with ice. Virginia dismounted and gestured to the tools they'd brought. "I started before dawn, but I didn't get too far."

Pete hefted the second shovel. "Don't fret, Miss Carter. Among the three of us, we'll have this door clear in no time. Let's tackle it, fellas."

The men began hacking into the snowbank as Virginia stood off to the side. The drift disappeared under the rhythm of their work. Moses paused to straighten his back, leaning on his shovel.

"Don't worry, ma'am. Your animals will be tended within the hour."

Virginia nodded, a smile breaking through her concern. "Thank you. My father may not be able to say it this morning, but this means a lot to us. To me."

Perry, sweat glistening on his brow despite the frigid air, grinned. "Well, we're not much for fancy gifts, but we figure lending a hand is worth more than a ribbon-wrapped package."

Virginia laughed. "It's a better gift than you know. Can I at least feed you some breakfast?"

"Not necessary, Miss Carter. We've got plenty of vittles on our wagon."

By the time the barn doors swung open, Virginia was already heading inside to fetch her animals feed and water. She rushed to the house and returned with three hot rolls, gleaming with butter.

"I know what you said, but I thought you might like these to help you warm up a bit," she said.

Pete took a chomp out of his roll before savoring its warmth. "Miss Carter, you make a fine breakfast roll. Almost makes me want to shovel more snow. Almost."

"Glad to hear it. And I appreciate what you've done. I couldn't have managed without you. My pappy, well he's still recovering from a battle wound he got from a Yankee bullet more than a year ago. It's been a real strain."

Moses glanced at her. "Sounds like he's doing what he can to recover from this war, same as most folks. Still, there's always room for grace when times are hard."

Virginia met his gaze, her eyes brightening. "Grace," she repeated. "It's not just somethin' you give when life's easy. It's what holds you stable when the world's gone wrong. Grace is the strength to offer kindness when you've every reason not to, and the courage to accept it when you're at your lowest. I reckon we all need a little more of it right now."

The men offered kind farewells before mounting their horses. They rode away as Perry glanced back at the small neighboring farmhouse. "Sometimes, it's the unexpected stops that remind us what matters."

Moses nodded, his gaze fixed on the horizon. "Kindness. Grace. That's what keeps the world from freezin' over. With any luck, some of that might spill over for the task ahead, fixing that wagon."

The sun cast a soft golden light over the snow-covered terrain by the time they returned to the barn. Fixing the wagon wheel couldn't wait for the warmth of day.

Perry knelt to examine the wheel again, running a gloved hand over the axle. "Yep. It's the lynchpin for sure. That plank loosened it up. Guess that explains the wobble. I'm going to put a new one in place, just to be sure."

Pete nodded, his breath fogging in the cold air. "Well, we're not goin' to tell Marcus about how his extra parts saved our hides. We'll end up owing him double. Now it's a matter of gettin' this wagon up so you can hammer a new pin into place."

Moses scanned the area, his eyes settling on a walnut branch jutting from a drift of snow near the barn. "There's our lever."

"And that rock by the barn door, that'll be our fulcrum," Pete said.

The men trudged through the snow to retrieve the items. Moses wedged one end of the sturdy branch beneath the rear axle while Pete shoved the rock into place, adjusting it for maximum leverage.

"All right," Moses said, gripping the branch firmly. "Pete, grab hold with me. Perry, you get that pin ready."

Perry nodded, retrieving the iron lynchpin and an iron mallet from their tool chest. "Ready when you are."

Moses and Pete pressed down, straining against the weight on the load. The rear slowly lifted, the axle rasping under the shift.

"Hold it steady!" Perry called, crouching beside the wheel. He pushed it tight and slid the new lynchpin into place. He delivered a series of firm strikes to drive the pin deep. The sharp clang of iron on iron echoed in the morning air, mingling with the sound of the men's labored breathing.

Moses adjusted his grip on the branch, his arms straining as he and Pete held the wagon aloft. "You almost done, Perry? We're fixin' to bust a gut back here."

"Almost!" Perry replied, delivering a final blow. The pin settled into place. He stood and examined his work, tapping the pin to ensure it was snug. "That ought to do it."

Perry wiped his hands on his coat and reached for a small tin of axle grease. He smeared the thick grease over the axle and the wheel opening, ensuring smooth movement. "I'll grease it up a bit more, and there shouldn't be any more wobbles from here to Memphis."

Perry gave the wheel a spin. It turned smoothly. "All right, fellas," he said with a grin. "Let's get this wagon moving. Memphis ain't getting any closer."

Moses and Pete eased the wagon down, the weight settling onto the newly secured wheel. Pete stretched his arms with a satisfied grunt. "Well, that's one way to warm up on a cold morning."

Moses dusted snow from his coat. "Not bad for a couple of trail-worn men with a walnut branch and a rock."

The men exchanged a nod, their spirits lifted by the small victory. With the wagon repaired and ready to roll, they hitched up the horses, confident their journey southward would now proceed a little smoother and warmer as the day wore on.

By the time they returned to the plank road, the snow had already begun to melt. Three miles later, it was barely visible.

From atop his horse, Pete adjusted his hat, squinting at the thinning snow along the roadside. "You know what that storm was?"

"I'm guessin' you're about to tell us," Moses laughed.

"That was a Wildcat storm. Comes blastin' through with a ferocious growl, throwin' everything it's got at you. But when you look around after, you realize it traveled on tiny cat feet, quiet, quick, and gone before you can reckon with it."

"Wildcat, huh?" Perry asked. "Sounds about right. Left a mess but didn't have the grit to stick around."

"Well, if that's the worst we've got to deal with between here and Memphis, I reckon we'll count ourselves lucky," Moses said.

Pete nodded, eyeing the repaired wagon wheel as it rolled along. "Lucky and a little smarter. Next Wildcat we see, we'll be ready."

The men shared a laugh as the horses plodded forward, the road muddy in places where the planks had given way. By the time they had covered another three miles, the snow had disappeared completely, leaving the world around them bathed in the soft glow of winter sunshine. Even the fiercest of Wildcat storms left behind clear skies and a path to press onward.

After several more days of travel, the world turned warmer as Pete, Perry, and Moses pressed southward. The horses moved steadily, their breath no longer visible in the daily breeze.

The route curved around a dense grove of pines, opening to a stretch of flat land where a caravan of wagons trundled northward.

Pete was the first to spot them. He squinted, shading his eyes. "Looks like a small group traveling north. Wonder where they're headin'."

Perry pulled the reins, slowing the wagon, Archibald seated at his side. Moses scanned the convoy of newcomers—a mix of people, wagons pulled by weary animals and loaded with a hodgepodge of belongings.

As the two groups met, a man with a broad-brimmed hat and a sun-leathered face waved them down. His voice carried across the space between them. "Afternoon, gentlemen. Travelers like us, I see."

Perry tipped his hat. "Afternoon. Headin' north?"

"Aye, that we are," the man said, stepping closer. "Name's Nathan Frye. My folks and I are movin' westward, toward the territories. Lookin' for land and better chances than what Memphis has to offer after the war."

Pete hopped off his horse and approached Nathan, eyeing the wagons behind him. "The territories, huh? That's a mighty long haul. What didn't you find in Memphis that's got you headin' clear across the plains?"

Nathan laughed, though there was little humor in it. "Oh, Memphis has its charm, sure enough. Fine food, music that could make the angels weep, and folks who know how to live. But charm don't put bread on the table, not for men like us. City's still torn from the war. And opportunity? It's thin as gruel. Out west, there's land to claim, a place to call your own without the shadow of the past breathin' down your neck."

A woman from Nathan's caravan stepped forward, a basket on her arm and a child clinging to her skirt. "Memphis is beautiful," she said, her southern voice soft. "We got a lifetime fill of smoked pork and bread pudding. Both were always worth a king's ransom, but even good meals don't last. We go in search of somethin' to build on, somethin' for the future."

Moses nodded, her words striking a chord. "And you think the West will give you that?"

Nathan shrugged. "It's a gamble, like all things. But I'd rather stake my claim on new soil than keep diggin' in old ground that won't yield."

The two groups exchanged glances. Perry cleared his throat. "We're heading to Memphis ourselves, chasing a different sort of dream."

Nathan's gaze sharpened. "I hope it's the kind of dream that likes a fine meal served on a cracked plate. Because that's what Memphis is. It looks pretty enough, but lean in close, and you'll see the war's left its scars on the city and its people. You best keep your wits about you at all times."

Pete smirked, glancing at Perry and Moses. "Sounds like the kind of place that might appeal to an old Arkansawyer like me."

The travelers shared a laugh, and Nathan's wife handed each man a small loaf of cornbread from her basket. "A little something for the road," she said. "To remind you of the good parts."

They each accepted the bread with nods of gratitude.

"Thank you, ma'am," Moses said. "And safe travels to you and your family."

"And to you," she replied.

Just then, a scream. Not far from someone behind the last wagon. Gunshots. Pete spun, heart pounding. A man came staggering out. A bullet wound to the shoulder, shirt bloody. "They're coming!" he shouted, spit flying.

Shit hit the wind. Nathan's face went pale. "Down! Now!"

A hail of gunshots tore through the hush, splitting wood, whistling past. Six riders burst into view, faces masked, guns up. Perry cursed, dragging Archibald off the wagon seat. Moses hit the dirt, pulling the woman and her child to the ground with him.

Bullets slammed into wagon wheels. Pete found himself face-down in the mud, adrenaline hot in his throat.

Nathan fired back, yelling, "Run! Go!" The woman's basket was stomped flat and the remaining cornbread scattered across the road.

In less than a minute, the riders vanished into the trees, leaving silence shattered, survivors counting each other, shaking, covered in mud and grit.

Nathan spat blood, eyes burning. "Goddamn Nighthawks," he growled. "That's what folks around here call 'em. Highway rats, born from the war and the hunger that came after. They wait for the desperate, the slow, the ones looking for a new start. Don't give 'em an inch, or they'll gut you for your boots."

He stared at Pete, deadly earnest. "You want dreams out here? You better have a gun in your hand at all times and eyes in the back of your goddamn head. The Nighthawks don't give second chances."

Nathan wiped blood from his lip, eyes burning. "This is the South," he spat. "You want dreams? Be ready to bleed for 'em."

Blood still spurted freely from the wounded man's shoulder, splattering dark red into the mud. Several members of the northbound group lifted the man into the back of a wagon and a woman wrapped the man's shoulder with a soiled bandage. Somewhere, out in the trees, a crow called. It was a harsh, mocking sound. For a moment, no one moved. Breath hung in the air, thick as gun smoke.

Perry broke the silence, voice hoarse. "Reckon we best keep moving. Eyes open and guns drawn."

Nathan nodded, the lines in his face deepening. "You do that. And remember, out here, it's not the land that'll kill you. It's the desperate bastards hidin' in the shadows, waiting for nightfall, but any time of the day works if they sense an opportunity for plunder. They're road pirates, pure and simple."

The groups parted ways. Perry felt a rush of adrenaline not unlike what drove him during the Battle of Leavenworth.

Pete spat into the dirt and wiped his mouth. "Guess Memphis ain't the only place where a man's gotta watch his back. But hell, at least in Memphis, we know to expect it. Out here, you can't tell what's sneaking up on you till it's too damn late."

"John Manchester warned me about this when he pulled me aside back in Gumbo Flats. I didn't want to cause any alarm so I kept it to myself. But now, I realize that was a mistake," Perry said.

"So all this time, you knew there'd be this kind of trouble, the kind that doesn't think twice about shooting you in the back?" Moses asked in a pointed manner.

Perry nodded. "Don't try to say you weren't already aware of the peril, Moses. John just made it a little sharper. He said the roads south were crawling with desperate men. Raiders. Nighthawks. I didn't want to spook anybody, but I think we all knew."

Pete jumped in. He grinned, though there was nothing soft in it. "Hell, Perry, next time a man whispers that kind of warnin', you let me know. I'd rather be spooked than catch a bullet in my backside. Trouble's been chasin' me since I could walk. I'd just rather see it comin', is all. Long as we keep our heads up and our powder dry, we'll sure as shit get to Memphis in one piece."

As the northbound travelers vanished over the next hill, the men remounted and continued their trek toward Memphis. Perry flicked the reins of the wagon and looked back over his shoulder. "Just remember, out here, luck's thinner than a shadow. Be deliberate in your actions. Expect this to happen again. Let's redouble our vigilance. Keep our eyes up, watch each other's backs, and we won't give the darkness a say in what happens next. That's how we make it to Memphis."

From that moment, every tree and shadow along the plank road held a threat. For the next few miles, nobody spoke. The road stretched before them. Perry kept the reins tight. Moses kept his eyes fixed southward. Pete scanned the tree line. They rode on, toward whatever truth Memphis and beyond was willing to yield.

"We're close," Moses said finally, breaking his silence. "I can almost feel Sally's arms around me. But when we get there, we need to move like that Wildcat storm we faced back yonder, fierce, on quick feet and gone before trouble catches our scent."

"Exactly," Pete said. "From this point forward, I want *us* to be the surprise. We will be the shadow they never see coming. We'll hit those plantations outside of Memphis like a bolt of lightning before a thunderclap. Reclaim what's yours and leave nothin' but rumors in our wake. That's how we survive. That's how we win."

CHAPTER 23

Mid-January 1866

HOUSE CALLS

THE WINTER MORNING back in St. Joseph was crisp but clear, the kind of day where the sun plays tricks on the mind, warming the land without the air. The snow that had blanketed the town during Christmas had long since melted, leaving behind a muddy patchwork of earth and frost.

Lucy and Millie made a short walk to St. Joseph's Catholic Church, which stood gray and silent in the morning chill, the stone steps rimmed in ice and the steeple stabbing the dull winter sky. Inside, breath steamed in the air, mingling with the smell of incense and muddy boots.

The two women pressed into a pew near the back, gloves threadbare, shawls drawn tight. The nave was half-full. Widows in black, men with hollow eyes, children clutching their mothers' hands, all gathered beneath the tall, stained glass windows. Candlelight flickered against their faces, shadows dancing across the plaster walls.

Father Keith Andrews, in plain Benedictine habit, ascended the pulpit. His voice was low and grave. It carried through the raw air. "We come together in the dead of winter—a season of waiting, of longing, when the world itself seems cold and barren."

He paused, glancing at the crucifix above the altar. "But January is not the end. In the Church's year, it's Epiphanytide. A time for revelation, hope and seeking light in the darkness. It time to remember that the Magi found hope not in palaces, but in a humble setting. So too, we search for light in our own modest places."

Lucy felt Millie shiver beside her. Father Andrews continued. "We are a people marked by loss—wives without husbands, children without fathers, fields and towns not far from here still scorched by war. We ache. But as the wise men pressed on through the night, guided only by a star, so must we."

He leaned forward, voice rough with conviction. "Hope is not loud, nor is it easy. Hope is quiet. It's a hand held, a loaf broken, a prayer whispered when the world is silent. Christ was not born into comfort. He was born into the chill, the straw, the threat. That is the lesson of the season."

A murmur rippled through the church as he raised his hand in blessing. "God meets us in the cold. He walks with us through January's shadows. Our task is not to banish the darkness, but to bear our light faithfully against it."

Millie whispered, "That's exactly what I needed to hear."

Lucy nodded, eyes shining with sudden, stubborn hope as the congregation rose to sing, voices thin but unbroken against the winter outside.

Returning to the Fontaine home after mass, Lucy stirred a hearty pot of oats near the hearth. Nearby, Millie hummed softly, mending a tiny flaw in a baby blanket with skill. The two women moved with purpose, bringing resilience and calm to uncertain days.

The rumble of carriage wheels broke the stillness, prompting Millie to glance up sharply. She set her sewing aside, stepping briskly toward the frost-kissed window. "Doc's here. Odd he's visiting on a Sunday."

Lucy wiped her hands briskly. on her apron. "Let's see if he's brought better news this time. I'd rather face facts head-on."

Doc Anderson stepped down from his buggy, Carrying his well-worn black bag, his patched coat flapped in the breeze. Lucy opened the door before he knocked.

"Morning, Doc," she greeted warmly. "Surprised to see you on a Sunday, but the coffee's hot."

"Much obliged," Doc replied. "That'll keep a doctor's system tickin', especially on a Sunday. Doctorin's kinda like farmin'. Neither offers the luxury of takin' the Lord's day off on a regular basis. You two look well. Let's see how things are coming along, shall we?"

The women exchanged empowering glances as Doc settled Millie on the parlor sofa, his movements deliberate yet gentle. He pulled out his pocket watch, timing her pulse with one hand while the other rested lightly on her wrist.

"Steady as ever. You've been eating well, I trust?"

"Lucy wouldn't allow otherwise," Millie said. "Keeps me fed like I'm a prize hog at the county fair."

Doc grinned, patting her hand. "Well, it's paying off. Let's check that little one now."

He leaned in, placing his hand gently on Millie's belly, his fingers deft as he felt for signs of movement. His face broke into a smile as he nodded.

"Baby has grown considerably since our last visit, and I felt some movement. You're carryin' ideally for the seventh month. How've you been feeling? Any discomfort, nausea, anything out of the ordinary?"

"Nothing too bad. A bit more tired than usual, but nothing I can't manage."

"That's normal. Your body's working hard. Keep resting when you can and keep up with your meals. Your little one's thriving."

Millie's face lit up. "That's a load off my mind."

He turned to Lucy, motioning for her to have a seat. Lucy sat, her hands folded over her lap with an expression of hope and apprehension.

"Your turn, young lady." He repeated the same steps, examining her with meticulous care. His hands moved over her belly with a gentle touch. He paused, concentrating, as if sensing something beyond what was visible. He scribbled into his notes.

"Lucy," he said after a moment, his face softening into a smile, "you've done a marvelous job of catching up. That little one's grown a lot, in fact, I'm not sure there's just one."

Lucy gasped at the thought. "I sure hope there's only one, Doc, but Pete and I will be happy with whatever the good Lord gives us. As long as you think the baby's healthy, that's all that matters."

"I felt a nice kick, so I know you've been taking my advice, haven't you? More butter, more milk, more rest?"

"I have, every word of it."

"Good. You're on the right track. Keep at it. Any questions or worries on your mind?"

Lucy hesitated and glanced at Millie before speaking. "Sometimes I feel a heaviness in my chest. Not pain, but a pressure. I don't know if it's worry or if it's something I should be concerned about."

"That's the burden of being a mother, Lucy. It's a heavy thing, bringing a life into this world. It's nothing to fear. Your body knows what to do, and you've got friends around you to lean on when it gets hard. Trust in that."

When the examinations were done, the women gathered around the small kitchen table, Doc cradling a cup of steaming coffee.

"You're both doing wonderfully," he said. "And your little ones are as fit as fiddles."

Millie and Lucy exchanged a glance, their smiles reflecting their shared relief.

"Thank you," Millie said. "We've been holding our breath for this appointment."

"An expectant mother's worry is as old as time itself."

After finishing his coffee, Doc got up to leave, but he turned at the door.

"This new world we've stumbled into is raw and unsure. But it's wide open. And that means your children won't just survive it, they'll shape it."

Millie and Lucy stood at the door as he climbed aboard his buggy and pulled away. The sky grew overcast, but the clouds in their hearts had lifted.

"We're gonna make it, Lucy."

The wooden pews at the African church outside Lowland groaned as families settled into their usual spots, hymnals gripped by hands weathered by work and life.

Gabe had been attending services regularly since Christmas. It was an unexpected shift in his routine, but one that he joyfully anticipated, especially since he knew Naomi would be there.

As he entered the church, he caught sight of her near the front. She wore a deep indigo dress with white trim, her bonnet tied beneath her chin. Her serene expression as she leafed through her hymnal stirred something in Gabe that felt new and unfamiliar—a sense of belonging, perhaps, or the hope of it.

Instead of taking his usual seat in the back, Gabe made his way down the aisle toward the front. When he reached her pew, he hesitated for a moment before tipping his hat and gesturing to the space beside her.

"Miss James, mind if I join you today?"

Naomi looked up, her dark eyes widening before a smile spread across her face. "Of course not, Mr. Watson. Please."

He slid into the pew beside her, the faint scent of lavender from her bonnet reaching him as he settled in. The congregation murmured as they noticed the two sitting together. A few heads turned, smiles exchanged between older members who had seen the quiet rapport building over the weeks.

As the service began, the pastor's voice rang out in a clear, deep timbre, leading the congregation through hymns and scripture. Gabe felt acutely aware of Naomi's presence beside him, her voice blending with the others in the room, but somehow standing out. It was soft yet filled with conviction and grace.

The service ended and the final hymn faded into the quiet rustle of people. Gabe turned to Naomi.

"Miss James, I don't believe I've ever had a Sunday quite like this. Sittin' here with you, it felt like the Lord's house was a little brighter today."

"Mr. Watson, you flatter me. I've enjoyed our visits since you have been coming more frequently. But I think maybe it's you sparking a bit of light yourself."

"I reckon I have. Haven't missed a sermon for more than a month. This place has a way of settlin' the mind. Truth be told, it's nice seein' a familiar face in the crowd."

"I'm so glad you're here, Gabe. Community feeds the soul in times like these."

The congregation filtered out of the church, some members stopping to exchange words with Reverend Hayes at the door. Gabe and Naomi stayed back, their steps unhurried as they walked out the door.

"Miss James," Gabe began. "I don't mean to be forward, but would it be too bold of me to ask if I might see you again outside of Sunday?"

Naomi tilted her head, studying him for a moment before smiling. "Well, Mr. Watson, I do believe that'd be just fine. I think it would be appropriate for you to meet my parents first. They aren't regular church-goin folks, but they are inspired by the Lord's grace. I know they'd be pleased to have you join us for supper. Let me check with them, but how about Thursday?"

Gabe's heart gave a small leap. "Sounds perfect, Naomi."

She nodded, her bonnet catching the sunlight as they walked toward the hitching posts. "I'll warn you now, my mother's cooking is magnificent, and she'll expect you to eat your fill."

Gabe laughed, his smile wide and unguarded. "I'll make sure I come hungry, then."

As they reached their horses, Naomi paused. "It's good to see someone takin' steps forward, Gabe. Feels like too many people are stuck lookin' back."

"I guess it's about time I started movin' forward. And maybe, maybe you're the reason I'm takin' that first step."

Naomi blushed, lowering her gaze. "Maybe it's not just the step, Gabe. Maybe it's where the path was always meant to lead. Sometimes, we don't choose the path, we're just finally brave enough to walk it."

With a tip of his hat and a promise to see her Thursday evening, Gabe mounted his horse. As he rode away, the church behind him and Naomi's smile were etched into his thoughts. A stir tickled his chest. It was the possibility of something new, something whole. The road ahead didn't feel quite so lonely.

Thursday evening, Gabe stood in front of the small mirror nailed to the wall of the Watson home. His reflection looked back at him with uncertainty. He adjusted the collar of his freshly washed shirt, its fabric still slightly damp from drying near the fire. He ruffled his hair and smiled. The effort highlighted the dimple on his left cheek. It was an inherited mark he'd long viewed as a peculiarly handsome quirk passed along by his father. He hoped Naomi might notice.

"Dinner with the James family," he said to himself. "A simple meal, Gabe. Don't make it more than it is."

But it felt like more. The invitation had lingered in his mind since Naomi had extended it, her words echoing like the final notes of a hymn. It wasn't only a chance to see her again, though that alone made his chest tighten. It was the prospect of stepping into her world, meeting the people who had shaped her. He wasn't sure it was an honor he deserved.

With a deep breath, he bundled up in his best coat and stepped outside. The sky streaked with purples and golds, a reminder of the fleeting day. He led his horse from the barn and cinched the saddle. As he left, the house faded behind him, and for the first time in months loneliness did not burden his mind.

The James family home was modest but welcoming, its warm light spilling out onto the porch and into the twilight. Gabe could hear faint laughter and the clinking of dishes as he approached, his nerves rising with each step closer. Naomi met him at the door, her smile as radiant as the lantern she held.

"You made it," she said.

"Wouldn't miss it," Gabe replied, tipping his hat as he stepped inside. The aroma of baked ham, sweet potatoes, and cornbread filled the air. The home's interior was simple with handmade quilts draped over the chairs.

Naomi's father, Elijah James, rose from his seat by the fire, his tall frame casting a long shadow. His handshake was firm, his weathered face framed by a salt-and-pepper beard. "So you're Gabe Watson," he said, his tone cordial but appraising. "Naomi's mentioned you."

"All good, I hope, sir."

"Reckon you'll have to find out over supper," Elijah said.

As they ate, the conversation flowed easily, Elijah asking Gabe about his life, his work, and his thoughts on the future. Gabe answered honestly. He talked about the farm, his service with the Jayhawkers during the war and the rescue mission that drew his father from home. He found himself glancing at Naomi, her presence both a comfort and a distraction.

Naomi's mother, Dora James, spoke with gentle authority. "I like to see a young man with a sense of purpose. Too many folks, especially our folks, wandering aimlessly these days, caught between the bad of what was and trying to figure out what might be."

"Can't say I've got it all figured out," Gabe admitted, "but I'm tryin' to make my way forward."

"That's all any of us can do, young man."

As the meal wound down, Elijah leaned back in his chair, a twinkle in his eye. "Naomi tells me you're quite the horseman. We could use a hand with a few stubborn colts out back sometime if you're willin'."

"I could manage that. Might even teach 'em a trick or two."

Naomi chimed in. "Careful, Papa, he might show them how to

outsmart you."

The room filled with laughter, and for a moment, Gabe felt as though he belonged, as though his past had been left outside, at least for the night.

After dinner, Gabe pushed open the front door, and Naomi stepped onto the porch, a blast of winter air curling around them. The floorboards groaned as a distant howl of wind rushed through bare branches. Naomi leaned against the railing, the lantern's glow casting long shadows across her face. She tipped her chin toward the sky, her eyes fixed on the stars as if searching for the wishes they might hold.

"Thank you for comin' tonight. It meant a lot to my parents. And to me."

Gabe rested his hands on the rail. "It's been a long time since I felt part of somethin'. Your parents made me feel welcome."

"Perhaps that's what you've been missin'. A place to belong."

"I think I've found the beginnin' to somethin' like that."

"The first step's always the hardest, but you took it, Gabe."

As they stood on the porch, the cold night stretching around them, Gabe reached out and grabbed Naomi's hand. He felt a glow of hope and warmth, fragile but undeniable. He saw a faint outline of a future. He suspected that Naomi might be at the heart of it.

CHAPTER 24

Mid-January 1866

MEMPHIS AND BEYOND

THE BUILDINGS IN MEMPHIS slumped, scarred and battered, as Perry, Pete, and Moses rode into the city. Coal soot streaked the buildings, many with sagging roofs and shattered windows. Doors hung open like hushed mouths.

The streets, thick with churned mud, bore the scars of wagon wheels and boot prints. Tattered banners of the Union occupation clung to weary store fronts. Smoke from distant chimneys offered the only sign of life in a place still haunted by the thunder of cannons and cries of the wounded.

The city had been a crucial Confederate stronghold on the Mississippi River, serving as a gateway to Tennessee's largest cotton and slave markets. Before the war, steamboats choked the Mississippi, their decks stacked high with cotton bales bound for market. Traders scurried along the docks counting profits in ledger books while enslaved laborers toiled under the sun. The city had stood as the Confederacy's gateway to wealth, its fortunes tied to the river's flow.

Then came the war on the river. In the summer of 1862, black smoke had billowed over the water as Union and Confederate gunboats clashed. Cannon fire sent splintered wood and torn bodies into the river's depths. On the bluffs, citizens watched in horror as their defenders faltered.

By evening, nine Union ships had crushed the Confederate fleet. The next morning, blue-coated soldiers marched through Memphis' streets, planting their flag in the city's heart. The war would rage on, but Memphis now belonged to the Union.

Two years later, in a gasp of desperation, General Nathan Bedford Forrest and his rebel cavalry thundered toward town, hooves kicking up dust on the winding roads. Pistols shined at their sides, sabers rattling with each gallop. Ahead, the city's dimly lit streets lay vulnerable, its Union defenders unaware of the storm about to break.

Forrest's men whispered their orders. Find the Yankee generals, free the prisoners, and sow chaos. If they struck hard, the Union would be forced to pull its troops back from Northern Mississippi to defend Memphis. Sweat, gunpowder and the promise of battle crackled in the humid air.

"Well, old Nathan failed, but he managed to escape, after leaving the city riddled by Confederate bullet holes," Pete said. "They called him the Wizard of the Saddle. But that adoration in no way excuses him from his atrocities."

"The mere thought of that man brings nothin' but darkness," Perry said. "The way he killed damn near everyone at Fort Pillow in April of '64, after they laid down their guns. It was pure slaughter. This whole region wears hardship like a tattered infantry coat, every stitch saturated with blood."

"It was black soldiers, men who took up arms to fight for freedom. Men like my Gabe," Moses said.

The streets of Memphis were silent. Perry spoke up. "Good thing the newspapermen didn't let that go. The story spread fast. Folks say it helped harden Lincoln's resolve to see the war through to the end."

Pete nodded. "Forrest lit a fire that burned stronger. Ain't that somethin'? Man tries to break a people, and all he does is make 'em more determined to stand."

"At what cost?" Moses asked. "All those lives lost—brothers, fathers, sons. For what? To prove that even in surrender, a man's life meant nothin' to Forrest and his kind?"

Pete's eyes met Moses' across the path. "You're right. Men like Forrest are destined to lose in the end. They can kill, they can burn, but they can't create. They leave nothin' behind but ruins."

Perry exhaled deeply, "I suspect that similar men are lurking in the dark alleys of this city, looking for any way to claw their way back."

"The federal forces can't let them," Moses said. "They need to build something bigger. Stronger. They need to repair this city so that for every life Forrest took, two lives will march forward with purpose. With freedom. They need to raise schools where chains once rattled, build roads where blood once ran."

As the men rode into the heart of the city they began to notice the people of Memphis. They moved like shadows, silent, hollow-eyed, their shoulders hunched under an invisible yoke. Along the broad sidewalks, their stares lingered on the passing strangers, not with curiosity, but with resentment sharpened by loss and anger dulled by exhaustion. The war had ended but defeat still skulked among them.

Pete adjusted his hat, leaning forward in his saddle. "These folks have been picked clean and they ain't yet found their hearts."

Perry nodded, his hand resting on the reins. "War'll do that. It's not the battles but what folks carry afterward."

Moses rode on, his posture straight, his face unreadable. His eyes took in every detail, from the broken cobblestones to the faded, bullet-riddled store signs. In his saddle bag, he carried the meticulously annotated documents that John had handed him back in Gumbo Flats and his good luck soybean seeds.

The men paused at a water trough to let the horses drink. Perry leaned on the wagon wheel, unfolding the map John had provided.

As the horses lowered their heads to drink, a sudden shout echoed from across the street—sharp, guttural, edged with fear. The men turned just as a door flew open and a ragged boy stumbled out, clutching a sack to his chest. Hot on his heels, two men in torn gray uniforms burst onto the boardwalk, pistols drawn, eyes wild with the hunger of men who had lost everything.

Time stuttered. Moses barely had a moment to shout a warning before one of the men's pistols cracked. The shot tore through the stillness, and Perry reeled in the wagon seat, a dark bloom of red spreading across the sleeve covering his left bicep. The horses reared, the water trough overturned, and chaos swept the street. Pete instinctively drew his own weapon, leveling it at the fleeing attackers, while Moses dropped to the ground, pulling Perry into the wagon's protection.

Townsfolk scattered, slamming doors and shuttering windows, but the echo of violence lingered, louder even than the gunfire.

After the dust and confusion, Pete pressed a hand to Perry's wound, feeling the hot blood seep between his fingers. "Stay with me." Pete worked fast, his hands steady despite the shock of the moment. He peeled back Perry's torn sleeve, inspecting the wound.

"Bullet went clean through," he muttered, relief in his eyes. "You got lucky, Perry. It'll be sore for a while, but you're going to be just fine."

Pete drew out a bandage from his saddlebag, wrapping it tight around Perry's bicep, then around his midsection for additional stability. The makeshift dressing soaked up the blood, and Pete gave it a final tug, knotting it off tightly.

Perry watched Pete's hands work, his breath returning to normal. He glanced down at the bloody bandage, then back up. He managed a crooked smile as he recovered from the initial shock.

"Didn't hardly feel it," Perry mumbled. "Like a little bee sting, I guess. Not the first time I've been shot, Pete, but sure didn't think I'd catch a bullet out of sheer bad luck."

With his right hand, Perry reached into his pocked and drew out Millie's rosary and recited a quick prayer.

"Let's pray that's the extent of it," Moses said. "Just being in the wrong place at the wrong time. You think you can manage the reins, Perry? We need to get the hell out of Memphis. Now."

"Yeh. The way Pete bandaged me up, I can rest my left arm against my side, but my left hand can still grip the reins. Let's hit the trail. We've got a mission ahead." He shoved the rosary back into his pocket.

Without another word, the men mounted up. Pete swung onto his horse, keeping a protective eye on Perry, while Moses took the lead. They left the water trough overturned in the street and didn't look back. The silent faces in the windows faded behind them as they rode hard, east to Germantown.

"Onward then. Time for us to make a little visit to a Mr. Silas Henson. He's the bastard who bought Sally and Michael. For his sake, I hope they're both alive and well. Then, we'll call on Jeremiah Collins. He's the man who took Samuel further south."

Perry's arm began to throb as the Henson plantation jumped from a clearing in the afternoon sun. The house stood tall, its once-bright columns smudged with grime, the paint peeling like old bark on a sycamore.

Beyond the grand home, small cabins hunched close to the earth, their doors ajar, revealing stacked crates and worn cots. Where the enslaved once slept in silence, voices now murmured. Freedmen were shaping new lives in the same cramped spaces, the scent of labor still thick in the air, but now paid labor.

With a slight wince of pain, Perry slowed the wagon, while Moses scanned the grounds for any sign of Sally or Michael. "This place appears still. Too still." His eyes locked on the row of cabins.

"Let's not waste time," Pete said. "The sooner we know, the quicker we act and the faster we get the hell out of here." He dismounted and shuffled his boots through the dusty path to the house. He climbed the front steps and knocked, the sound echoing through the paint-peeled door. After a moment, the door opened, revealing a tall black man in a neat but worn coat. His face was kind, his eyes bright with curiosity.

"Afternoon," Pete began, doffing his hat. "We're travelers lookin' to speak with Mr. Henson. Might he be home?"

The man shook his head. "Master Henson got himself killed during the war. I work for Mrs. Henson now. She's inside. May I ask what this matter's about?"

Pete hesitated, glancing back toward the wagon where Perry and Moses waited. "It's a family matter."

The doorman studied him for a moment, then nodded. "Wait here. I'll see if she's entertainin' visitors."

Moments later, the doorman returned, stepping aside as Mrs. Henson entered the doorway. She was an attractive woman of middling years, her face lined with loss but also dignity. She clutched a shawl wrapped around her shoulders, her eyes narrowing as she took in Pete, then at the wagon and the two figures in the distance.

"You've come about a family matter?" she asked. "Is this about my husband?"

Pete shook his head quickly. "No, ma'am. I'm sorry for any confusion. This is about another family. My friend over there." Pete gestured toward Moses. "He's come to seek his own."

Her eyes followed Pete's gesture, her face softening as she registered Moses' presence. "Go on."

"Ma'am, we've reason to believe that Sally and Michael—Moses' wife and son—may have been part of this estate during the war. He's come to ensure their safety and freedom."

Mrs. Henson's hand rose to her mouth. "Sally and Michael…" she repeated, her voice wavering. "Yes. Yes, they were here. They still are."

Pete's heart leapt. He turned and ran toward the wagon, unable to hide his enthusiasm. "Moses! Perry!" he called, waving them forward.

Perry steadied his arm as he climbed from the wagon. The men approached slowly. Mrs. Henson broke down into sobs, clutching the doorframe for support. "Oh, please," she cried, "please don't take them from me. I've lost so much already, my husband, my family. Sally and Michael, they are like family to me now. They've been great sources of comfort since the war ended and my husband failed to return. I've done everything I could to provide for them."

Pete's face hardened. "Ma'am, sorry for your loss, but Sally and Michael ain't your kin. They belong at that man's side. I respect the care you've shown, but it's time for them to go home."

Mrs. Henson wiped tears welling in her eyes, her composure returning. She looked at Moses, her eyes filled with sorrowful understanding. "You're right. It's not my place. I'll send for them."

She straightened, drawing herself up. "Wait here. I'll ask them to meet you in the parlor. Please come inside. I'll arrange a proper reunion."

The parlor was modest but clean, its furnishings worn but carefully maintained. A fire crackled in the hearth. Perry leaned against a wall and Pete sat in silence. Moses remained standing, his hands gripping the back of a chair as he stared into the flames.

"They're here and very much alive, Moses. You're gonna see 'em," Pete said.

Moses nodded, his knuckles tense against the wood of the chair. "It doesn't feel real yet," he admitted. "Not until I see their faces."

Footsteps sounded in the hall, and all three men turned toward the door. Mrs. Henson entered first. Behind her, a woman stepped into the room, her face sullen.

Sally carried herself with strength. A warmth poured from her deep brown eyes. Her face showed soft lines framed by curly hair streaked with bits of silver, lending her an air of grace untouched by life's severity. Sally's face retained a natural beauty Moses had instantly loved years before. She wore a simple cotton gown, slightly worn but clean, with an apron tied at her waist.

"Sally!" Moses shouted.

Sally froze. Here eyes searched his face as if trying to reconcile the years. Then, with a cry, she ran to him, throwing her arms around his neck. "Moses!" she sobbed, her hand reaching out to caress the dimple on his face. "I thought I'd never see you again." The cadence to her words was like that of a song sung long ago, a ballad of endurance and faith.

Moses held her, his tears falling freely. "I'm here. I'm here. I've come to bring you home."

As the two embraced, a larger figure appeared in the doorway with eyes wide and uncertain.

"Michael," Moses said, his voice trembling.

The young man stood tall and broad-shouldered, the image of youthful vigor and promise. He looked like a man shaped by labor and survival. His face was strikingly familiar, echoing his older brother Gabe with a strong jawline, and high cheek bones. A dimple creased his left cheek when he smiled, a trait that immediately marked him as a Watson.

Dressed simply with a sturdy shirt tucked into work trousers held up by suspenders, Michael wore the clothes like armor, his presence filling the space around him with magnetic energy. He looked every inch a younger version of Gabe, not just in appearance but in spirit, ready to carve out his place in a world that had tried to keep him bound.

"Is that my boy?" Moses asked, knowing the answer all along. "You must have grown a good half foot. Is that really you?"

As Sally broke her embrace with Moses, Michael ran to his father, embracing his shoulders.

"Papa," he whispered.

Moses pulled Sally back into the embrace, his breath shuddering as he buried his face in his son's shoulder. The weight he had carried for years, the fear, longing and doubt, eased if only for a moment. But even as joy swelled in his chest, a void lingered at the edges.

One embrace was missing. One voice still unheard. His fingers curled into fists. Samuel was out there, somewhere, waiting. And Moses wasn't done. Not yet. The room grew quiet.

"Sally. Michael," Moses began, his scarred hands resting on his knees, "I'm here to take you home."

Michael's eyes widened, and a mixture of joy and confusion flashed across his face. Sally's breath caught in her throat, her hands tightening around the edge of her apron. "Home? Back to Gumbo Flats?"

"No. After Gabe and I lost you, old man Manchester met his demise, and John gave us our freedom. As much as it tore at our souls, we knew we couldn't risk searching for you then. The world was too dangerous and uncertain. It would have been the death of us all. We made a hard choice. We headed west, to the freedom of Kansas Territory to start over. Build a new life. Start a farm of our own. I vowed, as soon as the fightin' stopped, I'd make this journey to find you. And now, I am here to see that through."

"Kansas?" Sally asked.

"Kansas," he repeated. "That's where we've settled, Sally. With Gabe. We've built a life there, a good one, an honest one. But it was never whole, not without you and the boys."

Michael's eyes widened, hope spreading across his face. "Gabe's well? You've both been waiting. Never forgetting."

"Gabe's alive and strong. He fought for the Union. Came back stronger than ever. He's ready to reunite with his little brother. I praise God above, I've found you, and I'm here to take you home. To land that we own and to a life worth livin'."

Tears welled in Sally's eyes, her hands shaking. "Gabe," she murmured, her voice cracking. "Oh, Moses, it's been so long. I thought... "Her words faltered, her emotions too overwhelming.

Moses took her hands in his own. "I know, Sally. I know. Now's the time to mend what's been broken. We're together again."

Sally's face clouded with a shadow of sorrow. "But what about Samuel." Her voice dropped, and she glanced down. "I haven't seen him since that day we were separated at the auction. They ripped him from my side like he was nothin'. Not a word, not a whisper of where he went."

Moses nodded, his voice calm but resolute. "That's why we're not done yet. We're goin' to find Samuel."

Michael, who had been beaming with joy, looked solemn.

"You know where he is, Papa?"

Moses leaned back. "We've got a lead. A man named Jeremiah Collins. He's a cotton planter south of here. He's the one who bought Samuel. That's where we're headed next."

Sally wiped her eyes, taking a deep, shaky breath. "You've found us after all these years. Now we're gonna find Samuel too?"

"Yes. We have to. This family ain't whole without Samuel. I won't rest until we bring him home."

Hope gleamed from Sally's eyes, a spark that had been missing for far too long. She nodded, gripping Moses' hands with renewed strength. "We'll find our son."

Michael stood, his face brimming with a resolve that mirrored his father's. "I'll help, Papa. Whatever you need."

"We're in this together, my son. Every step of the way."

CHAPTER 25

Mid-January 1866

THREADS OF FORGIVENESS

MOSES SQUARED HIS SHOULDERS and locked his eyes onto Sally and Michael. He exhaled and turned his head, motioning toward the men at his side.

"Sally, Michael," he said, reaching his right arm toward Perry and Pete, "meet the ones who never let me walk alone."

Moses shifted, clearing a path as Pete and Perry stepped forward. Pete's fingers brushed the brim of his hat. Beside him, Perry stood solid in spite of his wound. He gave a deliberate nod.

"This here is Pete Fontaine,"Moses said, resting a hand on Pete's shoulder. "Don't allow his sharp tongue or his southern accent to fool you. There ain't a finer man to have in your corner. And this is Perry Adams. He's our neighbor back in Kansas. Took a bullet to his arm back in Memphis, but he's a right fine farmer and the kind of man who won't leave a soul behind, no matter how rough the trail."

Pete spoke first. "Ma'am, young man, it's a pleasure. Your Moses here has been an unstoppable force. A man on a mission. I reckon he'd have dragged us the whole way to Memphis if our wagon had given out."

"Thank you, Mr. Fontaine, for lookin' out for my husband on his way here and for bringin' him to us."

Michael stepped forward, his grip firm as he shook Pete's

hand. "You've got my gratitude, sir. You and Mr. Adams both."

Perry raised his right hand in gentle dismissal. "No need for thanks, Michael. What your father's done and what all of you have endured, it's the kind of fight that makes men better by association. Back home, one of our buddies likes to call us the Three Musketeers."

Sally moved closer to Perry, still trying to accept the new reality unfolding around her. "Mr. Adams and Mr. Fontaine, you didn't have to come on this journey. You didn't have to face the risks or the road. But you did, for my husband, for us."

She paused, searching for words to convey the depth of her feelings in words but realizing nothing she said would be enough. "A man who gives so much of himself, who walks into danger to help another; that's the kind of courage this world needs now."

"Ma'am, your Moses has a way of inspiring folks to stand with him. He makes you want to do right. And truth be told, it's been an honor to walk this path with him," Perry said. "Like I said, the Three Musketeers."

"You've done God's work, Mr. Adams, whether you see it that way or not."

Moses looked between his family and his friends. "These two men have battled by my side to keep this mission alive."

Sally reached out, touching Perry's injured arm. "The Lord works in mysterious ways."

Astonishment washed over Pete's face. Never had he considered being viewed as an instrument of the Lord's work.

"If this don't put a fire in a man's belly, I don't know what will. But, we damn sure have one more stop before turning our wagon toward home."

Mrs. Henson stood near the doorway, her hands trembling. Her own feelings about the matter dissolving in the shadow of moment. For the first time that evening, the tension in her shoulders eased, replaced by something almost tender. She took a step forward, clearing her throat.

"Sally, Michael," she began. "I've done my best to look after you both. I hope you know that."

"We know, ma'am," Sally said. "You've been kind, even when the times weren't."

Mrs. Henson's lip quivered, but she steadied herself, her eyes lingering on Michael a second too long.

"Kindness doesn't erase the wrongs that brought us to this moment. I want you to know, I never considered you as anything less than the decent people you are. It's not my place to ask, but if you can, find room in your hearts to forgive me. Exonerate me for the ways I've failed you, for the liberties I expected and for the things I couldn't change."

Michael stepped forward. "Mrs. Henson, you will be missed, but this is our time to go home."

She nodded, swallowing hard. Her fingers fidgeted at her sides as though resisting the urge to reach for Michael. "I know. I see that now. I'll help you gather your things. Whatever you need." A breath caught in her throat as she met his eyes "You deserve this, all of it. A fresh start, a place with your family."

And yet, for the briefest moment, a tense moment hung between them unspoken. It was a whisper of what might have been if the time and the world had been different.

Mrs. Henson nodded, her eyes still settled on Michael with an intensity that didn't go unnoticed. She opened her mouth as if to say more, then pressed her lips together, hesitant.

Michael met her gaze, an unreadable glance behind his calm exterior. For a moment, the room held its breath. Then he reached out, a slow, deliberate movement crossing the line of taboo as he took her hand in his. "You were good to us, Mrs. Henson," he said, his voice almost intimate. "I won't forget that or anything else."

Sally's eyes brushed between them, then a knowing glance between her and Moses. Pete's eyes widened, shifting his weight as if he'd just caught the tail end of a tender drama.

Mrs. Henson exhaled, a flush creeping up her neck. She squeezed Michael's hand a second longer than necessary before pulling away.

"Take care of yourself," she whispered.

Michael dipped his head in farewell, then turned toward the waiting path. Behind him, Mrs. Henson's fingers tightened around the fabric of her skirt. Sally caught the way her eyes paused unblinking as Michael walked away.

Sally reached out, touching Mrs. Henson's hand. "We've survived, ma'am, and that's no small part thanks to you. We'll miss you and your home. I'll keep a place for forgiveness, like you've asked. But now it's time for us to go where we truly belong."

Mrs. Henson smiled weakly, her tears threatening to spill over. "You've both been part of this home, this farm, and me, in ways I never expected. I'll pray for your journey, and I'll pray for peace in your hearts."

Moses stepped forward then, his voice steady. "Mrs. Henson, your words mean a great deal. This ain't an easy goodbye, but it's a necessary one. Thank you for what you've done."

Mrs. Henson glanced at Sally before again turning to Michael. "Go, then. Find your freedom, your family, your future. May it be brighter than anything you've ever known here."

She turned away, dabbing at her eyes with a handkerchief, then looked back with a small but genuine smile. "You should go to the worker cabin and gather your things. There's no time to waste."

Sensing the need to redirect the scene, Pete jumped in. "Right you are, Mrs. Henson," he said, tipping his hat. "Perry and I'll see to the wagon while the Watson family gathers what belongings they have. It's only right they do that in private."

"I best get to it," Sally said. The eagerness in her steps betrayed her mixed emotions as she skipped toward the cabin, Moses and Michael close behind. She paused at the doorway, her hand brushing the worn wood as though coaxing it to forget the years of burden she had spent on Tennessee soil.

Sally moved inside the weathered doorway. The cabin was stark, its modest furnishings testifying to years of survival rather than comfort. One wheat straw bed rested against the left wall, alongside a small table with a single chair. A similar bed brushed against the wall on the right.

A wood-burning stove took half the space along the back wall. Sparse shelves above the primitive beds carried the meager sum of Sally's and Michael's belongings. It wasn't much, but it was theirs.

Michael ducked inside next, his broad shoulders brushing the doorframe. "We've got a lot to gather, but it won't take long," he said.

Sally nodded, her eyes sweeping the room and lingering on the little details: the patched quilt she'd mended so many times, the tin cups stacked on the shelf, the Bible she kept near her bed. Each item held a story, a memory of the life they'd encountered, a life of waiting, hoping for this moment.

Moses followed, his presence steadying every item and emotion in the room. He scanned the space, taking in the signs of the years Sally and Michael had survived without him. "Let's pack it all up. Every piece of it. What's yours, we're takin' with us."

Sally moved to the shelf and lifted the quilt, folding it with practiced hands. "This place..." she said, her voice trailing off. "It's been a holdin' ground. A place to survive, not to live. But now, finally, we have our true liberation."

Michael crouched by his bed and reached into the loose straw, pulling out a small wooden box. Inside were a handful of trinkets: a carved figure he'd whittled as a teenager and a well-worn harmonica. The wooden figure, resembling a soldier with rifle at the ready, was intended to be a gift for Samuel should they be reunited. He ran his fingers over the items with a bittersweet smile.

"Been a long time since I thought about what we could carry with us," he said, looking up at his parents. "Feels good to put that thought into action."

Michael picked up the harmonica and blew a series of notes—the first bars recognizable as being from a spiritual hymn called Swing Low, Sweet Chariot.

"Been working on this for a while," he paused. "Note-by-note. Now, I hope to have it all put in place by the time we reach Kansas." Michael played the same section again.

After hearing the song's familiar opening notes, Moses closed his eyes. The music stirred a twinge in his chest, the same kind of ache that comes from hope and sorrow intertwined.

"That's a fine sound, son. A sound of journeys and promises. Your mama and I used to sing that song under the stars back in Gumbo Flats, back when we thought freedom was just a dream. Now here you are, playin' it, and I reckon freedom's more than a wishful thought. It's our reality. You keep playin' that song along our path, and I'll take it as a sign we're gonna see Samuel sooner than we think."

Moses straightened, his glance far off but resolute. "Swing Low, Sweet Chariot," he said, almost to himself. "I reckon it's comin' for us all before long, but before it arrives, we have a lot of memories to make."

He stepped forward, placing a hand on Michael's shoulder. "Take with you every item you will need for the trip, but also those items that stir a memory, good or bad. Take every item that strengthens your soul and body. It's who you have been here and now it's comin' with us," Moses paused with a gentle smile. "But son, I'm afraid you're going to have to leave Mrs. Henson behind."

Michael stiffened beneath his father's hand. For a moment, he didn't breathe. He looked at Moses, searching for a reply. A slow heat crept up Michael's neck, knowing that his father could clearly see the situation that had been. "I know."

Moses gave his shoulder a reassuring squeeze before stepping back. "Good," he said. "Then let's go home."

On the other side of the cabin, Sally worked quickly, placing her items into neat piles. She picked up her Bible last, pausing as she held it close to her chest. "This has been my strength," she said. "When everything else seemed lost, it kept me goin'."

Moses nodded, pulling a length of hemp twine from his pocket. "Then we'll keep it with us. Always. It's part of our family story now."

As Sally and Michael continued sorting their possessions, Moses tied each bundle. The twine was tight and bit into his palms, but he welcomed the feeling. It grounded him, reminding him he was alive to see this reunion. Each knot represented one step closer to claiming their future as a family.

Outside, Perry leaned against the wagon wheel, scanning the horizon. "They may not have a lot of things they call their own, but they've got a lot of years to pack up in there." he said. "Glad we've got a little time."

Pete adjusted his hat. "Moses ain't gonna leave a stitch behind. Not now, not ever."

Back in the cabin, the three family members stood over the small piles they'd made. The room, now almost bare, was larger due to the absence of the things they would take on the road to their new home.

Sally let out a long breath, her hand brushing over one of the bundles. She turned to Moses. "It's strange, leavin' this place after all these years. I thought I'd feel relief, but mostly it's like I'm sayin' goodbye to a lost version of myself."

Moses stepped closer, wrapping an arm around her shoulders. "That version of you, it kept Michael safe."

Michael slung his bundle over his shoulder. "Ready when you are, Papa."

Moses smiled, hefting the parcels in one load. Never again did he want to set foot inside a building that had been used as slave quarters. "Let's load this up and move on."

They stepped outside and the cabin stood empty behind them, its purpose fulfilled. The sky above was wide and open, and the future waited, unknown but promising.

Moses and Michael carried the parcels to the back of the wagon. The twine bit into Moses' fingers again as he lifted the bundles into the back of the wagon. With each motion, he held each parcel close to his chest, as if shielding them from the meager surroundings they'd left behind. He nestled each one among the supply barrels and bedrolls to ensure they wouldn't shift.

"These might be the sum of what you have now," Moses said, "but trust me, once we get to Kansas, you'll have all the comforts life can offer. I'll see to that." It was like a promise forged in fire, each syllable another proof point to his unyielding determination.

Perry approached Moses. "You want to drive the Conestoga this stretch? Sally by your side? I think my arm's fine for me to take to the saddle."

Moses nodded, his eyes softening as he turned to Sally. "I'd like that. Been too long since we sat side by side like we should."

"The reins are yours. I'll ride alongside on Appy, and Michael can take your horse." Perry said. "That young man looks like he's got every reason to leave this place in the dust, and maybe one reason to look back."

Michael's grin broadened at the prospect of riding out on horseback. He climbed into the saddle like he had done it a thousand times. He shifted his weight and adjusted the reins. He straightened his back and broadened his shoulders, but as he turned in the saddle, his gaze drifted back to the porch. To her.

Mrs. Henson stood there, half-shadowed by the fading light, her hands clasped tight in front of her.

Michael's chest tightened, but he forced a breath. "I can't believe it," he said, though his voice carried an emotion deeper than mere excitement. "Leavin' this place for good feels like wakin' up from a dream."

Michael snapped the bridle to urge his horse forward, and as he looked down the trail, he welcomed the thought that even some pleasant dreams are better forgotten.

As the wagon rolled forward, on the porch, Mrs. Henson stood in silence. At first, her face was carved with sadness, but as the wagon passed through the gate, her expression shifted. She raised her hand high, waving vigorously.

"Go on, now!" she called. "Find the full measure of freedom waiting for you!" Her words carried an unexpected joy, a farewell that felt like a blessing.

Moses tipped his hat high into the air. Sally turned and waved goodbye. The plantation house and Mrs. Henson slowly faded into the distance.

Miles rolled by as the travelers headed south. Hernando, Mississippi, the last known location of Samuel, waited a day's ride ahead. As night fell, they found a small clearing near the road and set up camp.

Moses helped Sally and Michael settle in, unrolling blankets and ensuring their spot near the fire was warm and comfortable. Though it was the middle of January, a Dixie gulf breeze carried the promise of a milder night.

Michael leaned back, his eyes scanning the darkened sky. "I've been a free man for more than half a year, but I can breathe a little deeper out here."

He pulled out his old harmonica and blew notes about halfway through Swing Low, Sweet Chariot.

"Breathing deep is how freedom feels," Moses said. "And that song is its anthem. One puff at a time. Son, that is what you are delivering to all of us with that melody, a taste of hope that's been too long coming."

Pete listened, eyes reflecting the flicker of the campfire. He nodded. "Freedom's a lot like a song you play out under the open sky. It takes nerve, and heart, and the will to keep goin' even when your breath is short. But when it catches, it fills every nook and suddenly life doesn't feel so empty."

Perry grinned, resting his injured arm against Archibald and stretching his boots out toward the fire's warmth. "If that's so, we're tunin' up the best kind of tomorrow a soul could ask for."

They fell silent, the harmonica's notes floating up to the stars, each person lost in the music and the promise threaded through the darkness.

The fire's glow held back the mild Gulf breeze and prepared them for the next day's journey.

Moses stood and gazed toward the horizon. "Tomorrow, we ride with added purpose. Hernando's just another stop, but Samuel's the reason we keep movin'."

Sally, sitting beside Michael, looked up at Moses, her eyes shimmering. "We've waited long enough. We'll find him, Moses."

Moses threw on the night's final log. The fire crackled, sending a wave of sparks into the night sky. "Let's rest. Tomorrow, we close the distance between what was and what's intended."

He and Sally cuddled in blankets near the side of the wagon, thinking of the years they had missed together as well as the years to come.

CHAPTER 26

Mid-January 1866

FREEDOM'S FOOTSTEPS

MORNING UNFOLDED IN MUTED shades of gray, the last wisps of fog hugging the earth. The air carried a lingering dampness. Moses sat nearby, folding the map that had been their guide for much of the journey. His eyes lingered on Hernando, the name circled in pencil.

Sally and Michael packed their bedrolls near the wagon. The group ate a quickly prepared breakfast of biscuits and bacon around the morning fire. Talk shifted to the trail ahead.

"Hernando," Moses said. "The map says it's about five miles past the town to the Collins place. If the directions hold, we'll travel a road and then follow the tree line along a creek bed."

Sally looked at Moses, worry etched deep in her eyes. "What if Samuel isn't the same boy I remember? After all he's seen, all that time apart—what if he's changed?"

Michael squeezed her hand. Moses' eyes softened, and he placed his hand over hers. "He may have changed, Sally, but the bond between mother and son runs deeper than time or distance. Whatever he's faced, your love is the anchor he'll know when he sees you. That's a promise."

Pete, always quick with a wry remark, leaned back and looked out at the morning mist. "Strange how the road ahead can feel heavier the closer you get to what you've been lookin' for. And if Collins isn't willing to deal with us, we'll stack the deck against him. I'm always able to cut straight to some Southern convincin'," Pete said, making a fist.

Perry stood, brushing dust from his coat and glancing at the horizon. "If Collins wants trouble, he'll find we've got more backbone than most. And I know that a certain Missouri bartender doesn't have the ace of spades, the death card, tattooed on his arm for no reason. And you won't be going it alone, Pete. My arm's feeling a helluva lot better today. This bandage is coming off."

The group readied the wagon in silence, each movement carrying determination for what the next leg of the journey might bring. Pete hitched the horses. Moses saddled his horse and checked the bridle.

"Perry, if your arm's still feeling good, I'd like to take the wagon seat again today? It's really enjoyable to have Sally by my side."

"Not a problem, Moses. I think Appy enjoys having me back in the saddle."

Michael swung himself into the saddle of Moses' horse. Archy trudged around the camp, sniffing the ground and barking at a pair of quail flushed from the underbrush.

As they set out, the surrounding land shifted. Dormant cotton fields, some unpicked, and the rolling terrain of northern Mississippi came into view. The scars of the war lingered in abandoned homesteads, charred beams standing where homes once were, and overgrown paths that spoke of lives uprooted and fields abandoned.

The town of Hernando appeared on the horizon. The town, smaller and quieter than Memphis, carried its own kind of burden. It was a place caught between the old ways and an uncertain future. People moved along the streets, some leading mules laden with supplies, others sitting in the shade of storefronts, their faces etched with loss and the hard reality of Reconstruction.

From the wagon seat with Sally by his side, Moses fixed his gaze on the people of Hernando. "This land's seen a lot of sweat and blood. A lot of the winners have gone home. All that's left is losers. Rabbles who choose to hang on tend to seed anger and plot retribution."

The wagon rattled over packed dirt, trailing dust as it rolled through Hernando's quiet heart. Long shadows fell across worn storefronts, their faded signs nearly lost to time. Eyes tracked the travelers. Some were curious and some wary. Two children peeked from behind a water barrel, then dashed off, laughter slicing through the hush.

The wrinkled hands of older townsfolk rested on porch railings, their eyes shadowed beneath straw hats. Some leaned against porch posts, arms crossed. A rocking chair squeaked, its occupant unmoving, gaze locked on the passing wagon. White faces, black faces, all watching, measuring. The only sound was the slow churn of wagon wheels.

Trotting beside the wagon, Archy's ears flicked forward, his nose twitching. The sent was rich, meaty, irresistible. His muscles tensed, then, in a flash, he bolted toward a small butcher's stall outside the general store.

Behind the counter, a butcher with forearms like hams brought his cleaver down hard, splitting a slab of pork in a wet smack.

Archy was a blur.

"Archy! No!" Moses roared, but the dog was already airborne, jaws snapping around a ham hock before tearing off toward the wagon.

The butcher spun, cleaver flashing. His face darkened.

"That filthy mutt just swiped my best cut!"

He stormed after Archy, cleaver raised high, shouting, "Get that beast on a chain or I'll carve him up like a pork roast!"

Pete, quick on his feet, slid off his horse and approached the butcher with a disarming grin, hands raised. "Now, hold on there, friend. Let's not get carried away. That dog don't know better. He's got the manners of a squirrel. I'll make it right."

The butcher scowled, his thick mustache twitching with irritation. "Make it right? That hock was worth two dollars! You think I run a charity here?"

Pete nodded. "You're absolutely right," he said in his deepest Southern accent. "A man's work ought to be paid for, especially work as fine as this. That's some of the best pork I've seen since I left Arkansas.

I think old Archy was payin' you a compliment, sir. I'd pay a ransom for the chance to take a few bites myself, but you and I both know the value of a ham hock ain't two bucks."

Reaching into his front pocket, Pete pulled out a single silver dollar and flipped it into the air.

The butcher hesitated, his grip on the cleaver loosening as he snatched the coin in midflight with his other hand. "Well, it is good meat."

"I'm sure it is. In fact, it's a work of art, but it's not the Mona Lisa. Take the silver dollar and count yourself lucky. If you feel froggy and try to raise that cleaver again, you'll find out just how fast things can turn ugly."

The butcher's jaw tightened, but he stepped back. "If I see that dog near my stall again, there'll be hell to pay."

Pete held his gaze. "Try it and you'll find out who pays. We're done here."

Pete tipped his hat in a form of defiance and turned. He called Archibald with a sharp whistle and moved on without another word.

Archy slinked back to the wagon, gnawing at the pilfered ham hock with a look of pure satisfaction. Perry dismounted, grabbing the hock from the dog's jaws and tossed it into the back of the wagon.

"Archy, you're a wild mess," Perry muttered, glaring at the dog, who tilted his head as if he'd done nothing wrong.

Moses, visibly tense, shook his head. "We've got enough eyes on us as it is, gentlemen. Let's go before that butcher changes his mind and comes at us with his cleaver."

Pete hopped back onto his horse, his grin intact. "You worry too much, Moses. That butcher's an asshole and all bluster."

The group moved on, and more townsfolk stared after them, whispering among themselves. Tension hung in the air, but no one made a move to stop them.

Once they were clear of the street, Michael rode up to Moses. "Papa, that dog's gonna get us all in trouble one day."

Moses glanced at Archibald, who was now trotting alongside the wagon, tail wagging as if nothing had happened. "That dog's part of the plan. He's done his share on this trip. Don't judge him on the basis of one wild dash of hunger."

Moses continued, "Hey Perry, we better start feeding that dog a little extra. You know, something to keep him fat, happy, and satisfied."

"Well," Perry said dryly, "if we come through Hernando again, I think we should secure old Archy in the wagon."

"Or maybe we teach him to pay for his meals in advance," Pete said.

The group wasted no time pushing through the outskirts of Hernando. Archibald, unbothered by the chaos he'd caused, bounded ahead, his ears flapping in the breeze. The friends shared a collective sense of relief as the town faded behind them, their focus returning to the road.

Beyond Hernando, the land opened up again, the road winding past fields of cotton, many left unpicked. The Collins plantation was a mile ahead, marked by a weathered sign nailed to a fence post. The long road leading to the house was lined with oaks draped in Spanish moss. Moses' grip tightened on the reins as the wagon turned onto the path.

As they approached, the house came into view. It was a sprawling structure of whitewashed wood, its edges softened by age and neglect. Slave quarters, now abandoned and crumbling, stood in a cluster near the fields

Sally's voice broke the quiet, trembling with emotion. "This is it? This is where they brought Samuel? It's in such disrepair. I sure hope Samuel didn't experience the same neglect."

Moses brought the wagon to a halt near the house. He glanced at Perry, his expression solemn. "You ready for this?"

Perry nodded and patted his arm with a sense of confidence. "How about you, Moses?"

"Been ready since the day the old man sent him away."

Pete dismounted, handing his reins to Perry. "Let me do the talkin' first. These folks might not take kindly to a group like ours showin' up unannounced."

Moses looked at Pete, his eyes firm. "I ain't hidin' from this, Pete. Not now. Not ever."

Pete gave a small smile. "Didn't figure you for the hidin' type, Moses. But sometimes, a little diplomacy, or should I say Southern statesmanship, goes a long way."

Pete walked to the front door, while the others waited, holding their collective breath in anticipation. The heavy oak door was an imposing piece of craftsmanship, weathered but still commanding. A grand arch crowned the doorway, with a fan-shaped transom of etched glass that scattered faint patterns onto the porch below. Pete put his boot right in the middle of the fine reflection.

He pulled back the tarnished brass knocker and let it fly.

The journey to the Collins Plantation had been challenging, thanks to Archibald, but the moment of truth was now within reach. Whatever lay beyond that door—answers, resistance, or even hope—the rescuers were ready to face it.

After Pete's third knock, plantation owner Jeremiah Collins himself swung open the door with noted aggravation. His hulking frame filled the doorway like a barricade. His scowl was as weathered as the house's fading paint, his eyes narrow and suspicious under the shadow of a broad-brimmed hat. He leaned against the doorframe, arms crossed, a hunting rifle propped against the wall within reach.

"Well?" he barked, his voice rough as gravel as he scanned the horses and wagon in his front yard. "What business do you and this ragtag mob of misfits have on my property?"

Pete stepped forward, tipping his hat with a deliberate, practiced courtesy. "Mornin', sir. My name's Pete Fontaine. I mean no harm. Just lookin' for someone. Young man named Samuel Watson. We've reason to believe he might've passed through here."

Collins snorted and sneered. "Sam Watson? Not only did he pass through here, but for about six years he was the best field slave I had. Not anymore. He's gone. Hell, if you find him, you be sure to let me know."

"Seems we're getting off on the wrong foot here, sir."

"Well, that boy owes me about six months' worth of room and board. After the Yankees gave him his so-called freedom, he stayed in one of my cabins, eating my food, taking up my resources, and not payin' me a damn cent. Barely doin' a lick of work."

Overhearing the conversation, Moses stiffened in the wagon seat. Pete raised a calming hand.

"We're not here to cause trouble, Mr. Collins. Just hopin' for some information."

Collins ignored the attempt to cool his temper. "Information, huh? Here's some for you: that boy was trouble. He disappeared in the dead of night a week before Christmas and took off with one of my best saddle mares. He's the reason a large share of my cotton's rottin' in the fields unpicked, spoilin' in the boll."

Collins jabbed a finger in Pete's direction. "You seem like an upstanding Southern man, but how about those people," he said pointing a finger toward Moses and Sally. "They related to him? 'Cause if they are, I ought to hold them liable for his expenses. Damn thief in the night, takin' what didn't belong to him."

Pete's shoulders straightened, his face darkening. "Hold us liable?" His tone sharpened, each word delivered with a snap. "Now you listen here, Mr. Collins. We've got no legal obligation to you or your so-called debts. What Samuel did or didn't do ain't our concern. We're lookin' for a son and a brother, not signin' up to pay for your inferior cotton crop or anything else."

Collins bristled, his voice rising with indignation, eyeing his hunting rifle. "That bastard was the best field hand a man could ask for, long as I could keep him under control. After the war, it all went to hell. He got too big for his britches, thought freedom meant freeloadin'. His work ethic went to dust, and he became a liability. Don't think for a second I don't want my horse back or fair restitution for what that boy cost me."

Pete leaned closer. "Funny how you're real quick to call him a thief but nothin' about how you were livin' off his back before freedom was forced through your door."

Collins growled and for a moment, the tension in the air was so thick it felt like the faintest spark might set it ablaze. Pete shifted, his hand resting on his gun holster as he prepared for the worst. Moses' eyes burned with unspoken fury, his fists gripping the reins until his knuckles turned red.

Pete didn't flinch. "Now, if you've got anything useful to say about Samuel's whereabouts, we'd like to hear it. But if all you've got is barkin' and complainin', then we'll leave you to stew in the stubble of your rottin' cotton field."

Collins looked them over, his sneer deepening, but finally he stepped back. "I ain't seen him since he vanished. Guessing he was headed for the territories. If you find him, tell him I want my mare back and my damned money."

Pete backed away from the doorway, his focus on Collins. Backpedaling, he muttered loud enough for everyone to hear, "That man's got about as much grace as a rabid dog, and about half the sense."

Collins's sneer twisted into something darker, more malevolent, as Pete's words hit their mark. Without a word, Collins thrust his hand toward the rifle against the doorframe. He grabbed it and raised the barrel. The action was so sudden it made the horses snort.

Pete swung back around, his own hand instinctively going for the pistol at his hip. "You don't want to do this, Collins," Pete said as he raised his pistol.

Collins didn't answer. With wild eyes filled with fury, he leveled the rifle and fired a shot in Pete's direction. The bullet shot past Pete's left temple, grazing him enough to start a flow of blood. Pete didn't hesitate to squeeze his pistol's trigger. The crack of the shot split the wind, the echo vibrating through the trees.

Collins staggered back, a look of disbelief flashing across his face as the rifle fell from his hands. He clutched his chest, blood spreading across his shirt in a dark, widening stain. With a groan, he collapsed, hitting the floorboards of the porch with a heavy thud.

The world went quiet for a moment. Even the birds and wind paused in shock. Then the sound of hurried footsteps burst forth from inside the house. A small boy, not more than eight years old, rushed to the doorway, his blond hair sticking to his face.

"Daddy!" the boy cried, dropping to his knees beside Collins's prone body. "Daddy, wake up!" He shook the man's arm, his small hands smeared with his father's blood as he sobbed.

Pete, his pistol still in hand but lowered and bleeding from the wound to his head, crouched a few feet away, his face grim.

"Son," he said, in a voice carrying the tragedy of the moment, "it was self-defense. Your papa desired to take my life, and I couldn't let that happen."

The boy's tearful eyes snapped up to meet Pete's. "What did you do, mister? What did you do to my daddy?" His voice was a high-pitched wail, full of heartbreak and confusion.

Moses and Perry ran to the porch, seeing Pete's blood drip to the porch, their boots crunching against the road.

"Damn, are you OK, Pete? Looks like a graze wound," Perry's voice was tight, but his eyes flicked to the boy, and his initial anger melted into a softer but heavier tone.

He looked at Pete, then at Collins's lifeless body, then at the boy clinging to what was lost. Perry took a breath and stepped closer, lowering himself to the boy's level, searching for words.

"Listen to me, son. Your daddy made a choice, and it wasn't the right one. We all saw it. Pete didn't have a choice."

The boy turned back to his father, clutching his hand as Jeremiah's head lolled to the side. The man's eyes fluttered open, and he let out a rattling breath. "Jakey," he rasped, his voice faint. "Take care of your mother. I'm sorry...I couldn't..." With that, his chest fell still, and the boy let out a heart-wrenching cry, burying his face against his father's arm.

CHAPTER 27

Mid-January 1866

LOSS AND REDEMPTION

THE ACRID SCENT OF GUNPOWDER clung to the house like a burial shroud. Jeremiah Collins lay lifeless on the porch, his blood soaking into the cracks of the weathered wood as if the house itself were drinking in the life of the man who had ordered its construction.

Pete exhaled slowly. He holstered his pistol as his own blood continued to drip on the porch. His face was hard. Only after he glanced toward Jakey did his face soften with a hint of regret. "I didn't want it to end this way," he murmured, the words meant for the boy, but maybe even more for himself.

Moses stepped forward. He placed a hand on Pete's shoulder and wiped Pete's blood with a bandana. "You did what you had to. No more, no less. The man gave you no option."

Dirt and tears streaked Jakey's face. "He wasn't always mean," the boy choked out, his eyes fixed on his father's body. The boy's lips quivered, but no sound came. With a choking sob, he blurted, "He was mad all the time since comin' home. Everything changed."

Pete crouched down, bandana pressed to his temple, meeting Jakey's shocked stare. "War does terrible things to a man, son. That doesn't make what he did today right. I'm sorry you had to see this. Truly, I am."

The boy sniffled, wiping his nose with the sleeve of his too-large shirt. His eyes shifted to Pete seeking some assurance that this nightmare could somehow be undone.

The sound of more footsteps brought everyone's attention back to the doorway. A woman appeared, her face pale and cheeks hollow. Her hair tied under a kerchief. Her movements were hurried as her eyes darted between the scene on the porch and her son.

"Oh, no, no, no. Jeremiah!" she cried. She ran to Jakey, pulling him in, holding him close as though shielding him from the world.

She glared at Pete and the others, her voice shaking with anger and grief. "What did you do to my Jeremiah?"

Perry lifted his hands, his tone calm and measured. "Ma'am, your husband raised a gun and fired first. Came within a whisker of killing Pete here. Pete shot second. It was self-defense. Pete had no choice. We're all witnesses."

The woman's face crumpled, her arms tightening around the boy as her tears flowed. She glanced down at the lifeless body of her husband, her lips trembling as she tried to form words. "Jeremiah, he wasn't always like this."

Her voice cracked, and she ran a shaky hand over Jakey's hair, as though steadying herself in his presence. "He used to laugh, you know? Had a chuckle that could fill this house. He'd sing to Jakey here, songs he made up, silly songs that didn't even rhyme, just to make us smile. He worked so hard. Lord, how he toiled. This place was his life. We were his life. He would do anything for this farm, for us."

"Jeremiah was a dependable man," she continued, the words catching in her throat. She drew a shaky breath, her gaze shifting to Pete, grief carved deep into her features. "Before, Jeremiah was kind once. That was before the Northern invasion and everything fell apart."

The visitors stood silent, allowing the woman to express her grief. She pulled in another ragged breath. "The war broke him. Took the man I married and changed him into a stranger. He came home infuriated at the Union, at the Confederacy, at the whole damn world. It never left him. He couldn't let it go."

Her voice cracked. "I tried to reach him. I did. I held on, thinkin' the man I loved would come back to me. He got meaner. Mean to the neighbors, mean to me, mean to our former slaves, and eventually, cruel to his own son. I started to fear him more than I loved him."

She looked down at the boy clinging to her. "But this little one still loved his daddy. Even when Jeremiah's temper flared, Jakey here tried to see the positive side of him, tried to make him smile again."

"Ma'am, I'm sorry," Pete said, tying the bloody bandana around his head. "I don't take this lightly. He left me no choice. If he'd pulled that trigger with a touch more accuracy, I wouldn't be here."

The boy clung tighter to his mother, his face buried against her chest. "Mama, why couldn't Daddy ever be like he was before?" he sobbed.

She kissed the top of his head, her tears falling into his hair. "I don't know, baby. I don't know."

Moses, standing a few feet away, exhaled a long breath. He stepped forward. "Ma'am, I'm sorry for your loss, but your boy's got a chance to grow into the kind of man his daddy once was. A better man. Teach him to let go of what breaks him and hold on to what makes him strong."

The woman met Moses' gaze, a hint of strength returning. "I'll do my best. Sir, you look strangely familiar. You remind me of Sam. Are you kin to him?"

"Yes, ma'am. He's my son. Ripped away from me years ago. That's when your Jeremiah purchased him up in Memphis."

"Sam was always a solid young man, with the exception of stealing our mare,"

Pete squared his shoulders and looked into the woman's eyes. "Ma'am, I'd say that horse was likely past due payment. I don't figure Samuel owed Jeremiah anything. Freedom doesn't come with a debt."

"Samuel was a good boy when I lost him," Moses said. "I suspect Mr. Collins threw more at him than any young man should bear."

Moses paused, his eyes shifting to the boy clutching his mother's dress, then back to the woman. "I don't know what Sam endured here, ma'am, or what drove him to run, but I do know Sam was born into a world that didn't give him much choice. Everything he did—leaving, takin' your mare—was for survival. It wasn't right, but it was necessary."

The woman nodded. "I suppose I can understand that. Life hasn't always been kind to folks like you. This place has seen its fair share of calamity too."

Moses leaned forward. "I don't excuse what Sam did, ma'am, but he didn't steal his freedom. That was his birthright. Same as yours, mine, and this boy's here." He gestured to Jakey. "I still hope to find Sam. To bring him home. To give him a place where he doesn't have to run no more."

The woman's eyes glistened with tears as she glanced again at her husband's body, a sudden realization settling over her. She exhaled, wiping a tear from her cheek as she stared down at her young son.

"I'm not sure where to begin. Without Jeremiah. Without his hand on this farm. Without any help to plan a funeral. I doubt anyone would come. Jeremiah wasn't a kind man, but he was my husband. And he was this boy's father."

Jakey clung tighter to her skirt. "Mama, what's gonna happen to us?"

She knelt beside Jakey, pulling him into her arms. "We'll be all right, sweetheart," she whispered. "We'll figure it out. God'll provide a way, just like He always does."

Straightening, she looked back at Moses, resolute through her tears. "There's work to do. I'll need to bury him proper, see to the farm, and find a way to keep food on the table." Her eyes softened as they met his. "I won't let his hate pass down to this boy. That much I promise you."

"You're stronger than you think, ma'am. You've got the will to make it. I can see that clear as day."

The woman shook her head and looked once more at Jakey, brushing his hair back tenderly. "We'll manage. Somehow, we'll make it."

Perry stepped forward. "Ma'am, we'll leave you to make your arrangements. But if you've got any information about Samuel, any idea where he might've gone, it would mean the world to this man here."

"I don't know much. He left about a month ago, mid-December, under the cover of night. Took the mare and disappeared. Jeremiah figured he'd head west to the new states or the western territories. Said he probably wouldn't have the nerve to stay in the South."

With a final nod of understanding between them, the group turned back toward their wagon and horses. She called out, "Wait. There is something."

She disappeared inside the house, returning moments later with a small leather pouch. "He left this behind," she said, handing it to Moses. "I didn't know what to do with it, but maybe you will."

Moses opened the pouch, finding a rolled-up scroll of paper with a crude hand-drawn map. It looked like a roughly sketched outline of Missouri, with Kansas attached to the west. An uneven line was drawn up the eastern part of the state toward Gumbo Flats before disappearing into a trail of diminished ink. At the top of the paper the word "Hope" was scrawled. Moses' throat tightened as he traced the letters with his thumb.

"Thank you," he said. "And, Miss Collins, don't take this as an insult, but I want you to have this."

Moses reached into his pocket for a $20 double eagle coin. He placed it in her hand.

"It might not pay for your mare, but I hope it helps in some way."

The plantation visitors returned to their horses and wagon, but they lingered in the home's front lawn, the drama of the encounter pressing down on them.

For a moment, Pete remained behind, before walking to Moses' side. Pete's face was pale and his movements slow. He reached into his pocket for the wedding-petal locket Lucy had given him as a charm for the trip. He held the locket tightly in the palm of his hand suspecting it had somehow made the shot from Jeremiah's rifle veer slightly to the left.

"Moses, I'm not sure I'll ever shake this one. Even if it was justified.

I don't know if I will ever forget the look on Jakey's face. The terror in his eyes. It's a day he's never goin' to forget. I changed his life forever."

"It ain't easy, Pete. It shouldn't be, but you acted in self-defense. That's what matters."

Perry approached and clapped a hand on Pete's shoulder. "You're an honorable man, Pete. Don't let this moment make you doubt that. Now, let's stop that bleeding. It's my turn to do a little patchwork, my friend."

While Perry placed a fresh bandage around Pete's head, Moses studied the map drawn by Samuel. He tucked it into the saddle pouch that held his bag of lucky Gumbo Flats soybeans and some remaining gold coins. He climbed back into the wagon seat next to Sally. "Samuel's out there, and I mean to find him."

Perry tied Pete's bandage, looked at his friend and cleared his throat. "Moses, we've done all we can here. A full month is a long time for a man on the run. Sam's got a huge head start on us. There's no way to trace his steps from here."

Moses turned to Pete and Perry, his shoulders squared with determination. His eyes scanned the nearby fields and the horizon beyond as though Samuel might appear out of thin air. Moses shook his head. "But the map. You saw it. It has to mean something. I ain't givin' up on my boy. There's always a trail."

The silence between the three men was intense. Pete exchanged a glance with Perry, whose face mirrored the gravity of the moment.

"Moses," Pete interjected, stepping to his side. "We've followed every lead we had, combed through every piece of information. But a full month on the run, on horseback? That's like us chasin' smoke. We can't track Sam without more to go on."

"You think I don't know that? I get it, but he's my son. My blood. I can't leave him out there, not knowin' where he is."

"I understand, Moses. Believe me, I do. We've reached the end of this trail. We can't keep wanderin' aimless, hopin' for a miracle. The best thing we can do now is get you back to Kansas, regroup, and keep our ears open for news."

Moses looked between the two men, his face a mix of defiance and desperation. "No. Not good enough. Not for my boy."

Michael, riding just behind them, urged his horse forward. "Papa, listen to them. We've come so far, but we can't do this blind."

Michael's words hit Moses like a body blow from a sledgehammer. Michael's voice was as skeptical as Gabe's had been when the rescue plan was initially discussed. Moses turned sharply to his son, but Michael met his gaze without flinching. Moses opened his mouth to argue but found no logical reply. His hands closed into fists at his sides before relaxing again. His shoulders sagged as the truth sunk in.

"I know it's hard, Papa. It kills me too, thinkin' about Sam out there, making his way alone. Mr. Pete and Mr. Perry are right. If we keep chasin' shadows, we might not make it back ourselves."

Perry moved closer to Moses. "You've done more than most men ever could, Moses. This mission is far from over, but it's time to head back. Kansas is your cornerstone, the place where you've started to build somethin' strong. From there, we can keep lookin', keep hopin'. You've got to make it back to keep fightin'. There's no shame in takin' a step back, Moses. Sometimes that's how you find the next trail."

Moses closed his eyes for a moment, drawing in a long breath before exhaling. When he opened them, a flicker of sorrowful acceptance flashed from his face. "All right, we'll head back."

Michael nodded, a small smile of relief crossing his face. "None of us are giving up, Papa. We'll find him. Together."

"I just wanted to bring him home. I've planned his rescue for years, and now I feel like I've failed him."

"No, Papa," Michael said, stepping closer and gripping his father's arm. "You ain't failed him. You came all this way. You fought for us, for Ma and me, and now you'll fight for him too. I'll help, but we have to fight smart, not desperate."

Moses nodded, his throat tight with emotion.

The word "Hope," scrawled on Samuel's map, lingered as a beacon for the journey ahead. "All right. We'll head back."

The group fell into a heavy silence, Mrs. Collins and Jakey still kneeling in the shadow of the doorway, their lives irrevocably changed.

Perry broke the silence, "We've got a long road ahead, but let's be intentional about taking a safe path. I think the best route might be to head west into central Arkansas and then diagonally north through Missouri with a straight path back to St. Joe."

"Agreed, Perry," Pete said. "I think that'd be much safer, and if we can cut some corners, instead of heading to St. Louis and then west, it should make our path shorter in both distance and days. I have to admit, I'd like to revisit St. Louis on the return, but I would much rather take a path that takes us through my native Arkansas. It'll be like a little homecoming."

"What say you, Moses?" Perry asked.

Though still consumed by the discovery of Sam's hand-drawn map, Moses agreed. "At this point, I reckon it best to think about safety. Every step we take from here should be one closer to home."

"If we plan on about 20 miles a day, I figure we'll be back in St. Joe in about a month. I think that would please Lucy and Millie. We do have some important home fires burning."

Sally smiled from the wagon seat. "Mr. Adams, I'm lookin' forward to meetin' both those fine ladies. I'll be sure to thank them properly for lendin' their husbands to this mission. It couldn't have been easy for them, being expectant and all, but because of their sacrifice, Michael and I are free again and reunited with Moses."

She glanced at Michael and back at Perry. "We're headin' toward Kansas, toward a new life. And that's a future I'll never stop bein' grateful for."

Pete spoke up. "I know how to get us there. I know this territory well. We can cross the Mississippi by ferry and hit the plank roads across Arkansas. There's some pretty prime farmland along that path, and where there are farmers, there's a need to haul crops to market. If the plank roads run out, there will be well-marked trails connecting the towns. We can shoot up to Springfield. Once we escape those blasted Ozark Hills, we'll hit the Missouri River Valley. We can resupply as needed and we're practically home free."

"All we need to do is look out for rogues and ne'er-do-wells," Perry added.

"Surely we've already encountered our fair share," Pete said.

Moses snapped the reins to put the wagon in motion. As they began their return trip, the shadow of the Collins plantation house and the sadness it held faded into the distance.

CHAPTER 28

Two Weeks Earlier

SAMUEL'S JOURNEY

TWO WEEKS BEFORE MOSES and the rescue party set out from the Collins Plantation near Hernando, Samuel guided the Mississippi mare over the hills leading into Gumbo Flats. The horse, dust-caked and restless beneath him, wasn't his. He gripped the reins, eyes sweeping the rutted trail for familiar faces, for any trace of his father and brother. He vowed not to leave until he found them.

As he topped the ridge, Gumbo Flats stretched below him in the vast Missouri River bottomlands, the place where his relatives had lived and labored in bondage. From a distance, the farm looked far different than he remembered it. He recalled that the river had carved its fury into the valley land, leaving the grand house a skeleton, the slave quarters swallowed by silt.

On horseback, Samuel traced the familiar path, past the charred remains of a hillside corn crib and the skeleton of a barn. Below the ruins, the fields stretched far and wide. He inhaled, steadying himself. Only one path led to knowing whether his father and brother were still tending the farm for Old Man Manchester.

Samuel tightened his grip on the reins, feeling the mare shift beneath him, her muscles taut with the strain of the ride. He leaned forward, running a calloused hand down her damp neck and tightened his grip on the reins as loose stones tumbled beneath her hooves.

"You're holdin' up better than me, girl," he muttered. "Ain't no small thing, what we've come through."

The mare flicked an ear but kept moving, hooves pressing deep into the soft earth. He exhaled slow, scanning the valley.

"Stole you clean off Collins' land, but I reckon we were both stolen long before that." He gave her a firm pat. "You need a name that says somethin' about you."

The horse's dark mane blew in the breeze. A small smile came to Samuel's face.

"How 'bout Delta? It's a strong name. You're river-born, just like me."

He ran a hand along her mane. "Yeah, Delta suits you fine. Ain't no turning back now, girl. This is the last hill before that miserable plantation. You and me, we'll see this through. Now, let's go see if we're too late."

Samuel squinted, narrowing his gaze against the glare of the setting sun. In the valley, harvested corn plants stood in disciplined lines, their remaining leaves rustling in the breeze. Nearby fences, once leaning like drunkards, now stood straight, freshly mended. Someone was keeping the farm alive and breathing despite Old Man Manchester's weakness for the bottle.

They descended through a final grove of barren trees. Samuel's eyes met a most unpredictable sight. A fine, new home and a carriage house had sprouted from the moldering remains of the former structures. A plow lay inside the barn, its polished blade reflecting the sun.

They reached the house and Samuel swung his leg and climbed off of Delta. The horse's ears flicked nervously. He patted her neck, his thoughts far away. He revisited Gumbo Flats in hopes of finding some trace of his family, any clue to help make the connection to his kin, from whom he was ripped away along, with his mother and brother.

Old Man Manchester always claimed the separation was due to economic strain caused by the flood, but Samuel suspected something much deeper and more sinister.

The house was grander than he could have imagined. His memories of the old place still sent chills down his spine.

Samuel tethered Delta to a post and climbed the steps to the country home. Just as his fingers brushed the cool brass of the door knocker, the heavy oak door groaned. A figure stood framed in the flickering glow of lamplight, broad-shouldered, silver at the temples.

Standing on the home's front porch, Samuel looked vaguely familiar to John Manchester. He bore a striking resemblance to both Moses and Gabe, a perfect blend of the two men, as if he had inherited the best traits from each. He was tall and broad-shouldered, with a solid frame that spoke of years of hard labor but also a natural physical gift. His arms were muscular, his hands calloused from work, yet his movements had a quiet grace, a reflection of Moses' steady nature. He also shared the familiar Watson cheek dimple. John's eyes crinkled.

"Samuel?"

John's voice carried the warmth of a fire on a cold winter afternoon.

"Is that you? I never thought I'd see you here again."

Samuel nodded, his throat tightening. "Mr. Manchester, I'm happy to see you. But nothing else around here is familiar at all. Honestly, I was sure hopin' to find your father to maybe dig up some information about the whereabouts of my papa, Gabe and the rest of my family. I was kinda hoping they still might be in these parts."

"Well, Sam. You'd best come in, son. We've got a lot to talk about."

The two men sat in the dim parlor, the air still carrying a woody scent of newness. Samuel shifted in his chair. John leaned forward, resting his elbows on his knees, his eyes fixed on his guest.

"The Old Man passed on several years back, and when he did, I granted freedom to both your dad and your brother. I wanted to make amends for the way my father treated the rest of you."

"They freedmen now?"

"Yes, and so are you. They just got their freedom a few years ahead of time, before the war was over. About six years back, Moses and Gabe left here freedmen. That was right after my father," he hesitated. "Well, after things ended for him. They took off for Kansas, when it was still a territory. Built themselves a life out there. A farm, about seven miles north of a little town called Lowland, up in the northeast corner."

Samuel's heart quickened. "Kansas? They're alive, then? They're… they're free? Have you been to their farm?"

"Not yet, but I hope to see it someday."

"But, Mr. John, how do you know this?"

"I saw your papa not long ago, right before Christmas."

"You mean he came here, back to Gumbo Flats?"

"Sam, he's still as free as the wind and he can travel wherever he wants. He stopped here on his way to find you and the rest of your family. He was headed south. He's probably searching for you as we speak. He stopped here to gather some supplies and as much information as possible. I dug up a lot of documents a few months back. I had plenty to share, about you, your ma and Michael, and where you might be."

"How did Papa know?"

"I sent a telegram to county judges across Eastern Kansas. I told them I was looking for a man named Moses Watson, and I got a reply. Not long after that, your papa was at my door. I was able to give him names and maps that would lead him to all of you. I am thankful you survived your enslavement in Mississippi."

"Well, I have to say, I hate cotton, Mr. John, but I managed. Surely he didn't travel here alone."

"He did not, Sam. Your papa is a smart man. He brought a couple friends with him from Kansas and Missouri, white friends. I bet all three of them are on their way to that Collins plantation right now hoping to bring you home."

Samuel's chest tightened, his breath coming in short, sharp gasps as he processed the news. "Traveling to the Deep South? My papa?"

"Into the very heart of Dixie," John said. "But those two gentlemen with him, they're as wily as any bushwhacker in their path."

"I sure hope they find Ma and Michael. I had no idea where to look for them, or I would have done that myself."

"Understood, Sam. Blame is not on your shoulders. How could

you know?"

"Maybe I should try to catch up. Chase them down. It would be a long ride back, but I think I need to take that risk."

"I have a better plan, Sam. Reconnecting with your papa in the south would be nearly impossible. If they are between their intended stops, or if they are running ahead of schedule, it would be like searching for a needle in a haystack."

"Where else should I go?"

"I think the best thing for you to do is head north and west. Go to Kansas. Gabe's holding down the home front, waiting for your papa to return, hopefully with all the other Watsons. Heck, if you make good time, you might beat your papa back. Imagine the joy on his face to find you there with Gabe, waiting for him."

Samuel's eyes gleamed as he processed the suggestion. "You think he'd want that? Me to go to Kansas, instead of followin' south to try to connect?"

John leaned back, conviction in his eyes. "Son, your father's been fightin' for this reunion every day since my father and the institution of slavery tore your family apart. Head to Kansas, and you make that family whole again. That's what your papa wants more than anything. Trust me.

"The Missouri River's just north of here. Follow it west and north. It will take you within a stone's throw of your papa's farm in Northeast Kansas. I'd draw you a map, like I did for Moses, but I don't think you will need one. Another thing, Sam. I also gave your papa considerably more, but I will let him tell you the rest."

John dug into his vest pocket and tossed three gold pieces in the air.

"Sam, take this as a token of the new year. Plus, it'll help make your trek to the promised land of Kansas a bit less bumpy."

Samuel rose from the chair and caught the coins in one swoop. A new kind of determination was burning in his chest.

"Thank you, Mr. Manchester, for tellin' me this and for keepin' my papa's dream alive. I must confess, I got nothing in my possession to repay you for this grubstake of gold."

John stood with him, gripping his shoulder. "No worries. It's the least I can do. Your family and your future are calling, Samuel. Go to them. Make it right."

After his conversation with John, Samuel wasted no time. He led his ill-gotten mare, Delta, to the water trough, letting her drink deeply as he tightened the saddle and checked her hooves.

His hunger gnawed at him, but he ignored it, too consumed by the pull of his new destination. With a final glance at John's fine new home, he mounted the horse and rode north, the winter wind nipping at his face.

The ride across Missouri was grueling, the scenery a blur of bare trees, frost-covered fields, and frozen rivers. Each mile took him closer to the freedom his father had fought so hard to claim. Samuel pushed Delta hard, stopping only at trading posts for supplies and to rest Delta's legs and give her winter feed. The pull of family was stronger than exhaustion, stronger than the hunger that clawed at his belly.

At night, he built small fires. He slept fitfully, his dreams filled with fragments of the past: his mother's gentle hands, his father's deep voice, Gabe's laughter echoing across the fields.

Each successive day, the sun rose pale and cold, offering little warmth but guiding his path. Samuel avoided towns, fearing questions or confrontation. He was, after all, a horse thief, and men were strung up for far less. He stuck to back roads and wooded trails. Delta remained robust and willing, galloping for bursts, but always moving forward.

Samuel continued his cross-country ride. His mind raced with thoughts of what awaited in Kansas. Would Gabe recognize him after all these years? Would his father forgive him for stealing the Collins family's mare? He imagined the farm. Chickens and pigs and cows. He imagined the life his father and brother had built and wondered if there was a place for him in it.

All along the journey, Samuel clung to the memory of John's words: "Make that family whole again." It became his mantra, the rhythm that matched Delta's steady, 25-miles-per-day pace.

By the time Samuel reached the outskirts of Lowland his body ached from the journey, but his spirit was alive with anticipation. He had no idea about the reunion that awaited within the coming weeks. Time stood still for the moment.

Delta snorted beneath him, her coat damp with sweat despite the winter chill. He paused on a ridge overlooking the town, the glowing lanterns of the small settlement twinkling in the distance.

Samuel set up camp for the night against a rocky outcropping. From what John had told him, the Watson farm was a short ride north of town. His trip there would wait for the next morning. He was literally on the homestretch, and each step brought him closer to the life he had longed for, the family he had never stopped dreaming of.

The next morning, Sam neared the farm as the first rays of dawn broke over the horizon. His heart pounded as he approached a farmhouse. Could this be the place?

Nestled among the barren hardwood trees were a humble home, outbuildings, a smokehouse, and plenty of critters. A rooster greeted him with a rousing "Cock-a-doodle-doo." Smoke drifted from the home's chimney, a sign of life within. He tethered Delta to a post and climbed the steps, his hand trembling as he reached out to knock on the weathered door.

The door swung open, and there stood Gabe, his face a mix of shock and disbelief.

"Samuel?" Gabe whispered.

Samuel nodded, his voice failing him as tears streamed down his face.

Gabe stepped forward, pulling him into a fierce embrace. "You're home, brother. You're home."

Samuel had made it. The trip was over, but the story was far from finished. For now, he was where he belonged, with family, at least one member of it, free, and ready to face whatever came next.

"Where's everyone else?" Gabe asked with hesitation, fearing the worst.

"It's been a long, cold trip, Gabe. Let's go inside by the warmth of the fire and I will tell you what I know."

Gabe poured himself and Samuel cups of hot coffee from the woodstove as his brother put two sturdy chairs as close as possible to the fireplace.

"So, let's hear it, Sam," Gabe said.

Samuel leaned forward, elbows on his knees, as he laid out the facts, each one measured, each one true. He recounted his trip to Gumbo Flats, what John had told him and how he missed the rescue party by a breath. But he left the story of stealing Delta and his sudden decision to leave Mississippi unspoken, tucked behind more pressing truths.

"I had to reach Gumbo Flats. When I did, John told me all about the location of your farm. Papa told him all about it when they visited the old plantation before I got there. You wouldn't believe how the place has changed and for the better, Gabe. Fancy new home and a real carriage house. I guess you already know Old Man Manchester died."

"Happened while we were still there, Sam. Very tragic. But I'm glad you made it here in one piece. I'm sorry to hear that you missed Papa's arrival at your place of captivity."

"Me too, Gabe, but I had to get out of there while I was still alive. I was a free man. There was no reason for me to stay around, especially since the plantation master was in violent denial, and I do mean violent."

"You did the right thing, Sam. Papa's got good men with him. If there's any trouble down in Mississippi when they visit, I'm sure they'll handle it."

"Oh, Gabe, there will be trouble. I stole their horse."

"Ahhh, shit, Sam."

"I know. I only hope they see that my horse, Delta, was never theirs to begin with, just like me. I raised her as a foal. I hope my decision doesn't put them in danger."

"I guess all we can do is wait, hope and pray."

"I didn't go to church much in Mississippi, but I will join you in that prayer."

"Did Mr. John have any estimation of the timetable when we might see Papa? We might have to pray for a good while."

"He said Papa and his friends stopped in Gumbo Flats about a month before I got there. So, if you figure they were headed south, most likely close to Memphis, that would probably take at least a couple weeks. Then a path back to here maybe another month. Just a guess, but I'd say we should find out more in four to six weeks."

"Four to Six weeks? Hell, Sam, they've already been gone for what seems like a lifetime."

"Guess we'll have plenty of time to catch up, brother, and pray. And, truth be told, I can use some help getting this place in working order before Papa arrives. I've been a bit distracted lately."

"Oh? Tell me more Gabe."

"A young lady. Name's Naomi James. Met her at church on Christmas night. Never have I beheld such beauty. Her parents even like me."

"So, you a churchman now? No wonder you suggested prayer."

"I guess you could say that. Naomi's determined to make me a pious man."

"Well, then. God bless you, my brother. God bless you."

"How would you like to meet Naomi, Sam? Possibly attend a church service? I'll introduce you, and you can give us a family blessing so we can move toward a formal courtship."

Samuel grinned, as he leaned back in his chair. "I reckon if Naomi is the one turnin' you into a churchgoer, she must be somethin' remarkable. I'd be honored to meet her, Gabe. As for the family blessing, I think that's probably overdue."

"I'm not sayin' I don't expect Papa to come riding back really soon, but she's special and I don't want to lose her."

"I'm glad to do it, after I meet her, of course. I wouldn't be doin' it for just you and Naomi. I'd be doing it for all of us. Lord knows we could use some peace and joy after everything we've been through. But I gotta warn you, Gabe, if she's gonna be courted by my brother, she better be ready for the Watson family's brand of stubbornness. That runs deep."

Gabe and Samuel rode side by side that next Sunday morning toward the church. A sense of eagerness beat in rhythm with Gabe's pulse.

Samuel adjusted his reins, glancing at his older brother as they approached the humble church.

"So, this is the place?"

Gabe nodded, his face softening. "Yeah, this is where I've been findin' some peace lately. And where I met Naomi."

Samuel smirked. "I figured as much, dear brother. Let's see what your fuss is all about."

The two dismounted and tied their horses to a nearby post. The church's small bell rang, calling the faithful inside. Gabe fussed with his coat and hat, feeling the weight of the moment as they stepped toward the door. What would Naomi think about his younger brother?

Inside, the church was modest but warm, several wood stoves scattered through the building. Candles flickered along the walls, casting soft light on the faces of the gathered congregation. The air buzzed with quiet greetings and the faint rustle of hymnals.

Naomi stood near the left center aisle of the church, her bonnet neatly tied and her smile lighting up the room as she spotted Gabe.

Gabe led Samuel down the aisle, his heart thudding in his chest. Naomi turned, her eyes widening as she took in Samuel's face. The similarity between the two brothers was unmistakable. Samuel was younger and leaner, with a slightly rougher edge, and Gabe was more seasoned, his handsome features etched with wisdom and kindness of soul. Naomi's surprise melted into a warm smile.

"Naomi," Gabe began, "this is my brother, Samuel."

CHAPTER 29

Late January 1866

HARMONY AND DISORDER

NAOMI EXTENDED HER HAND, her gaze bouncing between Gabe and Samuel. "It's uncanny. The resemblance, I mean. But I see the differences, too. Gabe has a certain maturity about him." She glanced at Samuel with a teasing smile. "He's told me about you. Calls you the wild one."

Samuel responded with a laugh. "Honored to meet you, Miss Naomi. Gabe wasn't wrong about the wild part, but I'm workin' on it. I've been here for less than a week, and I fear Gabe's church-goin' ways haven't rubbed off on me yet. Some day when we have time, I have a few tales to share about how Gabe led me down that untamed path, but our trails have been quite different as of late."

"I'm sure you must have seen your share of hardship during those days."

"Yes, ma'am. Much more."

The congregation settled in and Reverend Hayes rose to the pulpit. Gabe motioned for Naomi to join them, and the three took a seat together. Samuel glanced at Naomi as she bowed her head in prayer, her reverence striking him with its sincerity. He leaned over to Gabe and whispered, "She's somethin' remarkable."

Gabe nodded. "You don't know the half of it."

Reverend Hayes' voice rose and fell like a melody, resonating through the small church with conviction.

"As we step into this new year," he said, his hands gripping the edges of the pulpit, "we must remember the power of beginnings. Every sunrise reminds us that the Lord's mercies are new every morning. As the sun rises on this year, so too must we rise—out of our pain, out of our fear, and into the life God has prepared for us."

He paused, scanning the room. "I tell you, good souls, that path ain't always smooth. It's beset by rocks and thorns. The journey is hard. Hear me when I say: the trials we face are not meant to break us but to shape us. To refine us like gold melting in a forge."

Members of the assembled gathering murmured their agreement, a low hum of "Amens" rippling through the pews.

"And as we move forward," the pastor continued, "let us not forget to carry hope in our hearts. For hope, my brothers and sisters, is the anchor of the soul. Faith is what steadies us when the storms rage. Belief keeps our feet shuffling when the road ahead seems without end."

He raised his hands. "So I say to you today: Hold on to hope. Treasure each other. Embrace the blessing of a better tomorrow, for family, God and our country in transition. A better day is ours if we choose to walk the path with faith."

The room fell into a worshipful silence as the final notes of the sermon settled into the hearts of those gathered. Reverend Hayes led the closing hymn, and Samuel found himself humming along, his voice blending with Gabe's as they joined the worshippers in singing Amazing Grace.

When we've been there ten thousand years,
Bright shining as the sun,
We've no less days to sing God's praise
Than when we first begun.

The song spoke to eternal hope, promising a future where peace and joy in God's presence replaced suffering and the struggles of earthly life. It resonated among the church folk as an affirmation of freedom and the perseverance to reach the brighter days ahead.

Following the closing hymn, Naomi, Gabe and Samuel gathered in a small circle outside the church doors to cut the wind's chill. The air bore the sounds of the congregation dispersing by horse, buggy and on foot.

Naomi adjusted her shawl, glancing shyly toward Gabe. Their eyes met like lightning bolts converging during a Kansas cloudburst.

Samuel slowly walked away to give the couple a moment of privacy. He approached his horse, Delta, and pulled her head closer to his. "Old girl, I think they're smitten."

Gabe cleared his throat, turning to Naomi. "Miss Naomi, there's somethin' I've been wantin' to ask you."

Naomi's smile grew, though her cheeks flushed slightly. "Yes, Mr. Watson?"

He reached for her hand, his voice shaking with emotion. "I'd like to court you formally. To show you my intentions are true. I want to earn your trust, your heart... and, God willin', your hand someday."

Naomi's eyes blinked before a radiant smile broke across her face. "Mr. Watson, you've already earned my trust. And my parents... well, they've been expectin' this. My father says you'll need to ask him properly, though. He's a man of tradition."

Gabe grinned, tipping his hat. "Then I'll see to it that I do just that."

Samuel stepped forward. He extended a handshake to Gabe and looked at Naomi. "Miss Naomi, I reckon this is where I step in. On behalf of the Watson family, I give you my full blessin'. Gabe here is stubborn, but he's got a good heart. If you've put up with him, even these few weeks since Christmas, you've got my respect."

Naomi laughed. "Thank you, Samuel. That means a great deal. I hope to get to know you better, to hear your life stories as the days go along."

Gabe shook his head, a mock glare at his brother. "Sam, you act like I'm some kind of burden to bear."

"You are, brother, but you're worth it. Otherwise, I wouldn't have risked life and limb to be by your side and under your roof. Haven't seen Papa in some years, but I can't wait to see what he says. I think he'll throw his big hands in the air, sit us all down, sip his coffee and say something like, 'Well, Naomi, it's a brave soul who courts one of my sons. They're like yearling colts—cute, clever, but prone to rummaging through trouble.' But there's no doubt he will also tell you that us Watson boys come with loyalty thicker than molasses, and humor that... well, sometimes it's an acquired taste."

Samuel tipped her a sly wink. "With Papa's stubbornness leading the charge, I reckon you won't be waitin' much longer to find out."

As they made ready to part, Gabe caught Naomi's eye. "Don't fret over what my papa might bark. I'll be speakin' to your father soon enough. And... thank you, Naomi. For believin' in me." Naomi brushed her fingers over Gabe's calloused hand. "And thank you, Gabe... for askin'."

Samuel gave a sharp whistle, and the two young men swung onto their horses. Dust kicked up behind them as they rode away, leaving Naomi standing there, her heart beating a little faster, a slow, glowing warmth unfurling in her chest.

The warm glow of lamplight spilled from the windows of The Outpost Tavern in nearby St. Joseph the very next evening. Inside, the chatter of regular patrons mingled with the gentle strains of music. Millie sat at the upright piano, her fingers dancing over the keys as she played a lively rendition of "Oh! Susanna," a tune fitting the charm of the rustic saloon and its guests. The scent of tobacco hung in the air, laced with the bitterness of stale beer and the warm, savory hint of roasted meat drifting from the kitchen.

Lucy stood behind the bar, her hands drawing forth mugs of beer as Hank moved among the tables, ensuring everyone had what they needed. The Outpost had become a haven for the townsfolk, a place to gather and exchange stories during the long winter nights.

Despite the cheer inside, Lucy's gaze frequently drifted to the door, her heart filled with hope that one day soon, Pete and Perry might walk through it. She caught Millie's eye across the room, and they exchanged a knowing smile. They were both counting the days.

As Millie's fingers struck the last note of the song, the room exploded with applause. Jeptha Nichols sat at the end of the bar nursing a sarsaparilla and raised his mug. "Play us another, Millie! You keep those keys singin' prettier than a songbird. Consider it a command performance from your resident genie."

Millie laughed, brushing a stray curl from her face. "All right, Jep, but you'll have to sing along if I do. Fair deal?"

"Deal!" Jep hollered to the amusement of the room.

The front door swung open with an aggressive bang, interrupting the saloon's joy and camaraderie. A man stepped inside, his boots thudding against the wooden floor. He was tall and wiry, with a pock-marked face. His eyes scanned the room before settling on Lucy.

"Evenin', ma'am," he rasped. "You Lucy Fontaine?"

"Depends who's askin' and why it matters," Lucy fired back, eyes cold as steel.

The intruder, Eugene Dawson, took a step forward. "Name's Dawson. And it matters 'cause the word is your husband, Pete Fontaine, is out bringin' more black folks into town. That true? We don't need no more troublemakers, nor their kind."

The room froze. Hank stiffened behind the bar, slamming down a glass beer mug. Millie stared in shock.

Before another breath passed, Lucy was on him, cast iron skillet swinging like judgment day.

"You cow-fuckin', lice-brained bastard!" she shrieked, landing a crack across his face that echoed through the room. "Rot in your own filth, you son of a bitch mutt!"

Millie dashed in, yanking Lucy back with both arms. "Lucy, no!"

Dawson staggered, wiping blood from his mouth, and sneered.

Jeptha looked across the bar directly at Dawson and gave him a glare cold enough to freeze hell.

Dawson sneered wider, spitting blood, and stepped toward Jeptha. "What you lookin' at, you piss-soaked drunkard?"

"Let me at him, Millie. He's a skunk-breathed shit eater," Lucy said.

Millie gave Lucy a full body embrace, walking her back behind the bar.

Hank stepped between Dawson and the bar, his broad shoulders a wall of calm authority. "Hold on there just a minute, Dawson. Jep here's my friend and Lucy's my boss. You so much as touch either one of them and you won't see another dawn," he growled. "You got a problem with Pete, you take it up directly with him when he gets back. If you got the guts. Comin' in here while he's gone and challenging his pregnant wife, that's a chickenshit move if ever there was one. But if you do challenge Pete, you better prepare for pain more than what you felt from Lucy's skillet. You ain't causin' trouble here tonight. End of story."

Dawson grunted, wiping the blood from his mouth on his sleeve. "I got no quarrel with you, Hank. But our citizens oughta know what's comin'. Fontaine's a troublemaker, bringin' in people who'll take what little work's left after this damn war."

Hank's words were steady as a hammer striking iron. "Pete Fontaine's a better man than you'll ever be, Dawson. He's doin' what's right, not what's easy. He's on a mission to bring some people home who've been separated. Family folks. They're Kansas farmers. They ain't gonna be taking any of the shit jobs that you and your fellow rabble might pursue. Shoveling horseshit and such. Now, you either sit the fuck down and keep a civil tongue, or you can find yourself a drink elsewhere."

"I won't drink in the presence of whores," Dawson said looking at Lucy. "Is that even Fontaine's baby you're carryin'?"

The words were enough, but Hank exploded into rage as Dawson lunged forward and took a swing at him.

Hank ducked, years of barroom brawls making him quicker than he looked as a large man. He countered with a punch to Dawson's gut, sending him stumbling backward into a table, cards and poker chips flying like a hailstorm.

The room erupted into chaos as chairs scraped and mugs clattered. A few men moved to help Hank, but he held up a hand. "I got this," he growled.

Dawson charged again, but Hank sidestepped, grabbing him by the collar and twisting him around. With a shove, he sent Dawson sprawling toward the door. "You ain't welcome here, Dawson," Hank said, his voice like thunder. "Get the hell out, you bastard."

Dawson scrambled to his feet and spat a mix of blood and tobacco juice on the floor. "You'll regret this, Hank. Mark my words."

Hank's hands hovered near his hip, where a holster rested on one side and a knife sheath on the other. "I don't want to hurt your weak ass more than Lucy already has, but you'll regret comin' back if you do. Now get out of here before I wipe that spit off the floor with your ass."

Dawson stumbled out the door, the sound of his boots fading into the night. Hank turned back to the room, his chest rising and falling with controlled breaths.

"Sorry about the commotion, friends," he said, brushing his hands together. "Next round's on the house. That includes Sarsaparilla for you, Jep."

Cheers erupted from the room, the tension dissolving into relief, gratitude and drinking.

The tavern returned to its usual hum of conversation. After calming Lucy for several minutes, Millie resumed her place at the piano, her mind shuffling as quickly as possible through memorized music. A flash of inspiration bounced from her eyes, and her fingers began to sculpt a reflective ballad across the keyboard. The haunting melody of "Shenandoah" began filling the room.

On cue, Jep arose from his barstool and broke into the solemn lyrics of the shanty about love gone wrong between a canoe-going fur trader and a fair Indian princess.

Oh Shenandoah, I hear you calling, Away, you rolling river.
Oh Shenandoah, I long to hear you, Away, I'm bound away.
'Cross the wide, Mis-sou-ri.
Mis-sou-ri, She's a mighty river, Away, you rolling river.
When she rolls down, her topsails shiver, Away, I'm bound away.
'Cross the wide, Mis-sou-ri.
Farewell my dearest, I'm bound to leave you, Away, you rolling river.
Oh Shenandoah, I'll not deceive you, Away, I'm bound away.
'Cross the wide, Mis-sou-ri.

The patrons, themselves seated nearly on the banks of the wide Mis-sou-ri, exploded in applause, and Jep took a dramatic bow.

Lucy applauded the performance and slid a mug of sarsaparilla down the bar to Jep. She moved to Hank's side, her hand resting on his arm.

"Thank you, Hank. You didn't have to stand up for Pete like that, but you did."

Hank shrugged and fought back laughter. "Well, ma'am, if memory serves, you took the first stand, and rightfully so. You wield a mean skillet. Your husband's got a way of makin' folks see the bigger picture. Ain't about to let a loudmouth asshole like Dawson tarnish that. Plus, it's why I'm here."

After finishing the tune and bowing to Jep, Millie crossed the room to join them.

"Lucy, remind me to never cross you in your moment of heated passion. I hate to think what you might call me. And thank you Hank, for putting the final punctuation into that melee. You've been more than just a help to this tavern. I hope you know how much we appreciate you."

Hank grinned, his cheeks flushing. "Aw, you ladies are somethin' else. Not that Lucy didn't have the situation totally under control, but I will always try to do my part to keep things runnin' smooth while Pete's away."

Lucy smiled. "And hopefully, he won't be away much longer. I hate to think what I might do next time something like that happens."

Millie nodded. "When they stumble through that door, I'm playin' every happy tune I know. And Hank, you'll have to make an appropriate first toast."

"If Miss Lucy don't beat me to it, but, yes, I'll certainly drink to that, Miss Millie." Hank laughed, raising an imaginary glass.

With Jep sipping on his sarsaparilla, still astonished after Lucy's and Hank's defensive actions, Millie, Lucy and Hank stood together, as the blaze in the bar's stone fireplace sent shadows across the room. Outside, the winter wind howled, but inside The Outpost, there was a sense of renewal that carried them through the long, dark evening.

CHAPTER 30

Late January, 1866

BURR OAK JUDGMENT

JEPTHA NICHOLS STEPPED from the warmth of The Outpost tavern into the bitter cold night. Shadows stretched long and thin beneath the frostbitten moon. The door swung shut behind him, muffling the laughter and music that had briefly wrapped him in a welcome hug. Outside, the wind met the spritely man like an old adversary, sharp, biting, and familiar. He welcomed the chill and its brutal honesty with the sober countenance of a man who had turned his life around.

After entertaining his friends at The Outpost with his spirited song, he was cheerful as always. His joy for life was hard-earned and well-kept. Once, that happiness had come from a bottle, often hollow and slurred. He had been a wreck of a man—a drunken, make-believe genie living inside a shattered lamp. His life had eroded into a ritual of granting favors to fools and devils in return for alcohol. Nights like this used to find him face-down in a ditch, forgotten by the world and wishing he could forget it right back, lucky to be alive the next morning.

But no more.

Now the cold wasn't punishment. It was proof. Though frail, it was evidence he was upright and breathing in a world that tolerated him, but only conditionally. Every sharp gust was a reminder that he'd climbed out of his ruin and forged a life of purpose. He even held a steady job working at Marcus Mixon's Trading Post.

Jeptha pulled his coat tight against the wind. He whistled Yankee

Doodle to keep his steps at a brisk pace. In that moment, beneath heaven's all-seeing stars, he walked like a man who had been broken and rebuilt stronger. His spine was straight, his heart clear and his soul unafraid.

Walking across the street toward his sparsely furnished room, the street was empty and silent. He felt a slight shift in the air before he saw them.

Three figures draped in white robes, faces hidden beneath stiff hoods, emerged from the alley like phantoms. They moved with cruel purpose, blocking his path beneath a sputtering street lantern across the street from The Outpost. The gleam of a knife caught his eye, its steel as cold as the souls that wielded it.

Jep halted, squaring his shoulders. "Step aside, boys," he said. "In spite of your best efforts, I know you are earthly souls who should know a man's got a right to walk home in peace."

But peace had abandoned the street on this night.

Eugene Dawson stepped forward, his voice thick with venom.

"Peace don't live here no more, Nichols, you old drunk. Not since you and your friends started bringin' dark folks where they don't belong. You've poisoned this town with your abolitionist lies. Thought maybe we'd remind you what your kind's place truly is."

Jep met Dawson's gaze, steady and unflinching.

"My place is wherever a free man plants his feet. This soil's free. Your side lost the war. And you might as well take off that dumbass hood, you cowardly bastard. I know it's you, Dawson. I heard your voice at The Outpost. If you want to drag this country backward, you're goin' to need a mighty hefty chain."

The first punch cracked across Jeptha's face, snapping his head sideways. Blood spattered across the frozen dirt street, staining the surface like spilled Catawba wine. He staggered but stood, spitting crimson at Dawson's feet.

"That all you got?" Jeptha rasped, chest heaving. "Cowards hiding beneath your grandmama's night clothes. How brave you must feel."

Dawson removed his hood. His face twisted in rage. "Shut him up!"

Fists and boots rained down. Jep's ribs cracked beneath the blows, his vision blurred, but still, between gasps, he laughed at them.

"You think hate makes you strong. It just makes you small."

That was it. Dawson ripped a rope noose from beneath his robe, shoving it roughly around Jep's neck. The fibers bit into his skin.

"You forgot your place, Nichols," Dawson hissed, tightening the noose. "This here oak's gonna remind you."

They dragged him across the street, his boots scraping grooves in the frozen mud. The burr oak waited, gnarled and ancient, its limbs twisted like the mercurial conscience of the town itself.

Dawson tossed the rope over a thick branch shooting over the street's edge and pulled until the line ground deep into flesh.

"Let this tree warn any fool who dares challenge the way things have always been in the eyes of God."

With one savage tug, the three men hoisted Jeptha off the ground. His entire body shook. His boots jerked once, twice, three times, then fell still.

The wind sighed through the branches, creaking like whispered prayers for predestined souls. The only other sound was the soft squeak of rope against limb, Jeptha's lifeless body swinging in the night. It was a cruel lullaby for a man beloved by all who frequented The Outpost Tavern.

Inside the tavern, laughter faded as the lanterns dimmed for the night's last call. Millie began wiping down the bar, humming softly, while Lucy gathered mugs, stacking them in neat rows.

Hank paused near the door, the weight of the night's earlier conflict with Eugene Dawson pressing against his chest. His gut cramped in pain. He sensed trouble was near. He could smell it on the wind. He shoved open the doors.

The cold hit him like a hammer blow, and the sight like a drop of mishandled nitroglycerin.

Beneath the silver eye of the moon, Jep's body swung from the burr oak tree across the street.

"God Almighty…" Hank shouted. His legs gave way beneath him for half a step. He stumbled forward, slipping on a patch of lingering ice in the doorway.

He shouted back inside the tavern. "Millie! Lucy! Out here! Now!"

The women burst outside, laughter still fading from their lips. And then they saw. Millie gasped and collapsed, knees hitting the frozen ground. "No. No. Please God, no!" Her voice cracked wide open as she buried her face in trembling hands.

Lucy staggered back against the doorframe, her breath stolen by horror. "They hung him. Jep. Right here outside our own front door. The place where we welcome all. The place where we love."

Hank stood beneath the body of his friend swinging in the cold winter breeze. He held up his arms in disbelief. His jaw wide open in shock, like a riverboat anchor stuck to a rusted chain.

"This was Dawson's work. Had to be." he growled. "No one else would crawl this low. No one else would twist a warped way of thinking' into a weapon against his own kind, just to send a message. This is all my fault. I should have let him spout his tantrum and leave in peace. Forgive me, Jep."

Hank quickly maneuvered the Fontaine's horse-drawn buggy beneath Jep's body. He reached up with a knife and sliced the rope, catching Jep's lifeless corpse and laying it gently inside the buggy's storage bed.

He pulled off his hat and bent his head toward Jep's cooling body. "Rest easy, old friend. Your fight's not over. Not while I draw breath."

He turned to the women, his voice sharp as the blade of a long-handled corn knife.

"I'll go notify the sheriff. But you two, dim all the lights and wait inside. Draw back the curtains so you can see all who might approach.

And Lucy, Pete's rifle's behind the bar. Grab it and be ready to pull the trigger."

Hank jumped into the buggy and raced down the street toward the city jail, keeping his eyes alert for any movement in the shadows. He sought any glimpse of cowards hiding along the street's dark edges. None were found.

Hank delivered Jeptha's body and filed a report at the jail. Sheriff Cyrus Cole knew of Jeptha's checkered past and could not look beyond it. He labeled the death self-induced, much to Hank's vocal opposition. Officially, the sheriff called the incident death by suicide. Overlooked was the fact that no pedestal or device could have been used by the soon-to-be-deceased Jeptha to execute the solitary deed.

Two days later, they prepared to bury Jeptha in Mount Mora Cemetery.

"Today, we bury Jep with every ounce of dignity that was stolen from him," Hank said to Lucy and Millie during the graveside service. "But tonight? Tonight, I burn their cowardly masks and set their robes to ash. I know who's responsible, and mark my words, I will swing a mighty sword of retribution. You ladies can call me a vigilante if you like, but I prefer angel of justice."

The cemetery sky hung heavy and gray, pressing down on the funeral attendees like a weary heart. Faces crowded around the casket. Nearly all were patrons of The Outpost. They had seen Jeptha's transformation and drew from it measures of admiration and inspiration. Nobody believed that good Ol' Jep would have taken his own life.

A slight dusting of snow began to fall in mournful flurries, softening the edges of every grave and fence post, muting the sound of the living. The wind held its breath in respect. People gathered in small clusters, bracing against the cold, their dark coats buttoned tight, heads bowed beneath wide-brimmed hats and woolen shawls. The sharp tang of cold filled their lungs, mingling with grief that sank deep in their bones. A collective fog of breath rose in a single cloud above the burial ground.

At the center of it all, Jeptha Nichols' coffin rested above a hole in the frozen earth. It was a plain pine box, dusted with snow. Modest by any measure, yet it shined, very Jep-like, against the desolate graveyard. The gleam did not originate from the casket's simple style, but from the soulful weight of the man it carried.

Father Keith Andrews stepped forward in a black cassock that fittingly matched the day's solemn tone. He made the sign of the cross and opened his worn Bible. His voice rose steady and strong.

"Children of God," he began, scanning the faces before him, "today we bury not just a man, but a light in this dark wilderness. Jeptha Nichols stood, as Job stood, battered by storms of trial and tribulation. He lost much in his life—comfort, peace, even safety—but never his mercy. Never his courage."

He paused, letting his words settle over the crowd.

"Some men speak of righteousness and conversion. Jeptha lived it. Where others clenched fists, he opened his heart. Where others built walls, he made bridges."

From the tree line beyond the graveyard, three dark figures watched in silence. Eugene Dawson and his men, their faces hidden beneath hats and bandanas, lurked like jackals at the forest's edge. They didn't mourn, they measured, calculating who stood defiant. Who might be next on their list.

Father Andrews raised his voice, sharp as the winter air.

"Who among us will pull his plow when the soil turns hard? Who will shield the innocent when hatred comes knocking again? If we do not rise, we have already fallen."

The graveyard held its collective breath.

Lucy stepped forward, tears freezing against her cheeks. In her gloved hands, she carried Jeptha's faded shopkeeper's apron— threadbare, stained with axel grease and flour from his recent work beside Marcus. She laid it atop the coffin, a sign of his conversion to honest sobriety.

"Rest easy, friend. We'll carry your fight from here."

Millie gripped Lucy's trembling hand, her own gaze fixed on the coffin, lips moving in silent prayer.

Marcus Mixon stepped up next, clearing his throat against the cold. His voice, steady as the grind of a millstone.

"Jeptha was a man who worked for me and beside me. He was a man who lifted me, day after day. When business was slow, when folks turned their backs, he stood his ground. Honest hands, steady heart. I didn't just lose an employee; I lost a true brother in this life."

An unknown mourner walked to the coffin and placed on its top a small wooden cross carved from a fallen branch from the burr oak tree where Jeptha died.

Then Hank walked up slowly. He bent at the waist, lowered his head and whispered.

"I promise you, Jep. This ain't the end. Not by a damn sight. You may be gone from this earth, but your fight's my fight now. I vow to finish it."

From the shadows, Eugene Dawson shifted, fingers twitching near his coat. The scene sliced through him like a blade. He spat tobacco juice bitterly into the snow, a stain against the white purity of the morning.

But no amount of hate could drown the hymn that rose from the mourners. Cracked, trembling voices sang "Shall We Gather at the River," thin at first, but swelling like a flood.

Yes, we'll gather at the river, The beautiful, the beautiful river.

Their voices rose above the barren trees, defying the bitter cold sky, daring the shadow of hate to strike again. And in the sparseness of that song, the echo of freedom rang quiet, steadfast, and true.

The wind off the Missouri River screamed through the streets of St. Joseph like a vengeful preacher, shouting damnation into the dark.

It sliced through the alleys and clacked against shutters with a promise of reckoning. Two blocks beyond the trembling glow of Charles Street's gas lamps was a place decency feared to tread. Eugene Dawson's home lurked in the shadows. It crouched low and mean, a rotting carcass of timber and spite.

In the dark of night, Hank dismounted beneath a grove of skeletal cottonwoods, their blackened limbs lashing out at the night sky like dragon claws. He paused, listening. Nothing but the wind and the faint creaking of rusty door hinges.

Perfect.

With boots shuffling softly through the new-fallen snow, Hank moved like a hungry wolf across the yard. Under each arm, like babies ready for bedtime, were canisters of highly flammable, adulterated kerosene. He hefted one and uncorked it with a twist. The smell hit him hard. It was sharp, oily, and unforgiving. Volatile, just like Dawson's hatred.

Dawson's house was dark as night as Hank poured one can and then another in careful, silent swooshes. Along the porch rails, under the eaves, across every dry plank and cracked shutter. The old wood soaked it in.

When his work was done, Hank stood back, trailing a thin line of the flammable fuel toward the cleared walkway like a liquid fuse ready to ignite. He pulled a stick-match from his coat and struck it against his boot.

For a moment, in his mind, he saw Jep's body, bloodied, swaying lifeless from the branch of the burr oak.

"This one's for you, my friend," Hank whispered. "May hell greet that son of a whoring witch with open and unforgiving arms."

Hank dropped the match and ran into the darkness. The flame danced, golden and wild. Fire shot down the kerosene trail with a hiss like a thousand serpents unleashed. The porch ignited first, flames scraping up the columns and curling over the roofline. Shutters burst and windows shattered. Smoke poured skyward like a funeral veil torn loose by the wind.

Then, as Hank mounted his horse and rode to the edge of an alley a block away, the house's entire exterior was engulfed.

Inside, Dawson woke choking on smoke and fear. He stumbled from his bed, pulling on his white robe like armor, ignorant of its doom. "What in God's name?" he coughed, staggering toward the door. When he threw it open. Pools of kerosene from the porch soaked into the robe and ignited.

Dawson's robe caught fire like dry brush. The night's silence erupted with his screams. The flames swallowed him whole. He stumbled into the street, arms flailing, face contorted in terror.

"Help me! Somebody! God Almighty, help me!" he shrieked, voice tearing through the night.

Doors cracked open along the block. Hesitant faces peered from shadows, but no soul dared step forward. No one came to save him. They knew what he was and whispered about what he had done.

The fire danced inside his robe, licking his flesh, burning his hair, scorching the hate from his bones. Hank watched from afar, his face cold and eyes empty, as Dawson stumbled back inside, falling to his knees inside the doorway, clawing at the wood frame like a drowning man grasping at a passing log.

"No mercy for the wicked," Hank whispered. "You wore your hate like a crown. Now choke on it."

At last, Dawson was reduced to a smoldering, oily heap of flesh and hate, his white robe reduced to ash and ruin. Behind him, the house groaned a final time, then gave in, collapsing inward. A tower of smoke and embers rose higher than the top branches of the lynching oak.

Then silence fell, broken only by the crackle of dying flames. The wind carried a bitter stench of justice through the sleeping town.

By dawn, all that remained was scorched earth, blackened beams, and whisps of smoke curling lazily into the morning sky. In the town, word spread like wildfire. Maybe it was a blaze set by vengeful spirits. Or perhaps it was a lantern knocked from a bedside table.

No one spoke Hank's name. Nobody saw him. But they remembered the inferno. And for weeks thereafter, they whispered that in the dreaded chill of winter, good fortune brought the flames of justice to the wretched house of a depraved man on a backstreet in St. Joseph.

The word "vengeance" was unspoken, but everyone knew that hate had met its reckoning beneath a cold, kerosene-lit sky.

CHAPTER 31

Two weeks earlier, Mid-January

THE ROAD HOME

THE JANUARY SUN ROSE with a golden Southern drawl over Mississippi. Unseasonable warmth blew in from the Gulf, a final embrace for the travelers as they began their return trek to the cold grip of Missouri.

The voyagers crossed the border into Tennessee with lifted spirits in the knowledge they were one state closer.

Behind them, the echoes of Mississippi gunshots lingered. Their visit to the Collins plantation in search of Samuel could only be remembered as a place where a flawed man met his tragic fate.

Sitting on the buckboard next to Sally, Moses snapped the reins, and the Conestoga continued its journey toward Memphis. Perry, Pete and Michael rode alongside on horseback. Archibald trotted forward, nose to the ground as if sniffing out the path home.

"It's good to be movin' again," Pete said.

"Feels like our first step toward home, but it's still bittersweet that we didn't retrieve Samuel," Moses replied, his eyes fixed on the road.

After three days of steady travel, the group arrived in Jonesboro, Arkansas, Pete's hometown. The town was modest but growing, its streets lined with rough wooden buildings and swarming with wagons and pedestrians.

"I'd like to make a quick stop," Pete said, dismounting his saddle near a small general store. "Won't be but a moment."

"This is your neck of the woods, Pete. Take your time," Perry said, climbing down from Appy to stretch his legs. Moses and Sally exchanged a glance, agreeing to give Pete his space.

Pete, the flesh wound to his temple still healing, opened the door and a cowbell chimed above the doorway. Inside the shop, Pete's eyes adjusted to the dim light. The scent of coffee and cured leather filled the air.

Behind the counter stood a grizzled man with a thick mustache and tired eyes. Pete spotted the man right away. It was his old friend, Maynard Pickens, a man who gave him sage advice as a young adult searching for a better life.

"Awesome Possum, Mr. Pickens," Pete yelled.

Maynard immediately recognized Pete's calling-card expression. "Pete Fontaine?" he questioned, squinting. "I'll be damned. Ain't seen you since well before the war started."

Pete removed his hat, his face carrying a mix of surprise and sadness. "Great to see you, Maynard. It's been far too long."

"What in tarnation happened to your head, Pete?"

"Just a little run-in with a tree branch, Maynard. No big deal."

The two men exchanged a brief handshake, but the tone grew heavy when Pete asked about his family.

"They're gone, Pete," Maynard said. "Cholera swept through like a tornado. Took the entire Fontaine clan with it."

Pete leaned on the counter, his knees buckling and knuckles whitening. "I should've been here."

Maynard shook his head. "Nothin' you could've done. People without adequate resources, like your folks, had little chance. You did what you had to, gettin' out when you did."

Pete nodded. Guilt wrinkled his forehead. He scratched his chin. "I reckon I owe you, Maynard. That advice you gave me all those years ago served me well."

Maynard tilted his head. "What suggestion was that, Pete? Lord knows I spouted a lot of ideals back then."

"You told me, 'A man can't change the wind, but he sure as hell can adjust his sails.' Took me a while to understand what that really meant, but I'll tell ya, it's carried me through more storms than I can count."

"Did I really say that? Must've been one of my good days. Glad it stuck, Pete. Have you done good for yourself?"

"I have. Got a lovely bride and we're expecting our first young'un in a couple months. I run a little tavern up in St. Joe, Missouri. Northwest corner of the state. The Outpost. The place ain't fancy, even by frontier standards, but it's revenue. Keeps a roof over me and Tennessee corn mash on my shelves."

"A tavern, huh? Never figured you for the barkeepin' type."

"Life's funny that way. If you ever find yourself up Missouri way, you've got room and board waitin' for you, and a good shot of that mash whiskey, on the house."

Maynard leaned across the counter, his handshake firm and warm. "Might take you up on that, Pete. I'm glad things turned out for you. Your folks would've been proud."

"Thank you for settin' me straight when I was too green to know better."

Pete tipped his hat and made his way to the door, the cowbell chiming as he stepped into the sunlight. Maynard watched him go, the faintest hint of a smile on his face, before turning back to his work, reflecting on the unexpected gift of an old friend walking back through the door.

Pete paused on the porch, staring out over the small town. When he rejoined the group, his usual wit was subdued.

"Everything all right?" Perry asked.

"More ghosts, that's all."

Leaving Jonesboro behind, the Conestoga turned west. The land rose steadily, transforming from flatter farmland into the rugged hills of the Ozark Mountains. The path was narrow, winding through dense oak forests and alongside rocky streams.

Michael pulled out his harmonica that evening as they camped near a babbling creek. He played the entire first verse of "Swing Low, Sweet Chariot", the melody weaving through the crisp night air.

"You've been practicin'," Moses said.

Michael grinned, the harmonica still in his hands. "Figured I'd get it just right for when we play it at home."

"You've got the sound of freedom in those notes. Keep that close to your heart, son."

Sally leaned against Moses, her eyes shimmering in the firelight. "That song's gonna carry us home, Moses. I don't know what home looks like, but I can't wait to see it and Gabe."

By the fourth day, they arrived in Mountain Home, Arkansas, a settlement nestled in the hills. The town offered a chance to resupply, and Perry took the lead, bartering for provisions.

As they prepared to leave, Sally lingered near a small church, its bell tower casting a long shadow over the dusty street.

"What's on your mind?" Moses asked, stepping beside her.

"Thinkin' about how far we've come, and how much further we've got to go," she said. "You know, Moses, I know we jumped the broom back at the plantation, but at some point, I think I'd like a real wedding. A church wedding."

Moses scratched the back of his neck, a slow grin spreading across his face as he looked at the church.

"Well now, Sally, I reckon if the good Lord invites a man like me into His house, then I don't see why we can't make that happen. There's a right fine African church not far from our home in Kansas."

He continued. "Honestly, I've thought about it too. Always figured you deserved better than a quick jump over a broom and a nod from the stars. A church wedding would really be somethin', wouldn't it? You in a fancy dress, me tryin' not to trip over my own feet. The whole town gatherin' just to see how I landed the finest woman in the county."

"You've got a way of talkin' sweet, Moses. But you mean it?"

"Sally, you're the reason I'm still standing here, breathin', fightin'. If you want a church ceremony, I'll move heaven and earth to give it to you. I'll make certain that church bell rings so loud, it'll shake the dust off the Kansas hills."

"Not sure it's a fitting thing for me to ask since our entire family can't be at our side. It wouldn't be right to hold such a ceremony without Sam. He's worth waiting for, if he can find us."

"Before we set a date, we'll wait a proper amount of time, in the event God sees it possible to light his path to our Kansas home. We've made it this far and I think Sam will too. One step at a time, Sally. One step at a time."

Crossing the Arkansas-Missouri state line brought little change in terrain or climate. For several more days, the group traveled the rugged and stubborn Ozarks. Travel was slow, but Pete enjoyed every moment.

"This here land reminds me of the old days. Used to walk through hills like this in pursuit of squirrel. I could pick them out of the treetops with amazing marksmanship. It was always a treat to bag one of those critters for the evening stew. Back then, even a scrawny squirrel felt like a feast for a family scratching out a living. I always had a dream for somethin' bigger."

"You found it," Perry said. "I think we all have."

"Sometimes I wonder what it would've been like if I'd stayed put in Arkansas."

"You'd have missed out on all this," Moses said, gesturing to the horses, and the open road.

"Fair point," Pete said. "And I'm sure the squirrel population is thankful I left too."

At the midpoint of their journey toward St. Joseph, the travelers broke over a hill and descended a hard-packed dirt and gravel road. The forest thinned and fields of prairie grass dotted with oak, walnut and elm trees framed the road. The terrain was transforming from the rugged Ozark Hills into open land.

They rode on, a sea of dormant grass and fallow corn fields on each side. Scattered cattle and sheep grazed in pastures lined by split-rail fences. Farmhouses and hay barns dotted nearly every mile along the route. Breaking over a final rise, a greater concentration of chimney smoke rose in multiple columns.

Perry drew out his trusty brass spyglass and peered into the distance.

"Pete, if I were to hazard a guess, I'd surmise that might be Springfield, Missouri, dead ahead."

"I think that's an astute observation, friend. And I must say, it's a fine sight! Civilization at last. I was startin' to think we'd been banished to wanderin' these hills for 40 years, like Moses in the desert. While we have our own Moses, the original didn't have to deal with a wagon axle beggin' for mercy every ten miles!"

Pete gave his horse's bridle a light flick. "Let's hope Springfield's got a decent plate of grub and a jug of elixir to wash down this trail dust. And if we're lucky, a blacksmith who's fast and cheap."

Pete leaned back in the saddle and glanced at Moses and Sally in the wagon seat. "Moses, my divinely named comrade, lead us forth to this so-called promised land! My backside's starting to think my exile to this saddle is permanent."

Approaching the outskirts of Springfield, echoes of life poured in from the village. The rumble of distant wagon wheels and the occasional sharp ring of metal to metal from a blacksmith's hammer signaled culture ahead. Archy responded in kind to the sound of barking dogs.

The Conestoga and horses descended into Springfield surrounded by the welcome sounds of laughter and townsfolk chatter. Dust swirled behind then as the group waved at children playing in small schoolyards. The aroma of fresh bread and stovetop stews wafted from nearby homes.

In the heart of Springfield, rows of new wooden buildings with false fronts lined the square, fresher than a hot rhubarb pie on a windowsill. There was a mix of larger homes, dry goods stores, a blacksmith, taverns and inns. The Greene County Courthouse anchored the square.

Along Main Street, business was brisk as shopkeepers dealt their wares and wagons rattled past. Springfield felt like a crossroads where the untamed Ozarks tipped their hat to the burgeoning heart of America.

Merchants called out to passersby, their voices blending with the visible invitation of goods displayed in shop windows. For weary travelers, it was a place to pause, replenish supplies, and prepare for the long miles remaining. It was a hub of life on the frontier's doorstep. Perry and Michael went to the blacksmith to have their horses' shoes checked. As they rode away, Pete turned to Moses.

"That son of yours is gettin' the hang of the saddle."

"I think he's gettin' the hang of a lot of things. He has a knack for horsemanship. That's what freedom does to your soul. It unleashes your spirit. Just look at how he's taken to his music. I can't wait to hear him toot on that damn harmonica tonight around the fire."

"Moses, watch your language" Sally chimed in, her voice warm. "He's got your determination, that's for sure."

Upon leaving Springfield hours later, the group turned northwest, the land opening into even wider stretches of prairie and gentle rolling hills. Their pace continued to quicken, but as they traveled north, the nights grew colder. They set up camp that night under a canopy of stars, and Pete shared a rare moment of reflection.

"I've spent most of my life runnin' from places and people. But this trip has taught me there ain't nothin' worth more than family, whether it's the one you're born into or the one you find along the way."

The morning storm arrived without warning, charging in like a raging buffalo. Dark clouds rolled in as a biting wind whipped across the tree-lined prairie swale. The air was just warm enough to turn the storm's fury into driving rain instead of snow. Rain fell in sheets, turning the valley creek they traveled along into a raging torrent.The wagon's wheels groaned and skidded, the horses whinnying in panic as winter lightning streaked across the sky.

"Hold steady!" Moses yelled, straining to keep the reins from slipping through his soaked hands.

The ground beneath them became a flood of rushing water as the creek overflowed, and a wall of water swept debris and branches into the road. The horses balked, and the wagon tilted slightly into the stream before slamming to a stop.

Michael led his mother to safety as Perry unhitched the horses from the Conestoga and led them to higher ground. Pete worked to unload supplies from the tilting wagon, hoping less weight might correct its stance. Moses waded into the water to move an underwater boulder that jammed one of the wheels.

"Moses, get back here!" Pete shouted, his voice lost to rushing current.

It was too late. The surging stream rose like a wall, knocking the wagon into Moses, catching him mid-stride and dragging him off his feet. The wagon stayed put, but Moses vanished under the churning surface, his shout for help lost in the chaos.

"Moses!" Pete leapt from the back of the wagon, plunging into the icy water with Perry right behind him.

"I can't see him!" Perry bellowed, his eyes scanning the foaming current. "Pete, watch out for the rocks!"

"Uh Roo Roo Roo."

Seeing a flash of denim, Archibald barked furiously from the riverbank, his floppy ears dripping with rain. The dog darted back and forth, his keen eyes locked on the river. With a sharp bark, he bolted downstream, sensing where the current was carrying Moses. Archy plunged into the water, his legs dogpaddling through the current.

"There!" Perry yelled, pointing toward midstream as Moses tumbled through the muddy rapids, his arms flailing.

Archibald swam toward Moses with fierce determination, his nose barely above water as he reached Moses. Clamping his jaws onto the denim of Moses' coat, the dog fought against the current, his muscles straining as he paddled toward the bank. Moses gasped for air, his hands weakly clutching the dog's fur.

"Come on, boy!" Perry urged, wading chest-deep into the water as Archibald dragged Moses toward the bank. "You can do it."

As the pair reached the water's edge, a log the size of a Civil War cannon careened down the flooding stream, striking Archibald hard against the head. The dog yelped, releasing his grip on Moses. Archy drifted into the current.

Pete grabbed Moses under the arms, dragging him to the riverbank.

"Archy!" Perry screamed, stumbling into the river only to be held back by Michael. "Archy, no! Come back! I promised Millie I'd keep you safe!" His cries echoed in the storm as Archibald's dark form disappeared in the rapids.

Michael steadied Perry, who was trembling with anguish. Moses coughed violently, water spilling from his lips, his face weak but alive.

"You're safe now," Pete said, his voice breaking as he laid Moses on the muddy ground. "Moses, that dog, saved your life."

Moses groaned, his chest heaving but his mind slightly incoherent. "The dog? Perry's dog?"

"I see him. I see Archy," Michael shouted. "But he's not swimming."

Perry jumped into Appy's saddle and the horse galloped downstream. They reached the point in the stream where Archy was wedged between the current and a tree, his head barely above water.

Perry jumped from his horse, rope in hand. He tied an end of the rope to Appy's saddle horn. Appy stood still as night as Perry looped the rope around his shoulder and headed into the flood. "I'm coming for you, Archy. Hang on, boy."

Perry reached Archy in the area calmed by the tree's presence. He wrapped the rope around his waist and the end loop around Archy. He slowly lifted the dog over his shoulder and walked his way back along the rope to shore, where Appy was a capable anchor on the other end.

Reaching the bank, Perry put Archy into a soft patch of grass by Appy's side. There was no breathing. No sign of life. Perry thumped Archy hard on the chest. "Come on, Archy, you old hound. Come back to me."

After a second thump, a gush of water exploded from Archy's snout. He was breathing but still unresponsive.

Perry knelt beside Archy and ran his hand over the dog's wet fur. Michael ran to his side.

"Is he OK, Perry? Is Archy goin' to make it?"

"I think so, Michael. He's a sturdy one. Now that the water's receding, the best thing I can do right now is carry him back to the Conestoga and wrap him in a woolen blanket."

Archy remained unresponsive as Perry lifted him into the wagon, which was again on land as the flood continued its retreat. Perry swaddled Archy in a gray blanket like he was a baby and leaned closer.

"Archy, you know I'm here. Open your eyes, give me a bark. Oh, how I would love to hear your 'Roo Roo Roo' right now."

Sally and the men gathered at the wagon. Michael reached out his hand and rubbed Archy's haunches.

"Archibald didn't do this out of duty. He did it because in his hound dog way, he loved us all. Archy saved my papa. He knew exactly what he was doing."

Pete, his arms around a stumbling Moses, awkwardly eased them both to the wagon's tailgate. They looked in on Perry and Archy, looking for any signs of life.

The storm eased. Perry inhaled sharply before letting out an anguished shout, his body trembling.

Moses, still weak, reached out a hand to Perry. "That dog, he's a hero. My hero. No matter what happens, don't you ever forget that,

Perry. Don't let anyone ever forget that."

"He's still breathing. I haven't given up on him yet."

"Perry," Michael said, "your dog did what none of us could. He gave us back my papa. That kind of courage doesn't just end. He's a fighter. You taught him that."

Perry slammed his fist into the wagon's sideboard. He sucked in a stuttering breath, blinking away rain and tears. "He's the best dog I ever had. Millie will want to know what he did, every last detail. I hope he's there when I tell her the story."

Minutes seemed like hours as the storm passed. Perry climbed from the wagon, glancing back at Archy whose chest was expanding and contracting slowly. But he remained motionless.

"I've done all I can do for Archy at this point. We need to head back to the trail. Let's re-hitch the horses and get as far away from this damnable valley as fast as we can. If it's OK with y'all, I'm going to ride back here with Archy and tie Appy to the wagon as we head out."

"You do that, Perry," Pete said. "You do whatever it takes to get his spirit back inside his furry self. I pray to God that he makes it."

"You're not the only one sending up that request, Pete."

The friends waited until the stream had fully retreated within its banks. They loaded the wagon and reharnessed Beulah and Barney for the road ahead.

Perry sat in the back of the wagon, elbows on his knees, watching Archy, as the wagon rolled up the hill and over the ridge. Every turn of the wagon's wheels defied the fury of nature. The light of mid-morning warmed the horizon, as Moses shouted to Perry. "Keep your eyes on that dog, Perry. Don't let him go nowhere. He didn't just save me. He reminded us all what it means to be willing to give everything. I owe him."

"He's still breathing. That's all that matters right now."

The group pressed onward. With every mile, Archibald's heroic actions steadied their resolve, a quiet reminder that even in the fiercest storm, courage and love could forge a path forward.

CHAPTER 32

Mid-February

THE SOUND OF HOPE

A LUMP WAS FIRMLY CAUGHT in Perry's throat, expecting the worst, afraid his promise to Millie to keep Archibald safe would be broken. For each of the three previous nights, Perry refused to leave his side. He stared at the stars through the rear opening in the wagon's canopy, willing the dog to wake up with every twinkle. But Archy just lay there, wrapped in the woolen blanket, withering like autumn leaves in the first frost.

But the travelers were getting closer to home. The Conestoga rolled on. They carved their path forward along the winding trail. The fateful storm had passed, but its aftermath still chased them like the stench of a wet cowhide.

Perry, sitting in the back of the wagon, kept his eyes locked on Archibald's unmoving form. Archy's chest rose and fell slightly. He was still breathing, but he hadn't moved a muscle. Perry reached out a hand to stroke his fur. He leaned in and whispered an old hunting tale, even placing a scrap of salted pork by the dog's nose. Nothing.

Michael clambered up beside him, peering down at the lifeless hound. "He's still fighting, ain't he?"

Perry swallowed hard. "I don't know, Michael. I just don't know." The wind feathered through the prairie grass, carrying with it his faith, now uncertain and fragile.

Perry dipped a cloth into a tin cup and squeezed cool water into

Archibald's mouth. The bulk of it ran onto the wooden floorboards. He watched for any sign, any whisper of life in the dog's shallow breathing. The act had become a ritual, every hour, every day. Perry's hands began to ache and wrinkle, but he never stopped. He couldn't.

Perry loaded up the rag with fresh water to wipe the dog's muzzle for what he feared might be the final time. As he dripped it into Archibald's mouth, the dog's body suddenly shuddered ever so slightly. But undeniably, it was a noticeable twitch. Then, Archibald's familiar brown eyes cracked open ever so slightly.

At first, Perry didn't believe it. He froze, heart hammering.

Then Archibald's eyelids lifted fully, his gaze locking onto Perry's. A weak, tired blink.

Perry shot to his feet so fast he nearly toppled out of the wagon. "He's back!" His voice rang loudly across the wagon, raw and urgent. "Archy's back!"

The wagon jolted to a halt. Footsteps pounded the earth as the others ran toward him.

Moses was first, pushing past Pete with urgency. His knees nearly buckled at the sight of the hound awake. "Praise the Lord," he breathed, pressing a shaking hand to his forehead. "And on the third day, he rose again. It's a dog-gone miracle."

Michael scrambled up beside Perry, his hands trembling as he reached for Archy. "Archy? You know us, boy?"

Archibald's dull eyes shifted ever so slightly toward Michael. His cracked nose twitched, his dry mouth barely parting. One deep breath. Then another.

And then, from deep in his throat, came the faintest, weakest, most beautiful sound Perry had ever heard.

"Roo..."

The group gasped. Sally covered her mouth. Moses shot his hands to heaven. Pete whooped and clapped like a child. Michael let out a sob of joy.

Perry laughed so hard he cried, so intense that his chest ached, his tears falling into Archy's fur. He ran his hand down the dog's ribs, feeling the warmth. "By Almighty God, I have now seen the glory."

Moses shook his head, grinning up at the sky. 'Well, I'd say that calls for a break. A hero deserves a proper welcome back.'

"Well, I wouldn't say he's totally back, yet, but this is good, damned good," Perry said.

No one argued. The group set down their packs and set up camp. They pulled out some of their remaining food and started a campfire. For the first time in a long while, they stopped, just to be together. Because Archibald was back.

The day wore on and the warmth of the afternoon settled over the open land as the group never strayed far from the wagon, their journey home momentarily forgotten. Archibald's return had cast a glow over them, a reprieve from the travails of the long, bitter road home.

Perry knelt beside Archy, running a hand over the hound's frail body. The dog's ribs jutted like the bones of a starved deer, his fur dull, his strength drained. His eyes, though open, were distant.

Perry exhaled hard. "He won't last long like this," he murmured, mostly to himself. Then he turned, searching for Pete. "He needs water and food. Pete, think you could whip up a pan of salted pork gravy?"

Pete looked at Perry with feigned curiosity. "Gravy? Ain't that your territory these days?"

"Ahh, come on, Pete. I have to get some water and food into Archy's belly if he's gonna have a chance at all," Perry said.

"Well, now, if you'd asked me for whiskey to jolt old Archy to his feet, I would politely decline. But gravy? Gravy I can do."

"Even after the trials of these last weeks, Pete, you can barely boil water without burning it," Moses said.

Pete placed a hand over his heart. "That's a damned lie and an insult to every barkeep on this side of the Mississippi." He grinned and punched Perry's shoulder. "Give me fifteen minutes, and I'll have that pup licking his chops."

Perry turned back to Archy, cupping the dog's head in his palm. "You hear that, old boy? It's not a ham hock, but you're about to partake in the best welcome-back meal this weary party has to offer, or at least somethin' that might stick to your ribs."

Pete rummaged through the food crate. Michael sat cross-legged by the fire.

"You really think he'll eat?" he asked.

Perry swallowed, staring down at Archy's frail frame. "I don't know. But I have to try."

Soon, the scent of frying pork filled the air. Pete stood focused over a cast-iron skillet, stirring a bubbling mix of fat, flour, and water.

"Almost there," he called, flicking his wrist as if he were some high-class chef instead of a trail-worn traveler with a rusty pan. "This is fine eatin', I tell you."

Perry didn't care for the theatrics, only for the steaming bowl Pete finally set into his hands. It glistened with golden goodness, its smell warm and inviting.

Perry turned to Archy, crouching low, spooning a bit of the doughy mix toward the dog's mouth. "Come on, boy," he encouraged. "Just a little."

Archibald didn't move.

Perry's heart sank, but he didn't give up. He touched the spoon to the dog's tongue, forcing a few thick chunks to slide into his mouth. Seconds ticked by, agonizing and slow.

Then, a lunge. A determined movement of the jaw. A swallow.

Pete gasped. "He's eating!"

A collective hush again fell over the group as they watched Perry slowly, carefully, offer more. Archy lapped at it weakly, each movement feeble but deliberate.

Perry let out his breath. "That's it, Archy," he whispered. "Just keep going."

Pete grinned, folding his arms. "Told you my gravy could bring a man, or a mutt, back from the brink."

"Let's not get carried away," Moses said. Sally gave him a good-natured elbow to the ribs.

But Perry wasn't listening. His focus remained on Archibald, on every careful chomp. The road ahead was still waiting, but for the first time in days, hope tasted real, even if it was powered by Pete's lack of cooking skills.

The next day, Archibald slowly sat up and drank water like a camel. He rose to his feet with a weak shudder. His legs wobbled, but he then shook his whole body, expelling the last foamy vestiges of death.

Ten days further down the trail, the path had grown more familiar. Perry continued to do his best to nurse his hound dog back to full health. Archibald's ribs were filling out. His legs growing stronger, but he continued to ride inside the Conestoga.

A rabbit hopping on the trail ahead was all it took. Archibald lunged toward the wagon's tailgate. Perry reached out his arms to try to stop him, but it was too late. The dog bounded to the ground. At first he whined when his paws hit the dirt, but he trotted at half speed toward the rabbit's path. He continued his half-hearted chase for a good twenty yards before stopping in his tracks.

Perry shot a whistle in his direction.

"Come on, Archy! Get back here!"

The dog snorted in self-defeat and returned to the wagon, but instead of jumping back up to the cargo bed, he started walking alongside and keeping pace.

Pete, riding closeby on his mare, gave a low whistle. "I'll be. Looks like someone's got his legs back."

Perry grinned, rubbing the trail dust from his face. "Not quite, but he's getting there. This was that pesky rabbit's lucky day. He wouldn't have had a chance with Archy at full speed."

Perry shouted at Moses to halt the wagon. He reached down and ruffled Archibald's ears. The dog wagged his tail and his eyes were sharp, continuing to scan the roadside brush for critters.

Perry saddled up Appy and climbed onto his horse's back for the remaining trip home.

Moses, up ahead, turned in the wagon seat. "Remember my dream that night back in the snowy barn, Perry. Just now, I recall I told Archy that if I was ever in trouble, I hoped he was there to pull me out. Well, he sure as hell did."

Sally tugged her bonnet tighter as the wind picked up. "Dreams, Moses, they ain't always just bedtime tales. Sometimes, they're whispers from the road ahead. Warnings. Or promises."

She nodded toward Archibald, trotting proud by the wagon's side. "And that old hound? Looks like he's chasing down a promise."

Perry grinned, but something settled in his chest. This wasn't chance. This was the kind of fate that walks on four legs and knows the way home.

Two miles further down the road, Archibald seemed emboldened by his newfound strength. He gave a sharp bark into the distance. "Uhh Roo Roo Roo." Only his hound dog ears could hear the gun shots.

Pete leaned forward, squinting. "Something's up."

The travelers slowed. Dust swirled ahead where the trail curved unseen around a rocky outcrop.

Perry set his jaw. "Stay close, Archy."

The dog let out a low growl.

Moses snapped the reins, urging the wagon forward at a cautious pace. The rest of the group followed, eyes fixed on the dust-streaked horizon. The silence felt too thick, the kind that settled before a storm. A crow cawed from a twisted oak near the trail's bend, its call sharp against the morning hush.

Archibald's ears twitched. He let out another low growl, his body tensed, nose working the air.

Perry reached for the rifle strapped to Appy's saddle. "Easy, boy," he murmured, scanning the brush for movement.

Then, they all heard it, multiple gunshots and they were growing louder.

Pete adjusted his hat, his grin tightening. "Hell. Seems like trouble don't much care if we expect it or not. Let's pull the wagon and the horses to the side of the trail, but this can't be good."

The sound of galloping hoofbeats reached them. Fast. A lot of them.

Moses yanked back on the reins, bringing the wagon to a sudden halt on the side of the trail. Dust swirled as they all turned their heads toward the bend.

A group of riders emerged—five men, rough-looking and wild-eyed—their mounts lathered with sweat. Guns drawn, bandanas pulled high over their faces. Outlaws.

Perry's pulse kicked up. His grip tightened on the rifle.

The outlaws barely spared the travelers a glance as they thundered past, urgency in every motion. Their horses' hooves sent clumps of dirt flying as they disappeared down the trail, leaving only dust and an urgent sense of danger.

Moments later, came another wave of riders—six men, this time, wearing badges that reflected in the morning sun. A lawman at the front pulled up sharply beside Perry, his mustache dusted with trail grit.

"You see which way they went?" he barked. "They say anything?"

"Seems to me, they didn't want to talk about it." Perry pointed down the path. "About a half-minute ahead of you. They went thataway. Fast."

The lawman nodded, tipping his hat. "Much obliged. It's the James Gang. Knocked off a bank in the city."

With a sharp cry to his men, the lawman and his posse were off, chasing the outlaws into the horizon.

Silence settled again. Moses exhaled, holstering his pistol.

Pete adjusted his hat. "Ain't every day you get front-row seats to a chase."

Perry looked down at Archibald, who had finally relaxed but still watched the road with wary eyes. "Yeah. It's time for God to take these reins and get us home. We're too close to be sidetracked now."

They crested the next hill and St. Joseph sprawled before them, lining the banks of the Missouri River. The sight brought a wave of relief. Trouble had a way of traveling fast. And sometimes, unlike the rest of their journey, this day it bypassed them and kept on going. After nearly a full month on the road from Memphis, it was late Wednesday morning, February 14th, St. Valentine's Day.

The familiar scenery of the frontier town came plainly into the travelers' views. With the exception of the close call with the outlaws and pursuing posse, the group had been riding in quiet anticipation for the better part of the morning, each lost in their own thoughts about what awaited. As the faint outlines of rooftops came into focus, Michael, still planted in the saddle, pulled his harmonica from his pocket, his fingers curling around the worn metal.

He cleared his throat, drawing everyone's attention. "I've been workin' on a little somethin'. Thought it might suit the moment."

Moses turned in his seat, his eyes narrowing with curiosity. "You been holdin' out on us, son?"

Michael grinned. "Maybe. But I wanted it to be just right for this exact moment."

He raised the harmonica to his lips, took a deep breath, and began to play the first notes of *Battle Hymn of the Republic*. The tune poured out, strong and steady, filling the morning with a triumphant melody that echoed into the roadside ditches.

Pete slowed his horse, turning to listen. "Well, I'll be. That young man's got more melodic spirit in him than a cavalry bugler."

"It's fitting," Perry said. "I'll give him that. Marchin' home with a victory tune."

Moses didn't speak. He leaned back in the wagon seat, his gaze fixed on the valley rooflines but his chest swelling with pride. The music carried memories and promises alike.

As Michael hit the final smoky notes, the crew fell into a silence, each member caught in the emotion of what lay ahead.

Moses broke the silence. "That was somethin' special, son. Feels like you captured the whole journey in a single song."

Michael tucked the harmonica into his pocket with a casual shrug. "Just wanted us to mark our triumphant entrance with somethin' more than wheels and hooves and a hound dog makin' noise. Thought we deserved a proper entrance."

Pete nodded. "What you gave us, Michael, was a musical reminder of what got us here."

The group shared a moment of hushed understanding as the doorstep of St. Joseph loomed closer. Michael reached for the harmonica again, his fingers itching for one more tune. Moses suspected it might be a full rendition of Swing Low, Sweet Chariot. He held up a hand in Michael's direction.

"Hold onto that one, son," he said. "Let that next song be for a special moment. I am confident we'll have many such occasions in our future."

Michael nodded, the harmonica slipping back into his pocket. "Reckon you're right, Papa. The best songs are still ahead of us."

The group urged their horses forward, the wagon rolling toward town, each of them feeling a stronger pull with every step. Sally and Moses exchanged a glance and hugged. The journey was nearing its end, the countless trials they had faced flooding their minds. But ahead lay the promise of reunion and the chance to reclaim their stakes in the soil and structure of freedom.

CHAPTER 33

Mid-February

STEALTHY ENTRANCE

ST. JOSEPH'S FRONTIER HEART beat with purpose. Boots rattled against boardwalks, a butcher hoisted fresh beef quarters onto iron hooks, and a wild-haired boy chased a rolling iron hoop down the street, laughing as it careened into a street-side water trough. The Conestoga eased down the main street, its canvas top rustling in the breeze. Perry, riding alongside on Appy, lifted a hand and leaned back in the saddle. "Hold up, Moses," Perry called.

Beulah and Barney came to a halt with a soft snort.

Pete leaned forward in his saddle. "What now, Perry? We're this close to The Outpost. You plannin' to keep our wives waitin' even longer?"

Perry flashed a mischievous grin. "I reckon I am, but for good reason." He paused for dramatic effect, gesturing toward Marcus's Trading Post just up the way. "Tell me, Pete, do you know what day it is?"

Pete squinted, rubbing his jaw in thought. "Tuesday? Wednesday? What's it matter? Days all blur together after months on the trail."

Perry shook his head. "It's Valentine's Day, my friend. And Marcus's shelves are bound to have just what we need to express our undying devotion. Me? I've got my heart set on peppermint sticks for Millie. Nothing says romance like tradition, and for us, peppermint sticks are the language of love."

Pete snorted, glancing down at his mud-streaked boots and dust-covered jacket. "Romance? In this condition? The way we look right now, we're more likely to scare 'em off than woo 'em. But you're right. It's all about the presentation."

Perry nodded toward the trading post dead ahead. "Then let's not waste a moment. It ain't every day you get to make a grand gesture. Let's freshen up our chances."

The group secured the wagon and horses outside the Trading Post, the promise of their reunion momentarily set aside for this errand of affection. Inside, the smell of beef jerky and freshly ground coffee beans mingled with the faint sweetness of peppermint near the counter.

Perry headed straight to the shelves where jars of the colorful candy sticks stood in neat rows. "There they are," he muttered, picking out a bundle of the striped treats. "Perfect. Just like the first night I saw her."

Pete ambled over, examining the goods. "You've got your peppermint. Now, what in God's green pasture am I supposed to get for Lucy? She ain't much for sweets."

Perry smirked. "Lucy's practical. See if Marcus has anything useful but still thoughtful. Maybe a new journal for her poems or some fine fabric for a baby blanket."

Pete nodded, wandering over to another shelf. He picked up a neatly folded bolt of indigo flannel. "This might do. Kinda matches her eyes." He held it up for Perry to see. "You think she'll like it?"

Perry grinned. "She'll love it. Thought counts, and that's a fine one."

Perry was still wrapping the peppermint sticks in brown paper when the shop door creaked open from the back room. Both men turned, expecting Marcus's usual hearty greeting—the booming laugh, the flourish of his apron. But what stepped through the curtain gave them pause.

Marcus, usually a blaze of colorful shirts and shopkeeper aprons, stood cloaked in black from collar to boot-heel. No smile touched his face. His dark eyes, normally sharp with mischief, held a distant quiet. Even his posture was different, straighter and restrained.

"Well, I'll be damned," Pete muttered beneath his breath. "Marcus? You join the clergy while we was away?"

Marcus managed a faint smile that didn't transfer to his eyes. "Not the clergy, Pete. Though I reckon the Lord and I've had words lately."

He moved behind the counter, his hands slow and deliberate as he adjusted the ledger. A black armband circled his left sleeve. The shop fell quiet, the cheerful energy of their errand evaporating.

Perry cleared his throat, setting the wrapped candy down gently. "What's happened, Marcus? You look like the walls of this place are crumbling on top of you."

Marcus rested his palms flat on the counter, staring down at the scarred wood grain before meeting their gaze.

"Jeptha Nichols is dead."

The words dropped like stones into a cattle pond, breaking the surface and sending ripples outward into silence.

Pete stepped back. "Dead? What... how? He was fine when we left. Hell, he was better than fine. Sober. Clear-eyed. Raising a ruckus in all the right ways."

Marcus's composure wavered. "They hung him, Pete. Right in the center of town. Strung him up from the old burr oak across from your tavern like a warning to every decent soul still breathing. Everyone thinks a fella named Eugene Dawson did it. He had ties to some new society that embraces a doctrine of hate."

Perry dragged a hand down his face. "Sweet Jesus. Jep. Why Jep? He was turning things around."

Marcus gave a shallow nod. "That's why they killed him. Dawson came into The Outpost starting shit, complaining about the mission you fellas were on to help Moses. Jep gave him a sideways glance, after Lucy clocked him in the mouth with a skillet. When Jep left the tavern, they grabbed him and lynched him. Still doesn't make a lick of sense."

Marcus paused. "I've put myself into a period of mourning my friend. Six weeks, by my own reckoning. Ain't nobody requiring it, but my heart won't let me wear color, just to honor Jep's memory."

Pete, still reeling, swallowed hard. "Six weeks. You're a helluva man, Marcus. I sure hope Dawson felt more pain in the end than my little Lucy smacking him a good one. Love that woman."

Perry spoke. "So, what about this Dawson fella? Is he still on the loose?"

"Nope. He's likely roasting in hell as we speak. He burnt to ash in his own house. Some kind of kerosene fire, they say. Some call it an accident. Others call it justice. I think it was hell callin' home one of its own."

Pete let out a low whistle, shaking his head. "Damn. This town's changing fast."

"It's gotta change, or we're all gonna drown in the rot," Marcus said.

He reached for the bolt of indigo flannel Pete still clutched in his hands.

"Homecoming gifts for the ladies?" Marcus asked.

"A combination of that and Valentine's Day," Perry said. "Thanks for keepin' the peppermint sticks stocked."

"Gentlemen, give them those gifts with a little more heart. They've been through a lot, but both are healthy and very pregnant. In spite of what's transpired, we've still got room for joy. It's what Jep would expect."

"There's plenty of reason for joy, Marcus. Our rescue mission to bring back Moses' family was largely successful."

"That's right. How could I almost forget to ask? Tell me about it," Marcus said as a genuine smile finally took the place of sorrow. "Sally, Michael and Samuel, was it?"

"Sally and Michael are outside with Moses as we speak. And more good news is that your Conestoga wagon made it all possible."

Marcus let out a long breath, his hands gripping the counter. "Thank the good Lord above. That's somethin'. That's somethin' real special. But what about Samuel, the middle son?"

"We didn't find him. We looked, but he'd already run from the plantation by the time we got there. Best we can figure, he might have headed this direction. You seen him?"

"Not even a shadow. But still, bringin' Sally and Michael home, that's no small thing. Moses must be over the moon."

Pete nodded. "He is. Man's been through hell. And as for Samuel, we're holdin' onto hope. If there's one thing we learned on this journey, it's that hope's got a way of smacking you in the noggin when you least expect it, kinda like Lucy's cast-iron skillet."

"I reckon you'll find Samuel when the time's right," Marcus said. "And the time is certainly right for you two to reunite with your wives. While it might be sufficient for them to lay eyes on your trail-weary cabooses, hedgin' your bets with those special gifts from my store is a good move."

"Whether you are in mourning or not, you're always a shrewd businessman, Marcus," Perry said.

Pete gave Marcus a smile. "And don't worry. We will not forget we owe you that favor, and I must say, the Conestoga was one of the biggest reasons we made it back unscathed."

"Needed to put in a new lynchpin, but all in all, she was as smooth as silk," Perry added.

"I'll tell you what I'll do, fellas. You hold true to that promise you owe me, and I'm just going to bestow that Conestoga on Moses. With a few more members in his household now, he's going to need it. But please make sure you tell him that I'm looking forward to meeting his family."

"Why don't you tell him yourself? Like I said, he's right outside."

Marcus's eyes widened as he bolted toward the shop door, the bell above the door jingling as he threw it open. His boots scuffed across the porch as his gaze swept the street, landing on Moses, Sally, and Michael standing near the wagon.

"Well, I'll be a mule's uncle!" Marcus boomed with delight. "Moses Watson, in the flesh! And this must be Sally and Michael. Lord have mercy."

Moses turned, his broad shoulders straightening as he nodded.

"Afternoon, Marcus. Been a long time."

"A long time?" Marcus barked a laugh, descending the steps with hurried strides. "Feels like a lifetime. And look at you, sir! You brought 'em home."

Sally stepped forward, her hand resting on Moses' arm. "I am honored to meet you, Mr. Marcus. I am so grateful to you. Moses told me all about your kindness, even when times weren't easy."

Marcus scratched the back of his head, his face flushing with modesty. "Ah, don't go makin' me out to be more than an imperfect man. It's these fellas that did the heavy liftin'," he gestured toward Pete and Perry, who were climbing back onto their horses, "I'll tell you, it's a joy to take in this sight. This is what makes all the hard times worth it."

Michael, his harmonica poking out of his pocket, extended a hand. "Thank you, sir. For everything."

Marcus gripped Michael's hand. "You're welcome, young man. And now that you're here, I hope to see you help your papa make that Kansas farm better than ever. Your papa and Gabe got a good thing started."

Pete and Perry climbed into their saddles following the introductions.

"Now, if you'll excuse us, Mr. Mixon, we've got some wives to surprise," Pete said.

"We'll be back for my buckboard wagon after the grand reunion," Perry said. "Thanks for keeping it safe while we were gone."

The group exchanged waves and smiles as Moses slapped the reins, and the Conestoga rolled forward. Marcus stood on the wooden sidewalk with a hand shading his eyes.

"You did good, Moses," he called after them. "You did real good."

Moses turned back briefly, raising a hand in acknowledgment before focusing his attention ahead. The journey had been long, the trials plenty, but as The Outpost's weathered sign came into view, Moses could only think about the joy that lay ahead for Pete and Perry as they were reunited with their wives.

The wagon wheels came to a halt in front of The Outpost at high noon, the horses shifting restlessly in the harness. Pete dismounted his horse and Perry slid off Appy. They stood by their horses for a moment, their eyes meeting in a quick exchange. This was the moment, and they determined to make it one of drama and surprise.

"Perry, you're the customer here, should you make the grand entrance?" Pete asked, clutching the bundle of indigo flannel in his hand.

Perry adjusted his hat, holding the small parcel of peppermint sticks like it was a prize jewel. "I think not, Mr. Fontaine. Seeing as this here's your establishment, I reckon you oughta be the one to lead the way."

"What a quandary we face. Maybe we should skip in together like a pair of unbridled schoolboys."

"Schoolboys we are definitely not. Let's go in together, but let's sneak in. More theater that way. They'll hate it and love it at the same time."

"Perfect. I can't wait to see the little baby bellies. Let's make our arrival worth their long wait."

The men stepped up onto the wooden porch and through the wide front door, side-by-side. Pete poked his head in to survey the surroundings, like a prairie dog scanning its den. The midday crowd paused but quickly resumed its chatter.

A faint melody from the piano floated through the air. Millie's head was buried in notes dancing across the sheet music. Her fingers marched across the keys with efficient accuracy. Perry's chest tightened at the sight of her so close, and yet Millie was unaware of his presence.

From the kitchen, Lucy shouted an order to Hank at the bar.

Perry and Pete moved quickly and quietly, keeping to the shadowed edges of the room. Perry motioned to Pete, and they sidled up to Hank, who was retrieving dishes from a nearby table. The moment Hank's eyes landed on them, his hand froze mid-motion, and a broad grin spread across his face.

Perry held a finger to his lips, leaning in. "Hank, we want this to be a surprise. Think you can help us with a little mischief?"

Hank's grin widened. "Gentlemen, you've come to the right man.

What do you have in mind?"

Perry held out one of the peppermint sticks. "This bribe is for the lovely pianist. Ask her for a request, a specific tune, 'Old Folks at Home.' Both have meaning from the day we first met. Tell her it's a request from an anonymous admirer."

Hank tucked the peppermint stick into his apron pocket. "I've seen a lot of things in my day, but this one takes the cake. You two, stay outta sight."

"Much obliged, Hank," Perry said.

As the sneaky friends retreated to a dark corner table, Hank sauntered over to Millie, who didn't look up from the piano as her hands danced across the keys. The familiar notes of a tavern standard drifted into the air.

"Millie," Hank said, leaning over the piano with a mock-serious expression. "This goes against every principle I have as a bartender, but I've got a request from a patron."

Millie glanced up, her hands never faltering. "A request, is it? What could possibly justify interrupting me mid-song?"

Hank set the peppermint stick gently on top of the upright piano. "This. And I think you know the tune to go with it."

Millie froze, her breath catching in her chest. Her fingers hovered above the keys as her eyes fixed on the peppermint stick. Slowly, she looked up at Hank, suspicion dawning in her gaze.

"Hank," she said, her voice trembling, "I know exactly the song that goes with a peppermint stick. But I'm not playing it. Not right now. I suspect this message comes from a certain scoundrel who's been away from my sight for far too long."

"Lucy," she shouted, "you might want to come out here. I think we have a situation on our hands. A pair of troublemakers in our midst."

Lucy appeared in the doorway from the kitchen, a towel slung over her shoulder, skillet in hand. "Last thing I need is more trouble. What's going on, Millie? Why'd you stop playing?"

Millie turned, her eyes scanning the room as a suspicious smile crept across her face.

Lucy's eyes widened, the towel and skillet dropping to the floor as she skipped across the room to stand beside Millie. "Where are they, Millie? Hank? Where?"

Hank leaned on the piano, his eyes twinkling. "Ladies, I reckon if you look real close, you might find your scoundrels lurking in the shadows."

Millie and Lucy turned as one, their eyes sweeping the dim corners of the room. Perry and Pete exchanged a glance, their stealthy plan unraveling, but neither could suppress the smiles breaking across their faces.

Together, they rose from their seats and shouted, "Beware, the ghosts of Gumbo Flats!"

Perry stepped forward. "Surprise, my love."

Millie's hands flew to her mouth as her eyes filled with tears. "Perry. Oh, Perry!"

Lucy, now heavy with child, didn't wait for Pete to move. She waddle-ran across the room, her arms wrapping tightly around him. "Pete Fontaine! You sly, no-good rascal! Don't you ever leave me guessing like that again."

Pete handed her the indigo material and reached into his pocket for the locket she had given him as a good-luck charm for the journey.

"Happy Valentine's Day, Lucy. I missed you so much, but your locket did its job."

Lucy kissed the locket, held the fabric high overhead and smirked. "Well, ain't this just perfect. Good luck to me. I missed you so much, Pete, but thanks to this little surprise of fabric, I'll be slaving over a sewing needle instead of napping before this baby comes. I wonder if the first word out of its mouth will be 'work.'"

The tavern erupted into laughter, applause and cheers from the lunchtime crowd.

Millie threw her very pregnant self into Perry's arms, her tears soaking into his shirt as he held her close.

"You're home," she whispered. "You're finally home."

Perry placed his hand on Millie's midsection and felt the sizeable bump. "I reckon I've traveled a thousand miles just to see your face again. Every road, every trail, it all led back here, to you. And now that I'm home, I aim to stay right where I belong to welcome this little one."

He brushed a tear from Millie's cheek and managed a gentle smile. "Now, I know I kept you waiting longer than any good husband should, but I brought you somethin' to sweeten the deal."

He reached into his pocket and held up the entire bundle of peppermint sticks. "A little something on this Valentine's Day to remind you that you've always been the sweetest part of my life."

Millie let out a soft laugh through her tears, taking the peppermint sticks in her trembling hands. "Perry Adams, you didn't need to bring me anything. You've got more flair than a traveling showman."

"Not really, Millie. At the moment, I feel a bit like a snake oil salesman. I almost failed in my promise to bring Archy home safe."

"What happened, Perry?"

"I almost lost him. A flash flood hit, swept Moses away, and Archy jumped in without a second thought. He kept Moses afloat till we could pull them out, but a log struck Archy hard. He was out cold for three days. We nursed him back. He's still healin' but almost back to normal. He's outside with Moses' family right now."

"You found them. You brought 'em back? When can I meet them?"

"We found Sally and Moses, but Samuel had already left by the time we got to the plantation where he'd been. We don't know where he went, but we'll continue a diligent search going forward. They wanted Pete and me to have a couple minutes with you and Lucy before they came inside."

"I can't wait to meet them, but, Perry," Millie turned sullen. "Have you heard what happened to poor, old Jep?"

"Marcus just filled us in. What a tragedy. But in the end, it sounds like God's fury was unleashed against his killer, that Dawson fella."

"It was heart-rending," Millie's voice caught, but she pressed on.

"But the good Lord has His timing when it comes to vengeance. Dawson burned alive. Some say a kerosene lantern tipped over. Truth is, nobody really knows. But that's the story folks tell."

She glanced sideways at Hank, "Ain't that right, Hank?"

Perry followed her look, raising an eyebrow. "That the whole story, Hank?"

Hank leaned back against the bar, an almost-evil grin curling at the corner of his mouth. He scratched his chin and said, easy as Sunday morning, "Fire's funny that way. Burns what needs burning. As for how it started, some things are better left between a man and his conscience."

CHAPTER 34

Mid-February

CLOSING THE CIRCLE

IN THE AFTERMATH of the reunion between wives and husbands, Millie's eyes scanned the room impatiently. Her breath halted as she searched the crowd. She wiped her hands on her apron, her gaze darting toward the door, expectant and eager.

"Where are they, Perry? Moses, Sally and Michael! They've been outside waiting far too long, and I want to see Archy too!"

"It's been a long journey for all of us. Moses thought a few more moments wasn't going to change the importance of the moment."

Millie pulled back slightly, her expression one of determination. "Perry Adams, what are we waiting for? Those folks must be cold and hungry after such a trip. Pete, Lucy," she called toward the bar, "would you offer me the kindness of inviting the Watsons in? We can't let them wait out there any longer."

"It would be my pleasure, ma'am," Pete said.

Lucy grabbed her towel and with a stern look snapped it at Pete. "What the hell are you waiting for, Mr. Fontaine. Bring 'em in."

Pete opened the wide door to the cold February air and called out. "Moses, Sally, Michael, come on in! We've got a fire going and plenty of food to share."

Moses stepped inside with Sally clutching his arm, her eyes wide as she took in the tavern's cozy warmth. Michael hesitated just a moment before stepping in behind them. Right behind him, Archibald bounded in.

Millie moved toward them, her hands outstretched. "Welcome. You must be Sally and Michael. I'm Millie Adams, the lucky woman who lassoed Perry about a year ago."

As he passed, Archibald paused at attention, tail wagging. Millie knelt down slowly. The dog licked her cheek. "Uhh Roo Roo Roo!"

Michael chuckled at the dog's eager greeting. Archibald gave a happy spin, then trotted in a wide circle, as if taking personal responsibility for their safe return.

Sally took Millie's hands in hers, her grip firm but warm. "Thank you, Mrs. Adams. I don't even have the words to say what your sacrifice over the last several months means."

Millie's eyes welled up as she looked into Sally's face. "It means you're home. For good. That's all that matters now. Come, sit by the fire. Let's get you warm."

Archibald trotted over and curled up by the fireplace.

Pete tapped Michael on the shoulder. "Young man, we've ridden side-by-side since Hernando. I know how famished I am, and you look like you could eat a whole hog by yourself. Lucky for us, I can smell a pot of stew in the kitchen."

Michael glanced at Pete. "Thank you, sir. No offense to you gentlemen, but it's been a long time since we've had a proper meal."

Lucy was ready to explode into action. "Well, let's fix that right now. We take care of our own."

Hank waved Lucy off. "Miss Lucy, you stay put. I'll round up bowls and spoons enough for everyone and then I'll bring out that stew pot, as well as beers and sarsaparillas."

Moses leaned forward. "Miss Millie, I'll tell you this: if it weren't for your husband, Mr. Fontaine and that dog of yours, I wouldn't have made it."

As Hank served drinks around the table, Pete raised his mug of beer. "A toast my friends: To Archy, to kin, to the road yet begun. May laughter find us and troubles soon run."

"I'll drink to that," Perry said, raising his mug.

"You all are welcome to spend the night in our home," Lucy said. "It's warm and there will be breakfast on the table. I think Hank can handle all the duties demanded here at The Outpost tomorrow."

Hank leaned back against the bar. He gave the bar towel a lazy spin before slinging it over his shoulder. "Yup, glad to keep watch over this place tomorrow. Pour a few drinks, stir up some laughter, and if trouble comes knockin', I'll serve up some fiery justice. If anyone tries to start trouble, I'll remind 'em I've got fists and Lucy's skillet, and I ain't afraid to use either."

The morning smell of frying pork sausage wafted through the air, pulling the friends from their beds one by one. Dawn streamed through the windows of Pete and Lucy's home, catching the steam rising from the cast-iron skillet atop the wood stove where Lucy and Sally stood. A pot of coffee bubbled nearby, and the table was already set.

Perry was the first to stumble into the kitchen, rubbing sleep from his eyes. "If heaven smells anything like this, you two will be helping Saint Peter guard the gate."

Sally turned, a wooden spoon in hand and a playful grin on her face. "Well, Mr. Adams, I reckon both Miss Lucy and I've had ample practice keepin' folks fed. Just give me a few more minutes and we'll be set. Y'all got a big day ahead. You'll need your strength."

Millie followed soon after. "After all these months, Lucy, I don't know how you muster the energy, pregnant and all. I'd have thought you'd be the one sittin' down to rest."

Lucy laughed. "Rest can wait. Right now, I just want to see my big extended family together, full and happy."

By the time Pete, Moses, and Michael joined them, the table held food edge-to-edge. The room came to life with clinking plates and warm conversation. Michael dug into his food with enthusiasm.

"I can't wait to see the farm, Papa," Michael said between bites. "To finally be at a place I can call home. I'm ready to help you and Gabe build on what you've already started."

Moses reached over and gripped his son's shoulder. "It's a good place, son. Hard work, but it's worth it. And wait till you reconnect with Gabe. He's been holdin' it together for us."

Sally looked up. "And our Samuel? Where do you reckon he is on this morning, Moses?"

"I don't know, Sally," Moses sighed. "But wherever he is, I pray he's found some peace."

The room grew quiet. Then Pete clapped his hands, breaking the spell. "Well, we won't find answers sittin' here, will we? Let's finish up and get y'all on the road."

After breakfast, the group gathered their things. Pete and Lucy stood on the porch, their arms around each other as they prepared to say goodbye. Millie approached Lucy, her eyes shimmering.

"You've been a rock, Lucy," Millie said, pulling her into a tight embrace. "I couldn't have asked for a better friend to watch over me while Perry was gone."

"And you've been my angel of strength, Millie," Lucy laughed. "Just know that I'll be countin' the days till we can sit as mothers and talk proper, about babies, and recipes, and everything else under the sun."

The two women lingered for a moment before parting, their shared bond stronger than ever.

Pete stepped forward next, pulling Perry into a hearty handshake. "Take care of that wife of yours, Perry. And don't let Jawbone Holler turn you soft."

Perry smirked. "You've got my word, Fontaine. Now, don't go stirring up too much trouble here without us."

As the farewells wrapped up, Moses helped Sally and Millie climb into the Conestoga. Perry and Michael mounted their saddle horses. Their last stop was to pick up Perry's buckboard wagon at the Trading Post.

As they approached the river on the far bank, the familiar landscape of Kansas stretched out before them. River bottoms led to rolling hills with bare trees clawing at the sky. It felt like a promise realized.

Moses turned to Sally. "This is where it all begins again. A new life. Our together life, chapter two."

Sally nodded, her eyes misting as she looked toward the western horizon. Millie gave her a firm hug.

The road stretched ahead, and with each mile the journey eased, replaced by the steady pull of home. For Perry and Millie that place was Jawbone Holler.

Arriving midafternoon, the group's first stop was the Watson farm. As they approached, the sight of Gabe tending the livestock created a wave of emotion. Moses jumped down from the Conestoga before it stopped, striding toward his eldest son. Gabe looked up, his face breaking into a wide grin as he dropped his tools and ran to embrace his father.

"Papa!" Gabe's voice cracked with emotion. "You're home."

"And I brought your mama and brother with me," Moses said, stepping aside as Sally and Michael ran to join the reunion.

After a flurry of embraces and joyful tears, Gabe turned to Moses. "There's something else you need to see, or should I say someone." Gabe sent out a holler in the general direction of the Watson home.

Before the words landed on the front porch, the rough door swung open. For a moment, time stopped. The figure in the doorway was unmistakable—tall, broad-shouldered, and with the same determined look that marked him as a Watson.

Samuel stepped forward, the afternoon light catching his features, and Moses felt a flutter in his chest.

"Samuel," Moses whispered, his voice breaking as he took a step toward his son.

Samuel grinned, his face filled with disbelief and joy. "Papa?

Mama? Michael?" His voice trembled with every word, as if speaking their names might awaken him from a dream.

Perry and Millie looked on as Moses crossed the yard in long strides, his heart pounding. When he reached Samuel, he grabbed his son's shoulders, his hands trembling. "It's really you," Moses said, his voice raw. "I prayed. I prayed every day."

Samuel nodded, his own eyes glistening. "I found my way here, Papa. John Manchester told me the way. I hoped you would not be far behind."

Sally reached them next, her sobs breaking the silence as she threw her arms around Samuel. "Oh, my boy, my Samuel! Look at you. Look how strong you've grown."

"Mama," Samuel said, holding her tightly. "I thought I'd never see you again. I had no idea where you were after the day we were separated in Memphis. I thought..." His words stopped short, replaced by the quiet strength of their embrace.

Michael, standing nearby, was frozen for a moment before stepping forward. "Samuel, it's really you," he said, his voice filled with awe. "I can't believe it. I've been waitin' so long to see you again."

Samuel turned to his younger brother, pulling him into a tight hug. "Michael, you've grown so much. You're taller than I am now."

The family stood together, all five of them locked in a circle of joy and disbelief. Perry and Millie watched with tears in their eyes.

From the middle of the pack, Gabe spoke. "There's more to this, Papa. Sam's got a story to tell. It's a miracle he made it here before you."

Samuel nodded, his expression somber as he pulled away. "Papa, I've been on a long road. I found my way to Gumbo Flats, hoping to find you or Gabe there. Instead, I met Mr. Manchester. He told me you were looking for me, headed south. He said you'd gone to find Mama and Michael. That's when he told me about the farm here in Kansas. I couldn't wait. I had to come."

Moses looked at him, his voice thick with emotion. "Son, the path you took wasn't an easy one, but it was the right one. I've been to the

Collins plantation. I know what you endured there."

Samuel's jaw tightened, his voice steady but filled with pain. "It wasn't just the plantation, Papa. It was the running. I knew I was riding a stolen horse. But through it all, I kept thinking about this, about us, standing here together again. That's what kept me moving."

Sally placed a hand on Samuel's cheek. "And you're here now, Samuel. You're here. That's all that matters."

As the Watsons continued their reunion, Perry and Millie stood in the distance, hands joined. "It seems like this farm's got a full house now," he said.

Millie leaned against Perry, her tears falling freely. "I've never seen anything so beautiful."

Moses pulled his family close once more. "We've got a farm to run and a future to build. I think we're going to need to add a couple rooms onto the house. And we'll do it together."

The Watsons gathered on the porch of their farmhouse, their hearts full. Samuel's return had completed the circle, and for the first time in years, the promise of a future free from fear felt real.

Gabe lit a lantern, the warm glow spilling across the porch. "Supper's gonna be simple tonight," he said. "But I reckon tomorrow, we'll feast."

Moses smiled, his arm wrapped around Sally. "And every day after, son. Every day after."

"Maybe not every day, Papa," Gabe said. "I have a few plans of my own. Me and Naomi."

"Naomi?" Sally asked.

"Yes, ma'am. And if you're willing, I'd like you to meet her Sunday. This Sunday in church."

Moses placed a hand on his son's shoulder. "Gabe, I've waited a long time to see you stand tall as a man."

"If the meeting goes well, I'd like your blessing for a whirlwind courtship. Already got her family's permission."

"We look forward to Sunday, Gabe. Let's meet her properly, but you don't need our permission. You're a free man. Free to pursue life with all its ups and downs, happy or sad, but always free."

Moses turned to Perry. "Things're about to get lively around here, Perry. But we still need to roll that Conestoga back to Marcus."

"No need for that. Marcus told me straight. You're supposed to keep it. Said you'd need it now."

"Well, I'll be. That wily shopkeeper's really tryin' hard to tarnish his stingy reputation, ain't he?"

"You and I both know that Marcus is all sass. Nothing more than a big softy. His disguise is slipping."

"It sure is."

"Now, I guess it's time that Millie and I found our way back home too. Got a house to reclaim and maybe a little nesting to do. Time to swap horses. I'll hitch up Beulah and Barney to our buckboard and take our leave. You enjoy your reunion. You've waited long enough."

CHAPTER 35

Mid-February

BACK TO THE HOLLER

MILLIE AND PERRY CLIMBED into the wagon seat, Appy tethered at the end and Archibald riding in the back. A full hour of sunlight remained in the winter sky as they hit the well-worn trail to their home in Jawbone Holler.

As the wagon crested the last rise, Millie gasped, her hand clutching Perry's arm. "There it is. Our little home."

The Adams farm was nestled in the familiar embrace of Jawbone Holler. The setting sun cast golden light across the wooden boards of the house, giving it a warm, glowing appearance.

Perry pulled the wagon to a stop in front of the house and sat for a moment, letting the sight wash over him. "Looks like she waited for us, Millie. Every board, every stone still standin', just like we left it."

Millie's eyes filled with tears as she climbed down from the wagon. "It's been less than four months, Perry, but it feels like it's been a lifetime. I can't believe we're finally back. Sure looks like Gabe kept everything in order while we were gone."

They walked to the front door together, Perry carrying a bag of essentials and Millie holding the peppermint sticks he'd bought for her in St. Joseph. He opened the door slowly, the creak of the hinges breaking the silence. Archibald was on their heels and ran into the main room.

After putting Buelah and Barney safely in the barn with fresh food and water, Perry returned to the house where Millie had lit lanterns in each room and started a fire in the cookstove, a pot of water on to boil.

The house was just as they had left it, though the air carried a faint musty chill from disuse. The familiar scent of cedarwood and dried herbs lingered. Small touches Gabe had added during their absence stood out—a neatly stacked pile of firewood near the hearth, a broom propped in the corner, and the faint scent of sage Gabe had burned trying to keep the air fresh.

Perry took a deep breath. "A little stale, but it still smells like home."

The flickering glow from the lanterns illuminated the familiar sights of their home—the woven rug Millie had made, the modest bookshelf filled with Perry's almanacs and journals, the kitchen table where they had shared countless meals, and the jawbone of Perry's beloved mule, Lukey, above the fireplace.

Without wasting any time, Perry moved to the fireplace, where he began stacking kindling. "Let's warm this place up." He struck a match, coaxing the flames to life, then into a full blaze.

Millie made her way to the piano in the corner, her fingers hovering over the keys before pressing down gently. The first note rang out and she smiled. "Oh, how I've missed these old keys."

Perry returned to the main room, leaning against the doorway to watch Millie at the piano. She played a few soft chords, testing the keys, before launching into a simple melody that filled the space with warmth.

"Your playing is as beautiful as ever," Perry said.

Millie turned to him, her smile radiant in the firelight. "This piano has been my anchor in so many ways, Perry. Sitting here, playing these notes, it feels like I've found myself again."

Perry crossed the room and knelt beside her, taking her hand. "You've always been here, Millie. Even when we were far from this place, you were my anchor. This home is just the shell. You're the heart of it."

They sat together with Archibald by the fire, their hands entwined, soaking in the peace of the moment. Millie leaned her head against

Perry's shoulder, her voice soft. "I prayed every night for your safe return, Perry. I prayed that we'd be sitting here again, just like this."

"And I thought of you every step of the way," Perry replied. "This house, this holler, it was always calling me back. You were calling me back."

Millie closed her eyes, letting Perry's presence wrap around her. "We've got so much to be thankful for, Perry. So much to look forward to."

Perry nodded, eyes reflecting the firelight. "We'll raise our child beneath this roof, build a life stone by stone and log by log. Whatever storms come, we'll weather them together. This place, this life, it's home. And nothing, not even a bad harvest, can take that from us now."

CHAPTER 36

Late February

A BUNDLE OF STICKS

BUNDLED AGAINST THE LATE February chill, the Watsons pulled up to the African church outside Lowland in the battle-tested Conestoga wagon. Inside, hymns rang out along with a mix of strong, steady voices interwoven by years of hard times and hard-won faith. It was survival set to music.

Naomi was seated with her parents. Her eyes lit up when she saw Gabe. She waved the Watsons over, making room for them to sit nearby. Moses and Sally exchanged a warm glance as they settled in. Michael looked around, soaking in the energy of the church crowd, while Gabe's gaze remained fixed on Naomi, who wore a simple but elegant dress of pale blue.

As the service began, Reverend Ezekiel Hayes stepped to the pulpit, his usual commanding presence filling the room. His booming voice carried over the congregation like a clarion call.

"My brothers and sisters, we are living in a time of rising. Across this land, the freedman community is building schools, churches, hospitals. These are foundations of strength and learning. Brothers and sisters are finding their Maroon."

The congregation erupted in a wave of "Amen!" and "Hallelujah!" as the reverend continued.

"Like those buildings of brick and stone, rise up to meet your challenges, not out of hate, but out of destiny, unity and love for the betterment of us all. The world will tell you to stay down. Know your place. The world will say you have no standing. But I say to you: rise up! Stand tall and proud, not as individuals, but as one people. Seek your Maroon, your place of holy gratitude.

"Through my extended contacts among the church brethren, I know of a settlement not far from here that goes back to territorial days. This is a place of peace for folks like us. It's called Quindaro. In territorial days it hid in plain sight along the south bank of the Mighty Missouri, on the doorstep of the larger settlement called Wyandotte. Quindaro hides no more."

Standing tall at the pulpit, Reverend Hayes leaned forward, his gaze intense. From under the pulpit he drew out a single stick, which he placed on his right, and a bundle of sticks, which he placed on his left.

"Brothers and sisters, the reason I place these sticks before you today is because in the native tongue of the Wyandot tribe, the original inhabitants of the site, the name Quindaro carries a powerful message in itself. It means bundle of sticks."

He grabbed the single stick and held it above his head. "Look at this stick. One solitary stick. It's strong in its own way but fragile all the same. Watch what happens."

With a sharp motion, he snapped the stick in half, the sound echoing through the small church. A murmur rippled through the pews as he picked up the bundle of sticks.

"Now, consider this bundle," he continued, lifting it high. "Bound together, united. Try as I might, I cannot break them. They hold firm. This, my friends, is the power of unity and the true meaning of the name Quindaro. Alone, we are vulnerable. But together, as one people, one bundle, we are unbreakable."

The congregation erupted with a resounding "Amen!"

Reverend Hayes leaned forward, his eyes sweeping the crowd. "Our journey as a people has not been easy. The road has been filled with trials and tribulations. But the lesson of the bundle is this: no matter what storms come, if we stand together, we will endure. We will rise, but we must do such in a spirit of peace with our white brothers and sisters."

He set the bundle down on the pulpit and continued with a fervor that filled the room. "Let me tell you more of this place called Quindaro. It's taken root out of strength through unity. Unlike territorial days, our days of captivity, it hides no longer. Today, it is a community, a sanctuary, a promise of what we can achieve when we rise together. To all Seekers of Freedom, it is the Maroon of all Maroons."

The congregation leaned forward, captivated by his words.

"We must build our own Quindaros across the land. Places where strength is found in each other, where freedom is not just a dream but a reality. Places where we can rise, not out of hate, but out of love. Not in isolation, but in unity. Not for ourselves alone, but for the betterment of all."

He stepped back, his gaze sweeping over the congregation once more. "Take the lesson of the bundle with you, my brothers and sisters. Let it guide you. Let it remind you that we are strong together, unbroken and unyielding. And may it light the path to a brighter tomorrow."

The room erupted into a chorus of amens as the reverend raised his hands in blessing, his face alight with hope. "Rise up, brothers and sisters! Rise up, for the future is calling, and we will meet it as one bundle."

The church shook to its rafters. The final hymn was sung with passion, the voices of the congregation lifting as one, carrying the message of hope and unity far beyond its walls.

After the service, the Watson and James families gathered near the rear of the church, the warm chatter of the growing congregation buzzing around them. Naomi greeted Gabe with a radiant smile, and her parents, Mr. and Mrs. James, welcomed the Watsons with warm handshakes and kind words.

Gabe cleared his throat, his palms sweating. He glanced at Moses, who gave him an encouraging nod. Sally squeezed his hand briefly before stepping aside to allow him to address Naomi's parents directly.

"Mr. and Mrs. James," Gabe began, his hands clasped in front of him. "I know I could wait longer, but my heart won't let me. Every day I've spent with Naomi has been a day I've seen the life I want to build with her, beside her, through every storm and season. I don't come to ask lightly. I've worked hard, and I'll keep workin' harder, but most of all, I promise to honor her, protect her, and never let a day go by without showin' her she's loved. I'd like to ask for your blessing for your daughter Naomi's hand in marriage."

Mrs. James' eyes shimmered as she looked to her husband. Mr. James studied Gabe for a long moment, then gave a slow nod. "You've already proved your word, son. And I've seen the way Naomi looks at you like you've already given her the life we prayed for. You've got our blessing."

Gabe exhaled, a quiet tremble in his breath. "Thank you. I'll carry that honor every day."

Naomi's mother reached out, touching his arm. "You make her happy, Gabe. That's all we could ever ask."

Gabe turned to Naomi, his heart pounding. "Naomi, I am not a man to take things for granted, so the final answer is yours to give." He knelt down on one knee, pulling a small wooden box from his pocket. Opening it, he revealed a simple golden band, the light catching on its polished surface. "Naomi James," he said, "will you do me the honor of becoming my wife?"

Naomi's hands flew to her mouth, tears welling in her eyes. "Yes," she whispered, then louder, "Yes, Gabe, I will."

The newly engaged couple embraced. Their joy caught the attention of the nearby congregation. Reverend Hayes approached with curiosity. "What's all this commotion?" he asked, his voice teasing.

Gabe stood, holding Naomi's hand. "Reverend, I just asked Naomi to be my wife, and she said yes."

"Well, praise the Lord! Looks like we've got a wedding to plan."

"Another thing, Reverend. This place called Quindaro, is it real? Is there good farmland close?"

"Absolutely, Gabe. It's in the bluffs overlooking the Mighty Missouri. Below, the valley offers ample farming opportunities. You thinking about a relocation, Gabe?"

Gabe glanced cautiously in the direction of his father. "Whatever Naomi and I decide to do, we will certainly make a decision together. Between the two of us, we are a small bundle of sticks."

Not hearing the conversation, Moses stepped forward to address the preacher. "Reverend, I'm Gabe's father. His mother, Sally here, and I were united in spirit while we were slaves back in Missouri, but we have never been properly married in the eyes of the Lord. Back on the plantation, we jumped the broom. It was all we could do at the time. But now, we'd like to ask Naomi and Gabe if they'd allow us to join their ceremony. A double wedding."

Naomi and Gabe exchanged a glance, their smiles widening. "Of course!" Naomi said, her voice full of excitement. "It would be an honor. I've always thought about a March wedding, Gabe. The start of a new growing season, full of potential and promise."

Gabe shook his head. "A finer time could not be chosen."

Reverend Hayes grinned broadly, his voice ringing out. "Well, isn't that somethin'? Two couples, one glorious day. We'll make it a celebration to remember. Better get to planning, folks. March is right around the corner and there's a lot to do."

As the families chatted, the congregation began to gather around, offering congratulations and well-wishes. Moses placed an arm around Sally. "This is it, Sally. A fresh start. Together. It's everything I dreamed of."

Sally leaned into him, her eyes shining. "And more, Moses. So much more."

The biting smell of livestock filled the air as Moses and Gabe showed Michael and Samuel the morning chore routine of tending the farm animals, from chickens to horses. The Watson farm buzzed with activity.

The sound of an approaching horseman broke the rhythm. Moses shaded his eyes with a hand and squinted toward the sound. Aboard the horse was a figure tall and formal, his black overcoat trailing behind him as his horse cantered closer.

"Gabe," Moses called. "Head up to the house and fetch your mama. Looks like we've got company."

As the rider drew near, Moses recognized the imposing figure of Judge Merriweather. He wiped his hands on his trousers and strode toward the gate, a welcoming smile breaking across his face.

"Judge Merriweather," Moses greeted, extending a firm hand as the judge dismounted. "What brings you to our little patch of heaven this morning?"

The judge gripped Moses' hand, his stern expression softening with warmth. "Moses Watson, it's a fine morning to pay a visit to good people. I heard all went well in Gumbo Flats and beyond. Also heard your family has been reunited. But today, I come bearing other news, though I'll admit, I'm not entirely sure of its particulars."

Moses gestured toward the home's doorway. "Well, then, let's get you a warm seat inside and some coffee. You've come all this way. Least we can do is make you comfortable."

By the time they reached the porch, Sally had joined them, her apron still dusted with flour. She offered a polite nod. "Good morning, sir. I'm Sally. It's an honor to have you at our home."

"The honor's mine, Mrs. Watson," the judge replied with a courteous bow. "I've heard much about the strength of this family and seeing it in action does my heart good."

They settled in the front room near the fireplace. Moses poured coffee from a blue enamel pot. "Now, Judge," Moses began, leaning forward, "you said you had news?"

The judge pulled a folded telegram from the inside pocket of his coat and handed it to Moses.

"Another telegram?"

"Yes, Moses. This one also came to me from Gumbo Flats by way of your friend John Manchester. He's arranged a transfer to the First State Bank of Lowland. A sum equal to the value of some gold that he deposited into a freedman account in Saint Louis. By the sound of it, though I don't know the specifics, Mr. Manchester insisted it be placed directly in your name."

Moses unfolded the paper. As he read the message, his hands began to tremble. He passed the telegram to Sally.

"Well, I'll be," Moses murmured. "I should not be surprised. John came through again. The mission I was on buried this matter in the back of my mind. I had forgotten, but it looks like John remembered."

Sally's eyes scanned the paper, her lips parting in surprise. "Moses, this amount could change everything."

Michael, Samuel, and Gabe emerged from the yard, drawn by the conversation. They gathered around as Moses explained the judge's news about the money.

Samuel grinned broadly. "Papa, that's a blessing, plain and simple. You can expand the farm, buy new equipment, maybe even some more land."

Gabe nodded. "You've always said this land is where we'd build our future. Looks like you've got the means to make that future even brighter."

The judge watched the reactions with a quiet satisfaction. "It's clear to me this gift has found the right hands. Moses, I've seen what greed can do to a man, but looking at all of you, I've no doubt this will be put to good use."

Moses leaned back in his chair. "Judge, this farm isn't just for me or my family. It's a foundation that will outlive us all. This money sent by John is about planting roots deep enough to hold through storms. It's for the soil, the work, and for generations to come. It's for building something that truly matters."

The judge stood, his hat held at his side. "Moses, if there's one thing I've learned, it's that the measure of a man isn't what he's given. It's what he does with that gift. And I believe you'll do something remarkable. I will personally see to it that an account is opened in your name at the Lowland bank."

Sally placed a hand on Moses' arm, her eyes shining. "We've already got all we need, Moses. This is just the Lord giving us a little extra, though we could possibly use a bit more room."

"You may be right about that, Sally. It's going to be a bit crowded under this roof. And with more mouths to feed, we might need a few more acres. We need to think about how this land can support all of us."

The judge placed his hat back on, nodding in agreement. "Moses, I couldn't have said it better myself. A farm like this isn't just a place to live. It's a way of life and a means to provide."

Samuel stepped forward, his youthful energy unmistakable. "Papa, I've been thinking too. If we're expanding, maybe you can add some fields for me to tend. Though I detest it so, I'm really good with cotton."

"There ain't gonna be any cotton on this farm, Sam. We are smack dab in the middle of corn country, and maybe a few plots to test out soybeans. I'm sure you'll be equally skilled with the crops most suited to our soil."

Moses glanced to the mantle above the fireplace. There sat the small leather bag containing the handful of soybean seeds he had brought back from the plantation in Gumbo Flats.

"I've seen what Perry can do growin' crops from his land, and I'm sure we can do the same, with a little advice from our neighbor."

Sam folded his arms. "It's not just about land, though. If we can get more tools, maybe even a mule team, we'd be able to plow and plant more efficiently. This is going to make a world of difference, Papa."

Moses stood, his chair creaking as he pushed it back, the serious tone of the conversation settling on his broad shoulders. "Boys, let's just take it one day, one week, one season at a time. You're right though.

Tools, fields, even mule teams, it's all important. But this farm's strength doesn't come from what we buy. It comes from what we give to it. Our labor, our care, and the spirit we pour into this soil. We've got to stay rooted in what matters, hard work, and trust in the Lord."

Samuel grinned, leaning against the doorframe. "Well, Papa, we sure have the determination. And if you want this farm to grow, I'm ready to give it everything I've got."

"You can count me in," Michael said.

Gabe did not offer his endorsement. He measured his words carefully. "You're gonna make this place better than it's ever been."

The judge's gaze moved from Moses to Sally and then to the boys. "You've got the right foundation here, Moses. And with the telegram transfer from Mr. Manchester, you've got the means to build on it. If there's one thing I've seen in my years on the bench, it's that families like yours can make the impossible a reality."

Moses nodded, his eyes meeting the judge's. "Judge Merriweather, I want to thank you for your support and your belief in me, and for bringing us this news."

The judge tipped his hat. "It's been my honor, Moses."

Sally smiled warmly. "You're welcome here anytime, Judge. And you'll always have a plate at our table."

"I'll hold you to that, Mrs. Watson."

Moses walked the judge to his horse, shaking his hand one last time. As the judge mounted and rode off toward Lowland, Moses turned back to his family.

"Gabe, Michael, Samuel, we've got work to do," Moses said with pride, crossing his arms. "If this farm's going to be the foundation for our future, it starts today. Let's make sure it's ready to stand for generations. We have fields to plow and cows to milk. And I think it's high time for us to take Butter back to Jawbone Holler."

CHAPTER 37

Early March

TWINKLES OF JOY

MILLIE'S SHARP GASP BROKE the morning silence. Perry snapped upright from bed, his breath caught in his throat. Millie's eyes were wide and glassy. One hand pressed the swell of her belly and the other dug into the mattress as if bracing for impact.

A second passed. Then another. No words. Just the rhythmic pulse of panic building between them. Perry reached for her, but Millie flinched just slightly, just enough to signal that something was wrong.

"Perry, I think it's time. My water's broken."

He blinked, sleep fleeing fast. "Time? As in…"

Her face twisted as a contraction shot through her lower back. "The baby's coming."

Perry shot upright, boots in hand before his feet hit the floor. "I'll ride for Ada Thompson—best midwife for twenty miles. I'll head to Lowland."

She gritted her teeth through another contraction, her hand gripping the bed sheet. "Listen to me, Perry. You're not riding all the way to Lowland and leaving me here. I mean send for her. I want you by my side. I'm scared."

Perry stopped fumbling, his eyes locking on hers. "Millie, darlin', I ain't goin' nowhere if that's what you want. But how am I supposed to get Ada here if I don't leave?"

Her fingers relaxed their grip as the contraction eased. "Go to the

Watson farm. Ask Moses or one of the boys to go to Lowland and bring her here. That'll be a lot quicker. I need you with me, but unless you plan to catch your own child, saddle the damn horse, go see Moses and get your tail back here."

"I'll ride like the wind. You just sit tight, and I'll make sure Moses or Gabe gets Ada here faster than you can blink."

Millie smiled faintly and reached for his hand, squeezing it tightly. "I'm not going anywhere, but you'd better hurry."

He leaned down, pressing a kiss to her forehead. "I'll be back before you know it. You just hold on for me, Millie."

Perry jammed his arms into his jacket, not bothering to button it, and dashed out the door, saddling Appy with precision and speed. His mind raced as fast as his heart. Millie's words echoed in his mind: I need you by my side. He rode toward the Watson farm.

Arriving, Perry's request to Moses was simple.

"Moses, Millie's in labor. Can one of your boys take the Conestoga into Lowland and dispatch Mrs. Thompson? She's the finest midwife Lowland has to offer."

"I'll do it myself," Moses said.

He hitched the wagon and set off at a brisk pace toward Lowland. The wagon wheels rattled against the uneven trail as he urged the horses forward, the urgency of Millie's labor driving him faster than he would have liked.

The journey was swift. Moses kept his focus, scanning the horizon for the modest home of Ada Thompson, nestled on the edge of town. He pulled up sharply outside her gate, stepping down before the wagon fully halted. A quick knock on her door brought Ada to the threshold, her gray hair tied back into a bun and her sleeves already rolled as if she had been expecting him.

"Millie's ready?" she asked simply.

"She is, Miss Ada," Moses replied, his voice firm. "We need you in Jawbone Holler."

Ada nodded, gathering her bag of birthing supplies in one smooth motion. "Let's not waste time."

She climbed into the wagon without another word, settling herself on the bench beside Moses as he snapped the reins. The horses lurched forward, their pace urgent, cutting the travel time as much as possible. The road back was familiar, the curves and dips of the terrain second nature. Moses kept his eyes fixed ahead, sparing only a glance to ensure Ada was steady in her seat.

They reached the Adams home in under two hours, the wagon pulling up just as Perry stepped outside to meet them. Without preamble or fanfare, Ada climbed down, bag in hand, and strode toward the house.

Moses exchanged a brief nod with Perry. "All yours now."

"Appreciate it, Moses."

Moses gave a small smile, turning the wagon back toward his own farm.

Inside the Adams home, the air was thick with anticipation and the faint aroma of the herbs Ada had brewed in a small pot on the stove. Perry paced the narrow hall, his boots echoing against the worn wooden floor. He paused by the door to the bedroom, listening to Millie's voice, calm but strained, as Ada offered soothing encouragement.

"You're doing well, Mrs. Adams," Ada said with the practiced ease of a midwife who had seen countless births. "Just a bit more, and we'll have your little one with us."

Perry pressed his palm against the doorframe, a flood of emotions welling in his chest. Joy, fear and hope swirled inside him.

"Perry Adams, if you're going to wear a hole in the floor, you best make sure it's easy to patch," the midwife said.

"I'd rather wear a hole here than miss the chance to see my baby born."

From within the room, Millie's sharp cry pierced the quiet, followed by the unmistakable sound of a newborn's wail. Perry's head snapped toward the door as Ada's voice carried out.

"Mr. Adams, you've got yourself a fine, healthy boy!"

Perry pushed the door open and stepped inside, his heart thundering as his eyes landed on Millie, her face radiant with exhaustion and joy. In her arms lay a tiny bundle, pink, wet and wriggling, with a soft fuzz of reddish hair crowning his head.

Perry knelt beside the bed, his calloused hands trembling as he reached out to touch his son's tiny fingers. "Millie," he whispered, his voice catching, "he's perfect."

"He's ours, Perry. Our little miracle."

Ada cleaned up quietly, giving the new parents space to marvel at their son. After a moment, she spoke softly. "Have you thought of a name?"

Perry glanced at Millie, their unspoken understanding passing between them in a heartbeat.

"Silas," Millie said gently. "Silas James Adams. After my father."

Perry's throat tightened, and he nodded. "Silas James," he repeated, the name carrying the authority of legacy and love.

The baby stirred in Millie's arms, letting out a soft coo. Perry leaned down, kissing Millie's forehead before resting his hand on his son's head.

"Welcome to the world, Silas James," he murmured. "We've been waiting for you."

Two afternoons later, a similar episode took place in St. Joseph, but instead of a midwife, Doc Anderson himself was dispatched to the Fontaine home.

Lucy sat in her bedroom, gripping Pete's hand with a strength that surprised even him. Doc Anderson stood at the foot of the bed, his sleeves rolled up and his expression calm but focused.

"You're doin' just fine, Lucy," Doc Anderson said. "Won't be long now. Just need you to keep that push up a little longer."

Pete wiped Lucy's damp forehead with a cloth. In a mix of emotions, he felt pride, worry and helplessness.

"You're incredible, darlin'. Just a bit longer, and we'll have our little one."

Lucy gave him a sharp look, a spark of her usual fire breaking through the pain. "Pete Fontaine, if you tell me to 'hold on a little longer' one more time, I might just throw you out of this room."

Pete brushed his hand across the back of his neck. "Yes, ma'am. I reckon that message is clear as daylight."

"No need to sweat bullets here, Pete. It might be best for you to wait in the parlor. Everything's under control," Doc Anderson instructed as he ushered Pete out of the room.

With a spirited shriek from Lucy and after one more push, the job was done.

Doc Anderson washed the baby in warm water with practiced precision. "Here we are, Miss Lucy. A strong, healthy girl. Just look at her."

Lucy let out a soft cry of relief as the doctor carefully handed her the baby girl.

Exhausted, Lucy yelled out at Pete. "Daddy, you better get in here. I have someone for you to meet."

Pete entered the room, his eyes wide as he looked at his daughter for the first time.

"She's perfect. Lucy, look at her. She's perfect."

After crying straight for a couple minutes, the baby finally let out a soft, gurgling whimper, her tiny hands grasping at the air. Lucy cradled her close, her tears mingling with her relief. "Welcome to the world, little Clara."

"Clara, huh? Sounds like the name of a little girl who's already too good for a papa the likes of me."

"Clara Rose Fontaine is gonna fit right in with the woman who said yes to you."

"And just like you, she's gonna rattle the stars."

Doc Anderson left, and night settled in. Pete rocked Clara. He whispered quiet promises to his tiny daughter. Lucy watched from the bed, her body drained but her gaze steady. She reached out, brushed a finger along Clara's cheek, then rested her hand over Pete's.

As the next morning broke, Moses stood outside his barn, securing Butter's halter. The cow huffed in the cool March air as she flicked her tail, seemingly indifferent to her impending journey.

"It's time to go home, old girl. You might be needed in Jawbone Holler."

Gabe emerged from the house, adjusting the reins on Moses' horse. "I think she's ready, Papa," he said, nodding toward Butter. "I'm gonna miss you, girl, but duty calls."

Moses tied one end of the lead rope around Butter's halter and the other to his saddle horn. He mounted the horse and headed toward the familiar path leading to Jawbone Holler. Gabe joined Michael and Samuel on the porch as Moses rode away, Butter in tow.

"Don't take all day, Papa!" Michael hollered. "Plenty of work to do when you get back! We got ourselves a double marriage ceremony to plan for too."

Moses turned in his saddle, raising a hand in acknowledgment. "We won't be long. But you boys make sure the feed bunk is full for the pigs."

"Will do, Papa," Samuel said.

The ride was peaceful as the warming air hinted of the rising spring. As Moses crested a hill that opened to a familiar meadow, he caught sight of the fox den nestled in the rocky slope. It was the same place he'd marked in his mind just before embarking on the rescue mission.

The den was quieter now. The scurry and play of kits, once so alive, had vanished. Instead, the two adult foxes sat side by side on a sunlit patch of earth. The male scanned his surroundings, his russet coat shimmering as he lifted his head, ears swiveling at a faint sound in the distance. The vixen, smaller and softer in her stance, remained still, her tail wrapped neatly around her feet.

Moses reined his horse to a stop and observed, his gaze fixed on the pair. The male fox stood and took a cautious step forward before turning back to nuzzle the vixen. She leaned into him, her movements serene. Their den stood empty, a hollow reminder of a season passed.

"They're alone now," Moses said to himself. "The young ones have gone. Struck out on their own. They had a whole brood last year, playful, curious. Full of life. But that season's done. And now, it's just the two of them, back to where they started."

The foxes moved together, slipping into the shadows of the hillside as though disappearing into the land itself. Moses' chest tightened as he let the sight linger in his mind.

"It's the way of things, isn't it?" he said to himself. "You raise them, pour your heart into making them ready. I'm thankful our boys will be together, not off to make their own way. But I reckon life asks us to prepare them for anything. To build them strong enough to leave if they wish, to trust they might carry a piece of their upbringin' with them."

As Moses resumed his ride with Butter in tow, the foxes had given him a glimpse of what might lay ahead, but he never thought that the Watson family might scatter, just as the kits had. He knew his family would remain strong, sinking roots deeply into the farm they would build together.

As his horse descended the hill, he tightened his grip on the reins and rode on.

His horse crested the final hills that led to Perry's farm, and the homestead came into view. Perry was outside, tending to a fence post with a hammer in hand. He straightened, wiping his forehead with the back of his hand.

"Look what the morning's brought in! Butter, my old friend, and you to boot, Moses."

Moses dismounted first, leading Butter forward with an easy hand. "Perry, it's time to return what's yours. Butter's served Gabe well in our absence, but it's time for her homecoming."

Perry gave the cow a fond pat on her side. "Moses, the newest member of the Adams farm crew has arrived. You got Ada here just in time. Little Silas made his appearance not long after you left. If you have time, you're welcome to see the little fella."

"Congratulations, Perry, but I think I'll give Millie and little Silas some privacy. I just wanted to return Butter, and now, I'm glad I did."

"She's been missed, I won't lie. But I'm glad she was a welcome guest on your farm. Gabe did a great job caring for her. But, Moses, I could have retrieved Butter myself. You didn't come all this way just to bring her back, did you?"

Moses swung down from his saddle. "Not quite. I've news to share. I wanted to tell you the day I dropped off Miss Ada to deliver Silas, but I knew you already had enough on your mind."

"Don't keep me in suspense. What's this all about?"

Moses stepped forward. "I'm here to invite you to somethin' special. The African Church is hosting a double wedding three Saturdays from now. Gabe and Naomi, Sally and me. We're tying the knot properly this time."

Perry's face lit up, and he let out a low whistle. "Now that's news worth riding all this way for. A double wedding, huh? That's a grand occasion if I've ever heard of one."

"I'd appreciate you helping us spreading the word. We're expecting Pete and Lucy, Marcus, Hank. We hope they'll all be there. It'll be good to have a few familiar faces in the crowd. Friends who've stood with us like lanterns in the dark."

Perry nodded, his expression sobering. "You've got my word. I'll make sure folks know. This isn't just a wedding. It's a celebration of everything that's come out of these last few months."

"And one more thing. My friend John came through again. Remember that gold in the mystery chest? He had that money transferred to the

Lowland Bank. It's all in my name, but I feel like I owe you a share for what you did for me."

Perry shook his head. "You owe me nothing, Moses, but your friendship. What we did, we did together. That chest found its way to the right hands. Use it to build somethin' that lasts. Somethin' worth all the trouble we went through."

"That's exactly what Sally and I plan to do."

Butter tugged idly at the lead rope. Perry patted the cow's flank and laughed. "Butter, I reckon you'll have to forgive me if I get a little too caught up in taking care of Little Silas to milk you on time."

Moses grinned. "She'll understand. She's a forgiving type."

CHAPTER 38

Late March 1866

FOREVER FROM THE DUST

THE LAST SATURDAY OF MARCH, double wedding day, arrived with a warm spring glow. The African Church was alive with energy, its walls resonating with voices, laughter, and the occasional hum of a hymn as the congregation warmed up their voices.

Outside, the promise of new beginnings floated on the breeze, mingling with the scent of budding trees, early flowers and freshly turned soil in nearby fields.

The church pews were packed with familiar faces. Perry sat proudly beside Millie, who cradled Silas in her arms, the baby snug in a neatly wrapped blanket. Pete and Lucy shared the same pew, Clara nestled against her mother's chest. Marcus and Hank claimed spots on the aisle.

Across from him, Marcus caught sight of babies and leaned over to Hank. "Look at that," he said, nodding toward Perry and Pete. "Life isn't going to be the same for those two. Glad those days are past me, but just in case, Hank, if I start talking about settling down or picking out baby names, you've got full permission to drag me into the woods and leave me there."

"Feels to me like Old Pete might not be stirring the pot with quite as much vigor going forward."

At the front of the church, Gabe stood tall beside Moses. Both men were dressed in their finest clothes. Beside them in equally dapper attire were Michael and Samuel. Naomi, radiant and serene, stood beside

Sally and her own mother, who clutched a small bouquet of spring wildflowers. The wedding party formed a bundle of unity and hope.

As the congregation settled, Rev. Hayes stepped forward to the altar. He raised his hands, his deep voice calling the room to order. "Brothers and sisters," he began, "we are gathered here not just to witness the union of one couple, but two. And we're here to celebrate what love can build—a foundation, a family, a future."

Scattered "amens" murmured through the congregation, all heads nodding as he continued.

"Marriage is a covenant, not just between two souls, but among all who witness it. It's a vow that reaches beyond the couple, anchoring itself in the hearts of friends, and neighbors. Love, when shared, becomes something greater. It becomes strength. Today, we don't just celebrate two unions, we affirm the power of unity. When lives are bound in trust, in hope, in love, they form something unshakable. In that bond, we find resilience. In that promise, we find light. And from this day forward, these four hearts carry all of us forward together."

Pete leaned toward Perry. "This preacher man sure knows how to make a fella think. Almost makes me wanna renew my vows right here and now."

"What do you mean, almost, Buster?" Lucy jabbed him with an elbow. "First you pack me into a wagon and haul me across counties while I'm still stitched from birthing your child, and now you're hedging on forever? Boy, you better start practicing your 'I do's'. You're gonna be saying 'em again tonight, and with feeling."

"Focus, Pete," Perry said with a smile. "I know it's rough for a man of your significant stature, but today ain't about you."

Reverend Hayes turned to the couples. "Naomi and Gabe. Sally and Moses. Do you stand before this congregation and before God, ready to pledge yourselves to one another, to walk this road as partners, through all trials and triumphs?"

"We do!"

Reverend Hayes approached each of the couples for formal

responses as well. As the individual vows were recited, the room held its breath with joy and hope swirling around the moment. Reverend Hayes pronounced the two couples united as husband and wife under God, and the gathering erupted into cheers and applause.

From his spot in the wedding party, Michael pulled his harmonica from his pocket. He lifted it to his lips and blew the familiar notes of "Swing Low, Sweet Chariot." As the smoky notes faded, Rev. Hayes called out, "Brothers and sisters, these couples remind us of what we can achieve when we stand together. Now go forth. Celebrate, rejoice, and carry this spirit into the world!"

Two men seated at the front arose and walked to the sides of the church to retrieve two brooms. The first one placed on the floor for Gabe and Naomi. As the young couple moved forward, Gabe took Naomi's hand, and with youthful agility they jumped the broom.

The first man removed the ceremonial broom as the second man placed the other on the floor for Moses and Sally. With a careful and deliberate motion, Moses held out his hand, which Sally grasped with intention. They walked carefully together toward their broom and in a spritely action, the older couple hopped up and forward in a unified fashion. Like the many years before, they jumped the broom, but this time in the sanctioned presence of God.

The congregation surged forward to greet both sets of newlyweds.

Naomi's parents enveloped her and Gabe in tight embraces, their eyes shining with pride. Pete and Lucy approached Moses and Sally, Pete slapping Moses on the back.

"Moses, you old rascal," Pete said with a grin. "You've gone and made it official. Sure took you long enough."

"Good things are worth the wait, Pete."

Lucy held Sally's hands. "I couldn't be happier for you. You've got yourself a great man."

"We both have great men," Naomi said, joining the conversation. "And a perfect family."

Perry and Millie stepped forward with little Silas. "This right here is what it's all about," Perry said. "New beginnings sprouting like spring crops."

Millie, still recovering from childbirth, smiled at Sally and Naomi. "The road here hasn't been easy for any of us," she said, holding Silas close. "But look at the love, hope, and resilience where there was once only struggle."

Naomi tilted her head. "That's a beautiful way to put it, Miss Millie."

Millie nodded, her hand brushing Silas's small head. "And it's true. You strike out with human intention. You falter. You fall. And then you turn it over to God."

Perry glanced at Moses. "From here to Gumbo Flats to Memphis and Hernando and back to Jawbone Holler, we leaned on each other. Now you have an entire family to lean on, but Millie and I are here by your side whenever you need us."

The families gathered beneath a sprawling oak behind the church. Gabe stood with Naomi, his arm around her waist, resolve in his eyes as he addressed Moses and Sally.

"Mama, Papa," he began. "Naomi and I have been talking."

Moses nodded, the breeze ruffling his collar. "Yes, son, what is it?"

"We're heading to Quindaro."

Moses blinked. His mouth parted, but no words came. He looked at Sally, then back at Gabe, as if checking that the world hadn't shifted underfoot.

"Quin...Quindaro?" he echoed, the name catching like a sandbur in his throat. His hands went to his hips, then dropped, then crossed, then dropped again.

Gabe nodded. "Good farmland down there. Rich river land. And Naomi wants to continue her studies at the little college they just built. She's got her heart set on becoming a teacher."

Sally placed a hand on Gabe's cheek, her eyes brimming with pride. "A teacher. My son and his bride carving out a future in a place fed by the flames of freedom."

Moses looked at his son, then at Naomi, a touch of sorrow pouring from his eyes. He let out a slow breath. "Gabe, I'd planned to take some of the money that John sent us and buy you, Michael and Samuel pieces of land next to ours."

Gabe stepped forward, his voice steady. "You and Mama are everything to me. Your intention is generous, and I don't take it lightly. But Naomi and I, we've got to plant where the soil fits what we're growing. I heard you say that to Sam. Quindaro's calling us. Not just with land, but with purpose. Naomi's future is there, and I won't have her dreams shrink to fit the lines someone else drew. I'm not turning away from you, Papa. I'm carrying everything you gave me—the wisdom, the confidence, the gumption—and putting it to work."

"I had a picture in my mind, Gabe. Your life unfolding by my side, like two furrows behind a plow, straight and sure. But you're right. A seed won't take if the ground's not right."

Moses turned to Naomi. "This world needs the kind of teaching only you can give. And that kind of knowing, real knowing, it don't yet grow here. Maybe the land I dreamed of for you ain't marked on any map. Maybe it's wherever you two choose to plant roots. If Quindaro's where your purpose calls you, then that's where we'll help you build."

Gabe smiled and nodded. "You didn't just raise me, Papa. You showed me what it means to stay focused on your target. We'll carry that with us, every step."

Moses looked around, his heart full as he continued to digest Gabe's news. Perhaps, he realized, the Watsons were like that family of foxes after all. Kits raised and scattering to the wind.

He gripped Gabe's hand. "Go son. Make your mark in Quindaro. But don't forget, no matter how far you go, this will always be home. There will always be a place under our roof. And you better visit us as often as possible."

The passing of days and the eventual parting of Gabe and Naomi failed to dim the renewed glow of purpose in Moses' heart. The morning after their departure, inside the Watson home, Moses reached above the hearth and pulled down the weathered leather bag of stray soybean seeds he'd gathered at Gumbo Flats.

He shook the bag, stuffed it into his pocket and stepped onto the porch. He grabbed a hoe leaning against the porch rail and walked toward the freshly plowed field nearest his home. The sun rose behind him, casting shadows across the furrows.

Spring was for planting.

Moses' scarred hands gripped the hoe's wooden handle. Hands that were once bound and beaten now worked out of choice, not command. Again, he looked at his palms. Clenching and unclenching. The scars had become less significant than a single hair on the back of his hand. They no longer defined him; they simply were.

The ghosts of his past, every single one, had been exiled.

He knelt, pressing his hands into the soil, feeling its warmth. He scooped a handful, letting it fall through his fingers, each bit a testament. This wasn't Gumbo Flats. This Kansas soil didn't cling like burden. Though dry, it held firm like promise.

With the hoe's handle, Moses poked a small hole into the soil. From the leather bag, he drew out a single soybean seed, smooth, round and sure. He dropped it in, covering it gently with a scoop of his palm.

He looked to the southern horizon, where Gabe and Naomi had gone. But this ground, this place, once wild, now whispered his name in a voice that resounded wide, damn open.

With family secure, the mystery of life no longer burdened his soul. He had found his answers, not in understanding his scars, but in what he had built in spite of them.

He rose. Soil on his knees. A lump in his throat. Hat to chest. Face to sky.

"This is my offering."

No more words.

Only promise. Intention. Presence.

He walked toward the house, steps steady. Behind him, the dry soil

cradled the seed. The field needed rain.
Over his shoulder, the seed waited.
But Moses no longer did.

(THE END)

ACKNOWLEDGMENTS

I CONTINUE TO BELIEVE in the power of writing with intentional but measured flair. Writing is a solitary journey, but leans on encouragement and guidance from others. As my mission to complete this stand-alone sequel to *Jawbone Holler* has been realized, I feel compelled to express my deepest gratitude to those who kindled my flame for writing.

I am thankful for all the lessons I learned from the Benedictine professors during college in Atchison, KS, including the monks and sisters who were drawn to the vocation of education. The transformation I experienced at Benedictine College continues to fuel my life.

For the steadfast support of my sisters who pushed me along the way, Marilyn, Doris, Nona and with heartfelt memories of my departed sisters, Donna and Mary, I am grateful. And for the support of friends and supporters, Joe Boeh, Cam Camfield, Bill Eckman, John Schlageck and Chris Chinn, I am thankful. And for all my friends who carry the Ad Astra spirit of the Sunflower State, you are a special people and I am honored to count myself among you.

I continue to be indebted to each of my children, Trace Thornton, Troy Thornton and Taylor McCord, for believing in the old man each step of the way. The blessings offered by all three of these "kids" has been a driving force throughout my life.

To my wife, Denise Brazier Thornton, your love, support, and guidance have been my anchor in the stormy seas of writing. Your belief in me, especially during those few fleeting moments of self-doubt, gave me the strength to push onward.

I am eternally grateful for the friendship and support of my colleagues at Stratovation Group. Your friendship and trust keep me ticking and moving forward with intention.

And, as always, I wish I could express my gratitude to my departed parents, Dorothy and Marion Thornton, for the stories of inspiration and for the unwavering support and love they bestowed on me through-out my life.

Writing **The Ghosts of Gumbo Flats** has been a passion project, and it was a story begging for the voice of Moses, the steadiness of Perry and the assertiveness of Pete, and, of course, the strength and courage of the women, Lucy and Millie, they left behind to make the trip. This would not have been possible without the belief from those around me, through whom my soul is fortified. May my words honor the gifts you have all shared, and may they serve as a testament to the unwavering power of the human spirit and that intangible quality of being a Kansan.

With heartfelt appreciation,

Mace Thornton

ABOUT THE AUTHOR

MACE THORNTON IS A FORMER JOURNALIST, an author, and strategic communications specialist. A native of Troy, Kansas, he grew up on a small farm in the Missouri River Hills of northeast Kansas. With a degree in journalism from Benedictine College in Atchison, among his passions are writing, sports and the people of agriculture. His award-winning journalism and commentaries have been published across the nation.

Mace's career took him far away from his home state for more than three decades, but he now lives a little closer, in the St. Louis area, with his wife, Denise, and their spirted rescue pup, Anna Mae. In addition to writing, he is a partner at Stratovation Group, a research, marketing and communications firm headquartered in Columbus, Ohio.

Like *The Ghosts of Gumbo Flats*, the soul of his debut novel, *Jawbone Holler,* was drawn from the hills where he was raised and the stories that echo through the people who embrace them. He is also co-author of a novel with Rogers Brazier, *West Bottoms,* set in Kansas City against a backdrop of Dust Bowl era scandal and misguided passion.

The Thorntons have three adult children scattered to the corners of our great nation, Trace (and Amy) in Virginia, Troy (and Katrina) in Washington State, and Taylor (Shawn and precious granddaughter, Grace) in Georgia.